ONLY A MONSTER

VANESSA LEN

An Imprint of HarperCollinsPublishers

ALSO BY VANESSA LEN

Never a Hero

HarperTeen is an imprint of HarperCollins Publishers.

Library of Congress Control Number: 2021943917
ISBN 978-0-06-302465-6

Typography by Jessie Gang
22 23 24 25 26 LBC 5 4 3 2 1
❖
First paperback edition, 2023

For my family, with love

PROLOGUE

When Joan was six, she decided she was going to be Superman when she grew up. She told Dad she needed the costume so she could practice. Dad had never liked spending money, but he painted an *S* on Joan's blue T-shirt and found a red napkin she could use as a cape. Joan wore them to bed every night.

"Superman?" Gran scoffed when Joan came to stay with her in London that summer. "You're not a hero, Joan." She bent her gray head confidingly. "You're a monster." She said *monster* like being a monster was as special as being an elf.

Gran was making up Joan's bed in the guest bedroom, and Joan was helping by stuffing the pillows into their cases. The room smelled like fresh laundry. Morning sun filled it to the corners.

"Monsters look like giant spiders," Joan said. "Or like robots." She'd seen enough cartoons to know. Gran sometimes told jokes without smiling. Maybe this was one of those times.

But Gran's eyes weren't shiny with a held-in joke. They were serious. "That's pretend monsters," she said. "Real monsters look like me and you."

Joan and Gran didn't actually look that much alike.

Joan took after Dad's side of the family—the Changs. Dad had moved to England from Malaysia when he was eighteen. He had round, freckled cheeks and narrow eyes and smooth black hair like Joan's.

Gran looked like the photos of Mum. She had curly hair that hung around her head in a cloud, and green eyes that were too sharp for her face. Sometimes Joan saw that same suspicious expression on her own face in the mirror. *The Hunt family look*, Gran called it.

Gran finished smoothing the duvet and sat on the edge of Joan's bed. It put her and Joan at the same height.

"Monsters are the bad guys," Joan said skeptically. In cartoons, monsters lurked under your bed. They had scary laughs that went on too long. They *ate* people. At school Mrs. Ellery had told Joan that Chinese people ate cats. Joan had kind of felt like a bad guy then—but with the same bubble of resistance that she felt now. She wasn't. She *wasn't*.

For some reason, that made Gran smile. "You remind me of your mum sometimes."

Joan didn't know what that had to do with monsters. Still, she held her breath, hoping Gran would say more. Mum had died when Joan was a baby, and Gran hardly ever talked about her. At home, there were photos of Mum above the TV and on the living room wall. But Gran didn't have photos of anyone in her house. She had paintings of fields and old ruins.

"Dad said she was clever," Joan ventured.

"Very." Gran pushed Joan's hair back from her face. "Clever and stubborn. She didn't believe things without proof either."

Before Joan could ask what that meant, Gran reached up into the air above them as if she were plucking an apple from a tree. The hairs on the back of Joan's neck rose, although she couldn't have said why.

When Gran opened her hand, she was holding something that gleamed gold like the morning sun. A coin, but not a coin that Joan had ever seen before. On one side, there was a winged lion; on the other, a crown.

"I know how you did that," Joan said. It was called *sleight of hand*. Joan's cousin Ruth had shown her how to do it with a button. You could make something appear and disappear by hiding it between your fingers and then flipping it into your palm.

Gran dropped the coin into Joan's hand. It was heavier than it looked. "Can you show me?" she said. "Can you make it disappear?"

Ruth's trick had been hard. Joan had only gotten it right twice, and she must have dropped the button a hundred times. Still, Gran's face was expectant, so Joan put the coin into the arch between her thumb and forefinger, balancing it.

"No," Gran said. "The way I did it." She moved the coin into the center of Joan's palm and closed Joan's fingers over it. "The monster way."

I'm not, Joan thought. *I'm not a bad guy.* And Gran wasn't either. Joan had spent almost every summer with Gran for as long as she could remember. When Joan had nightmares, Gran sat up with her. When Joan had found an injured bird in the park, Gran had wrapped it in her scarf and looked after it until it could fly again. A person like that wasn't a monster.

Joan concentrated on the weight of the coin until she couldn't feel it anymore. She opened her fingers, showing Gran her empty palm.

Gran's smile was warm. "The monster way," she said approvingly. She added: "There's a rule that goes with that trick."

"A rule?" Joan said. At home, with Dad, there were rules about what you should and shouldn't do. Stealing was wrong. Helping people was right. Lying was wrong. Listening to teachers was right.

The Hunts had rules too, but it was like they'd agreed to a whole different set of them. Stealing wasn't a big deal, and neither was lying—as long as you were doing it to strangers. Paying debts was right. Being loyal to your family was right.

"We hide in plain sight," Gran said. "Do you know what that means?"

Around them, the house seemed very quiet. Even the birds outside the window had stopped chirping. Joan shook her head.

The warmth was still there, but Gran's expression turned serious. "It means that no one can know what the Hunts are," she said. "What you are." She lowered her voice. "You must never tell anyone about monsters."

ONE

Joan smoothed down her hair and did a last mirror check in Gran's upstairs hallway. She had a date today. With *Nick*. In the mirror, her eyes went soft and happy. Joan had been volunteering at a museum with him over the summer break. She'd had a crush on him all summer, but *everyone* at work had a crush on Nick.

He'd asked Joan out yesterday, biting his lip and nervous, as if he thought she might say no. As if just being in a room with him didn't make her heart stutter.

Now they were going to spend a whole day together, starting with breakfast at a café on Kensington High Street. Joan checked her phone. An hour to go.

She was nervous too, she admitted. A waiting-for-the-ride-to-start mix of nerves and excitement. She and Nick had been getting closer and closer over the summer, but this felt like the beginning of something new.

Laughter rose from downstairs, and Joan took a deep, centering breath. Her cousins were already up. Their familiar, comforting bickering washed over her as she descended the stairs.

"Best forged painting in the National Gallery," her cousin Bertie was saying.

"Easy," her other cousin, Ruth, said. "Monet's *Water-Lily Pond.*"

"That's not forged!" Bertie said.

"I rest my case."

"You can't just say a random painting!"

Joan was already smiling as she reached the bottom of the stairs. Most of the year, she lived with Dad in Milton Keynes. She liked her quiet life with him, but she liked this too—the noise and clatter of Gran's place. She stayed with Gran every summer, and she looked forward to it every time.

In the kitchen, Ruth was perched on the broken radiator under the window. At seventeen, Ruth was a year older than Joan and their other cousin, Bertie, but this morning she looked like a kid. She was still in her pajamas: gray flannel bottoms and a *Transformers* T-shirt with the Decepticon logo: big beaky robot mouth. Her dark curls framed her face.

"Is there any tea in that cupboard?" Ruth asked Bertie.

Bertie craned to check, one eye on his frying pan of mushrooms and tomatoes. "Only that smoky stuff Uncle Gus drinks." He seemed to be dressed for a 1920s boating trip on the Thames, straw hat covering his black hair. All the Hunts had eccentric fashion sense.

"That stuff tastes like a—" Ruth cut herself off as she caught sight of Joan in the kitchen doorway. She took in Joan's new dress and sleek hair, and her face lit up, a slow illumination of glee.

"Ruth," Joan protested. "Don't start."

But Ruth was already crowing. "Look at you!"

"You got a job interview?" Bertie asked Joan. "I thought you were still volunteering at that museum."

"I'm having breakfast with someone," Joan said. She was already red. She could feel it.

"She got dressed up for a *date*," Ruth said. She put her hand over her heart. "It's the ultimate nerd romance. They're going to the V and A after breakfast! They're going to look at *medieval textiles* together!"

"Nerd romance?" Joan protested, but she couldn't stop herself from smiling again. "You know the V and A has other stuff too. There's historical wallpaper . . . ceramics . . ."

"A story for the ages," Ruth said. She leaned back against the window, hand still over her heart. "Two history geeks volunteer at a museum over the summer break. And then one day they're mopping floors together, and they *look* at each other over their mops . . ."

Joan snorted. She went over to steal a corner of uneaten toast from Ruth's plate. "You should come help out sometime," she told them both. "It's actually really fun. We learned how to repair broken ceramics the other day."

"One day, I'm going to record you so you can hear what you sound like," Ruth said. She made stiff robot arms. "I am Joan. I love community service. I'm so square, I only cross the road when the traffic light says I can."

"Yes. That is exactly what I sound like," Joan said.

Ruth grinned. She might have been a year older than

Joan, but their relationship had always been flipped. Ruth saw rules as other people's problems. Joan was always playing the older sister—taking shoplifted things from Ruth's pockets and reshelving them, and dragging Ruth to the end of the street so that they could cross at the lights.

Aren't you a Goody-Two-shoes, Ruth would say, but she was fond about it. They'd known each other far too long to think they could ever change each other's natures.

"Go on," Bertie said to Joan, and he sounded just as fond now. He put the whole pan of mushrooms and tomatoes on the kitchen table. "Tell us everything."

"Let us live the nerd romance vicariously," Ruth said.

Joan kicked idly at Ruth's shoe. "I like him," she told them both.

"Really," Ruth said, with the indulgent patience of someone who'd been hearing about Nick all summer. She reached over to take a mushroom from the pan.

"You know the rest. We're having breakfast this morning. And then we'll walk up to the V and A."

"Uh-huh," Ruth said. "And then are you two history nerds going to sneak behind the exhibits and . . ." She mouthed at the mushroom, licking it with exaggerated tongue curls. "Mmm—mmm—"

"Ruth!" Bertie complained. "I cooked those mushrooms."

"Mmm—mmm—"

Gran's dry voice sounded from the stairs. "Do I want to know?" she said.

"Anyway, got to go!" Joan said, before the whole family

could start up. "I'll see you later."

And now Uncle Gus and Aunt Ada were coming down the stairs behind Gran. "Go where?" Uncle Gus said.

"She has a date!" Ruth called to him.

"Wait, I want to hear about this!" Aunt Ada called back.

Joan fled the kitchen. "Talk to you later!" she yelled from the hallway.

"A date with who?" she heard Ada ask the others.

"That boy she has a crush on!" Ruth said.

Bertie belted out in song: *"She's going to kiss her summer crush in front of the medieval textiles!"*

Joan cracked up. "Bye! Goodbye!" she shouted, and shut the door.

She was still smiling as she walked up Lexham Mews. She turned onto Earl's Court Road and then Kensington High Street. It had been a warm summer, and the hazy air promised another hot day.

A message from Nick popped up just as Joan got to the café: *I'm on the Tube!* Joan took a deep, happy breath. He was running early too—less than fifteen minutes away. She bit her lip. She still couldn't believe she was about to spend a whole day alone with him.

She got a cup of tea at the counter and took it over to a table by the window. Sun streamed in, warm against her face. She went to message Nick back, and as she did, she felt a rush of air as the door opened behind her.

There was a thundering crash then that would have caused

an eruption of jeers in Joan's school lunchroom. Joan turned, along with the rest of the café.

A man was standing in front of an upturned table, eyes wide and bewildered. Bits of broken plate and glass lay strewn over the floor. He blinked down at the mess, as if he thought someone else had made it. "I want to buy flowers," he mumbled.

A waiter near Joan groaned. "Not this again." He raised his voice to one of the other staff members. "Ray, get the vacuum out! That drunk's back!" To the man he said, wearily: "You can't get flowers here. I keep telling you. There hasn't been a florist here for years."

Joan stood slowly. She'd recognized the man. "Hey, he isn't drunk," she told the waiter.

Mr. Solt was Gran's neighbor from up the road. Last week, he'd wandered into Gran's house in this same confused way. His daughter Ellie had been in tears when she'd arrived. *He has dementia,* she'd said to Gran. *It's got so much worse since Mum died last year. He doesn't even know what year it is half the time.*

"Mr. Solt?" Joan went over to him, her shoes crunching on broken glass. There was glass everywhere. Mr. Solt was wearing soft slippers; inside them, his feet were bare. He must have walked all the way from his house wearing them.

"Where's the florist?" Mr. Solt's face creased in confusion. He was a big man in his seventies—bald, with hulking shoulders. Right now, though, he was all hunched up like a little boy. He looked like he wanted to cry.

Joan tried to coax him back from the glass. "Why don't

I call Ellie?" she suggested to him. "She can get you some flowers, and you can go home." She glanced at her phone. Nick would be here in around ten minutes. "It's all right," she said to the waiter over her shoulder. "I'm going to call his daughter."

She touched Mr. Solt's arm, tentative, and, to her relief, he allowed her to guide him away from the glass and out the door.

Outside, it was a sunny day with a rare cloudless blue sky. It was early enough that most of the shops on Kensington High Street were still closed.

"Let's find you somewhere to sit," Joan said to Mr. Solt. But when she looked around, she couldn't see any benches. She settled for the strip of wall between the café and the bank next door. "Do you want to lean against the wall while we wait?" she suggested. Mr. Solt blinked at her. "We're going to wait here," Joan explained. "I'm going to call Ellie, and we're going to wait for her."

Mr. Solt stood there, still staring down at Joan without expression. Joan felt a strange sense of unease then. Something terrible was about to happen, she thought, and then wondered why she'd thought it.

"Mr. Solt?" she said.

He staggered, and his hands shot out, grabbing Joan's shoulders. She jerked back instinctively, and his heavy grip tightened.

And then it was weirdly like they were scuffling, even though Mr. Solt was only trying to get his balance back.

Joan looked over her shoulder, trying to see through the

café windows, but she was angled away, closer to the bank. A motor vroomed tinnily to life from inside the café. A vacuum cleaner. Joan looked the other way—the way Nick would walk up. But Kensington High Street was emptier than she'd ever seen it.

Mr. Solt bore down on Joan's shoulders. Joan's legs shook with the effort of holding him up. She was ridiculously reminded of the time she'd tried to take the mattress off her bed and had collapsed under its weight. She'd had to shout for Dad to get it off her, and he'd laughed so hard afterward he'd had to hold on to the door frame.

She tried to laugh now. It came out high and nervous. She wasn't scared, she told herself. Not exactly. Mr. Solt was just confused and trying to get his balance back. In a second, they'd both find their feet.

She wondered how she'd even tell Nick about this when he arrived. *This weird thing happened before you got here. Mr. Solt kind of lost his balance, and so did I, and then we were just stumbling around in the middle of Kensington High Street together.*

Except that then Joan's knees buckled. *"Mr. Solt!"* she blurted. Mr. Solt frowned. For a second, awareness sparked in his eyes. He pushed Joan away from him with a confused shove. She stumbled backward, flailing her hand up to grab his shoulder, his shirt, *anything* to keep her feet.

Joan's back hit the wall with a painful thump, and for a moment all she could see was that cloudless blue sky.

And then there was a kind of snap.

And everything went dark, as if someone had switched off the lights.

Joan could hear herself breathing loudly. She felt totally disoriented. She reached out in the dark, trying to feel for where she was, and as she did, flares of light roared past her, making her flinch.

She stumbled back. The lights had been a car.

Her eyes were beginning to adjust now, but the feeling of disorientation was only getting worse. She couldn't make sense of what she was seeing.

On the other side of the road, there was a burger shop. Joan knew it well. She'd walked past it dozens of times before.

She turned slowly. The café stood behind her, dark and empty. There was a *Closed* sign in the window. She hadn't moved, she realized. She was still here. Still standing on the exact same spot where Mr. Solt had pushed her.

Only Mr. Solt was gone.

Joan stared. A moment ago, she'd been waiting for Nick to arrive. The sun had been shining on her face. It had been morning.

But where the sky had been blue, now it was black. The stars were out. The moon.

It was night.

TWO

Joan looked disbelievingly at the black sky. Night had fallen—not with a gradual sunset, but in an instant, as though someone had thrown a blanket over the world.

She couldn't make sense of it. A moment ago, she'd been waiting for Nick to arrive, and now . . .

She went to check the time and realized with another rush of confusion that she wasn't holding her phone. She had a vague memory then of it slipping from her grip in the scuffle.

A car zoomed past, lighting up the street. The spot where her phone had fallen was empty. Joan took a stumbling step, disoriented.

A curl of panic started in the pit of her stomach. She was supposed to meet Nick here for breakfast. But now the café was empty, chairs stacked inside. Her eye caught on that *Closed* sign again.

God, what had just *happened*?

Mr. Solt had pushed her and then . . . Joan tried to remember. And then nothing. Then it had been night.

The sound of voices made her start back. A group of girls

tottered past her along Kensington High Street, chatting and laughing. They were all dressed up and clutching at each other to stay upright, like they were in the middle of a big night out. "Ooh, sorry," one of them said when she walked too close to Joan.

Joan's heart skittered as she watched them go. It was obvious that they were just enjoying their night; nothing strange had happened to them.

Joan closed her eyes, hoping the world would right itself when she opened them again. That it would be morning. That Nick would be walking toward her, up the road. But when she opened her eyes again, the sky was still black. The shops of Kensington High Street were still closed for the night, their windows dark. And it *felt* like night. The temperature had dropped at the same moment that the world had gone dark.

Joan pinched her arm. It hurt. The air was cold. The ground under her feet was firm. She wasn't dreaming.

But if this was real . . . Joan turned back to the dark windows of the shop behind her. There was a sign there with the café's hours: seven a.m. to nine p.m. If this was real, that meant there was a gap in her memory at least thirteen hours long.

Joan pushed down a surge of panic. She reached into her pocket for her phone, needing to talk to Nick—to tell him she was here—and then remembered again that her phone was gone.

Another surge of panic hit her. And then it was too much. She was alone in the dark with no memory of the day. She suddenly wanted to go home to Gran. She felt like a little kid again—like she'd fallen and hurt herself. Like if she could just get home, Gran would give her a hug, and then everything would be okay.

Joan stumbled back down Kensington High Street and then Earl's Court Road. All the familiar streets looked different in the dark. The shops were like empty shells. What time was it? It felt *late*.

What had *happened*? Had she been knocked out? Had she been drugged? Had she imagined it all? Each possibility scared her more.

In a rush of panic, she stopped and patted at her clothes. She was still fully dressed, she discovered in relief, still dressed for her date with Nick—sundress and sandals.

Could she be sleepwalking? She'd never done that before.

But underneath all her speculation, there was another question—one that she was afraid to think about too much: *What did Mr. Solt do to me?*

Mr. Solt's house loomed near the corner of Lexham Mews. Joan cringed away from it, afraid Mr. Solt might come out the door. She broke into a run, tripping on the uneven path outside his house. And then she ran the rest of the way back home, tumbling onto Gran's doorstep in the dark.

She got the door open and then locked it behind her. She checked the lock and then checked it again. When she turned, she expected to find the house dark and quiet. But to her surprise, there was a well of light coming from the kitchen. Someone was still awake.

Gran was at the kitchen table, drinking cocoa. More cocoa bubbled on the stove. Joan hesitated in the doorway, not sure if she was in trouble. The clock said it was just past one a.m. Dad would have freaked out if Joan had stayed out that late without calling him.

"Hello, love," Gran said without looking up. "Come and sit down." There was another mug of cocoa on the table, Joan saw now. It was steaming.

"I—" Joan didn't know what to say. *Gran, I think maybe I was drugged. Or maybe I hit my head and got knocked out.* Neither of those things seemed true. "Something happened," she managed. "Someone did something to me."

"Sit down, my love," Gran said, more gently. She slid the cocoa over to Joan.

Joan sat slowly and put her hands around the mug. It was very hot.

Gran looked softer than usual in the dim light. She was in a flannel dressing gown, and her hair was a curly gray halo. She waited for Joan to sip the cocoa and then she asked: "What happened? Tell me exactly."

Joan tried to remember, and panic bubbled up inside her again. The whole day was missing from her memory. There was just nothing there. "Mr. Solt did something to me," she said. "He did something. He—he pushed me against the wall. And then . . ." She hit the blank place in her mind again. "And then I don't remember." The words blurted out of her. "Gran, I don't remember anything that happened since this morning."

"He pushed you." Gran sounded reassuringly calm. "Did you push him back?"

"What?" Joan said. It was such an unexpected question that for a moment she didn't know how to answer. "No."

"But you touched him." Gran put a finger against the nape of her own neck. "Here."

Joan started to say no again and then remembered how she'd flung her hand up to keep her balance. She had a vivid sense memory of the edge of her hand knocking against Mr. Solt's neck.

"It was day," Gran said. "And then it was night, with nothing in between."

Joan stared at her. That was exactly what it had been like. "He did something to me," she whispered.

"He didn't do something to you," Gran said. "You did something to him."

"What?" Joan said.

"My love, I told you what you were when you were six years old."

Joan shook her head. She couldn't take her eyes off Gran's face.

Gran leaned closer. "You're a monster, Joan."

On the stove, cocoa was still bubbling. Joan could hear the slow tick of the clock. The whole world seemed to have narrowed to Gran's green eyes.

"You mean I can make things disappear?" Joan said. "Disappear and reappear?" She wasn't very good at it. If anything, that ability had diminished over the years. Gran and Uncle Gus could make whole paintings vanish, but Joan had never managed anything much bigger than a coin.

In the yellow kitchen light, Gran's eyes were as luminous as a cat's. "That's the Hunt family power," she said. "Each monster family has its own power. But all monsters have a power in common. We can travel. That's what you did."

"Travel?"

"Humans are bound in time," Gran said. "Monsters are not. You stole time from that man and then you used it to travel from this morning to tonight. You traveled in time."

Joan wanted to laugh. She wanted Gran to start laughing. But Gran was just looking at her. "What are you talking about?" she said.

"Life," Gran clarified. "You stole a few hours of life from him."

"No," Joan said. She didn't understand.

"You didn't take much," Gran said. "Half a day, perhaps. He'll die half a day earlier than he was supposed to."

"No!" Stealing life from humans . . . Joan's family had always called themselves monsters, but Gran was making it sound like they were *monsters*. Like they preyed on humans. Yeah, they shoplifted sometimes. Ruth could pick a bike lock. Bertie snuck into movies through the back door. But they weren't *monsters*.

"I didn't," Joan said. "I didn't steal life from him. I wouldn't. None of us would. And traveling in time . . . well, that's . . ."

Joan saw Uncle Gus's hat then, on the kitchen bench. It was

like all of Gus's hats: beautifully kept. This one was a chestnut color with a rich brown band. Gus was slimly built with a kind of 1950s style. He liked sharp suits and hats. Even his hair was old-fashioned: neatly smoothed and parted to the side.

Joan thought about what Aunt Ada had been wearing yesterday morning. Ada had an eclectic wardrobe, and Joan had always liked it. Yesterday she'd been up early, wearing a mechanic-style jumpsuit and a scarf in her hair with a knot at the top. The day before, she'd been in a white dress, like she was going to a 1920s garden party.

Like she was going to travel back in time to a 1920s garden party.

Joan pushed away from the table. The scrape of her chair was loud in the silence.

"Joan," Gran said.

Joan gripped the edge of the table. She shook her head again. She didn't even know what she was trying to deny.

Gran held out something. It was Joan's phone, the one she'd dropped in the scuffle with Mr. Solt. The screen was cracked.

"Don't forget the rule," Gran said. "No one can know what we are. What you are. You must never tell anyone about monsters."

Upstairs, Joan's room was just as she'd left it that morning— bed unmade with her pajamas strewn over the pillow. She stared down at her phone, at the long, jagged crack across the screen. Someone had turned it off. Gran had known to wait up for Joan tonight, and apparently she'd known to retrieve Joan's phone as well. Joan swallowed.

She turned her phone back on. When it lit up, she felt like a bucket of cold water had been thrown over her. There were messages from Nick.

She wanted to cry suddenly. She'd wanted to spend the day with him so much, and she'd missed their date. Not only that, but she'd hurt him. She'd stood him up.

Throat tight, she scrolled through the messages. The first was the one she'd seen that morning. She'd been about to answer it when Mr. Solt had arrived.

I'm on the Tube!

I'm here!

Everything okay? Are we still having breakfast?

Joan, are you okay?

Joan swallowed around the lump in her throat. The first message had been sent at 7:39 a.m.; the last at 6:23 p.m. She stared at her phone, not sure what to say. In the end, she went with:

I'm so sorry. I'm okay. A family thing came up.

You stole time from that man, Gran had said, *and then you used it to travel from this morning to tonight. You traveled in time.*

Joan sat heavily on her bed. Her first terrible instinct was to put her arms over her head and block everything out. This couldn't be real. She couldn't bear it to be.

Gran had said that Joan had stolen time from Mr. Solt, that he was going to die earlier than he would have because of her.

But that couldn't be true. Joan wouldn't hurt him. She never would.

And the rest of it was . . . just impossible.

But the alarm clock said one fifteen a.m. That was real. And Joan had left for the café not an hour ago. That was real too.

Monsters. Joan's family had always called themselves that. Why hadn't Joan ever asked why?

She watched the alarm clock blink. The minutes ticked over at the same speed they always did. One forty-five a.m. Two thirty a.m. It felt unnatural to be this wide awake so deep into the night. It felt like being jet-lagged.

And that thought brought memories with it. Like how Ruth sometimes seemed hyper and then an hour later exhausted enough to fall into bed and sleep all night. Like how Bertie could change outfits five times in a day.

Ruth and Bertie . . . If this was true, then they'd known all along. *They'd* stolen life from people. *He'll die half a day earlier than he was supposed to,* Gran had said about Mr. Solt. Gran hadn't even seemed to care. Like she really was a monster. The thought was unbearable.

Six thirty a.m. Seven thirty a.m. Sometime after that, Joan must have fallen asleep.

She dreamed that she was outside the café again with Mr. Solt. Only this time, when he pushed her, she turned and put her hands around his neck and *squeezed.* He choked and struggled, but as big as he was, she was somehow stronger than him this time.

And then, like a flicked switch, day turned into night.

Mr. Solt's voice came out of the darkness. *You're a monster.*

Joan woke up with a start. The curtains were open, and the sky outside was startlingly white. Joan reached up to cup her own neck, and felt the fragile flex of it when she swallowed. What kind of a dream was that? What kind of a person would have a dream like that?

Downstairs, in the kitchen, Ruth was eating toast with Marmite. The kitchen clock said three thirty. Joan couldn't make sense of it. Ruth was eating breakfast. It was bright outside. The clock said three thirty. Those things didn't go together. And then her sense of time abruptly reoriented: three thirty in the afternoon.

Ruth looked up. "Hey!" she said. "I can't believe you didn't wake me up when you got home! Tell me about your date with the hot nerd! Tell me everything." She sounded so normal that Joan felt another swoop of disorientation. "Was it amazing?" Ruth said. "Did you . . ." She pursed her lips in an exaggerated kiss.

"I missed it," Joan heard herself say.

"You missed it?" Ruth's amusement faded. "You missed your *date*? What do you mean? You were so excited."

Joan stared at her. Ruth's hair was all teased up. Her jacket had big shoulder pads, and her makeup was a little smeared. She looked like she'd just come home from a 1980s costume party.

Or from the 1980s.

"It's true, isn't it?" Joan said slowly.

Ruth was starting to frown. "What's true?"

"We're monsters," Joan said. "*Real* monsters. Our family steals life from humans."

Joan couldn't look away from Ruth's familiar face. She'd known Ruth her whole life—since before she could talk. Sometimes, in the summers, they'd shared a room. She'd argued with Ruth over stupid things, and made up with her again. Stayed up with her all night, talking about everything. Joan's throat felt chokingly tight. *Laugh*, she thought to Ruth. *Please. Or be confused. Or deny it. Tell me I've lost it completely.*

Please, Ruth. Please. Tell me it isn't true.

Ruth opened her mouth and closed it, as if she wasn't sure what to say. It was strange to see her looking so uncertain. She was usually so confident about everything. "Someone told you?" she said finally.

Horror settled in the pit of Joan's stomach. It was true. What Gran had said last night was true. "Why didn't *you* tell me?" she blurted.

The color was leaving Ruth's face. "Joan . . ."

"You've been stealing life from people?" Joan said. "Gran has? Bertie has?" The whole Hunt family. Joan's stomach gurgled like she might be sick. "Ruth, that's so wrong! That's really wrong! That's *evil*!" A horrible thought struck her. "Did you ever steal life from my dad? From me?"

Ruth looked shocked. "Of *course* not. How could you think that?"

Joan backed into the hallway. Her stomach lurched. She really was going to be sick.

"Hey!" Ruth said. She scrambled out of her seat. "Where are you going? You'll want to talk to Gran, okay?"

"Talk to Gran?" Joan said, incredulous. "I don't want to talk to any of you." She needed to get out of this house. She needed to get away from her family.

"Joan—"

"*No!*" Joan's voice cracked. She backed up more. "I never want to see *any* of you ever again!"

THREE

Last night, Joan had run past Mr. Solt's house, afraid of him. Now, as she passed it, she ducked her head, ashamed. *He didn't do something to you*, Gran had said. *You did something to him.*

Joan wished suddenly and desperately that she could go home—really go home. Not to Gran, but to Dad in Milton Keynes. But Dad was on holiday in Malaysia right now, visiting the other side of Joan's family. A friend of Dad's was house-sitting for them.

Joan felt as though she'd taken a step outside the real world. Over there in the real world, Dad was in Malaysia. Over there, Joan's friends were in the middle of their summer break.

And here . . . here, Joan's family had been stealing human life all this time, and Joan had never known it. Here, Joan had stolen life from someone yesterday too.

Joan turned the corner out of Gran's street and realized that she had no idea where she was going. If she called Dad, if she tried to go home to Milton Keynes, if she called a friend and asked to stay, there'd be questions. Questions she didn't know how to answer.

With nowhere else to go, she found herself heading to Holland House, the museum where she'd been volunteering. To Nick.

Holland House was an estate in Kensington that had been restored and transformed into a living museum. Each room was a perfect re-creation of the house's Georgian heyday. Inside, costumed historians guided tourists around the house and talked about how the occupants had once lived. Outside, there were picnic gardens, and a hedge maze for the kids.

Joan had been volunteering there three days a week since the start of the summer. The work was mostly cleaning and gardening, but Joan loved it. History was her favorite subject at school. Her friends talked about being actors and singers. Joan's dream was to work in a museum.

She walked the familiar route to Holland House. Around her, the world seemed surreally normal. The empty shells along Earl's Court Road looked like ordinary shops again. Even the blue skies of yesterday morning had turned back to London's more usual gloom. It was as though yesterday had never happened.

Joan reached Kensington High Street. On the other side of the road, the wrought-iron gates of Holland House stood open. It was late enough in the afternoon that tourists were leaving for the day, streaming out into Kensington.

It was strange to walk in against the current. Joan felt as if she were going the wrong way. Maybe she was. What would she even say to Nick when she saw him? From his point of view, she'd ignored his messages and stood him up. Then, today, she'd missed her volunteer shift without calling in. What if he didn't even want to talk to her? Joan swallowed hard at the thought.

As she made her way up the elm-lined path to the house, tourists passed her with empty picnic baskets and souvenirs from the gift shop. Kids ran by, waving foam swords, their parents following more sedately behind.

As always, Holland House came into view in pieces. Red brick broke through the veil of trees, then white trim and shining windows, before the path gave way to smooth lawn and the house was revealed in full.

The living museum of Holland House was a redbrick-and-stone manor draped in ivy. The roofline was gently gabled and turreted, and on the lawn outside there was a fountain and roaming peacocks.

Joan stood on the cusp of the lawn now. She'd somehow expected the house to seem different. But it looked just as it had two days ago. The whole world looked the same: Gran's kitchen and Earl's Court Road. It was Joan who'd changed.

Now she knew that underneath the facade of ordinary London, there were monsters.

Joan climbed the back staircase that the staff used. Afternoon light filtered through the windows. The air smelled of sun-warmed polish and wood.

Nick was working in the library. It was a long gallery space that stretched the entire width of the house. Bookshelves and oil paintings filled the walls. At one end of the gallery, windows looked out onto a formal garden; at the other, the front courtyard.

Joan hesitated in the doorway. Nick's back was to her. He was working alone, wiping down a picture frame with a soft dusting cloth. It was a little warm in the library, and his shirtsleeves were rolled up to the crooks of his elbows. Joan couldn't take her eyes off the sliver of bare skin between his collar and his hairline. *You touched him here*, Gran had said of Mr. Solt.

The surreal feeling was even stronger now. Joan remembered the first time she'd met Nick—her first day volunteering here. It had been a sunny Saturday at the start of summer. That morning, the crowds at the house had grown and grown until it seemed as if half of London were picnicking on the grounds, and inching shoulder to shoulder through the hedge maze. On Joan's lunch break, she'd retreated to the house, climbed the back staircase, and found herself alone here in this library. She had closed her eyes and breathed in the smell of paper and books bound in leather. The reprieve had been an intense relief.

A floorboard had creaked, and she'd opened her eyes again to find a boy walking into the library. He'd been a little older than her—seventeen, maybe. Her first thought was that he was classically handsome: clean-cut, with dark hair and a square jaw. And then he'd looked at her, and Joan had felt warmth roll over her, as if she'd stepped into a sunbeam.

Later she would learn that he was kind. That he never lied.

That he talked to everyone with the same respect and interest.

Joan shifted her weight now, and the floorboard creaked. For a moment, memory and reality converged as Nick turned.

Joan's heart skipped a beat as his dark eyes met hers. "I'm so sorry," she said. "I'm so sorry I didn't meet up with you yesterday."

Nick pushed a hand through his hair. In some lights, it was almost black—*Mr. Darcy black*, their friend Astrid called it. The window behind him had lightened it. "It's okay," he said. And the words were casual, but there was a vulnerable note underneath. He seemed braced for rejection.

"There was a family thing," Joan said. That wasn't exactly a lie, but it sounded like one. "And . . . and I'm sorry I didn't answer your messages. I lost my phone. . . ." She heard herself trail off. *But I found it again.*

You must never tell anyone about monsters, Gran had said. For the first time, Joan wondered if this secret would always stand between her and people she cared about. Here with Nick, and at home with Dad.

She imagined Nick waiting for her at that café. She hadn't responded to any of his messages. But she knew him. He'd have waited and waited, just in case. How long had he been there before he'd realized that she wasn't coming?

Are you okay? he'd asked in his last message.

She imagined him getting that curt message from her hours later that night. *A family thing came up.*

"Joan . . ." Nick was still standing there, waiting for more.

Now Joan saw the realization dawn on him slowly, along with the hurt of it. She wasn't going to give him a better explanation.

Downstairs, doors were closing. Footsteps tromped to the main entrance. The last of the tourists were leaving for the day.

Joan scrubbed a hand over her face. It was all too overwhelming. She needed something real. "I could . . ." She gestured awkwardly at the dusting cloth in Nick's hand. He blinked down at it, as if he'd forgotten he was holding it. "I could finish up in here. I know it doesn't make up for the shift I missed, but . . ."

Nick searched her face. "You don't have to do that."

"It won't take long," Joan said. She went over to the cleaning kit. She could feel Nick's eyes on her as she rummaged for a cloth. She was being all weird, she knew. And she was only putting off the inevitable.

The picture frame was wooden with rose carvings. Joan cleaned it as they'd been taught, getting the dust out of the fiddly carved bits, careful not to touch the painting itself. The silence was heavy. She tensed, waiting for him to say it: *You really hurt me. That's not okay, Joan.* Or maybe he'd just leave.

She heard Nick's footsteps. Slow, like the way she'd walked to Mr. Solt. He wasn't walking away.

He stopped beside her. She felt overly aware of him: broad-shouldered and square-jawed. "Joan?" His voice was a soft rumble. "What happened yesterday?"

Joan's throat felt thick. How often did her family do it, she wondered. How much life did they steal—and from who? Had Ruth stolen time from neighbors? From people Joan knew?

She wished for a reckless second that she could actually confess everything to Nick. She always felt better when she talked to him. And what Gran had told her last night was so frightening that she needed to tell someone. But she could never tell Nick. He was human, and Gran had reminded her of the rule last night: *You must never tell anyone about monsters.*

Downstairs, staff called goodbyes to each other. More doors were closing. People were going home. "I just came here to say I'm sorry." Joan had to force the words out. Her throat felt so tight.

She shouldn't have come here at all, she realized now. She hadn't known who to turn to, but she shouldn't have turned to Nick. The truth was, she'd stepped into a strange and dangerous new world last night. One Nick didn't belong in.

Nick didn't answer for a long moment. Joan saw the emotions cross his face. Had he guessed that when she left, she wouldn't be back?

Joan's chest hurt. *I like him*, she'd said to Ruth. But that wasn't what she felt. When she'd met him, it was like she'd recognized him. Like she'd known him her whole life. And when he'd asked her out, she'd felt like a new part of her had opened up. She hadn't even known she could feel like that.

The thought of leaving now—of never seeing him again—made her heart break. But she knew that she had to. She knew herself. She wouldn't be able to lie to him. She'd already had a reckless urge to confess. She felt it still.

"Joan," Nick said. They were standing so close. "Don't," he

said. There was something raw in his dark eyes. "Don't just go."

So he *had* guessed.

I have to, Joan thought. *I don't trust myself around you. I'm scared of what I'll tell you. I'm scared of what I am.*

But when he said, "Please," Joan found herself nodding.

Staff weren't supposed to stay after hours. Joan felt strange about breaking that rule—she was usually a letter-of-the-law kind of person, and Nick was too. They retreated to the far end of the library to sit side by side on the bare wooden floor under the window—where they couldn't damage anything.

Nick found a hazelnut Dairy Milk bar in his bag and laid down his jacket as an improvised picnic blanket. "Wouldn't want to drop any crumbs," he said solemnly. His collar slid down as he smoothed out the jacket, and Joan tried not to look at his pale neck.

Nick's fingers brushed against hers as he passed her the chocolate. Joan suppressed a flinch. She'd taken time from Mr. Solt just by touching his neck. She would never forgive herself if she hurt Nick like that too.

By tacit agreement, they avoided the topic of yesterday. Instead they made halting small talk. "Were you gardening today?" Joan said. It came out sounding as awkward as she felt.

There were a hundred unspoken questions in Nick's eyes, but he answered her. "Still doing that audit for the insurance company." He'd been born in Yorkshire and still had a faint northern accent. It sounded stronger when he was tired. Joan could hear it now. "I cataloged that room you like—with all the little paintings."

"The Miniature Room," Joan said. It must have taken him ages to catalog all the curios. That was a two-person job, and he'd had to do it alone today. No wonder he was tired. She looked down at the floor. Her guilt felt like a live thing inside her. She'd hurt Mr. Solt yesterday. She'd hurt Nick. She might not have intended to, but she had. Was this what monsters did?

As they exchanged more awkward small talk, the air felt heavy with unspoken things. The conversation they weren't having seemed louder than the one they were.

Joan drew her knees up. Around them, the house got quieter and quieter, until even the settling creaks of the floor seemed to still. They were the only ones left in the house.

Across the room, the late-afternoon sun splashed against the half-dusted painting. "I didn't finish dusting the frame," Joan realized. There was half an hour of work left on it. "I'll do it before we go."

Nick's voice was gentle. "I'll do it tomorrow."

Tomorrow. Joan didn't know how to think about tomorrow. She could barely imagine tonight. She let her head fall back against the wall. The painting was nearly life-size, but from here it looked like one of the miniatures. It was a portrait of a man in Regency-era hunting clothes. He was standing under an oak tree, chin at a haughty tilt.

Nick followed Joan's gaze. "Astrid calls him Hottie McTottie," he said, and Joan was surprised into a laugh. To be honest, though, she'd always thought the man in the portrait looked more cruel than anything. There was a corpse of a fox at his feet, and the tip of his shoe was on the fox's neck. The artist had painted his eyes as cold and predatory. "They say he once owned the house," Nick said.

Joan pictured all the empty rooms around them. "Can you imagine what it must have been like when just one family lived here?" she wondered. "So much space."

Nick looked up at the ceiling: a series of skylights, interspersed with silver stars against evening blue. "I can't imagine growing up here," he said. "My family had a tiny place when I was small. Eight of us in a two-bedroom flat." He sounded more relaxed as he said that—more like they were having a normal conversation.

"Eight?" Joan said, surprised. He'd spoken a little about his brothers and sisters before, but Joan hadn't realized there were so many of them.

"Three brothers and two sisters," he said. "My brothers and I all slept in the TV room until I was seven. But we didn't mind. It was nice, you know? Cozy."

"Yeah," Joan said, thinking of when she stayed with Gran. She liked Dad's serene house, but she liked living with the Hunts in summer too. She always had, anyway. She wasn't sure how she felt now. She closed her eyes for a moment. The back of her throat felt tight with tears.

Nick hesitated. Joan could tell what he wanted to ask. She braced herself, dreading the question. But Nick just shifted slightly so that they were sitting closer, their arms touching.

They sat like that while Joan collected herself. "What's your family like?" she managed.

Nick hesitated again. She could feel his eyes on her. "We didn't have much, growing up," he said. "My parents taught us to look after each other. To be good to each other. To help people in need. I believe it—I believe we should help people if we can." Someone else might have had a self-mocking tone—to show they knew it was hokey. But Nick just said it. Like he meant it.

Joan looked down at her hands—the hands that had stolen life yesterday. She'd always believed that too. Earnestly, like Nick. She wanted to be like that. She'd thought she *was* like that.

After that conversation with Gran, Joan had felt as if she was turning into something she didn't understand. Now, talking to Nick, she wondered if there might be a way to find herself again. To just be Joan. *Could* she, even knowing what she was?

"My dad always taught me that too," she said.

She told Nick about Dad and her extended family in Malaysia. About how she was an only child. And then—more tentatively—about being one of three cousins the same age when she stayed with the Hunts.

They talked for a long time. The conversation meandered from family to people at the house and then to anyone that occurred to them. When the words finally petered out again, Joan was relieved to find that the awkwardness was gone. The silence felt normal. Comfortable.

"I don't usually talk about myself this much," Nick said. He sounded uncertain, as though he was afraid he'd been boring her.

Joan leaned her head against the wall beside his. "I like talking to you," she said. She thought about how tentative he'd been when he'd asked her out. He was *so* good-looking. Movie star good-looking. There must have been people falling all over him at home, but he seemed as new to this as she was.

"I like being with you," Joan said. "I—Nick, I *really* wanted to go on that date. I really wanted to. I got all dressed up." She wasn't dressed up now, she realized wryly. She'd barely thought about clothes when she'd gotten up. She'd pulled on a dress over a tank top and bike shorts.

"Yeah?" Nick smiled, a little shy. "I got dressed up too. Not like a suit, but . . . there was a nice jacket."

Joan turned her head to look at him properly. "Yeah?" she echoed. The curators had put Nick in a Regency costume once, when one of the professional actors had been sick. The trousers had been tight around his thighs, the jacket straining around his muscled shoulders.

Joan heard the rhythm of her own breath change first. Nick touched her cheek and then Joan couldn't breathe at all. She'd never kissed anyone before. Nick's warm hand shifted to tilt up her head. She felt Nick's shaky breath—a warm puff against her mouth. He was nervous too.

Joan's breath caught as his mouth touched hers. Nick lifted up just enough to smile at her again. She smiled back. She suddenly didn't feel nervous at all. She pushed her hands into Nick's hair and kissed him. She felt warm and shivery all over. She shifted her weight, sliding her hands down to—

She jerked away fast, shocked at herself. She couldn't touch his neck.

"Hmm?" Nick seemed dazed from the kiss. "Joan?" Then he sat up a little, frowning. "Did you hear that?"

Joan registered it too then. Tires crunching over gravel. It was a sound she'd never heard here. Cars weren't allowed this close to the house. Lights washed in through the windows.

Joan scrambled to her feet and so did Nick. The sun had started to set. How long had they been sitting here, talking?

There was a black car in the courtyard below. "I didn't know they held functions here," Joan said. Three more cars were arriving. A distant warning bell went off in her mind. Where had she seen cars like that before?

Nick still seemed to be feeling the kiss. He took a deep breath, visibly gathered himself. His thick hair was rumpled from Joan's hands. "We should probably go."

Joan didn't fancy gate-crashing anything either. Nick offered his hand. Joan hesitated, but took it. Touching hands was safe, she reminded herself. It felt good to touch him—an echo of the shivery feeling from the kiss.

"We can go out the back way," Joan said. She led him up the library. "They won't even see us. They'll come in from—"

She stopped, staring through the open doorway.

In the passage outside the library, a man was stepping out

of thin air with the casual stride of someone out for a stroll. He had shoulder-length black hair and a long, vulture-like face. He was half turned away from Joan. As his back foot appeared, he brushed at his suit with finicky care.

If he turned even a little, he'd see them. Joan squeezed Nick's hand, willing him to stay silent. Willing him not to have seen what she'd seen. But Nick had. He was staring, eyes wide. The man had appeared out of thin air. Nick squeezed her hand back hard.

Those black cars. Joan remembered now where she'd seen cars like that before.

Two years ago, she'd arrived at Gran's place for the summer and found a buzz of energy in the air. And not the usual buzz of good humor among the Hunts—the house had felt alive with tension.

"The Olivers are in town this year," Ruth had explained to Joan. "Everyone's on edge."

"What do you mean?" Joan had said.

"The *Olivers*," Ruth had said, as if Joan should know what that meant. When Joan had looked at her blankly, Ruth had added: "Another family of monsters. Posh gits who drive around in black Jaguars. They hate us and we hate them."

"Another family of monsters?" Joan had said. "Monsters like us?"

"Not like us," Ruth had said. "The Olivers are really bad. Cruel."

Joan had seen those cars once later that summer. As she'd

walked down the street, three of them had rolled past, sleek and black. Inside the last, Joan had glimpsed a gray-suited man in the driver's seat, wearing a proper chauffeur's hat. In the back seat, a boy had sat alone. He'd been around Joan's age, golden-haired and beautiful. And as he'd passed, Joan had seen that he was sneering, as though he despised the whole world.

Cruel, Joan thought now. What would the Olivers do if they caught Joan and Nick here?

A woman appeared beside the vulture-faced man. And then more and more people were popping into existence—in the passage and in the rooms beyond: the Yellow Drawing Room, the Gilt Room.

Joan couldn't shut the door—not without making a sound. It was old and creaky and whined when it closed. She could only step back into the library, careful not to touch the creaky floorboard. She coaxed Nick back with her, hoping their movements would be masked by all the arrivals.

As she stepped back, there was a sound behind her. A third footstep—a footstep neither she nor Nick had taken.

Joan turned slowly. Where the library had been empty, now there were people all down the long gallery. Joan heard Nick breathe in, sharp and shocked.

A man grabbed Joan's shoulder with a heavy hand. "Why is it," he said, "that whenever we come to this time, we find the place infested with rats?"

FOUR

They were monsters.

If Joan had fostered any doubt about the truth, she couldn't doubt it anymore. They'd appeared out of thin air. Joan must have looked just like that yesterday when she'd traveled from morning to night.

Seven of them were standing in the long gallery, elegantly dressed in early twentieth-century suits and gowns. Joan's eyes caught on details. A white silk scarf draped over a black jacket. Silver beading on a blue dress. Black leather shoes with a mirror sheen.

"Did you see that?" Nick whispered to Joan. "Did you see them appear out of the air?"

Joan felt sick. "Yes." She wished she could tell him what was happening. She wished she knew more herself. She couldn't stop thinking of Ruth's words. *The Olivers are really bad. Cruel.*

In the silence, footsteps sounded, slow and deliberate. The vulture-faced man stepped in from the passage. His shoulder-length hair was as black as a raven's wing.

The man behind Joan gripped her shoulder tighter. "Lucien.

These two were here when we arrived. They saw us arrive."

Joan shivered at the way he said it. She had a horrible fore-boding feeling. *You must never tell anyone about monsters,* Gran had said. And now Nick had seen them. What did that mean?

"We're—we're volunteers here," Nick said. "We clean the house. We catalog the books. We don't have anything you'd—"

The man who'd spoken struck Nick hard across the face.

"Don't!" Joan said, shocked. She flung up a hand, as if she could belatedly stop Nick from being hit. Someone gripped her shoulder and dragged her back. Joan clutched desperately at Nick's hand, but couldn't hold on as she was pulled away. There was blood on Nick's mouth: a horrible smear of red.

Joan's voice had drawn the attention of the vulture-faced man. Lucien. He closed the gap between them and grabbed her chin. There was a scuffle between Nick and two men. Lucien ignored it, forcing Joan's chin up. "This girl is one of us," he said.

"A monster?" one of the others asked.

Nick stopped struggling and stared, his dark eyes huge. "A monster?" He sounded bewildered. "What?"

"I'm not—" Joan started to say, but Lucien squeezed her face, making her gasp.

"Don't try to deny it," Lucien said. "I can see what you are. I have the Oliver power. You're a monster and your little friend here is human." As he spoke, his eyes narrowed as if he'd noticed something else. Some prickling instinct made Joan follow his gaze down to her bracelet. It was a simple gold chain with a small charm—a gold fox with a silver tongue. Gran had given it to her years ago. *The Hunt family symbol*, she'd said.

Lucien's mouth twisted. "Search them," he said roughly.

Two men did, with efficiency. One of them found Joan's phone. Joan wrenched it away while he was still fumbling for it. She typed fast to Ruth: *Olivers at hh*. But as she tried to hit send, the man tore the phone from her. He crossed the room in a stride, opened a window, and dropped the phone out. There was a distant smash of glass in the courtyard below. Beside Joan, Nick managed to reach the corded phone on the desk, but then that was torn away too.

And then their arms were caught and they were muscled out of the library. Joan fought, the heels of her sneakers skidding and squealing against the wooden floor. "Let us go!" She could hear the rising panic in her voice. "Leave us alone! Let us go!"

They were dragged into the Gilt Room—two rooms over from the library, and the most ornate room in the house, a jewelry box of red velvet and oil paintings with gilded frames and gleaming gold leaf.

At least three dozen people had gathered, as though for a cocktail party. All of them turned to stare as Joan and Nick were hustled in. Joan was humiliatingly aware of her flushed, sweaty face. Her hair had loosened from its tie. Nick was disheveled too. There was blood on his mouth, and the struggle had rucked up his hair.

In contrast, the glamour of the Gilt Room fit the Olivers like a glove. They lounged casually on the velvet chairs and leaned against the blue-and-gold wainscoted walls as though it all belonged to them.

The most intimidating of them all was a blond man standing alone by the great marble fireplace—unlit in this warm weather. With a shock, Joan realized she'd seen him before. His portrait was in the library—the cold-eyed man in Regency-era hunting clothes. In real life, he was imposingly tall, with the same long face as Lucien. But where Lucien's face was vulture-like, this man's features were handsome and refined.

Joan looked at Nick. He hadn't recognized the man as being from the portrait—of course he hadn't. He didn't know that these people had stepped into this house from another time. Joan wished that she were still holding Nick's hand. She wanted to signal to Nick to run. But where could they run to? There were Olivers everywhere.

"Edmund," Lucien said to the cold-eyed man.

The man beckoned to Lucien without speaking. His posture was as arrogant as a king's.

"We found them in the library," Lucien said. He pushed Joan and Nick forward. "They say they're volunteers here. But look." He dragged up Joan's wrist to show Edmund her bracelet with its silver-tongued fox charm. "The girl's a Hunt."

The word *Hunt* rippled around the room in tones of distaste. As Joan followed the ripple, she saw a boy her own age, golden-haired and haughty. He was standing by one of the arched windows. *Hunt*, he mouthed at her with contempt.

"A Hunt," Edmund echoed. His family might have been roused, but his own voice was very cold. He examined Joan from his great height, as though examining a specimen. "Half-human, half-monster," he said to her musingly. "If your mother were an Oliver, you'd have been voided in the womb. But the Hunts have such tolerance for abominations."

Joan stared up at him, shaken. People had said things all her life about her being half-Chinese and half-English. But Edmund's flat tone and cold expression had somehow been as frightening as an overt threat. She had the feeling he wouldn't blink before killing her.

"What should we do with them?" Lucien said. "The boy saw us arrive."

He'd said that in the library too. As though Nick was a problem that would have to be dealt with. Joan scanned for an escape route, trying not to be too obvious.

Edmund's heavy hand landed on her shoulder, making her jump. He bent to examine her. "You traveled for the first time," he said to her. "Recently, I think." He bent closer—close enough that Joan could see the color of his eyes: the light gray of clouds on a gloomy day. For a long moment, she was caught in his gaze, like prey in the sights of a predator.

In the dim light of the chandeliers, she might have been the only person close enough to see his eyes widen. "It's true, then," he murmured. "The Hunts have been keeping secrets."

"What do you mean?" Joan whispered. What secrets?

"Edmund?" Lucien said. "The boy."

Edmund was still staring at Joan. He straightened slowly. To Joan's dismay, his attention turned to Nick. "You saw us arrive, boy?" he said.

"No!" Joan blurted. Edmund's expression was just like it had been in the painting: predatory. She thought about that image of the dead animal under his foot. "He didn't!" Joan said.

But Nick had already started to answer too. "I—I saw everyone appear out of the air."

Joan felt a sick swoop in the pit of her stomach. *You must never tell anyone about monsters,* Gran had said. But what happened to humans who found out?

Exits. There were five doors leading out of the Gilt Room— two doors to the east, two to the west, and one directly ahead. But Olivers were blocking every one of them.

"Dear me," Edmund said to Nick. "Everyone appearing from the air . . . That must have been awfully frightening." The words were warm, but his eyes were still a predator's. "You must be wondering who we are." He lowered his voice, as if divulging a secret. "We're monsters," he whispered. "We steal life from humans like you."

"Monsters?" Nick whispered back.

He was so vulnerable, and he didn't know it. A human, in a room full of people who could steal his life from him with a touch. Joan couldn't bear it.

"I know what you're thinking," Edmund said to Nick. "You're thinking that monsters don't exist. But of course you'd think that. Any human who learns the truth of our existence is killed."

Cold dread washed over Joan. She threw herself toward Nick, but Lucien wrenched her back. "No!" She fought Lucien desperately. "Let him go! You can't hurt him!" This couldn't be happening. Nick shouldn't even have been here—he was only here because she'd come to see him so late. And now . . . She sucked in a panicked breath. Were they going to kill him? They *couldn't.*

Nick was struggling too, head rearing like a spooked horse as Olivers closed in on him. "Joan!" he shouted. *"Joan!"* He managed to throw off one man, but a second slammed a casual fist into his jaw.

Nick slumped, knees sagging; the blow had knocked him unconscious. Olivers grabbed his arms, preventing him from slipping to the floor. Someone shoved his head down so that it lolled, baring his pale neck.

You touched him here, Gran had said.

"No!" Joan gasped. *No, no, no.* There was a knife in Lucien's belt. It looked ornamental; the handle was shaped like a mermaid—silver with blue enamel eyes. Without letting herself think about it, Joan threw her weight back against Lucien. He shoved her away instinctively.

Edmund made an irritated sound. "Control her," he told Lucien.

Lucien flushed and reached for her. But it was too late. Joan had the knife. She thrust it toward Lucien and was relieved when he backed up and Edmund did too, their hands rising. It seemed that monsters were as afraid of a blade as humans.

"Let him go!" Joan told the men holding Nick. But she couldn't fight them all. She took a step toward Edmund instead. "Let him *go*." She was surprised by the menace in her own voice. And she meant it. If they killed Nick, she'd *hurt* them—as many of them as she could before she was overpowered.

Edmund's eyebrows went up. "Dear me," he said dryly. "You seem fond of the human boy. I suppose that perversion must run in the family." Joan gripped the knife tighter. Edmund looked at Lucien. "Careless of you, brother, to lose your knife to a girl."

Lucien's gloomy face seemed to belong more to one of the wall paintings than to a living man. He took his time answering, and when he did, it was with an irritated drawl. "She's hardly a threat. One knife against forty people."

Joan judged the distance between herself and Edmund. He'd backed away from the fireplace, too far away for Joan to lunge at. Everyone had moved away from her. Now what was she going to do? Nick was unconscious. She tried not to let panic overwhelm her, but her heart felt like a hammer in her chest. She needed to *think*.

"One knife against forty?" Edmund repeated to Lucien. "Well. That sounds rather unsporting."

"Unsporting?" Lucien said, puzzled.

"One blade against another would be fairer, don't you think?" Edmund said.

When Edmund lifted his hand to indicate the sword above

the fireplace, Joan went light-headed with fear. She'd dusted that sword a dozen times. According to the tour guides, it was a replica of one that had belonged to the house's namesake, the first Earl of Holland. He'd been executed for his allegiance to Charles I.

"What am I to do with that?" Lucien sounded puzzled.

"Well, I suspect we can't kill *her* by touching her," Edmund said. "I would say there's too much monster in her for that." His eyes were bright, belying his even tone, and Joan wondered if she might be sick.

"This is tedious," another voice said suddenly. Joan was surprised to see that it was the blond boy. The one who'd mouthed *Hunt* with disgust. He was standing alone in an arched recess. Behind him, a window rose to the full height of the arch. The recess was deep enough to hold a comfortable armchair, but the boy had avoided it. "Should we not just let them go?" the boy said to Edmund. "Half-human or not, the girl is wearing the Hunt mark. They've claimed her as one of them. It hardly seems worth escalating matters for sport."

He wasn't alone in his objection. The other Olivers were shifting their weight, uncomfortable too—it seemed that only Edmund had a taste for blood.

"Aaron, this is a surprise," Edmund said mildly to the boy. "Are you actually expressing an opinion?"

There was a long silence. Long enough for Joan to hope that the boy—Aaron—would help her and Nick. That he'd stop this. But in the end it was Edmund who spoke again. "*Leave.*"

"Father—"

"We'll speak of this in the morning," Edmund said.

There was a dark flush on Aaron's cheeks, but he hesitated.

"Help us!" Joan begged Aaron. He didn't meet her eyes. "*Please*. You can't let him do this. He's going to kill us!"

"Aaron," Edmund said softly. His tone made Joan think of a snake sliding over grass.

Aaron dropped his head. Then, to Joan's despair, he turned and walked out of the room.

Joan turned back to Edmund. "Why are you *doing* this?" Because Nick had seen them arrive? Because Joan was a Hunt, and the two families hated each other?

"Why?" Edmund's eyes were as cold and gray as stone. "Because it will leaven my evening." But for some reason, Joan flashed back to the way his eyes had widened when he'd peered down at her. *The Hunts have been keeping secrets*, he'd said. "And because *you* should never have been born." This was said with sincerity and loathing.

Metal scraped. Joan jerked her eyes back toward the fireplace. Lucien had pulled the sword from its bracket. Silver flashed as he drew the blade. He thrust it into the air, the blade moving faster than Joan's eyes could follow. It was clear that he knew how to use it.

Joan gripped the knife. This couldn't be happening. A few feet away, Nick was slumped unconscious, held up between two men. His familiar body was limp, as if he were dead already. Just a little while ago, they'd kissed. This couldn't be *happening*.

"Do it," Edmund said to Lucien. The impatience in his voice made Joan shudder. She wondered how much it would hurt when Lucien stabbed her. Would it be like when you cut yourself, and nothing hurt at all for a few seconds? Would she be dead before the pain came? Maybe Nick wouldn't feel anything either. Maybe he'd be unconscious for it all.

Joan didn't really believe that, though. Edmund seemed the type who enjoyed seeing other people suffer.

"You don't have to do what he says," she told Lucien. In her head, the words had felt steady, but out loud, her voice dipped in and out like a faulty speaker. "You know this is wrong." Lucien didn't respond to her, so Joan turned to the rest of the family. "You can't just watch us die," she said desperately. But everyone was avoiding her eyes.

"Enough hesitation, Lucien," Edmund said. "End this. Or do you need someone to knock *her* out too?"

Lucien flushed dark red. He turned to Joan. He raised his sword and prowled toward her. Joan's hands went cold and numb.

She stumbled back. Velvet chairs scraped behind her as people got out of the way. "This is murder!" she said.

"Quiet!" Lucien snapped at her. He thrust the sword. Joan dove back, shocked when she avoided the blow. But she wasn't fast enough to dodge the next. The blade caught her side. The pain struck a moment later. She heard herself make a stunned sound. Blood began to seep, thick and wet.

Joan slashed desperately at Lucien. He punched her wrist

with his fist, an agonizing slam, weighted with his sword. Joan grunted in pain and the knife flew from her hand.

The sharp edge of the sword came again. Joan dodged, and only just evaded it.

The next blow was too fast. Joan had one clear thought as the blade raced toward her. She was going to die. She flinched.

But the blow didn't come.

Joan looked up slowly. There was someone standing between her and Lucien.

It was Nick. He held Lucien's wrist in the cage of his fist, as if he'd caught Lucien's arm mid-strike. Joan stared.

Nick tilted his hand sharply, and Lucien's sword fell. Nick caught the hilt before it could hit the floor. Then, in one smooth movement, he thrust the sword into Lucien's chest, matter-of-fact.

Lucien's eyes went wide with disbelief. Blood bloomed across his shirt. Nick withdrew the sword and plunged it again, and Lucien slumped to the floor, very still. Nick wrenched the sword out again.

In the aftermath, all Joan could hear were her own loud breaths. In, out; in, out—the way Nick had stabbed Lucien with the sword. The room was silent. The whole thing had happened in seconds—so fast that Lucien hadn't even cried out.

Nick turned to Joan. "Are you all right?" he said to her. His dark-eyed gaze was focused on her, ignoring the threat of the Olivers, as if she were the only person in the room. "Did he hurt you?"

"What?" Joan stared at him. *I grabbed a knife. I wanted to rescue you*, she imagined blurting absurdly. And then her focus sharpened and she couldn't take her eyes off Nick's face. He looked just like he always did—square-jawed and broad-shouldered and earnest. *Open as a can of peas*, Gran would have said.

"I'm so sorry," Nick said. "I shouldn't have let that happen. I didn't expect them to knock me out."

Joan looked over his shoulder. The two men who'd been holding him were lying on the floor, as still as Lucien. "How did you—" she started and then stopped. She didn't know how to keep going. Were those men dead too? Had Nick just *killed three men?*

"He *did* hurt you." Nick stepped closer to look at where Lucien had sliced into her side.

Joan stumbled back from him instinctively. The movement caused a flare of pain that made her breathe in, sharp. Nick's weight shifted toward her as if he wanted to step closer. He was holding the sword loosely by his side. His shirtsleeves were still rolled up, and she flashed back to him holding the dusting cloth in that same way. She couldn't stop staring at him. She'd spent every other day with Nick for weeks. She *knew* him. Didn't she?

"I think Lucien was a proper swordsman," she said disbelievingly. A trained swordsman.

Nick regarded her. "He was very good," he agreed.

"You killed him," Joan said. "Nick, you *killed* him." She could hear the bewilderment in her own voice. "You took his sword from him and you killed him."

"He was very good," Nick said again. "But I was trained from childhood."

"Trained to do *what*?"

"To kill monsters."

Joan stumbled back another step. Humans didn't know about monsters. No one was trained to kill them. She could feel all the Olivers staring. *Your hot nerd*, Ruth had called Nick when Joan had talked about him. *Your history nerd. Your crush from work.*

"Who are you?" Joan said.

"Try not to move," Nick said. His weight shifted again as though he wanted to step closer to her but was afraid she might run. "You're bleeding, Joan."

Joan couldn't stop staring at him. "Who *are* you?" she repeated.

He didn't answer her. And as Joan stared into his steady eyes, a memory came to her. A sweltering summer night when she and Ruth couldn't sleep.

Tell us a bedtime story, Ruth had said to Gran. *Tell us a story about the human hero.*

Joan backed up another step. The heel of her foot caught on something. She looked down. It was Lucien's shoe. That was an angle you didn't usually see of a person, she thought stupidly. The bottom of their shoes.

She imagined Lucien standing up and brushing the dust from his trousers. She imagined him taking the sword from Nick. But he didn't move. He was as still and blank-faced as a doll. A minute ago he'd been trying to kill her. And now there was nothing behind his eyes. There was blood all over his chest. An image flashed into Joan's mind of the whole Oliver household slumped on the floor like dolls.

"*Run,*" she said suddenly. She hadn't even known she was going to say it. Her voice sounded loud in the silent room. She barely knew who she was saying it to. "Everyone needs to run!" There were rustles and shifting noises, people moving uncertainly. No one was sure enough to make the first move. But they had to. They *had* to. Joan was suddenly sure of it. "For God's sake!" she said. "You all have to get out of here! *Run.*"

"All right, that's enough." Edmund stepped forward from the fireplace. Joan jerked around to look at him. She'd almost forgotten he was there. His voice was that of a parent who'd come upon children arguing. It stopped the shuffling in the crowd as abruptly as if he'd flicked a switch.

Edmund raised his arm. He had a gun, Joan saw with horror. He pointed it very deliberately at Nick. "*No!*" Joan said. The gun moved to Joan.

"*Don't!*" Nick said, just as sharply.

Edmund raised his eyebrows. "Don't?"

"I saw you steal time from a tourist once," Nick said to Edmund. His voice was soft with contained anger. "You touched her neck. Right here." Nick touched his own nape. Joan stared at him. "How much time did you steal from her?" Nick asked. "Twenty years? Thirty? How much of her life did you take from her?"

"Not as much as I'll take from you," Edmund said, low and dangerous.

"You won't take any more time," Nick said. "Not from me or anyone else. Never again."

Edmund seemed almost amused. "Why? Because *you'll* stop me?"

"Yes."

"I don't know who think you are, but I'm the one with the gun." It was still trained on Joan. Edmund mimed shooting it at her. "Bang," he said softly. Joan jerked back. She couldn't breathe.

Nick aborted a movement beside her. Joan saw his fist clench.

"You know what?" Edmund said, addressing Nick genially. "I'm *not* going to kill you."

Joan exhaled hard. Edmund looked at her and laughed again. "Oh, you I'll kill," he told her. "But him . . ." He turned back to Nick. His voice went soft. "You killed three Olivers tonight. I'll have to make you pay for it." He angled the gun thoughtfully. "Perhaps I'll start by stripping a decade from your life. I could travel on your own time and slaughter your family while you're still weak and young. I'll let you watch. And then . . . a child has so much time in it. I'll take you home with me after I kill them. Keep you locked up in my house, available anytime an Oliver wants to travel. We can bleed you slowly."

Joan felt sick. "*You* should be locked up," she whispered.

Edmund lifted the gun fast, aiming it at Joan's head. Nick was faster. He threw the sword.

Edmund's gun clattered to the floor. His body followed in a slow crumple. The sword's blade was deep in his chest. He blinked once, shocked, and opened his mouth as though he was going to speak. And then his eyes glazed into blankness.

For a moment, everything was very still. And then, as though someone had pressed play, people were shoving each other to get out of the room.

"They won't escape," Nick said. "I signaled my people when we were first caught. They'll kill any monster they find on the grounds."

"People?" Joan whispered. He'd signaled people? She had a flash of memory of Nick hitting numbers on that corded phone before it had been wrenched from him. There were people coming? How many of them? She turned reflexively to the window.

Night had fallen. In reflection, the Gilt Room's gold and silver leaf formed a constellation of speckled lights. Nick's image stood in the middle of it, and—Joan took a second to register her own face. She'd never seen herself so scared.

She forced her expression into something more normal. She needed to keep it together. She had to *think*. "Look." Her voice wobbled, but she knew if she said the right thing—the *exact* right thing—no one else would die. Nick just had to understand. "Edmund was bad," she said. "Properly bad. But—but the other Olivers just seemed—I mean, you saw them. They were scared of him. They didn't want him to kill us. They're just people. Like me. I'm just a person. I mean, sure, we're monsters, but we're not like . . ." She raised her hands and made bear claws. "Not like 'Grr!'"

Nick was looking at her. Joan felt her chest loosen slightly. He was listening.

"I mean, I would know, right?" Joan said. "Dad's side of the family is human. Mum's side are monsters. But, really, both sides are the same. When you get right down to the bones of it, they're the same. They love each other. They laugh. Sometimes they argue. But they're all just people. If you talk to them. If you just explain to them—"

"I'm sorry," Nick said.

It took Joan a moment to understand what he was saying. She felt her game face drop. "You're going to kill them all?"

He wouldn't. Would he? She'd once seen him rescue a wasp from behind a curtain—everyone else had wanted to squash it. Nick had set it free. Except . . . now there were four bodies in the room. And Nick had done that. He'd started out unarmed, and he'd killed four people in minutes. Like it was nothing.

"You're really going to kill them all?" she repeated. Realization hit her. "You're going to kill *me*?" she whispered. She took another step back.

"*No*," Nick said, fast. "No, Joan. You were trying to protect me. I—I can give you safe passage out of the house tonight."

The way he said it made Joan wonder if he actually felt something for her. "You didn't need protecting."

"You thought I did," he said.

"Nick—"

"Edmund said that you traveled for the first time recently." Nick's dark eyes were very serious. "Was it an accident? Is that what happened to you yesterday? Is that why you were so upset when you came back today?"

Joan couldn't answer.

"It *was* an accident, wasn't it?" For a moment, Joan thought she saw agony in his eyes. "Joan, I'll give you safe passage out of the house tonight. But understand that if you ever steal time from a human again, I will kill you myself. I won't hesitate."

Joan's throat closed up. *You're a monster, Joan.* "And that's that?" she said hoarsely. She remembered the first time she'd seen him, in the library. She'd looked up at him, and she'd felt as though she'd known him her whole life. And now . . . "You're going to murder all these people, just like that?" she said. "Without trying to talk to them? Without anything?"

"Not only them," Nick said.

Joan went still. "What?"

Nick made a slight movement, as if he'd stopped an instinct to step between her and the door. "Please," he said. "Please stay in this room. I can only protect you if you stay in this room."

"If you hurt my family . . ." Joan couldn't finish the sentence.

"I sent the signal to my people," Nick said. "It's already started. We're hunting down every monster in this city tonight."

Joan went cold all over. For a long moment, she couldn't speak at all. When she did, it came out in a scared rush. "Nick, you *can't*," she whispered. "You *can't*." She imagined people knocking on Gran's door. Grabbing her. Hurting her and Ruth. Bertie. "You *can't*." When Nick didn't respond, Joan heard herself take a sharp breath. "You hate us that much?"

"It's not about hate," Nick said. But his mouth went tight, as though that wasn't quite true. "I only kill monsters who steal human life."

Downstairs, a door slammed. Someone screamed. Joan shuddered.

Nick glanced toward the sound. "Joan, *please*." Was Joan imagining the emotion in his voice? "Stay in this room. My people are all over these grounds. They're all over this neighborhood. You can't help your family. You'll be killed if you leave here. You're only safe if you stay here in this room tonight."

"Don't do this," Joan said, pleading with him. "Nick, don't hurt my family. You and me, we're—we're friends. Aren't we?"

"Monsters killed my whole family," Nick said. Joan stared at him. He'd talked about his family just tonight. *Eight of us in a two-bedroom flat*, he'd said. "I can't allow monsters to harm humans," he said. "I'll kill every one who does. Every one I can find."

Joan was running to the door before she'd even realized she'd moved.

FIVE

The Gilt Room's thick carpet muted Joan's racing footsteps enough that when she crossed into the Yellow Drawing Room, she startled at the slap-slap-slap of her own feet hitting the parquet floor. It was too loud. She wrenched her shoes off.

The room was surreally untouched by the events of the evening. The Yellow Drawing Room was one of those rooms you passed through on the way to somewhere else. Everything was a novelty of yellow: the walls, the chairs, even the thick-piled divan in the corner.

A jumble of memories clamored for Joan's attention. The sword in Nick's hand. *Monsters killed my whole family.* His mouth against hers. She shook her head, trying to clear it. No, no. Not right now. She couldn't think about any of that now. She *had* to warn her family that he was coming.

There was a glint under the divan. Joan bent. Someone had dropped their phone in their rush to flee.

It opened on the lock screen. Joan found the emergency options and dialed. She held the phone to her ear and waited. She could hear the wind sighing through the room. Her stillness had given stage to the subtle sounds of the house. A clock ticked on the mantelpiece. Floorboards popped. Some distant device hummed. There was no sound from the phone.

Joan looked at the screen properly. No signal. Was something blocking it? She squeezed the edges hard enough to hurt.

Muffled thuds sounded suddenly from downstairs. Someone was running. Two someones. Joan went to the mantelpiece and grabbed a candlestick—one of the heavy bronze ones that took an hour each to polish. She eased the door open.

The slice of light showed the passage between the library and the old servants' staircase. Downstairs, someone screamed and then suddenly stopped. There were more running footsteps. Joan couldn't tell whether they were near or far.

Joan held her breath and padded down the spiral staircase, soft in her socks. The old wood creaked, making her throat close up.

There was another distant scream and Joan's knees started to shake. How was she going to get out of the house? Nick knew it as well as she did—there'd be people watching the doors. He even knew about the old servants' passages.

She gripped the candlestick hard. But as she reached the bottom of the staircase, there was still no one in sight. She crept farther in. The door to the Linen Room was cracked open, showing the room all set up for tourists, one cupboard artfully open with shelves of folded tablecloths and sheets.

Joan held her breath and listened. Nothing. Where was everyone? Was this some kind of nightmare? If not for the pain in her wrist and the warm blood oozing down her side, she might have believed that none of this was really happening.

Something nearby creaked, making Joan's breath catch. She ducked quickly into the Linen Room. It was empty. Then the Valet Room. Empty. Then into Sabine's Room: the big bedroom suite beyond. Empty.

No. Not empty.

To Joan's horror, Ruth was at the back of the room, near the sofa set. Outside, the moon was shrouded by clouds, but there was enough light to see that Ruth's face was very pale.

"No," Joan breathed. No. *Ruth.* "What are you doing here? You can't *be* here." She stumbled toward her.

"You messaged for help," Ruth said. She hadn't moved from where she was standing.

Joan remembered typing desperately on her phone before it had been torn from her grip. She'd been reaching for the send button; she must have hit it. Her breath hitched. She'd yelled at Ruth this afternoon. She'd told Ruth she was evil, that she never wanted to see her again. But when Joan had needed help, Ruth had come.

"And I called everyone else," Ruth said.

"Everyone else?" Joan said. "Who—" The words caught in her throat. Her eyes had adjusted enough to see that there were dark stains on the carpet by the sofa. Joan stumbled closer.

"Joan, *don't*," Ruth said. "Don't come back here. Just stay where you are."

Joan shook her head. She heard herself make a strange,

deep sound as she rounded the corner of the sofa.

Gran was slumped on the sofa seat, legs splayed at an awkward angle, her shirt collar soaked with blood. One of her shoes had fallen off. It lay upturned by her stockinged foot.

"*No*. No, no, no." Joan had been on her way to warn her family about Nick. They couldn't be here. This couldn't be happening.

There was a folded blanket on Gran's chest. Joan had registered Ruth's stance as odd—slightly stooped. And now she saw why. Ruth was pressing down on the blanket with both hands.

"Everyone's dead." Ruth sounded like she was trying to break it gently, but her voice sounded strange and stilted, like when she did robot impressions. Ruth had the best robot voice. "Uncle Augustus. Bertie. Aunt Ada. Everyone's dead."

"No." Joan shook her head. "No." She couldn't seem to focus her eyes properly. Everything around her seemed blurry and unreal. She'd been on her way to warn them. They *couldn't* be dead. There was blood soaking through the blanket. Blood all over Ruth's hands.

"Joan." Ruth's voice jolted her. "I think Gran's dying," Ruth said, still with that strange, stilted tone. Her eyes were glazed. "She's lost so much blood."

"We just—" Joan could hear how weird her voice sounded too. "Okay, we have to call an ambulance. We need to call lots of ambulances. And then. Okay, this is what we're going to do. We're going to call an ambulance."

"The phones aren't working," Ruth said.

Joan blinked at her. "But we have to—"

"*No.*"

Joan and Ruth both started at the sound of Gran's voice.

Joan bent over, feeling weak. She hadn't wanted to admit it to herself, but she'd half thought Gran was already dead. She'd been so still.

Ruth gasped out a sound somewhere nearer to grief. "Gran."

"Don't involve humans," Gran murmured. Her eyes fluttered open. "You need to get out of this house."

"Who *did* this?" Ruth demanded. "Was it the Olivers? Because it if *was*—" She faltered. "Except I thought I saw Victor Oliver in the garden. I thought I saw Mattea."

"It wasn't them," Joan said.

"Then *who?*"

"Once upon a time," Gran murmured, "there was a boy who was born to kill monsters. A hero."

"What?" Ruth wiped her eyes against her shoulder. "The human hero? Those are bedtime stories. Oh God, Gran. You've lost so much blood."

A hero. In her mind's eye, Joan saw Nick push a sword into Lucien's chest. She saw him hurl the sword at Edmund. She swallowed. "I saw him kill people."

"You saw him?" Gran said sharply. "Did he see you?"

Joan hesitated. *He spared me because I tried to save him. Or maybe he felt something for me, like I felt something for him.* She couldn't bring herself to say it. "I escaped."

Gran gave her a long look, as though she knew Joan was

withholding something. "The Olivers?" she asked.

"Dead. Or fled."

"Dead," Gran said flatly. She took a pained breath. "My loves. You need to get out of this house. Ruth, lock the doors. Then get that window open. Wide enough for you and Joan."

"But the window—" Ruth's voice cracked. "The window is all the way over there. What if you die while I'm gone?"

Gran almost smiled. "Then you'll be filled with a lifetime of regret at your slowness at window opening," she said. "You'll compensate by never closing a window again. You'll shiver every winter for the rest of your life."

Ruth usually got grumpy when Gran was sarcastic, but now her mouth trembled. Joan wanted to look away. Ruth hated crying in front of people.

Gran's expression softened. "Oh, Ruth." Her fingers twitched as though she wanted to touch Ruth's arm but didn't have the strength.

"Please," Ruth whispered to her. "You don't have long."

"It's all right," Gran said gently. "I'll wait for you."

Ruth and Gran seemed to have some kind of silent conversation then. At the end of it, Gran's mouth curled up slightly, and Ruth rolled her eyes. "You're a bossy old woman," she said. She turned to Joan, her jaw set. "Put your hands where mine are."

Joan shuffled closer. She put her hands over Ruth's. Gran's blood was warm and sticky, and there was so much of it that it was hard to grip Ruth's hands. Joan couldn't believe this was happening.

"Press down," Ruth said. She slid her hands from under Joan's. "Press down really hard."

Joan pressed. She had to be hurting Gran, but Gran didn't make a sound.

"Gran . . . ," Ruth started.

"Go," Gran said. "I'll be here when you come back."

Joan stared down at the stained blanket under her hands. There was blood everywhere. All over the floor. All over Gran. All over Joan's hands now.

"Can Ruth hear us?" Gran whispered.

The room was big enough to be a bedroom and sitting room combined. Ruth was on the other side of it, propping a heavy chair under a doorknob. Joan shook her head. Her hair fell across her face, and she shrugged it away impatiently. "You shouldn't speak," she told Gran. "You should rest. We'll have the window open soon. We'll get you out."

"Don't be a fool," Gran murmured. Her words were so soft that Joan could hardly hear her, close as she was. "I didn't send Ruth away so I could rest." The rise and fall of her chest was unsteady under Joan's hands. She was struggling to breathe. "I was supposed to have so much more time to prepare you. I thought I'd be fighting beside you."

She wasn't making sense. "Gran, please," Joan said. "You need to save your strength."

"Hush," Gran said. "I will speak. You will not." Despite the pain, Gran's green eyes were as sharp as ever. "Only you can stop the hero, Joan."

Joan stared at Gran. She had to be delirious.

"I'm so sorry, my love, but—" Gran tried to take a breath and choked. Again and then again.

"*Gran,*" Joan said. She felt as though she were holding Gran together with her bare hands and couldn't hold her hard enough.

Gran caught her breath. "Can Ruth hear us?" she rasped. The effort of speaking seemed to be exhausting her.

Ruth was by one of the windows now. Joan drew a breath to call for her, but Gran put her hand over Joan's. "No," Gran managed. "Just—" Her face tightened with agony. She tried again. "Just. Can she hear us?"

Joan shook her head.

"Joan, you're in very grave danger." Gran's voice was getting weaker. Joan had to strain to hear her. "Graver than you know. Someday soon you'll come into an ability. A power."

"The Hunt—"

"Not the Hunt power," Gran whispered. "Another. You can trust no one with the knowledge of it."

Joan looked over at Ruth. She was still working on the window.

"No," Gran whispered. "Not Ruth. Not anyone. Promise me you'll tell no one of it."

Joan could trust Ruth with anything. "But Ruth—"

Gran's hand came up to clasp Joan's wrist. The ruby on her wedding ring glinted dully, the same color as all the blood. "Promise me," Gran ground out. "*Say* it."

"I promise," Joan whispered hoarsely.

Gran sighed in apparent relief. Her hand slipped from Joan's wrist.

She'd left something behind. Joan stared down numbly. Gran had placed a fine-chained gold necklace with a pendant over Joan's wrist. It was draped loosely over Joan's Hunt bracelet, and the two chains seemed to blur together as Joan stared at them.

After a time, she heard Ruth's pattering footsteps and then Ruth threw herself down to the floor. Dark curls were stuck to her forehead. "Gran, I got the window open."

Gran didn't respond. Her eyes were closed.

Ruth touched Gran's shoulder gently. "Gran, we can get you out. Joan and I can lift you."

Gran didn't open her eyes.

Ruth gave Joan an uneasy look. She touched Gran's cheek and then hovered her palm above Gran's mouth and nose.

Gran was dead, Joan thought blankly. She was dead.

"But she . . ." Ruth sounded bewildered. "She told me she'd wait for me."

Joan wanted to tell her that Gran had tried, but all she could think of was Gran saying *Only you can stop the hero.* Gran had been delirious.

A sound slowly entered Joan's awareness. A muffled thumping. She'd been hearing it for a while, she realized. How long? She felt out of sync with the world. "Ruth, we have to get up," she heard herself say.

"Huh?" Ruth blinked. Her eyes focused dully on Joan.

"Hey." She squeezed Joan's arm. "Stop."

Joan looked down. She was pressing Gran's chest, as though she could still stanch the blood. She released the tension in her arms. Everything ached. She felt like she'd been ill for a week. Her hands and arms were a butcher's shop.

The gold necklace was still draped loosely over her wrist, incongruously delicate. Joan touched it, leaving bloodied fingerprints, very dark against the gold.

The thumping sound was getting louder. Joan shook herself. She shoved the chain into her pocket and forced herself to her feet. *Thump*. The door to the passage jumped on its hinges. "Ruth," she said. "We have to go."

Ruth was staring at Gran's face, looking as numb as Joan felt. "We can't leave Gran here."

Joan didn't want to either. The thought of leaving Gran with people who hated monsters was unbearable. But Gran had always been practical. "Ruth, she'd want us to go." With each thump of the door, a larger slice of light was showing. Joan grabbed Ruth's hand and dragged her up. "We have to go."

She half shoved, half pulled Ruth over to the window. She pushed the curtain aside and recoiled. There was a body outside, lying in the colonnade: a woman with long black hair. She was wearing a blue dress with silver beading.

"I know," Ruth said shakily. "It's Marie Oliver."

Joan wiped her face with the back of her hand. The gap in the window wasn't nearly big enough. She gave the glass a shove. It barely moved. Had anyone even opened it in the last hundred years?

"I think we can squeeze through," Ruth said. "Don't you think?"

Joan stared at her. The gap wasn't big enough for a child. She pictured Ruth stuck in the window while Nick's people stabbed her like they'd stabbed Gran. Her stomach rolled. If anyone was going to get stuck, she wasn't going to let it be Ruth.

She climbed up onto the sill. The wooden flat of it bit into her stomach as she forced herself into the gap. As soon as she started pushing, she knew she wasn't going to fit. Her side dragged against something sharp, making her grunt. The seeping warmth that followed told her that the wound in her side had torn wider. And then she *couldn't* go any farther. She was stuck just like she'd pictured. A fish on a hook for anyone passing. She struggled desperately.

"Shit." Ruth shoved at Joan's side, making Joan pant in pain. "Oh God. I can't move you." Joan struggled harder. "Oh my God," Ruth whispered, panicked. "Oh my God." She shoved Joan again. She shoved her again. She shoved her *hard*. And then something tore in Joan's dress, and Joan fell to the ground in an inelegant flop.

Joan lay there for a moment, trying to breathe through the pain. On the ground beside her, the dead woman lay, eyes wide open, looking up at nothing. Joan felt a sob rise in her throat like bile. She squeezed her eyes shut for a second and then forced herself to her feet.

"Give me your hands," she said to Ruth shakily. "I'll need to pull you hard."

"Here." Ruth passed something through the gap. It was the heavy bronze candlestick that Joan had taken from the mantelpiece.

Joan tucked it under one arm. "Give me your hands. *Hurry.*" Whoever had killed Marie Oliver might be just around the corner. "And be careful. There's a nail sticking up."

"Fuck, this is narrow," Ruth said. "I don't think I'll fit."

"You'll fit," Joan promised. "I'll pull you through."

A loud crash sounded. The room lit up. "Ruth!" Joan tried to catch Ruth's hands, but Ruth had already scrabbled back, turning to face the intruders. *"Ruth!"* Joan screamed. She didn't even care if anyone heard her. "Ruth, get on the sill! I'll pull you out!"

"Joan, run," Ruth ordered. Her voice sounded weird. Fierce and stern. Almost like Gran's voice.

"No!" Joan shouted. People in black were swarming into the room. "Ruth!" One of the figures caught Ruth's arms. A knife flashed. *"No!"* Joan screamed.

Ruth struggled, flailing an arm free. One of the figures slumped to the floor, and then the knife plunged into Ruth's gut. She made a horrible, agonized sound. Her shocked eyes met Joan's through the window.

"No!" Joan heard herself cry.

And then there was just empty space where Ruth had been. She was gone.

A face appeared in the window. "There's another one out there!" they shouted.

Glass shattered, and Joan *ran*, bursting out of the colonnade into the South Garden. It was incongruously cheerful. The trees were lit with fairy lights, and the hydrangeas were in full bloom, in ice-cream shades of pink and white.

Joan had run the wrong way, she realized, terrified. She should have gone north. To the south there was only open lawn and the hedge maze.

The fastest way out was across the lawn and then down the path to the southwest gate. But there'd be nowhere to hide. She would be out in the open for at least five minutes, even if she ran as hard as she could.

That left the maze.

Someone shouted behind her and Joan hurled herself across the garden, crushing hydrangeas as she ran. The perfume of them rose, fresh and sweet. There were bodies lying among the flowers. Joan glimpsed a man with a mermaid tattoo curled delicately around his wrist. A woman with long red hair.

Joan risked a glance back. A figure in black appeared from around the corner of the house. Joan threw herself into the mouth of the maze. Had they seen her going in? She had to assume they had.

She ran, stumbling into the hedge walls in her haste to turn corners. And then she just ran and ran until she had to stop, hands on her knees, sucking in air and trying to quiet herself. Her own wheezing breaths sounded like Gran's last gasps. Like

Ruth's agonized grunt. She was still shoeless, she realized then, and still clutching the heavy candlestick like a runner's baton. Her dress was torn from where it had caught on the window ledge.

Joan wanted to lie down and cry. Her family. Oh God, her *family*. She wanted to pretend this wasn't happening. She imagined what Gran would say to her now. Her incredulous expression. *Joan, you're running for your life, girl. So bloody run!*

Joan stumbled forward.

She wasn't sure when she began to hear the other sounds. At first they could have been hedge leaves rustling in the wind. But soon the thud of steps was unmistakable. There was someone else in the maze with her, running too.

And someone was in pursuit of them, perhaps no more than a turn behind.

Every now and then, the maze brought them close enough for Joan to hear them clearly—the broken gasp of someone who'd been running too fast for too long; the steady breaths of someone who'd been trained to chase.

Joan peered into the thick press of the hedge, but the night was too dark. There was no way to tell how far away the runner and chaser were. The other side of the hedge wall could be miles of twisting paths away, or a single turn.

Then the sounds of running stopped abruptly. "Oh God. Please don't. *Please* don't." A boy's voice.

Joan caught herself before she gasped out loud. It sounded as though the boy were right next to her.

Joan walked forward carefully and then hesitated. She had no idea where she was in the maze. Everywhere she looked, the view was the same: dense hedge walls and dirt path.

"Please," the boy said, hoarse. "Please."

Joan crept around the corner. And there they were—Aaron Oliver, trapped in a dead end, facing one of Nick's men.

In the moonlight, Aaron's golden hair looked almost white. There was a tattoo on the back of his pursuer's neck—a snarling wolf. The man's posture was relaxed and confident as he walked toward Aaron. He drew a long knife from his belt.

Aaron saw Joan and froze. Joan knew exactly what he was thinking. He'd left her to die back at the house.

Two steps, Joan thought. Two steps back the way she'd come, and she'd be safe again. Two steps, and she'd be out of sight.

Joan took two steps. Aaron's eyes widened. She slammed the heavy candlestick into the back of the man's head.

The man rocked on his feet. He seemed shocked but unhurt. He grabbed Joan's hair and jerked her head back, knife coming up. Joan swung the candlestick hard into his face. There was a sickening crack like a twig breaking. The man stumbled, and Joan swung at him again, as hard as she could, connecting with his jaw. He fell, and she fell with him, feet tangling with his. The candlestick slid from her grasp, and she scrabbled after it desperately.

"He's out." Aaron's voice. "You hit him rather hard."

Joan's vision focused. "Oh my God," she heard herself say. The man was lying on his side, unconscious. His face was a bloody mess. Joan put her hands on her knees and breathed.

Aaron's feet appeared in front of her eyes. "I think I'm going to be sick," Joan told him. Then she turned away and retched, hunched over, at the base of the hedge.

When she was done, Aaron offered his hand, gingerly, as though he didn't really want to touch her.

"Fuck you," Joan said. Her stomach was still rolling.

"Why did you help me?" Aaron said.

Joan got herself upright, ignoring Aaron's question and his outstretched hand. She felt like she'd been pummeled in the stomach. She avoided looking at the man lying in the dead end. "I don't know how to get out of the maze from here," she said.

"I do," Aaron said. When Joan looked up, he'd rearranged his expression to something more familiarly supercilious. "I grew up in this house."

Grew up in this house? Joan couldn't make sense of that, but she didn't care enough to think about it. "Then get us out of here."

Aaron grabbed her sleeve as she turned.

"Don't *touch* me!" she said reflexively.

Aaron tugged the pinch of cloth in an exaggerated gesture to show that he wasn't touching skin. "Wrong way."

It took Joan a second to understand him. "We can't go back to the house," she said, confused.

"I need to find my father," Aaron said. "He'll take care of . . ." He nodded at the unconscious man. "That." At Joan's blank look, he added, a little awkwardly, "No harm will come to you now, of course. You saved my life. My family will pay the debt."

Aaron didn't know.

The night around them seemed very quiet. "We can't go back," Joan said. She took a breath. "Your father is dead."

Aaron went still. He let go of her sleeve. "What?"

Joan saw Gran again in her mind's eye. Gran was back there in that room. Joan had just left her lying there. And Ruth . . . Joan squeezed her eyes shut. "Your father is dead."

"No, he isn't."

Joan opened her mouth, and then couldn't think of what to say. *I'm sorry.* That's what she'd normally say if someone's father had died. Only, she wasn't sorry. Edmund had wanted her to die, horribly, for his own amusement. Aaron had just walked away; he'd *left* her to die. "It was fast," Joan said.

Aaron straightened the cuffs of his jacket. They didn't need it. He was neat and ordered and unrumpled. Someone stumbling onto the scene would never have guessed he'd just been running for his life. "You're wrong."

Joan thought again about the way Edmund had died. The sword wedged deep into his chest. She took a slow breath, hoping not to retch again. "I'm really not."

"You think I don't know—" Aaron bit off the words as his voice started to rise. "You think I don't know when my own father is going to die?" He was clearly forcing himself to stay calm, to stay ordered. "I know my family history. This isn't when he dies. It isn't today."

There wasn't *time* for this, Joan thought, frustrated. Standing here, where Nick's people could come upon them from any angle, was unbearable. "The boy who was with me," Joan said urgently. "The human boy. He killed Lucien. Then he killed your father. His people are all over the estate. They're killing us."

"Us?"

"*Monsters*," Joan said. And then she remembered how Edmund had called her an abomination because she was half-human. She wanted to scream suddenly. She wanted to grab Aaron by the shirt and drag him out of there. But she didn't know the way. "*Listen* to me," she said. "My gran is dead. My family. Your family. They're all—" Her voice broke. "They're all dead. And if we don't get out of here, we're going to die too. They're *killing* us."

Aaron stared down at the unconscious man. The wolf tattoo on the back of the man's neck was stark black against his skin.

"Aaron," Joan said. Without view of Aaron's face, she had no idea what he was thinking.

After a long moment, Aaron spoke. "I saw people in the South Garden." He sounded as though he were pulling the words reluctantly from somewhere deep. "Ivette. Victor. I saw people in the Green Lane. They were just lying there." He lifted his head, focused on Joan. He frowned. "You look like you've been in a car accident."

Joan blinked down at herself. Then she wished she hadn't. Gran had bled so much that her dress was stiff with it.

"Are you hurt?" Aaron said.

"No." Then Joan remembered Lucien and the sword. Well, not too badly. At least, she hoped. She fished in her pocket for the phone she'd found and the necklace Gran had given her. She started to remove her dress.

"What are you doing?" Aaron sounded horrified.

"I can't walk around covered in blood," Joan said. She tugged the dress over her head and caught his scandalized expression. "I'm not *naked* underneath." She gestured at her bike shorts and tank top.

"Oh," Aaron said, face stiff.

Joan balled up the bloody dress and shoved it under the hedge next to the unconscious man. A message. *Dear Nick, I took out your guy. Love, Joan.*

"How do we get out of here?" she said.

Aaron gestured ahead. Joan waited for him to turn his back, then fastened the necklace around her neck, tucking it under her tank top.

A Hunt and an Oliver cooperating. Yesterday, Joan's family would have said that was impossible. *We hate them and they hate us.* A few minutes ago, fighting against Lucien, Joan would have agreed.

But today, Joan had gone up against the Oliver family and lived. Today, Nick had saved her life. Then he'd revealed himself to be a threat beyond imagining. What was one more impossible thing?

SIX

Joan walked out under the leafy archway, past the cheerful *You escaped the maze!* sign. She found herself in darkness, in a field at the edge of the grounds. Dandelion heads brushed her ankles in the long grass. She couldn't see any sign of Nick or his people.

From here, Holland House was the size of her palm. The windows glowed like candles. The house looked welcoming, even homey.

Aaron came to stand beside her, just a shape in the darkness. He looked at the house. He'd said it had been his childhood home.

It was too dark to see his face.

Joan touched his elbow. He didn't react. But when she headed for the road, he followed.

Kensington High Street was all lights and cars and people, the cheerful bustle surreal after the silent gray of the maze. Joan stood at the curb, staring at the ordinariness of it all: kebabs and burgers and black cabs.

A car started nearby, making her jump. It crawled along the road, as though the occupants were lost—or looking for someone. Joan glanced at Aaron, and by unspoken agreement they both slid into the shadows of a doorway.

They made it to Kensington Gardens by a ragged route of back streets, avoiding any slow-rolling cars and vans. Kensington Gardens was closed for the night. Aaron gave Joan a boost over the fence, and she landed with a thud that flared the sword wound into sharp pain. She bent over and breathed.

A moment later, Aaron landed beside her, and she made herself straighten. "Do you think we were followed?" Aaron whispered.

"I don't know," Joan whispered back. The gardens were very dark. The streetlights penetrated a little, but beyond their sphere, Joan could hardly even see trees.

"Keep an eye out," Aaron said. "At night, police patrol the park with dogs."

"How do you know that?"

He scowled. "Do you actually require the amusing anecdote now? Or can we continue to run for our lives?"

I don't want to be running with you at all, Joan wanted to tell him. *You left me to die*. But he was right that they couldn't just stand here, talking, where anyone could stumble on them.

"Let's head for the Serpentine," Joan said. The moonlight on the lake might give them enough light to navigate across the uneven ground without having to rely on phones for light.

"Dogs can track across water."

"That's not why—" Joan started, and then cut herself off. He had a way of talking that made her want to argue with him. "Let's just go," she said shortly.

They walked in silence. Joan's socks quickly became soaked with dew. She welcomed the discomfort. It kept her mind here, in the park, in the present. Her feet were wet and cold. Better to think about that than to think about Gran's slack mouth. About the people lying dead among the flowers. About the sound Ruth had made when the knife had punched into her. About Nick's face when he'd said: *If you ever steal time from a human again, I will kill you myself.*

They followed the dull shine of the Serpentine as it wound through the park. Eventually, Aaron touched Joan's arm to stop her.

"What is it?" Joan whispered. The brush was thick here, almost wild. Joan could hear the lap of the water in the darkness. She was shivering in spite of the exercise. Had Aaron heard something nearby? She hadn't. She folded her arms around herself and felt sticky warmth at her side. She was still bleeding. It seemed like a bad idea to get themselves wet and even colder.

"You're injured," Aaron whispered.

"What?" Joan wished she could see him better. It was so dark.

"The way you're walking. Did the attackers do it?"

Joan was incredulous. "Your *uncle* did it."

Aaron's pause was barely perceptible. "How bad is it?"

"Can we please just keep walking."

"Don't be a fool. How bad is it?"

Joan looked up at the dark sky, wishing she were here with

anyone else. *God, if only Bertie or Ruth*— She bit the inside of her cheek hard to stop the thought. She grabbed the base of her tank top and peeled it up.

Aaron thumbed his phone on, shielding the light with his body. There was a cut on Joan's side. It had bled—a lot. So much that it was difficult to see how deep it was.

Aaron swore under his breath. "We need to find somewhere to stay for the night."

"You mean together?" Joan said, surprised. She'd assumed they'd part ways as soon as they left the park.

In the harsh light of the phone, Aaron seemed as surprised as she was. He recovered quickly, his face becoming a sneering mask. "Fine with me if you want to split up."

"I didn't say that."

"It's not like I want to hang about with you either."

"God," Joan said, sharper than she'd intended. "Is it hard work being such a prat all the time?"

Aaron's smile didn't get anywhere near his eyes. "Not really."

Joan ground her teeth to keep herself from getting too loud. "Let's just sleep here in the park," she suggested. "It's as good as anywhere." Kensington Gardens was big enough to hide two people if they stayed quiet. "We could take turns sleeping and keeping watch."

"I'm not sleeping on the *ground*."

Joan couldn't help but huff a laugh. "Well, okay, Your Highness. Let's check in to the Savoy."

Aaron took off his suit jacket. To Joan's surprise, he offered it to her. She shook her head. She was cold, but not nearly cold enough to wear Aaron Oliver's jacket.

"There's blood all over you," he said.

Joan looked down at herself. Her tank top was a mess. And her arms. Her hands . . . It was mostly Gran's blood.

"Here." Aaron draped the jacket around her. It was light gray wool and far too big for her. The warmth was immediate and the relief intense. Joan's first instinct was gratitude, and then she was annoyed at herself for it.

Aaron turned off his phone screen. The contrast made the night very black. "We can't go to a hotel," he said, as if she'd been serious about the Savoy. "We're far too memorable, looking like this. They'd only have to ask around."

Joan pictured the area around them. A vague memory came to her. There was a place north of here where Gran met people sometimes—when she didn't want it known that she was meeting them. "I might know somewhere," she said.

"Somewhere safe?" Aaron said.

"I don't know," Joan admitted. "But probably safer than here."

It turned out to be a longer walk than Joan had remembered. By the time she found the right street, her teeth were chattering again, and Aaron was looking over his shoulder more than he was watching the way ahead.

The streetlights were broken here—and recently. Glass

was spattered on the ground. Aaron walked around the shards with fastidious care. "Isn't this nice," he said. "You've managed to home in on the one piece of slum around here. Trust a Hunt."

Joan wished she'd paid more attention when she'd come here with Gran. All the houses on the row looked the same. She went up to one of the doors with more confidence than she felt.

To her relief, the door wasn't locked, and the foyer was familiar—a tiny reception area the size of Gran's bathroom. The smell was familiar too. Ancient cigarettes and damp. The carpet stuck to Joan's socks, adding brown furry muck to the mud and grass.

Joan rang the bell at the desk. A woman emerged from the staff door. She had gray hair and cat-eye glasses, and she didn't blink at Joan and Aaron's mismatched clothes. Her name tag said *Vera*.

"Room for two, please," Joan said.

Vera pointed at a handwritten sign taped to the counter. *Cash only. Hourly and nightly rates. Payment up front.*

"That's you," Joan said to Aaron.

Aaron looked sour. His expression was as clear as a thought bubble: he couldn't believe that he was here in this foyer, with Joan and Vera.

"Two beds," Aaron said.

"*Two* beds?" Vera seemed far more surprised at that than at the contrast between Joan's muddy socks and Aaron's Savile Row suit.

Joan felt her face heating up. Aaron seemed flustered too,

for the first time since Joan had met him. "I trust you can accommodate," he said. He pulled a wallet from his back pocket. Joan glimpsed strange banknotes. Old-fashioned notes. Transparent notes. He thumbed through them and then pulled out two recognizable twenties.

Vera shrugged. She slid a numbered key under the glass and pointed at the fire door. "Lift's broken."

"I'd have preferred sleeping under a bridge," Aaron told Joan as they tromped up the stairs. Cockroaches scuttered alongside them.

"Nick won't look for us here," Joan said.

"Nick." Aaron looked at her sideways.

"I—I knew him before tonight," she said.

She looked away from Aaron's sharpening gaze. "We were—" She stopped at the stab of pain in her chest, harsher and sharper than the pain in her side. She'd kissed Nick just before all this. She'd wanted it so much. "I knew him," she managed.

Aaron was still looking at her. Joan had the unsettling impression that he was seeing more than he should have. Then his eyes dropped to a yellow stain on the fraying carpet and he grimaced. "Well, of course he won't look for us here. No one would come here. Rats wouldn't. Health inspectors clearly haven't."

He was back to his annoying superiority, but for just a second Joan had seen something underneath that careless exterior:

something more insightful and intelligent than she'd realized, and more alien. It occurred to her that he wasn't human. And that, for all that she was half-monster herself, she didn't really know what a monster was.

The stairs ended in a long corridor with peeling wallpaper that showed layers of older patterns underneath: blue paisley and sallow orange. The edges of the carpet were nibbled to threads—Aaron had been wrong about the rats.

Joan found their door number and then leaned against the wall while Aaron struggled with the stiff lock. The pain from the sword wound was starting to get to her. She touched her side underneath Aaron's jacket and found fresh blood on her fingertips. *Shit.*

Aaron reached inside. There was a click. A single dim bulb illuminated the room. Two beds. A private bathroom with an uncurtained shower and a toilet. Everything they needed. Better than Joan had expected.

"Oh, this is unmitigated hell," Aaron said. The view through the window was the dark glass of an office building. He stared at it grimly and then snapped the curtain shut.

"What's wrong with it?" Joan said.

Aaron pointed at the ceiling. There was a cloudlike brown stain on it. "What's that?"

"A fresco," Joan said. As Aaron wandered into the bathroom, she considered their situation. The lock might have been stiff, but the door was as thin as her finger. There was a single flimsy bolt.

She shrugged off Aaron's jacket and squeezed herself between the two beds. Then she shoved the nearest one. It didn't want to go at first. She forced it, inch by grinding inch, until it was up against the door. With any luck, that would slow down anyone trying to kick the thing in. The jolt of pain hit her belatedly. She leaned on the bed and breathed. *Goddamn Lucien.*

"Here," someone said, right beside her, and Joan flinched. For a second, all she could see were Edmund's cruel gray eyes. The round muzzle of the gun.

She raised her hand instinctively to push him away.

"Fine. Do it yourself, then," he said, and Joan's vision cleared. It was Aaron, his mouth disdainful. He dumped a first-aid kit on the bed along with a hand towel and a bowl of soapy water. "What kind of hotel has a first-aid kit in the bathroom, and no robes?" he said. "Nice place you've brought us to."

Joan stared at him as he picked up his jacket from the bedside table. She wasn't scared of him, she told herself. She'd been afraid of his father, but she'd seen Aaron at his basest self. He was a coward. He might have been more than a head taller than her, but if it came down to a fight between them, she was sure that she could take him.

Aaron didn't seem to notice the way she was looking at him. He made a show of shaking out the jacket and walking to the wardrobe. "Really," he said. "Clothes should be hung. Not tossed aside like wrapping paper."

Joan pulled herself together enough to say: "Not exactly important right now, is it?"

"It's important to look respectable. We represent our families."

Their families were dead. He seemed to remember it at the same moment she did. He stood, frozen, a hand on the open wardrobe door. "Well," he said. He closed the wardrobe with more force than necessary. "These coat hangers are wholly inadequate."

The first-aid kit had been raided before—it was that kind of place. Joan sat on the bed and sorted through what was left. Bandages. Tape. Antiseptic. Scissors.

She peeled up the mess of her tank top. Aaron hissed. "It's not all mine," Joan said. She suspected it was mostly Gran's.

Aaron came over to sit on the bed opposite hers. There was a small gap between them—so small that they were practically kicking each other. "What exactly happened back there at the house?" he said.

Joan looked up at him. He was stupidly good-looking. In his designer suit, he made this poky little room seem almost glamorous. His hair shone like a crown.

"You mean after you left the Gilt Room?" she said.

He hesitated. "Yes."

"After you left me to die?"

His chin came up, and he met her eyes without apology. "Yes."

"Well . . ." Joan dampened the towel in the soapy water and started to clean herself up. It hurt. A lot. Her jaw felt clenched tight enough to break teeth. "After that, your uncle tried to stick a sword in me. Then my friend Nick killed *him* and put that sword through your father's heart." She put the towel back into the bowl. The line of the cut was revealing itself along her side. She remembered the sword coming toward her. "I ran," she said. "And . . ." Her composure wavered. "And I found my gran dying. Then I ran again and found you in the maze. Is that what you wanted to know?"

Aaron's face was reddening. "Yes."

"Did you think we were friends because we escaped together?"

"Of course we're not friends."

Joan wanted to laugh. Of *course* not. She was half-Hunt. And, worse, half-human. Edmund had shown her exactly what the Olivers thought of that. She tore open an antiseptic wipe and swabbed it over herself. It stung like being sliced open again.

"Listen," Aaron said, "I know you're new to this."

Joan paused, feeling a new wariness. What did *that* mean?

"I'm an Oliver," Aaron said. "We can see if someone is a monster or a human just by looking at them—our family power. And you . . . you stink of new-car smell."

Joan was reminded again that she knew close to nothing about this world. It was a familiar sensation. She'd grown up between Dad's house and Gran's. Half-human, half-monster. Half-Chinese, half-English. It all felt the same sometimes. Joan was more than a stranger, but less than a true insider. She stood on a threshold, neither outside nor in.

"You've barely traveled, have you?" Aaron said.

"First time yesterday," Joan admitted. "It was an accident."

"Well, baby monster . . ." Aaron leaned forward, intense and serious. "I don't know how much your family has taught you, but you saved my life, and monsters don't take such debts lightly. Of *course* you and I aren't friends. Until I pay you back, you're more to me than that." There was no gratitude in his pale gray eyes, only that odd intensity—almost anger—as though Joan had burdened him with something instead of saving his life.

Joan didn't want him to feel indebted any more than he did. "I stopped you from getting stabbed," she said, "and you showed me the way out of the maze. We're even. There's nothing owed."

"Well, that answers that," Aaron said.

"What?"

"How much your family taught you."

Joan really, really didn't want to discuss her family with Aaron Oliver. Her hand shook as she smoothed a bandage down. She added waterproof tape and went to have a shower.

The bathroom was tiny. In the mirror, Joan's reflection looked glassy-eyed. There was blood on her chin and all over her arms and hands. Under her fingernails. In her hair. She started to shake again as she stripped.

Just a few days ago, they'd all had dinner together at Gran's little kitchen table. Uncle Gus had made lentils with fresh tomatoes. And Ruth had said to Joan: *How's your crush from work?* And Aunt Ada had said: *What crush? What's this?* And Bertie had said: *Ooh, what's he like? Show us a photo! Is he nice?*

Joan had another flash of memory. Of pleading with Nick.

Don't do this, Nick. Don't hurt my family.

She turned on the water as hot as it went. Then she scrubbed and scrubbed. She kept scrubbing until the water ran clear and her skin hurt, and even after that.

When all the blood was gone, she turned the tap off and slid to the tiled floor. She pulled her knees to her chest. The position tugged painfully at her cut side, but she couldn't bring herself to care. Here, in the quiet, she could hear Gran's last harsh breaths again. When she closed her eyes, she could see all those people lying dead among the flowers.

Once upon a time, Gran had said, *there was a boy who was born to kill monsters. A hero.*

Joan had been so angry with her family earlier today. For their silence. For the secrets they'd hidden from her. And now they were gone. Nick had killed them.

Joan pictured Nick's face, square-jawed and honest. She drew her knees tighter against her body. In movies, heroes killed monsters all the time. When the camera moved from the monsters' bodies, you never had to think about them again.

But when *you* were the monster, when the monsters killed were the people you loved . . .

Joan kept her eyes open. She watched water crawl toward the drain, making long lines on the tiles.

When she got back to the bedroom, Aaron was lying on top of his bedcovers, shoes off but still clothed. "I tried to call emergency services," he said. He was holding his phone. His throat bobbed up and down as he swallowed. "The dispatcher kept asking *who* I was. *Where* I was. Whether anyone else had survived and where they were. I hung up."

"Do you think they traced the call?" Joan asked. What was the extent of Nick's reach? How many people did he *have*?

"I don't know." Aaron sounded exhausted. "I've been trying to call the other families. No one's answering." He dropped the phone onto the bed and put both hands over his face. "Who attacked us?" he said. "How can this be happening?"

Joan remembered again that sweltering night when she and Ruth had been sleepless, sick with a fever. Ruth had been eight, and Joan seven. Gran had sat up with them, cooling their faces with damp cloths. The air had been heavy with the smell of impending rain.

Tell us a story, Ruth had said. *Tell us a story about the human hero.*

You have a morbid sensibility, Gran had said, but she'd been smiling.

Aaron was shaking his head. "This night is all wrong," he said now. "It's all wrong."

"I can't bear it either," Joan whispered. Her family must have been in pain when they'd died. They must have been so scared.

"You don't understand," Aaron said. "I'm saying this night is *wrong*. The Oliver records say nothing of an attack. The people I saw dead . . . those deaths are wrong. It's all wrong. They weren't supposed to die tonight."

The Oliver records. Joan felt as though a crack were opening up in the world, giving her a glimpse of something beyond—something vast and strange. A new world where the future was recorded as if it were past.

But . . . "It doesn't matter what the records say," Joan told him. "It happened. We were there."

"Don't you understand what I'm saying?"

"No," Joan told him. Why did he even care about the accuracy of a stupid book? His family had died tonight and so had hers. "Your records are wrong," she said. "Obviously."

Aaron's expression said this was pure, outrageous blasphemy. "You have no idea what you're talking about." He got up and stalked to the bathroom.

After a few minutes, the shower started.

Joan looked up at the stain on the ceiling and considered her options. She should find somewhere else to stay for the night. It didn't make sense to stick with Aaron. He despised her, and the feeling was mutual. And, according to Ruth, the Hunts and the Olivers had always been enemies.

And yet . . . If she was honest with herself, she didn't want to be alone tonight. Not with the sound of Gran's dying breaths still in her ears. Even Aaron Oliver's company would be better than that.

Aaron's shower seemed to take forever. Joan closed her eyes. She didn't sleep. The clock ticked on the wall, marking the seconds. Eventually, the water stopped. The bathroom door squeaked.

Joan opened her eyes. Aaron was coming out of the bathroom, shirt half-buttoned. His hair was darker when it was wet.

He'd put all his clothes back on—as Joan had. They were both still dressed to flee.

"We have to leave in the morning," Aaron said. He'd obviously been thinking about it in the shower.

Joan realized then that she'd been holding out some small hope that tomorrow could end with Dad picking her up at an airport far, far away from here. But that couldn't happen. It wasn't safe for Dad to be around her.

"I don't think he'll stop until he kills us all," she said.

"I know." Aaron stared down at his hands. "We don't have a choice, then, do we? We have to leave this time."

A jolt ran through Joan at his words. She felt like a struck bell.

If they traveled back in time, they could warn everyone. They could save everyone.

But now, in this quiet room, she remembered how monsters traveled. To leave this time, they'd have to steal time from humans.

And it mattered. Joan couldn't lie to herself. She'd have given *anything* for even five more minutes with Gran. With any member of her family. Every day of life mattered. Every minute mattered.

Could she really do this? Could she deliberately steal time from someone's life?

She looked down at her hands in her lap, and saw they were shaking.

"Yes," she said. A feeling of wrongness welled up inside her. She couldn't do this. This was wrong. This was really wrong.

This was something only a monster would do.

She pushed down the wrongness until all she could feel of it was a lingering horror. If only a monster would do this, then she could do this. She *was* a monster, wasn't she?

She lifted her head and met Aaron's eyes. "Yes," she said. "We have to stop this from happening. We have to go back."

SEVEN

———◆———

Joan woke to sun streaming on her face. She heard rustling sounds nearby; someone was opening the curtains. "No," she grumbled. "Five more minutes."

"Wake up," a boy said.

Joan opened her eyes fast and scrambled to sit up. She was in a strange, small room. A hotel room. Then it all came back to her in a gut punch. Gran was dead. Bertie. Aunt Ada. Uncle Gus. She remembered the sound Ruth had made when they'd stabbed her.

And Nick . . . Nick had done it. That felt like another punch.

Aaron Oliver was leaning against the wardrobe door. He was fully dressed, one hand in his pocket. "Get up," he said coolly. "We've almost slept through it."

"Slept through what?" Joan said.

Aaron looked clean and crisp, even though he was in the same clothes as yesterday. Joan looked down at herself. She was filthy. Her black tank top was stiff with dried blood.

"Here." Aaron threw something at her. It was his jacket again. "And here," he added. He unlocked his phone and dropped it into her hand.

"What's that for?"

"Is there anyone you still care about in this time?" he said. "Anyone still alive?"

Joan's stomach dropped. *Oh.*

She'd been avoiding thinking about Dad. Whenever she did, she found herself too close to losing it. Dad was the real world. He was school runs and Friday night sci-fi movies; he didn't belong in this nightmare. He didn't know about any of this. She shook her head.

"It's up to you," Aaron said. "But this could be the last time you speak to them."

The room was disgusting in the daylight. There were cigarette burns on the carpet and weird streaky stains on the quilts. Joan didn't let herself look too closely at them.

"Make it quick," Aaron said. "We need to be at the Pit in forty minutes."

"The Pit?"

Aaron gave her an impatient look. "It's where we're going to steal human time."

Aaron gave her what privacy he could, standing with his back to her, staring out the window, hands in his pockets.

Joan checked herself with the camera app. Her expression was strange, but her face wasn't scratched up or anything. Good enough. As she dialed, Aaron shifted his weight.

In her mind's eye, she saw Edmund lift his gun again and point it at her head. She watched Nick hurl the sword into Edmund's chest.

"Hello?"

Joan jumped. "Dad?"

The video appeared. Dad's familiar, sensible face. "Hi, Joan!" He beamed. He was wearing his new glasses with the thick black frames. He was having afternoon tea at Aunty Wei Ling's place. There was thick toast and kaya jam on his plate, and plastic bags of mangosteen and longan.

For a second Joan was right on the edge of bawling. She bit the inside of her cheek hard.

"It's Joan," Dad said to someone off-screen, and then Aunty Wei Ling's voice went: "Say hello to Joan!"

"Hello!" Joan's two-year-old cousin, Bao Bao, shouted. The image shook, and then Dad's face blurred away, and Bao Bao's pointy little face filled the screen. "Nǐ hǎo. Nǐ hǎo."

"Nǐ hǎo, Bao Bao," Joan said.

Bao Bao said something then in Hakka, or maybe Mandarin. Joan couldn't always tell the difference.

"English, ah!" Aunty Wei Ling said. "Joan speak English."

The screen tipped over again. Joan saw the ceiling with its big slow-moving fan, and then a blur of the rest of the table—coffee, a bowl of half-boiled eggs, and then Dad again, smiling.

"Having a good time in London?" he asked.

Joan made herself nod. She'd never wanted to be somewhere as badly as she wanted to be there at Aunty Wei Ling's house with Dad—eating toast with eggs and kaya jam and drinking coffee that tasted like flavored sugar.

"We're going to that crab place you like for dinner," Dad said.

"Next time, you have a holiday here!" Aunty Wei Ling shouted off-screen, and Dad laughed.

"What else have you been doing?" Joan asked.

She listened greedily as Dad talked about a trip to the bird park yesterday. Bao Bao had seen a cassowary. He came to stand beside Dad and held up his hand above his head to show Joan how tall it had been. It was from Australia. They were going to an island tomorrow. Joan smiled in what she hoped were the right places and wished that they would talk forever.

"You're quiet today," Dad said to her.

There was movement behind the phone as Aaron shifted again. Joan glanced at him. He made a wrap-it-up gesture.

"Yeah, just woke up. Still sleepy." Joan made herself smile. Then she made herself say the next bit. "I have to go, Dad. Just wanted to say hi."

"Okay," Dad said. "Call you later?"

Joan nodded. She wanted to say, *No, don't hang up. Stay talking to me forever.* She wanted to say, *Don't ever let anyone touch you on the back of the neck.* But that would sound crazy.

If she told her Dad about the monsters, maybe Dad would believe her and maybe he wouldn't. Either way, he'd be worried enough to call Gran, and when he didn't get an answer, he might even fly back here. He'd put himself in danger, and that couldn't happen.

"See you soon, okay?" he said.

Joan nodded. "Bye, Dad," she managed. She ended the call. The black screen reflected her face. She turned the phone over, not wanting to look at herself.

Aaron stepped away from the wall. "What about your mum? Or was she in the house last night?"

"She died when I was a baby." Joan wiped her face against her arm. "You want to call anyone?"

Aaron shook his head. Joan blinked. He had no family left at all? No friends, even? "Let's go," he said.

They arrived just after ten.

"The Pit," Aaron said.

"This is Buckingham Palace," Joan said.

"This is a festering hole of misery and petty theft," Aaron corrected her. He caught an elbow in the stomach from a tourist. His lips tightened. "A pit."

There were people everywhere: crowded onto the Victoria Memorial under the great stone statue of Victoria and pressed against the palace gates. From the festive atmosphere and the faint sound of drums, the Changing of the Guard was about to begin.

"Why are we here if you don't like it?" Joan said, confused.

"To take time," Aaron said. He led her into the crowd. At Joan's blank look, he said: "You know how this works, right? We take time from humans, and we use it to travel."

"I know," Joan snapped, even though she only knew what Gran had told her two nights ago. Aaron had a way of talking to people as though they were beneath him. It made Joan want to push back at him about everything.

"The time comes off the end of their lives," Aaron said. "If we take a year, they'll die a year earlier than they should have."

Joan swallowed. The feeling of wrongness was back in the pit of her stomach.

"Stealing time is always a risk," Aaron continued. "You don't know how long anyone has left. If you try to take more time from someone than they have, they'll drop dead right there in front of you."

"Drop dead?" Joan said numbly.

"Yes, and we don't want to draw that kind of attention." Aaron's tone was utterly practical. He could have been talking about getting caught picking a neighbor's flowers. "So we reduce the risk by taking a little bit of time from a lot of different people."

It still didn't explain why they'd come here to Buckingham Palace. A Tube station would have been just as crowded. And they'd stopped off at Primark on the way to buy Joan a T-shirt, jeans, and some shoes. For some reason, Aaron had also bought an ugly floppy hat and two bottles of water. Why hadn't they taken time there?

Aaron seemed to know what she was thinking. "We can't just pop over to the local grocery and steal time," he said. "If a monster did that—if they kept taking time from the same place, the same group of humans—those humans would die earlier than the general population. That would create a statistical anomaly that could draw the attention of human authorities. And *our* authorities—monster authorities—they *don't* like that. That's why you should always take time from visitors." He gestured at the crowd around them. "Tourists."

Tourists. Joan looked at the crowd. Everyone here was dressed for a holiday—comfortable shoes and light jackets.

"There are a lot of different techniques," Aaron said, "but to be honest, most of them are just for show. The important thing is to touch the back of the person's neck. Any part of your hand will do—fingers, thumb, palm. Then concentrate on an amount of time. No other thoughts. Clear your mind of everything else. Just one touch, nice and fast, and move on. The ratio is one to one. Take a day, and you can travel a day."

Joan's stomach was really starting to hurt. "Okay, so. So, we go back two days. You warn your family, and I'll warn mine."

"Days?" Aaron frowned. "We can't go back two days."

"What?"

"You can't be in the same time twice. The timeline doesn't allow it. If we want to go back, we'll have to go back to before you were born. And you're, what—seventeen?"

"What?"

"*How old are you?*" Aaron said slower, as if she were stupid.

"Sixteen."

"I'm seventeen. So that's seventeen years. But for safety, you should always add a few years. Let's say twenty years."

Joan stared at him. "But. But we only need to go back a couple of days. To before our families were killed."

"Well, we can't."

"But." Joan couldn't take it in. "We can't go back twenty years! We can't take that much time. That'd be like killing someone!"

"Keep your voice down," Aaron said, and Joan realized that people were staring at them. Aaron tugged her farther into the crowd. "We're not killing anyone," he murmured into her ear. "We're not taking twenty years from a single person. That's why we came *here*. We're going to take a little time from a lot of people."

Joan looked around at the crowd. These were all *people*. They'd come here for a bit of spectacle and a few photos. Maybe afterward they'd have a soft serve with a Flake. What kind of person would steal life from them? Only a monster would do that.

"Can you do it or not?" Aaron sounded impatient.

If she didn't do it, then Gran and Ruth and Bertie and Aunt Ada and Uncle Gus were dead. They were really dead. They really would have died last night. Joan squeezed her hands into fists and nodded.

"Then watch and learn," Aaron said.

With little effort, Aaron transformed himself into a tourist. He untucked his nice shirt, making it look almost comfortable. He put on the ugly floppy hat he'd bought. Then he pushed into the crowd, phone raised, taking photos of the palace. As he walked, the edge of his hand caught a woman's neck—apparently accidentally. He walked a little farther and then stopped suddenly to take another photo, making people stumble into him from behind. Aaron stumbled in turn, hand flinging up for balance, brushing people's necks. Joan saw him mouth *sorry, sorry* as he pushed his phone by people's ears to get the right angle. It looked like an accident every time.

After a few minutes, he pushed his way back to Joan. It took him a while. The crowd was still growing.

"Your turn," he said. "Ten days from each person. That's two school weeks. Monday to Friday. Then Monday to Friday again."

Joan's stomach churned. "Two school weeks," she echoed. Back of the neck. It was difficult to summon the idea of school. It felt like something from a whole other world.

Aaron passed his water bottle over a man's shoulder. The man gave Aaron an irritated look as the bottle went by his ear. Joan reached for it, her hand shaking. The man was around thirty years old and wearing a T-shirt with a dinosaur on it: a T. rex on a children's slide, its little arms waving in delight.

Joan let the edge of her hand brush the man's neck. It was awkward touching a stranger like this. He was sweating slightly. His hand came up to swat at the touch. Joan snatched her hand away.

It's okay, Aaron mouthed. Around them, the rumble of the crowd was beginning to rise. The drums and trumpets were getting louder. Joan craned around people's shoulders and heads and raised arms and phones. She glimpsed red coats on the long strip of the Mall. The new guards were coming.

Aaron stopped abruptly. A woman in a sun hat collided with him. Joan collided with the woman in turn, almost tripping over her shoes. Aaron gave Joan a meaningful look.

Joan let her hand fall against the woman's shoulder, as though regaining balance. She shifted her thumb to touch the woman's neck. She could feel Aaron's eyes on her.

Take time, she told herself.

She couldn't feel anything.

I'm taking time, she thought hopefully.

Through the crowd, she could see more red coats and tall tufted hats. The *thump, thump, thump* of the drums was getting closer.

A flash of movement caught her eyes. Aaron was gesturing at her to drop her hand. Joan had been too slow.

Joan pushed down the beginnings of panic. What if she couldn't figure this out?

"Breathe," Aaron murmured. "You just need to concentrate." He moved away again, putting a man between them. He held up his water bottle, and Joan reached over the man's shoulder for it.

The new man was heavyset, with dark hair. Joan let the edge of her hand shift against his neck. *Concentrate*, she told herself fiercely.

She squeezed her eyes shut. She wasn't here in a crowd, outside Buckingham Palace. She was at home in Milton Keynes. It was a school morning. Monday morning. She imagined fumbling with the alarm. Pulling on her blue-and-mustard uniform. The bell on Monday afternoon. Tuesday. Then Mr. Larch's noisy history class on Wednesday. Thursday. The happy sound of the last bell on Friday afternoon. Then Monday again. Wednesday again. Friday again.

Nothing happened. Joan tightened her grip on the bottle. She was trying her hardest, and it still wasn't working.

She opened her eyes and shook her head at Aaron.

She moved to shift away from the man, and then she was choking on it. Time ran into her like a jolt of strong coffee, like butterflies before an exam. Energy, intense and insistent, flowed through her. It felt horrible. It felt incredible.

Someone was there suddenly. Aaron. He tugged her hand, guiding it away from the man's neck.

"Are you all right?" he asked.

Joan breathed out shakily. She nodded.

Aaron took time as naturally as breathing. Joan struggled with every take. She knew she was being too slow. She could see Aaron becoming more and more tense as the ceremony drew closer. His eyes were everywhere—tracking every phone, scanning the crowd.

As the guards reached the palace, the crowd became so dense that it was difficult to move. Joan slowed down even more. She took time, then painstakingly shifted and squeezed to the next person.

She tried to concentrate on the mechanical act of it, but as she did, she found her mind returning to the Gilt Room. To Nick's grave face as he'd said: *If you ever steal time from a human again, I will kill you myself. I won't hesitate.*

She was stealing time from these people. She was a monster. She felt so fucking ugly inside. And at the same time, she wanted to scream at Nick: *Why did you have to kill my family?*

The next man was wearing a hoodie. Strange for such a warm day. Joan pushed the hood aside.

There was a tattoo on the back of his neck. A snarling wolf. Joan gasped. She'd seen that wolf before. The man in the maze had had the same tattoo.

This man turned fast, perhaps feeling the cool air on his neck. He reached for Joan, but she was already propelling herself into the crowd. She could hear him struggling after her as she muscled herself through the crush of people to the low fence that cut off the memorial from the road.

"Stay behind the barricades!" a cop shouted.

Joan leaped over the barricade, ignoring the "Oi!" behind her. She sprinted across the street. Here the crowd was even more dense. People were pressed ten deep, right up against the palace fence.

Someone grabbed Joan's arm. She threw a wild punch.

"It's me! It's me!" Aaron looked weirdly disheveled. He'd lost the floppy hat somewhere. He dragged her farther into the crowd, toward the fence.

"They're here!" Joan said. She looked over her shoulder, trying to pick them out from the crowd. "They're here!"

"I know." Aaron's grip tightened painfully around Joan's arm. "Do you have enough time to go?"

"I don't know." Was Nick here? Joan couldn't see the man with the tattoo. She couldn't see Nick.

Aaron's grip shifted so that he and Joan were holding hands.

It surprised Joan enough that she turned back to him. "What are you doing?"

"We have to leave now!"

"But . . . I don't know if I've taken enough time."

"*Look.* There." Aaron pointed. He sounded as scared as Joan felt. "There. There." People jumped over the barricades and ran toward them. A pack of wolves converging. "I'll do destination," Aaron said, "but you have to jump too. As long as we're holding hands, we'll go together. Are you ready?"

Joan nodded, even though she had no idea what she was actually supposed to do.

"Okay, *now,*" Aaron said.

Joan couldn't take her eyes off the men running toward them. Aaron had said to jump. She imagined herself jumping. Nothing happened.

"Do it!" Aaron said. "They're coming!"

Joan visualized jumping again. Nothing happened.

"I'm doing the hard part!" Aaron said. "You just have to jump!"

Joan jumped for real, jostling everyone around her. People turned and stared.

"What the hell are you doing?" Aaron said.

"You said to jump."

"Through time!"

Joan heard herself make a sound that might have been a laugh and might just have been terror. She thought frantically back to that morning with Mr. Solt, when he'd pushed her and day had turned into night. She couldn't remember doing anything—it had just happened. Nick's people were in the crowd now. Joan still couldn't see Nick. "You need to go without me," she said.

"Don't be stupid!" Aaron said. "Jump!"

"I don't know how!"

"You annoying, backward, time-mired Hunt. Jump!"

She imagined jumping again. Nothing. "You have to go!" she said. "They're almost here!"

"Look at me," Aaron said.

"It's too late!" The sword wound in Joan's side ached: a reminder of how much this was going to hurt. "You have to go!"

"Don't look at them," Aaron said. "Look at *me*."

Joan swallowed and lifted her head to look at him.

"You can do this," Aaron said. His face was very serious. His eyes were gray, Joan thought distantly. Like the sky before rain. "You've done it before. You know how."

"I really don't," Joan whispered. Oh God, there were more people leaping over the barricades now. "Aaron, you have to go."

"Look at *me*," Aaron said. Joan forced her gaze back to him. "Yeah, just like that. Tell me why you were working at Holland House."

"What? What are you talking about? Holland House?"

"You volunteered at Holland House." Aaron seemed so calm. "Why?"

"What are you *talking* about?"

"Just think," Aaron said. "Why?"

"Why?" Joan took a breath. "I don't know. I don't know, okay? I just did. I like history."

"You like history."

"*Yes*," Joan said impatiently. "Aaron, they're coming."

"You liked the re-creations of history at the house," Aaron said.

"Yes. I—yes."

"Holland House showed you another time," Aaron said. "And you were drawn to it. It wasn't the real thing. It was just a cardboard cutout, but it was as close as you could get to being in another time."

Joan stared at him. She remembered the first time she'd walked into the house. She'd loved it—immediately and irrationally. It had been restored to its Georgian heyday, and Joan had felt as though she'd stepped into another time.

"Traveling to other times is your birthright, Joan," Aaron said. "It's in your blood. You've been stuck here a long time, but you don't have to be. Remember the feeling you had? When you first walked into the house. Do you remember?"

Nick's people were almost upon them. Joan saw the shine of a knife.

"Do you remember?" Aaron asked.

Joan felt it again then. The yearning she'd felt when she'd first arrived at Holland House. Her heart wrenched with it. "I remember," she whispered.

The knife slashed toward her.

And the world shifted.

EIGHT

For a long moment, Joan couldn't hear anything but her own harsh breaths. Nick's people had vanished. She pressed her hand against her throat, where the knife had been about to slash her. She turned her palm over. Her skin felt strangely tender with anticipated pain. But there was no blood.

Nick's people were gone. The knife was gone.

No. *She* was gone.

Buckingham Palace seemed unchanged. People were still jostling for position to see the guards. The great statue of Victoria still sat on her throne.

But the man beside Joan had an old-fashioned camera, its thick strap looped around his neck. A second ago everyone had been holding up phones. Now no one was. And there were other differences too. Clothes were looser; hair was bigger.

Joan took a breath. She was breathing air from another time. She was standing with people from another time.

The sounds of the world came back in a rush—the drums, the trumpets, the marching footsteps of the guards. The ceremony was on top of them. No one seemed to have noticed that two people had arrived out of nowhere.

"We did it." Joan could hear the muted shock in her voice. "We traveled."

"*I* traveled," Aaron said dryly. "Dragging you along."

A woman nearby gave them both a curious look. Joan realized she was still holding Aaron's hand at the same moment he did. He tore his grip from hers as if she'd burned him. Joan rolled her eyes.

The Changing of the Guard was ending now in a last thunder of drums and trumpets. And it was suddenly all too loud. A lifted camera made Joan flinch. She was safe, but her body didn't believe it. Not yet.

She needed to breathe clear air. With effort, she pushed her way out of the crush, until the crowd finally yielded and she found herself in open space.

And then her breath stopped in her throat. Here, the past lay all around her. Cars circled the memorial in an unbroken stream, wide and boxy and low to the ground as she'd only ever seen in movies.

She was in the past. She turned a slow circle, following the cars. She was in the *past*. On the horizon, there was an empty space where the London Eye should have been: a missing tooth on the skyline.

The last turn brought her face-to-face with Aaron. He was watching her with an unexpectedly soft expression that disappeared as she focused on him. "Have you finished staring?" His voice was studied boredom. *This is nothing. I do this all the time.*

"Yes," Joan said. Her eyes returned to the piece of sky where the London Eye should have been. "No."

The world felt infinite. She could go anywhere. Any*when*. She could travel back to the Regency. To the Restoration. To the Roman Empire. She could see Pompeii before it fell. She could see— Then she remembered how they'd gotten here. She shuddered. No, she could never do that.

Tourists strolled around them. Girls and boys snuck Aaron a second look. Even with his hair all messed up, he was good-looking enough to turn heads. If these people only knew what he was, what Joan was—what she'd just fantasized about doing—they'd run screaming from them both.

Joan took a step toward the road, and then realized that she'd started for the Tube, to get to Gran's house in Kensington. She stopped, disoriented.

Gran moved every year. Here, in this time, Joan had no idea where the Hunt family lived. She had no idea where anyone was. When she'd imagined going back in time, she'd imagined going back a few days to warn everyone. Now she was decades in the past, before she was even born.

She wished suddenly that she could go home—not to Gran's. *Home* home, to Dad's, in Milton Keynes. She'd tell him everything, and he'd make a big pot of rice porridge with lots of ginger, like he did when she was sick. They'd scoop it into the little bowls from the top of the cupboard. Dad would crack an egg into Joan's bowl, and he'd tell her that everything would be okay.

But there was no home in this time. Right now, Dad was still living in Malaysia—he hadn't moved to England yet. If Joan went home to Milton Keynes, a stranger would answer the door.

"Are you about to lose it?" Aaron sounded more curious than concerned.

"No," Joan said.

"Because you look like you're freaking out."

"Yeah, well, I'm not," Joan said. It came out as embarrassingly emphatic.

She expected Aaron to mock her, but his eyes turned back to the clumps of tourists. "We can't stay here," he said. "We just appeared out of thin air. Someone might have noticed."

No one was even looking at them. Around them, people were either following the marching guards or peeling away. But of the two of them, Aaron knew this world. Aaron knew people here. Joan needed him. She hated that she needed him.

Aaron turned toward St. James's Park. The relieved guards were marching back down the long red stretch of the Mall. Thinning streams of tourists followed them, still taking photos with those big boxy cameras.

"Wait," Joan said, and only realized she'd spoken when Aaron turned back to her. "Where are we going?" she said. "We can't go to your family."

Aaron was silent for so long that Joan thought he wasn't going to answer at all.

"I know," he said finally. His expression was closed off. Joan waited for him to elaborate. But instead he started again toward the park.

Joan stared at his back for a long moment before following.

It was a sunnier day than the one they'd left. St. James's Park was a patchwork of picnic blankets and deck chairs, and people eating sandwiches and soft serves.

Conversation blended with kids shrieking and a tinny cricket match streaming from someone's—Joan blinked. Coming from a silver box the size of a bread bin.

This wasn't her London, she remembered again.

After that, all she could see were differences. The drape of people's clothes, the haircuts. Even the air smelled different in this time—like cigarettes and tar. The cars sounded different. When Joan closed her eyes, she could have been in a different city.

And something inside her was drawn to it—just as she'd been drawn to Holland House. She wanted to keep traveling, to see London grow stranger and stranger until there wasn't even a London here anymore. And then to keep going beyond that. To see the Iron Age, the Bronze Age.

Or to travel forward. To see wonders. *Time travel is in your blood*, Aaron had said.

"Hey!" Aaron's hand clamped over her arm.

Joan blinked at him, feeling weirdly muzzy. His grip hurt, but in the same distant way that her arm had hurt the time she'd broken it and Dr. de Witt had prescribed a wildly strong painkiller that had made her head float.

Aaron's face was right up close then, eyes wide. "Joan?" His voice sounded far away, as though he were speaking through a long pipe. "Hey, stay with me."

"Shouldn't," she mumbled. "Your family tried to kill me."

At school, Mr. Larch had said that there were once elephants and camels in St. James's Park. And crocodiles. King Charles II had played French croquet here. And before that, it had been a hunting ground. Wild deer and ducks for the king's table.

"Joan." The suddenness of Aaron's voice jolted her again. "Are you with me? Can you hear anything?"

"Can hear your stupid voice." Her own voice came out weirdly dreamy.

Aaron's small smile hit her right in the gut. It was unfair for him to be so good-looking, she thought distantly, when he was so disagreeable all the time.

"Can you feel me touching you?" he said.

His hand was on her arm. Joan opened her mouth to say that of course she could feel it. But the truth was, she could hardly feel her body at all. And Aaron's voice was the only thing she *could* hear clearly. Where a moment ago the park had been full of bird chatter and people talking, now everything seemed muffled. Panic stirred inside her, but even that felt far away and cotton-wooled. "What's happening?" she mumbled.

"You're all right," Aaron said. "But you need to listen to me very carefully. You have to stay in the moment. *This* moment. Pick out one detail from the park. What can you hear?"

"I don't—" She tried to pick out a thread from the muffled mess of her senses, but everything wisped away like smoke. "I don't know."

"I can hear the wind in the trees," Aaron said. And again his voice was the only clear thing. "Now you."

Joan struggled to focus. There *was* a sound floating above the others. Something high and sweet. She had to struggle even harder to find the word that went with it. "Bird," she managed. It was like talking underwater. She saw Aaron's hand tighten, but she still couldn't feel it.

"Good," he said. "What else? I can hear people talking."

Joan made another exhausting effort. It was like being stuck inside a dream, unable to wake up. "Cars."

"One more."

Joan struggled again. "Water. Fountain."

She wasn't sure how long they stood there together, naming sounds in the park. Aaron's hand gradually solidified against her skin, temperature coming back first so that she felt the warmth of him before anything else. The conversations around them reemerged, and then got louder and louder, like someone was turning the volume up. Joan took a breath that tasted like bitter rubber and fuel, and nearly choked on it.

Aaron squeezed her arm, and this time she definitely felt it. "There," he said. "There you are."

Joan took another choking breath. The fog in her head was clearing. She shook her head, trying to clear it faster. "What's going on?"

"You nearly died."

"*What?*"

"You tried to travel without taking time first."

"No," Joan said, confused. "I took time at the Pit. I must have had some leftover."

"It doesn't work like that," Aaron said. "Once you jump, it's gone. You jumped and then you tried to jump again. You didn't know how to put on the brakes."

"No, I just felt . . ." All Joan had felt was a yearning—a pull in her chest. The same pull she'd felt in the Pit. But if that was how you jumped, how were you supposed to stop yourself from traveling accidentally? How could you stop yourself from feeling a feeling?

"You should eat something," Aaron said. "Food from this time will ground you. Until then, you need to focus on the details. Smell, sound, temperature. Stay in the present. Don't think about anything but now."

But when *was* now? Suddenly, Joan had to know. She pulled away from Aaron with an almost frantic desperation. She had to find something—anything—with a date.

There was a rubbish bin beside the path. She rifled through it, pushing aside empty crisp packets, the remains of sandwiches. Half a Galaxy bar.

"Um." Aaron sounded mildly horrified. "When I said eat something, I didn't mean other people's refuse."

"Heh," Joan said absently. A Coke can. A crumpled Twiglets packet. No newspapers, no magazines. Damn.

"Is this a human thing?" Aaron said. "Caressing rubbish? I don't spend much time with humans."

"I'm looking for—" Joan glared at him. "*No*, it's not a human thing. I'm looking for the date."

Aaron's eyebrows lifted. "In the bin?"

"There might be a newspaper in there." Joan was starting to feel defensive. "In the movies, people always find the date in the newspaper. It happens in *Doctor Who* all the time. They do it in *Back to the Future*."

"What on earth is *Back to the Future*?"

Joan bit her lip, but the laugh spluttered out of her, half-hysterical. They'd traveled in time. Now she was here with this ridiculous posh boy who didn't even watch movies.

"I fail to see what's so amusing," Aaron said.

"What in the name of Eton is *Back to the Future*?" Joan said. "What is it? What is it, old bean?"

"I don't— Well, that's childish. I don't sound like that."

"You sound exactly like that."

Aaron huffed. "Oh, take your hands out of the bin! We don't need a newspaper to determine the date." He gave the picnickers and joggers a look of professional assessment—the kind of look that Ruth might give a lock she was about to pick. "It's 1993," he said.

Joan opened her mouth at his audacity. "You can't know that just by looking."

"Big hair, but not giant hair," Aaron said. "And no neon. So we're not in the eighties. No Rachel haircuts either, so this must be pre-*Friends*. That's a window of 1990 to 1994. After that, it's easy enough to narrow it down. That man's phone." Aaron pointed out the guy, still chatting on his phone. "BT Jade—it came out in 1993. So we could be in 1993 or 1994, but look at his watch. Look at his shoes. Brand-new. He likes new things. It's 1993."

Joan was impressed in spite of herself. *"Friends?"* she said. In the back of her mind, though, she was doing the sums.

"The Rachel haircut is a time marker," Aaron said. "Like St. Paul's or the new Globe. Why are you making that face?" He scrunched his mouth. Joan could only assume he was mimicking her own expression.

"You overshot!" she said. "We were only supposed to travel back twenty years!"

"So what if I did." Aaron folded his arms loftily. "You're lucky we got out at all. You were an utter deadweight."

"But—"

"My point," he said, "is that you don't need to rummage through other people's crisp packets as if you were a rabid squirrel."

Joan could hardly hear him. She stared at their surroundings. Across the grass, the lake barely rippled. A woman walked by with a pram. The baby would be an adult in Joan's time. Older than Joan herself. That elderly man might be dead.

And the strangest thing about it all was the absolute solidity of the world. The air smelled of cars and tar; the ground was hard under her feet. This was real. She was undeniably here—in a time before her own birth.

"What are we going to do?" she said. "We have to stop Nick." She felt a strange mix of urgency and helplessness. They were so far away from what had happened. "We need to warn everyone about what's coming."

And Nick wasn't here at all, she realized then. Not anywhere in the world in this time. She was surprised by her hollow feeling of loss. He hadn't been born yet. She could look for him everywhere, and he'd be nowhere.

"Before we do anything, we need to eat," Aaron said. "You almost traveled without taking time first. You almost died. Do you understand that? I always knew the Hunts were irresponsible, but failing to educate you in basic safety—"

"Don't talk about my family." Joan had meant to snap it, but it came out low and dangerous. The secrets that had been kept from her felt like a raw place inside her. Just being with Aaron—seeing how easily he negotiated this world—made her feel even more raw. "You of all people."

"Yes, me of all people indeed," Aaron said. "Your family taught you a lot about the monster world, did they?"

"I know a bit," Joan said defensively.

"Like what? Who can you trust in this time? You have no ID. Where are you going to get it? You have nowhere to sleep tonight, no money. No friends. And the Hunts are impossible to find."

"I can take care of myself."

"Which family's territory are we standing in right now?

What does that mean? What are the King's Laws? What happens if you break them?"

Joan pushed down a wave of helplessness. She didn't want to have to rely on Aaron bloody Oliver. His father had tried to kill her. Aaron would have let it happen. He'd just walked away.

"You traveled in time," Aaron said. "You're not in the human world anymore. If you want to survive, then you'll need to learn about the monster world *very* fast."

"I wish it were from anyone but you." She hadn't meant to say it out loud, but it was true.

"Oh, believe me, I know." Aaron turned and started walking again.

NINE

Signs of the nineties were everywhere: brick walls papered with *Jurassic Park* posters and the fluttering rags of older ones. *Groundhog Day*. Nirvana. The cars, the clothes, even the traffic lights looked different. It was like—and yet so unlike—the London that Joan knew. The police were fancy-dress versions of themselves, all in bobby hats and smart jackets. People's clothes were baggy and strange.

Aaron led Joan through Covent Garden, head raised as though he owned the whole city. At some point he'd transformed himself from a dowdy tourist back to a wealthy schoolboy.

As he had last night, he avoided the main roads, taking shortcuts Joan hadn't known existed—through hidden courtyards and walled parks. By the time he stopped, she was thoroughly lost. They could have been in Covent Garden or Temple or farther out.

Aaron had brought them to a passage between buildings, narrow enough that Joan could touch the stone walls on both sides when she stretched. The sky was a thin strip of gray above. It was as cool as a cellar here. This part of London felt very old. Chimneys blew out woody smoke.

There was a door in the wall—small and squat and black—with a brass plaque beside it, a sea serpent engulfing a sailing ship. The kind of image you might see on a medieval map to mark uncharted territory.

"This is one of our inns," Aaron said.

Joan touched the plaque. "Here be dragons?" she said.

Aaron's smile was amused, almost soft, as though he'd forgotten for a second that he didn't like her. Joan's stomach twisted strangely. She was nervous, she thought.

"Is this your first time in a monster place?" he said.

Joan wet her dry lips. She nodded.

"Dragons need not fear other dragons," Aaron said, and Joan's stomach did that strange twist again. She knew that wasn't true. Aaron's own family had shown her that.

But she took a deep breath and opened the door.

Her first impression was of an old-fashioned pub: glossy wood and stained glass. There were tables in every nook, crammed with people in the clothes of a dozen eras. Laughter and conversation filled the room.

But there were oddities too: rushes and herbs were strewn underfoot, and the air was smoky, almost barnyard. Joan could smell hay, crushed fennel, and lemon balm, as well as rosemary and rich roasting meat. A hearth in the corner held a bubbling cauldron of stew. Joan's stomach rumbled.

Her next impression was almost cathedral. The far wall was a series of stained-glass windows. In them, map monsters swam in an ocean of blue glass: a bearded fish, a spiny dragon, a great beast with scales and tusks. Blue light spilled from the windows, turning the wooden floor into rippling shallows.

As Joan stood there, a man emerged from a back room. He was Black with graying hair and a handsome, unlined face. He scanned the room with an air of authority, and then strode over to two men, sandy-haired and muscular, sitting near the hearth. "Did I see money change hands in my inn?" His tone was calm; Joan was reminded of a school principal. She guessed he was the owner of this place.

The two big men ducked their heads, seeming as chastened as scolded children. "Sorry, Innkeeper. Just off-loading my phone," one of them said.

"Does this look like a market?" The innkeeper gestured to the door. "Out." He didn't bother to watch the men go, although they did—scurrying obediently away. He turned his attention to Joan and Aaron, taking in their hairstyles, their shoes, the cut of their clothes. "Just arrived?" he said.

Aaron nodded. "Are there any rooms available?"

"We'll find you something," the innkeeper said. "Rooms come with food," he added briskly. "Help yourselves to bowls. Someone will bring you a key."

Aaron led Joan to the hearth and took two bowls from the mantelpiece above it. He ladled stew from the cauldron. It smelled delicious: savory and rich. Joan could see carrots and onions and maybe duck.

They found a table in an out-of-the-way corner. When Joan pulled the chair, it dragged against the floor, the sound momentarily rising above the chatter in the room. Aaron raised an eyebrow and shifted his own chair. Silently, of course. He had the graceful precision of a cat.

"Do we really need a room?" Joan said. She'd imagined they'd just tell someone about the massacre, and that would be that.

"Food first," Aaron said. "You don't know how to ground yourself on your own yet. Eating food from a new time is an easy shortcut." He blew on his own spoon and ate a bite. "This is good," he said grudgingly.

"So how will this work, then?" Joan said. She ate her own stew. The flavors were unexpectedly Christmassy: orange peel and cinnamon and cloves. She kind of liked the combination. "Once we warn someone, will it just be like—" She snapped her fingers. "Like last night never happened? Like you and I won't even remember any of this happening?" It was a strange thought. She and Aaron might never know that they'd once sat here alone at a table, eating a meal together. That they'd once helped each other.

There was plate of fresh bread on the table. Aaron took a roll and scored a cross in the crust. He pushed a pat of butter into the scoring, and then passed the roll to Joan. He took another for himself. "Eat that too."

The bread was dense and very dark, and warm enough that the butter had already melted into it. Joan looked around as she chewed.

Just like the city outside, the inn was familiar and strange at the same time. People stepped in and out of the air with casual ease—as if they were merely stepping from one room to another.

At the closest table, two women were playing a game that looked like chess—but when Joan peered more closely, the pieces seemed wrong: an elephant, a medieval cannon.

It was all so disorienting. And yet . . .

Some things were familiar. Joan licked butter from her thumb. It was heavily salted and as sour as yogurt. She'd only ever tasted butter like that at Gran's house. She bent to breathe in the familiar scent of it.

"We call it whole-milk butter," Aaron said.

She could have been eating Gran's food. "My gran makes butter like this. I thought it was a family thing."

Aaron shrugged. "It's a monster thing."

A monster thing. When all this was over—when the events of last night were undone—maybe this taste would become a family thing again. And that was a strange thought too. Maybe Joan would never learn that there was a greater context to these parts of her life. A culture.

Laughter erupted at one of the tables. "Hathaways," Aaron said, sounding annoyed. The laughter was coming from a rowdy table in the center of the room. There were a dozen people there. Like all the groups in the inn, the Hathaways seemed to be a mix of races; their only real similarity was their muscular build—men and women both. Most of them seemed to have pets: Joan spotted a gray cat on a man's lap; a sleepy pug curled under a chair. As she watched, a black cat jumped onto the Hathaway table and stalked between cups and bowls. Joan opened her mouth to ask Aaron another question, but right then a woman stepped out of the air near the Hathaway table. Her hairstyle was distinctive: curls at her forehead and coiled plaits at the back of her head.

"That woman's hair," Joan said slowly. Where had she seen hairstyles like that before?

Aaron glanced over and shrugged. "We really should eat before we talk."

Joan answered her own question. "Statues."

"Joan," Aaron said. "Keep eating."

"Ancient Roman statues."

"*Joan.*" Aaron leaned in until all Joan could see was his face. "You're right," he said. "From her hairstyle, I would say she arrived from circa 100 AD." His voice took on an almost seductive quality. "I went there once, you know? To the Temple of Venus on Velian Hill. It was such a hot day that the flower offerings wilted in their vases. The perfume of roses and myrtle was like wine."

"What?" Joan tried to focus on him. Her head felt muzzy.

"The stream of worshippers didn't stop," Aaron said. "There were so many offerings that jewelry and flowers piled up on the floor."

The smoky hearth was losing its scent. "Stop it," Joan said thickly.

"Newlyweds brought in a bull with gilded horns," Aaron

said. "I stayed for the sacrifice. Do you want to hear about that?"

"*No.*" She felt as though she were falling. What had Aaron told her at St. James's Park? Focus on the details. She put her palm shakily against the table. She could barely feel the wood. Her throat contracted in a terrified sound that she couldn't hear. *Details.* There were scratches in the gloss of the table. Beside one of the bowls, Aaron's fist was clenched tight enough to whiten his knuckles. There was a shallow cut on Joan's own hand— across her thumb. That must have happened in the sword fight.

The smell of the hearth returned slowly until the air was smoky enough to make Joan cough. "Why did you do that to me?" she demanded.

Aaron smiled slightly, but his eyes were flat. "Right now, anyone could do that to you. A Jane Austen book cover could do that to you."

"What is *wrong* with you?"

"What is wrong with *me*?" Aaron had the gall to sound irritated. "I'm trying to help you." He added, conceding, "You did well that time. You came back from it quickly."

The problem was he looked so much like a human boy that Joan kept expecting him to act like one. But he wasn't a human boy. He was a monster, raised by monsters. "You know what?" She stood up. "I don't want your help." He'd brought her here to this time. She didn't need anything more from him than that.

"Where are you going?" He frowned.

"Just don't," she said. "Don't help. Don't do anything else for me." She felt his eyes on her as she walked away.

Joan had noticed a flow of people coming and going near the back, even though the signs for the lavatory pointed the opposite way.

Sure enough, there was a back door. Joan opened it, expecting another nondescript laneway, but to her surprise, it opened onto a cobblestoned square with bow-fronted shops and tall brick buildings. *Front door,* she revised.

Streets led away from the square. Looking down one of them, Joan saw more buildings and what looked like a park that ended in a wall. Joan imagined that wall enclosing all of this. *A monster place,* she thought, *hidden away.*

It had started to rain while Joan had been inside. Now big splotches fell onto the cobblestones, darkening them. The sky had grayed. Here and there, people popped in and out of existence. The ones appearing ducked their heads from the rain and scrambled into buildings.

Joan stopped one woman as she hurried toward the inn. "Excuse me," she said. "Do you know where I can find the Hunt family?"

The woman's eyebrows drew together. "What do you want with those thieves?" She pushed past Joan roughly and went inside.

Joan stared after her, shaken. The Olivers hated her family. Had the woman been an Oliver? Or did lots of people hate the Hunts? It was an unsettling thought.

Around the square, there were all kinds of shops, selling

cakes, tea, jewelry. One seemed to specialize in hats, apparently of every era: top hats, floral hats, straw bonnets, baseball caps. Another sold confectionary, its window display a cornucopia of whole glacé pineapples and oranges. Interspersed among the fruit, there were sugar sculptures—a translucent tiger, a brightly colored parrot. They were lit from within by what looked like real, shifting flames. Joan had never seen anything like them.

She walked on. About half the new arrivals were hurrying out of the rain and into the inn.

Many of the others headed in another direction, running down one of the streets. The rain started to properly pelt down. Joan jogged across the cobblestones, following them. Water splashed up from puddles, soaking her ankles.

The trail of people led her to a covered market with a grand Victorian facade. Above the open entrance, the name Ravencroft Market was carved in stone along with three-dimensional birds and leaves. Joan walked in. The floor inside was a continuation of the cobbled street. An ornate glass ceiling arched above, the color of a summer sky. Here and there, leadwork ravens soared among the glass.

Joan's hair dripped as she passed racks and racks of clothes. She could have walked out of the market as a Roman centurion or a lady of the Regency or in nineties grunge.

There was food too—an eel-and-pie stall, a curry stall. Joan's stomach rumbled again. She wished she'd taken the bread roll with her. She continued past tables of spices and herbs.

Homemade bottles labeled *garum*. Bunches of spiky banana-like fruit. Dried yellowish leaves labeled *silphium*. Unfamiliar chocolate bars. It reminded Joan of the Chinese grocer she and Dad went to: a place to get things that weren't on the high street.

Garum, she thought idly. That had been a condiment in ancient Rome, a little like fish sauce. Joan had read about it. And just like that, the muzzy feeling was back. *Focus*, Joan told herself, pushing down fluttering panic. *Focus on details*. But everywhere she looked, there were objects from other times. A centurion shield, slung over someone's back. A rough wooden bow, unstrung.

"*Oi*," someone called out. Joan jumped, startled out of the muzziness.

A stall owner was looking at her—a man in his early twenties. He had sandy hair and the muscular build of a boxer. "You selling that contraband?" he said.

"Contraband?" Joan said. The man's card table was covered with bulky nineties phones and watches, cameras, and other electronics.

The man gestured at the phone poking out of Joan's jeans pocket. "You're in the nineties, love. Drop that thing outside these walls, and you'll hear about it from the Court. But I'll take it off your hands."

It was the phone Joan had found in the Yellow Drawing Room. She'd almost forgotten about it.

"You have the pass code?" the man asked.

Joan shook her head.

"I'll give you a hundred for it."

A flash of memory came to Joan of Gran buying a sausage roll at Greggs one day. Gran had winked at Joan and then offered the man half the asking price for it. At the time, Joan had squirmed with embarrassment. Who *did* that? Now she just wished Gran were here.

"Five hundred," Joan said for the hell of it, because the audacity of it would have made Gran laugh.

"Oh, fuck off," the guy said. "You think I'm running a charity?"

"Two hundred," Joan said. "Screen's not even cracked."

The guy grimaced. "One seventy," he said. "No more than that." He jerked his chin. "I'd give you more for that necklace, though."

Joan reached instinctively to touch the chain. Gran had given her the necklace last night before she'd died. Joan swallowed and shook her head.

"Go on," the man said, "name a price."

It was the only connection Joan still had to Gran. Gran had touched this chain. Gran's blood had been on this chain. Joan shook her head again.

The man shrugged. "Suit yourself." He handed Joan some strange notes, and Joan gave him the phone in return.

She examined the notes curiously. They were clear plastic with golden images at their center: a crown, a winged lion. Laid over each other, they seemed to form part of an unfamiliar coat of arms. Was this monster money? "Can I have some of this in local cash?" she asked, partly to gauge the exchange rate.

"What am I—a currency exchange?" the guy grumbled. But he took back a twenty and gave Joan forty pounds in more recognizable money.

Joan pocketed the cash. As she turned, a familiar voice drawled: "Well, look at you. Selling stolen goods like a true Hunt."

Aaron was standing by the table, arms folded casually. But his hair was wet and dark like it had been last night after his shower. Had he run out here looking for her?

Aaron surveyed the man's watches and phones with clear disdain. "Hope you're not going to spend it here," he said to Joan.

"I'm going to the post office down the street," Joan said. "I saw the sign—it said they deliver to other times. I'm going to write myself a letter."

"What on earth for?"

"To stop Nick, of course," Joan said. "To warn myself so I can save my family."

Aaron barked a laugh, spontaneous and harsh.

"Why is that funny?" Joan demanded, even though Aaron hadn't sounded amused, exactly. If anything, the laugh had sounded pained. She had an uneasy feeling suddenly—like the feeling she'd had when she'd taken time at the Pit.

"Oh, it's not funny at all." Aaron gestured for Joan to lead the way. "By all means, write a letter and save us all from heroes."

The uneasy feeling increased as Joan went back out into the rain. Aaron followed her in silence. The post office wasn't far, but by the time they got to it, water was falling from the eaves in sheets, spattering as it hit the ground.

"Ooh, you two got caught in it," the woman at the post office said when Joan pushed open the door. She had a soft northern accent that reminded Joan of Nick. She was sorting what looked like wedding invitations, popping them into different drawers, labeled with fifty-year ranges: 1900–1949; 1950–1999; 2000–2049. She gestured: "Postcards over there," she said. "Lovely one of Steffi Graf winning Wimbledon this year."

"Could I send a letter, please?" Joan said.

"A letter?" the woman said. "Isn't that nice? Love a letter. More people should write letters." She gestured at a shelf with sheets of paper and envelopes.

Joan could feel Aaron's eyes on her. The post office was set up like a little living room: there was a love seat and a low coffee table in a pink-painted alcove. Joan sat on the love seat, and, after a moment, Aaron's weight settled beside her.

Joan breathed out. *Dear Joan*, she wrote. It felt strange to address herself.

She hadn't realized how difficult it would be to write out the events of last night. Her hand shook as she told herself how the Olivers had arrived. How she'd sent a message to her family. How the Hunts had come to help her and how they'd died. She told herself about Nick. Aaron's gaze on her felt like a physical presence as she wrote.

It was going to be okay, she thought to herself. After this letter was delivered, last night wouldn't have happened. As soon as her past self got the letter, she'd prevent the massacre. She'd warn Gran and her family. They'd all stop Nick together.

"Do you think I need to say anything else?" she whispered to Aaron.

He hadn't spoken since they'd left the market, but he'd been reading over Joan's shoulder. Now he said heavily, "No."

Joan signed her name. Then she took a deep breath and went back to the counter.

At what point would time reset itself? Would it be when she handed the letter to the woman at the counter? When it was delivered?

The woman took the letter and one of Joan's strange monster bank notes and handed over some change: more notes and coins.

Now, Joan thought. She'd be back at home with Gran and everyone would be alive again *now*.

Outside, the rain continued to pelt down. Seconds ticked by. "Can I please send a copy to my gran as well?" Joan said.

The woman showed her how to use the copier. Joan wrote down Gran's address from last year and a date for last summer. The woman took back some of the coins.

Now, Joan thought. It was all going to be undone *now*.

The woman put both letters into the 2000–2049 drawer.

"You're sure this will be delivered at the right time?" Joan said.

"Guaranteed, or your money back," the woman said cheerfully.

Now. Now. *Now.*

Nothing. The clock on the wall ticked off the passage of time. Nothing changed.

"Can I help you with anything else?" the woman said.

Joan startled when Aaron touched her elbow. "No, thank you," Aaron said to the woman. To Joan he said: "Why don't we go back to the inn." Joan almost imagined something gentle in his voice.

Joan's unease grew as she opened the door out into the rain again, until the feeling was thick and heavy in her stomach. Until it was so strong that she had to stop in the middle of that strange, hidden, trafficless street, with the rain pouring down on her.

"Joan," Aaron said. To her surprise, he walked out from under the eave to join her. His white shirt turned sodden, sticking to his skin. She could see the edge of a dark tattoo just where his hip started.

"Is that post office a scam?" Joan said. "Is that why you laughed at me?"

"I didn't," Aaron said. "I didn't laugh at you. And it's not a scam. The post office sends messages to different times."

"Then . . . how long do we have to wait?"

"Let's go inside," Aaron said. The gentleness was back in his voice. "We have a room upstairs. We can dry off up there."

Joan's hair felt heavy and cold down her back. The bandage was a clear outline around her waist. She knew why she was standing out here. The rain was soothingly relentless. She didn't know why Aaron was standing with her. He was thoroughly drenched now too. She hadn't known him long, but she knew that he liked to look ordered and in control.

"If I ask you a question, will you tell me the truth?" she said.

Water dripped from Aaron's darkened hair, his shirtsleeves, the cuffs of his trousers. "Yes."

"Will those letters save our families?"

The tired pity in his eyes made Joan's throat close up. He shook his head. The sound of the rain drowned out his voice so that his answer was only a shape on his lips. "No."

The unease inside her felt like a clawing animal. Her throat felt so tight she could barely speak. She forced out the next words. "Then how do we save them?"

The pity in Aaron's face deepened into something awful and weary and *old*. And Joan suddenly didn't want him to answer. She was already shaking her head when he did.

"Nothing you do will save them," he said.

"No," Joan said. *No*. That didn't make sense. There were a thousand things she could do now that she was here in this time. She could warn Gran face-to-face. Or she could hire a law firm to deliver messages to herself and her family, to every one of Gran's addresses, every year. She had years and years to find ways to stop that night from happening.

Nick wouldn't catch anyone by surprise. No one would die. *That* made sense.

"Joan . . . ," Aaron said.

But Joan suddenly couldn't bear his presence. "No!" she said. She turned and ran, skidding and slipping on the wet cobblestones.

She could hear him calling after her, but she didn't want to hear anything else he said. He was a liar. He'd left her to die last night. He was as cruel as his father.

She wrenched open the door to the inn, peripherally aware of everyone turning to stare at her. She supposed she must look a fright—soaked to the skin and wild. She scanned the room, searching for familiar eyes. For *the Hunt family look*. For silver-tongued fox charms and tattoos. For any sign of her own family. There were dozens and dozens of people in here. One of them had to be a Hunt.

All she needed was to find Gran's younger self in this time—to find *any* Hunt in this time. She just needed to tell them face-to-face. No letters, no middlemen. *That* would stop all this.

She headed to where the innkeeper was standing behind a glossy wooden bar. He was sipping coffee, eyes on his patrons. Joan had the impression of a benevolent mayor.

"I need to find someone from the Hunt family," Joan said.

The innkeeper gave her a long look. "The Hunts don't like to be found."

Joan fumbled for the cash in her pocket and put a transparent-and-gold note on the bar. The one that said 50. "Dorothy Hunt," she said. That was Gran's name.

"Some people *shouldn't* be found."

Joan put another 50 down. "Any Hunt will do," she said, "but if Dorothy is in this time, then I want to talk to *her*."

The innkeeper made a sound at the back of his throat that might have been disapproval, but when Joan looked down, the cash was gone.

Joan had hoped that the clawing feeling inside her would be eased by that, but if anything, it worsened it. She scanned the room yet again. She knew it was stupid to keep checking, but—

She saw the tattoo first—a delicate mermaid curled around a man's wrist. She lifted her eyes to his face.

She'd only seen him once before, but he was shockingly familiar. He'd been in his fifties when he'd died in the garden at Holland House. Now he was in his early twenties, and he had a round boyish face, a smirky mouth, and blond hair that was already thinning.

For a long moment, the overlaid image was more real than the inn. She could see it all. The dark garden at Holland House. The maze ahead of her. This man lying on his side, eyes open, one arm flung out, his mermaid tattoo stark against his pale wrist. The scent of crushed flowers seemed to fill the inn.

He'd *been* there. She could warn *him*.

There was a gust of cold wet spray as the door opened and closed.

Joan was distantly aware of Aaron saying her name urgently, but she was already moving.

The man looked up as Joan approached him, his curious expression turning to distaste as he took in Joan's bracelet: the gold fox charm with its little silver tongue.

"I—I know." Joan raised her hands placatingly. "I know I'm a Hunt. I know you're an Oliver. But listen to me. Please. Something terrible is going to happen. But we can stop it."

The man pushed his chair away. Joan grabbed at his sleeve as he stood. "Wait," she said. "*Listen* to me. Listen. A human is going to be born. He's going to kill *so* many people. He's going to kill you!"

Just like in the post office, she found herself thinking *now, now, last night will be undone now* as she told him the details of the date, the place, the time, all the people who would die.

And just like at the post office, nothing changed at the end of it.

She was doing this all wrong. She could feel it. She was saying the wrong things. She could feel herself breaking unspoken rules, conventions she didn't understand. But she couldn't stop. She was sure that if she just said the right thing in the right way—if she could make him understand—then everything would be fixed.

There was a change in the quality of the light. Joan knew without looking that Aaron had stepped into the space behind her. She had the feeling that he was blocking her from the view of other patrons.

"*Tell* him," she begged Aaron. Surely an Oliver would listen to another Oliver.

"Aaron?" The man looked Aaron up and down, mouth twisted in a sneer. "Does the head of our house know that his son is slumming at the Serpentine Inn with a Hunt? Or have you fallen even further than we'd imagined?"

Aaron's hand shook slightly as he went to adjust his shirt cuffs. He seemed to remember the state he was in—jacketless and still soaked, his shirt painted to his chest. He lowered his hands.

The man opened his mouth to speak again, but Joan interrupted. "For God's sake, *listen* to me!" she said. The clawing feeling had risen to her throat. Nothing mattered but what Nick was going to do. "You need to listen to me! You need to tell everyone that a human is coming—a human who kills monsters!"

The man jerked his sleeve from Joan's grip. He straightened his own cuffs. "Get this mad bitch out of my way," he said to Aaron evenly.

"Aaron, tell him!" Joan said. But to her shock, Aaron took her shoulder and pulled her firmly aside so that the man could pass.

Joan was vaguely aware of Aaron corralling her up a short staircase.

"What are you doing?" she demanded. "Let go of me! We have to go after him! We have to go back down there!"

And then they were in a suite with big windows looking out onto the stormy street.

Aaron slammed the door behind them, and Joan rounded on him. "You didn't even help me!" she said. "Why did you drag me away? We have to warn him!"

"It doesn't work like that!" Aaron said.

"Of course it works like that!" Joan said. "If we warn people, they can stop Nick! Everything will go back to how it was! We won't even have stolen that time. Everything will be undone."

"God, you are so fucking . . ." Aaron's voice went hoarse. "So fucking *raw*. We can't change what happened, Joan!"

"What are you *talking* about?"

"The timeline protects itself," Aaron said. "It corrects itself."

"What does that even mean?"

"Those letters you sent will be lost or misdelivered. Victor will ignore what you said. No matter what you do or who you tell, that massacre will happen."

Joan shook her head. "No," she said. "No, you're wrong."

"You can't stop your family from dying," Aaron said. "You just can't."

"You're wrong, you're wrong!" Joan barely knew what she was saying. She felt as though she were choking. "You didn't even talk to that man downstairs! You could have convinced him!"

"Can't you feel I'm telling the truth?" Aaron said. "You must be able to feel it—the resistance of the timeline. It's all around us."

Joan couldn't feel anything. "We came here to help them!" she said. "That's the whole reason we came back!"

"That's the reason *you* came back!"

"What are you talking about?" Joan demanded. "What are you . . ." But their conversations were coming back to her. Aaron had never said that he'd help her undo the massacre, she realized slowly. It was Joan who'd talked about saving their families. She stared at him. "No."

"We had to run," Aaron said. "If we'd stayed there, we'd have died. Would you have left just to flee?"

"I don't believe you," she whispered. She couldn't. "We have to undo it. We—we stole so much time." More than sixty years of human life between them. "We have to undo it together."

"Well, we can't," Aaron said, "because it doesn't work like that." And the words were cold, but he sounded as upset as Joan felt. He turned and stalked to the bedroom, slamming the door behind him.

Joan stared out the window onto the monster street below. Rain was still pouring down. The cobblestones were shiny and black. Aaron had to be wrong. He had to be. This couldn't be how it was—Joan's family dead, those people in the Pit . . . Joan couldn't really have shortened their lives.

Through the window, movement caught her eye. Across the street, the post office door was opening. A man stepped out into the rain, carrying a sack of mail. Joan's breath stopped.

The man hefted the bag, clearly struggling with it in the wet. Then he took a step and vanished, bag and all.

Now, Joan thought. She knelt on the window seat, trying to get a better look. *Now*. Aaron had been wrong. Those letters would be delivered. And it would be all over *now*.

Five seconds passed. Ten seconds. Joan was still kneeling on the window seat in her wet clothes. Twenty seconds.

There was something on the ground where the man had been standing. Joan pressed closer to the window, trying to see through the streaming rain. There were two things. Two white envelopes.

You must be able to feel it, Aaron had said. *The resistance of the timeline. It's all around us.* Now, in the back of Joan's mind, the word *resistance* snagged. With the same sense with which she'd felt the yearning of time travel, she could feel something in the world. Aaron had made it sound like a natural force. A resistance. But Joan's sense of it was more of a great beast stirring. Something that when pushed would push back.

As rain continued to fall, Joan watched the two envelopes slowly take on water. She watched them discolor and distort with the weight of it. Then she watched them fall apart until they were no more than pulp in the gutter.

On the street, monsters continued to appear and disappear. They ran from the rain in their top hats and hooped skirts, in their nineties grunge and eighties hair.

As Joan watched, Aaron's expression came back to her. She remembered how he'd looked at her as they'd stood in the rain—with that awful, old, weary expression.

"Joan!" Aaron whispered in her ear.

Joan startled awake. It took her a second to get her bearings. She hadn't even realized she was falling asleep. She was curled up on the window seat. There was a blanket over her now. It was night outside. The only light in the room was the jumping colors of a television.

"What's that noise?" Aaron whispered.

Joan tried to gather her thoughts. She was disoriented and confused. Something was playing on the TV. Music. "*Totoro?*"

"No. I mean, yes, but—" Aaron stalked away and pressed a button on the remote. The music continued. Aaron mashed at the remote. "Urgh—" He bent down and wrenched the plug from the back of the television.

The room was suddenly silent and dark.

And then Joan heard it too—a *click-click-click* of someone picking a lock. In the moonlight, the doorknob bobbled. And then Joan was awake. She was very awake.

She scrambled up, pointing at the wobbling doorknob. Aaron's eyes widened in understanding.

There was a heavy vase by the door. Joan lifted it, tensed and ready. Aaron picked up a cushion from the sofa and positioned himself on the other side of the door.

What the—? Joan mouthed at him. What was he going to do with a cushion? Smother the intruder?

Aaron mimed an *I don't know.* He looked around for something to replace it with.

But it was too late. The lock snicked. The door opened. Joan hurled the vase.

"Whoa!" The person dodged and the porcelain smashed against the corridor wall. "Well, hello to you too, Joan."

Joan stared at familiar green eyes. A familiar cloud of dark hair. "Ruth?"

TEN

"We should probably hug," Ruth said, in her wry way.

Joan threw herself at her, and then she just lost it for a while. When she finally drew back, she'd left a damp patch on Ruth's shoulder bigger than her whole face. Ruth looked at it and wrinkled her nose.

Joan laughed shakily. "Shut up."

Ruth examined the room, stopping as she reached Aaron. "Why are you here with an Oliver?" she said to Joan. There was a funny note in her voice.

"Oh." Joan found Aaron staring back at Ruth, narrow-eyed as a cat. "Aaron, this is my cousin Ruth," she said uncomfortably. "Aaron and I escaped together," she said to Ruth. "And you. I thought . . ." She couldn't say it. She'd seen the knife thrust into Ruth's gut.

"I know." Ruth loosened up slightly. "You just went all tragedy over my jacket."

Joan felt like she was a kind word from going all tragedy again. She butted her head into Ruth's shoulder. She was *alive*. "How'd you find us?" Joan managed.

"Couple of people owed me." Ruth touched Joan's hair with her fingertips—gently, the way you might touch a painting. "God, look at you. I heard rumors you'd escaped. I hoped."

"You found us so quickly, though."

"Quickly?" Ruth said. Her forehead creased. "Joan, I've been searching for you for nearly two years."

There was a puckered scar at the base of Ruth's rib cage where she'd been stabbed. Her hair was longer than it had been yesterday. And there were other differences, now that Joan knew to look. She seemed tired, and there was a jadedness in her eyes that hadn't been there before. She'd been in this time long enough to look the part: black jacket and black jeans, a slash of bright red lipstick.

"Two years . . . ," Joan said. The crevasse of Ruth's scar was deep; she must have been so close to death. "But how—"

"We can talk later," Ruth said. "Right now, we need to go."

"Go?" Joan said. From downstairs, voices rose, raucous and drunk. Ruth's eyes flicked to the door. That was different too. Ruth was usually brazenly confident, but this version of her seemed as watchful as an animal. "Go where?" Joan said.

"Somewhere with fewer eyes and ears. Get your things."

"I don't have things." Joan let Ruth tug her into the corridor.

Ruth put up her arm to bar Aaron from following. "Not you," she said.

Aaron seemed more resigned than surprised. "Goodbye, Joan."

Joan pushed Ruth's arm down. "He has to come with us!"

Ruth shook her head. "I know you escaped together, but you don't know the Olivers. They're all ruthless. This one would throw you to the wolves if he thought it would please his family to see you torn apart."

But Joan thought about how watchful Ruth seemed. "Why are you worried about eyes and ears?" she said. "What are you afraid of?" When Ruth didn't answer, she said: "If you don't think this place is safe, then he has to come with us."

From downstairs, voices rose again. Ruth flinched, head turning toward the staircase.

As Joan turned too, she caught Aaron watching her with the same wary, uncomprehending expression he'd had in the maze. As if he couldn't understand her at all.

"Ruth," Joan said. "If we need to go, then let's go."

Ruth shook her head again. But she beckoned to both of them. "I'll be keeping *my* eyes on *you*," she said to Aaron.

Outside, it was still raining. Old-fashioned streetlamps made the cobblestones shine. Joan hadn't really noticed the discomfort of her wet clothes earlier, but now her jeans chafed as she jogged with Ruth down one street and then another. Her T-shirt was cold and tacky.

Joan had expected Ruth to take them out of the complex, but to her surprise Ruth led them to the covered market. Aaron seemed surprised too. "The inn wasn't safe, but *this* is safe?" he said with disdain.

Ruth glared at him. "How long have *you* been at this? If

you know so much, why don't you just fuck off and take care of yourself?"

Aaron glared back. He opened his mouth to answer. Joan interjected before he could. "I thought you said we had to be careful of eyes and ears," she said to Ruth.

That made Ruth glance around again with that new wariness she had. She sped up. "Come on," she said. "This way."

Ruth took them up a winding iron staircase. Joan looked down onto the market as they climbed. It was a different market at night. The racks of clothes were gone, and there were tarps over the goods tables. In their place, more food stalls had opened. The air was fragrant with onions and sausages, fried spices, fresh donuts with hot jam. People sat around on low plastic stools, eating and drinking and talking. It reminded Joan of the food markets in Malaysia.

Ruth led them across a landing with a wrought-iron balustrade and an open view of the market below. There were gilded features within the black of the balustrade: curling vines and leaves.

"I didn't know there was a hotel up here," Aaron said.

"There isn't," Ruth said. "These are the stall owners' quarters. I found an empty one."

"*Found?*" Aaron said. "You mean you're squatting?"

Ruth slipped a couple of tools from her pocket and picked open the last door on the landing in three deft clicks. "You're welcome, Your Majesty," she said to him, sweeping her hand toward the open door.

"You Hunts," Aaron said, but he stalked into the room.

Joan followed him in. Without lights, she couldn't see much. A semicircular window took up most of the wall overlooking the street. It was divided into hinged panes: stained glass, like the windows at the inn. Joan made out the design: ravens in a leafless tree.

Aaron pushed open one of the panes, cutting the tree's branches. Joan craned. The inn was several streets away: not visible from here. She couldn't see much at all through the streaming rain.

"Close that," Ruth said. She waited for Aaron to do it. "Lights on," she said, and the room illuminated.

It was a studio flat with its own bathroom: A rumpled bed, partitioned away by a bookshelf. A kitchenette with a breakfast table. A white sofa and matching armchair. A coffee table.

The main feature was a carpet, which filled the whole space. The design reminded Joan of a medieval tapestry, except that the colors were more vibrant than anything she'd seen in a museum—bright reds and midnight blues. There were woven images of monstrous creatures attacking humans: people consumed by dragon fire; people with serpents wrapped around them like rope. It occurred to Joan that she'd seen similar portrayals, in galleries, of humans slaying dragons and other fantastic creatures. Both kinds of images made her stomach squirm.

Joan watched Ruth lock the door and check that all the hinged windows were firmly closed. That wasn't like Ruth. She wasn't paranoid like that.

Joan looked around. At home, Ruth left stuff lying everywhere, but there was barely any sign of her here. Just a mug and a plate on the breakfast table. Nothing of her own.

There was so much that Joan wanted to ask her. *How did Bertie and Uncle Gus and Aunt Ada die?* And *Why didn't you ever tell me about monsters—about what monsters really were?* But those were family conversations. They couldn't talk like that in front of Aaron. She had other questions too. *What's happened to you in the last two years?* And *Why do you look like you're still on the run?*

She chose the one that seemed easiest. "What are you afraid of?"

Ruth pushed a hand through her curls. Wet with rain, they brushed her shoulders. "How long has it been for you?" she asked. "Since the attack?"

"We escaped last night," Joan said.

Ruth made a soft, shocked sound. "Last night?" She came over to where Joan was leaning on the back of the sofa.

Joan nodded, trying not to get all emotional again. She'd thought that Ruth had died last night. She'd thought that all the Hunts were gone. It was hard to let herself believe that Ruth was really here.

Ruth poked at Joan's foot with her own. She'd done that all the time when they were little—just to be annoying. This time, though, it was almost unbearably comforting. Joan was so grateful that Ruth was alive.

"You were overheard saying some things at the inn," Ruth said. "Things that aren't safe to talk about."

"You mean about the massacre?" Joan said, and once again Ruth's eyes flicked to the door as if afraid they might be overheard even here. It was disconcerting. The Ruth she knew was never afraid of anything. But Joan was beginning to understand that this wasn't the Ruth she knew. Not exactly.

"Why isn't it safe?" Aaron said. He was leaning against the wall by the door, as if he hadn't quite decided whether to stay or go.

Ruth didn't answer. The suspicion she seemed to carry with her now was stark on her face.

"Oh, I don't trust you either, poppet," Aaron said.

"Call me that again," Ruth dared him, and Aaron smiled at her, all teeth.

Joan was dismayed. She'd known that their families loathed each other, but she hadn't expected Ruth and Aaron to be at each other's throats so quickly.

"I know who you are," Ruth said to him. She made it sound like an accusation. "Your father is the head of the Oliver family. I know all about you."

Aaron lounged against the wall, a picture of casual arrogance. *A lot of people know who I am*, his expression said.

"You're Edmund Oliver's youngest son," Ruth said. "The only Oliver son. You should have been the next head of the Oliver family, but you were removed from the line of succession."

The phrasing was odd: *Edmund Oliver's youngest son. The only Oliver son.* There was no chance for Joan to ask about it, though, because Aaron was already talking.

"Gosh," Aaron said. "You do know all about me. And I don't

know anything about you. No, that's quite all right," he said as Ruth's mouth opened. "I don't care to know."

"What'd you do that was slimy enough to get disinherited from the Olivers?" Ruth said to Aaron. "Here I thought your family didn't have any standards."

"Stop it," Joan told them.

Aaron glared at Ruth. "Coming from someone whose family is full of thieves and liars," he said.

Joan had a flash of standing in the Gilt Room, surrounded by Olivers sneering at her. "*Stop* it!" she said. "Just stop! Both of you!" There must have been something in her voice, because they both blinked at her. "We can't *be* like this."

"Like what?" Aaron said. "Like Olivers and Hunts in a room together?"

"*Yes.*" Joan pushed away from the sofa and went to the kitchenette across the room. She filled the kettle. "Yesterday, there was a feud between us. Today, there isn't."

Ruth's laugh was bitter. "Joan, it doesn't work like that. . . . Olivers are nasty, sneering, human-hating snakes! You don't know what they're like!"

Joan did know. She glanced at Aaron, but he avoided her eyes. When he spoke, he sounded subdued. "The enmity between our families spans a thousand years," he said. "It's not going to end tonight."

"Olivers can't be trusted," Ruth said.

Aaron's voice sharpened. "*Hunts* can't be trusted," he said. "Olivers keep our word. Hunts are liars. Hunts—"

"*Stop,*" Joan said again. "Just *stop.*" The counter was cold against her back. She looked from Ruth to Aaron. They were barely three paces apart, neither looking at the other. "You're both still thinking like you did before the massacre," she said, frustrated. "But everything's different now!"

"It isn't!" Ruth said.

"God, Ruth, it is! Nick killed our families! *Both* of our families! He didn't care which one we were from. Don't you remember? There were only two sides that night: us and him."

Aaron and Ruth just stood there, staring at her. Joan wanted to shake them.

"Don't you see?" she said. "The three of us might be the only people who survived the massacre. We might be the only ones who know what happened. The only ones who can stop him."

She didn't say the rest: they were the only ones who could save their families. She'd lose it if Aaron argued with her about that right now.

There was a long silence. It stretched and stretched. Behind Joan, the kettle bubbled and spat and then switched itself off. From downstairs, she could hear the sounds of the market: people talking, sellers calling.

And still Ruth and Aaron stood there, not looking at each other, not looking at Joan. Joan's heart began to sink. The hatred between their families ran too deep.

Then Ruth spoke abruptly. "We weren't the only survivors."

"What?" Aaron said. There was hope in his voice, but Joan could see how Ruth was gripping the back of the sofa, her knuckles white.

"We weren't the only survivors," Ruth said. "But you're the only ones I've found alive." She glanced at the door again. And this time, Joan felt a chill start to spread through her.

"What do you mean?" Aaron said.

"Someone is hunting down anyone who escaped," Ruth said. "Someone is silencing anyone who tries to tell the tale of it. You spoke about the massacre in public today. You can't ever do that again."

Joan made tea. The ordinary ritual of it was comforting. Beside her, Ruth reached into the air, taking out food she'd bought at the market—pies and mushy peas, still piping hot. The Hunt family power. And that was comforting too. At Gran's place, everyone had had stashes of food like that—except Joan, of course. Her Hunt power had faded over the years.

As Ruth reached for another pie, Joan found herself suddenly remembering what Gran had said last night. *Someday soon, you'll come into a power. Not the Hunt power. Another.* What had Gran meant by that? But that memory was quickly chased by another memory—Gran's blood seeping all over Joan's hands. Gran's harsh breaths rattling in and out. Joan heard her own breath hitch.

"Joan?" Ruth said, jolting Joan out of it.

"Yeah." Joan wasn't there, she reminded herself. She was here.

Ruth reached back into the air and retrieved a knob of ginger—freshly peeled. Joan blinked at it. "For your tea," Ruth said. She dropped it carefully into one of the mugs. "I know you like ginger in your tea."

Joan took a deep breath and let it out. "I'm so happy you're here," she whispered.

Ruth didn't quite smile, but for a moment that new hard look in her eyes softened to fondness. "I'm glad I found you."

Joan brought the teapot and mugs over to the coffee table. Ruth laid out pies. "Bacon and egg," she said. "Steak and ale, steak and kidney, cheddar and leek." She unloaded tubs of mushy peas too, and chips with gravy.

Ruth and Joan squeezed onto the sofa together. Aaron took the armchair. For a little while, they all just sat there, looking at the dark window, drinking too-hot tea, and eating.

Aaron drank his tea black and unsweetened. Ruth dropped three sugar cubes into her mug. She hovered her hand over the rising steam. Joan's heart tightened at the familiarity of the gesture—Ruth always did that when she felt cold.

Aaron broke the silence first. "The attack isn't recorded in the Oliver histories." He lowered his mug to the table, hand shaking a little. Joan remembered what else he'd said: his father's death hadn't matched the records either. "This is all wrong," he said. "None of this is supposed to be happening." He'd said that last night too. *This night is all wrong.*

"It's not just the Oliver records," Ruth said. "I've seen other families' records of that night. They all say the same thing."

"You've seen other families' records?" Aaron sounded a little shocked.

"Listen to what I'm saying," Ruth said. "*They all say the same thing*. Not just the same false events, but recorded with the same words. I've seen it in the Hunt records, the Hathaway records, the Patel records."

This night is all wrong. The families each recorded all the events of history, but Nick's attack wasn't in any of them. There was only one explanation. Someone had concealed the attack. "You think the records have been tampered with," Joan said.

Aaron shook his head. "That isn't possible. Only the family archivists record events. And they would never collaborate."

"I know," Ruth said.

Aaron's gray eyes were wide. "The family histories must be perfect. Because if they're not, doubt could be cast on every recorded event."

"I know," Ruth said again.

"If we can't trust the records, then we can't trust anything." Aaron's voice was rising. "Any event could be wrong. Any death. There'd be no way to know what's going to happen on any given day."

"You mean like being human?" Joan said.

Aaron stared at her. "Yes." He sounded taken aback. His eyes were a little wild. "It would be as bad as being human."

It's not so bad, Joan wanted to tell him, but she could see that he wouldn't be able to hear it. He seemed shaken by the prospect of an unpredictable future. It was the opposite for Joan. The thought of an unchangeable future written in a book was a claustrophobic horror.

She leaned over to put her own mug down. Her wound

pulled as she stretched, a fresh reminder that Nick's attack had only been last night for her and Aaron.

"Who's doing this?" she asked Ruth. Someone was falsifying records. Someone was hunting down survivors. "Who's trying to cover up the attack?"

"I don't know," Ruth said.

Joan remembered the disbelief in Gran's voice last night. *I was supposed to have so much more time to prepare you.* Joan closed her eyes. She remembered how Gran had gasped in pain. She remembered the sound Ruth had made when she'd been stabbed. Her own breath hitched as she pictured that deep, twisting wound under Ruth's rib cage. "I thought you were dead," she whispered to Ruth.

Ruth ducked her head. "When I saw you at Holland House that night, I—" Her voice cracked. "I'd thought *you* were already dead. All the others were dying or dead when I found them. Bertie . . . Uncle Gus. Aunt Ada. Gran."

Joan took a long, shuddering breath. *You messaged for help,* Ruth had told her that night. *And I called everyone else.*

Ruth must have known what Joan was thinking, because she squeezed Joan's hand. "You know it wouldn't have mattered whether you'd sent that message for help or not. The other families were attacked too. He would have found us wherever we were."

Joan squeezed Ruth's hand back. "I still wish I'd never sent it," she managed.

"I know," Ruth whispered. "And I wish I'd been there

sooner. When I got there . . . Uncle Gus and Aunt Ada were already dead. Bertie was barely alive. I tried to call an ambulance, but my phone didn't work. I held his hand."

Joan swallowed around the lump in her throat. God, *Bertie*. She couldn't believe this had happened. Was *going* to happen.

"How could those humans have known so much about us?" Aaron asked. "How did they find us?"

"I don't know," Ruth said.

"You went looking into the records afterward, though?" Joan said.

Ruth nodded.

"Did you learn any more about the attack?"

"You mean, did I learn any more about *him*?" Ruth said.

Him.

Joan swallowed. She'd been trying not to think about Nick directly. Now she felt a flash of anger, followed by pain. It hurt to think about him. She didn't want to think about him.

A memory came to her anyway. Not of the night itself, but of before that. Of a morning when she and Nick had arrived at work before anybody else. They'd cleaned the Gilt Room together. Joan had dusted the picture frames and Nick had mopped the floor, his shirtsleeves rolled up. The morning sun had been soft and warm. And Joan had thought, *If every day were like this, I'd be happy forever.*

She heard her breath shudder out. "Did you learn anything about him?"

"I never actually saw him, you know?" Ruth said. "I only heard *you* talk about him." Her mouth twisted, sad and wry. "You talked about him so much that summer. I remember I used to tease you about him. God, that was so long ago."

It had been two days ago for Joan.

"He doesn't seem to exist," Ruth said now. "I know he was working at Holland House because you said so. But there are no employee records of him. I tried to trace him through security footage near the house. He somehow never appears."

Joan waited for more, but Ruth had stopped. "What else?" she said.

"You're the one who knew him, Joan." Ruth's voice was gentle.

"I didn't," Joan whispered. She remembered how it had felt when they'd met. Like she'd known him her whole life. Like she could trust him with her life. She'd just known. But she'd been wrong. She'd never felt so sure and been so wrong.

Her throat felt tight. Last night, she and Nick had sat together under the window in the Holland House library. Nick had touched her cheek and she'd leaned up to kiss him. When the Olivers had attacked, he'd saved her life. And then he'd stood in front of her and said: *If you ever steal time from a human again, I will kill you myself.*

"I haven't learned anything about him," Ruth said. "Not his real name, not who his parents are, not how he came to learn about monsters. I don't know who he is."

Once upon a time, Joan thought, *there was a boy who was born to kill monsters. A hero.* "Gran used to tell us stories," she said. "Do you remember?"

"Joan . . ." Ruth was already shaking her head.

"About a human boy who was destined to kill monsters."

"Those are just stories," Ruth said. "They're just bedtime stories for children."

Joan looked at Aaron. He was watching her with an expression she couldn't quite read. "That man in the maze," she said to him. "He had a tattoo." She touched the back of her neck. "Here, where a monster would see it if they tried to take time. A warning. You didn't believe that your father was dead until you saw that tattoo. And then you *knew.*"

Aaron couldn't seem to take his eyes from hers. "It was the hero's emblem from the stories," he said. "The wolf." Joan felt the hairs on the back of her neck rise. That was in the stories Gran had told her too.

"The human hero is a mythical figure," Ruth said. "Like King Arthur. He isn't real."

But Joan could see it in her eyes. She was remembering the same sweltering night that Joan had been remembering. Years ago, Joan and Ruth had fallen sick with a fever, and hadn't been able to sleep. Gran had sat up with them all night and told them a story about the hero—one Joan had never heard before.

"In the myths," Aaron said now, "the human hero is the end of days. He kills the first monster, unraveling us all so that monsters never exist. We're never born."

"Those are fairy tales," Ruth said.

"Yes," Aaron agreed.

"The timeline can't be changed," Ruth said, "so he can't kill the first monster. He can't stop us from being born."

"No."

"Okay," Joan said. "Okay." Ruth had gone so pale that the only color on her face was the slash of red lipstick. Joan wished again that Gran were here to explain everything in that reassuring, dry way of hers. But Gran wasn't here. Gran was dead, and if Joan didn't do something, then Gran would stay dead.

"What do we know?" Joan said, trying to focus. "There was an attack by humans. Ruth hasn't found any other survivors. There are false events in the historical records. Is that all?"

Ruth hesitated. Her eyes turned unerringly to the door again.

"Ruth?" Joan said slowly. Maybe she didn't fully know this new Ruth yet. But she knew *her* Ruth. Her Ruth wouldn't just have been running for two years. Her Ruth would have been looking back at her pursuers, trying to work out who they were.

"I don't know anything else," Ruth said. "Not for sure."

"Not for sure?" Joan said.

In the pause that followed, the building seemed very quiet. The rain was slowing outside, just a patter against the roof now. Joan couldn't even hear the market sellers downstairs.

"I thought I saw something once," Ruth said. "Just after I escaped. After I landed in the eighties."

"My family still lived in Holland House in the eighties," Aaron said.

"Yeah, I know," Ruth said with a tired half smile. "I was bleeding all over the shop and had to get your stupid window open again. And I knew if I passed out, your family would find me. Almost bled out before I got to the road."

Joan pressed closer to Ruth. Ruth was sort of smiling about it, but she'd been even closer to death than Joan had realized.

"Next thing I know," Ruth said, "I'm in hospital, and the girl in the bed next to mine is telling me to shut up." She swallowed. "I'd been babbling about the massacre. Annoying everyone in the ward. I didn't know what I was saying."

Ruth had woken up all alone. At least Joan and Aaron had had each other last night.

"They wheeled me out for a scan," Ruth said, "and that's when I saw *her*, walking in the direction of my room."

"Her?" Aaron said.

"A blonde woman with a long swan neck," Ruth said. "Walking down the hallway of the hospital ward like she owned it. And there were three men with her. Wearing pins with winged-lion insignia."

Joan started to ask what that meant and then stopped when she saw that all the color had drained from Aaron's face.

"When they brought me back to my room," Ruth said, "the girl in the other bed was gone. They said she must have checked herself out. But I don't think she did."

"You saw Court Guards at the hospital?" Aaron said, hushed.

"I don't know for sure," Ruth said. "I was all drugged up

and really out of it. But afterward . . . Every time I followed rumors of survivors, I found whispers of Court Guards. And a blonde woman."

Something creaked on the landing outside. They all jerked their heads to look at the door—as Ruth had been doing all night.

A door nearby opened and closed. A lock slid shut. Joan breathed out. She heard Aaron's and Ruth's breaths ease out too.

"We should get some rest," Ruth said. "Stall owners are going to bed. Best to have our lights on and off on the same schedule as them."

Ruth's watch said it was nearly four a.m. Joan didn't know what time it was according to her own body clock.

Without much discussion, they'd agreed that Joan and Ruth would share the bed. Aaron would have the sofa. Now Joan lay awake in the dark. She wasn't tired at all. Outside the room, the building creaked and settled. Footsteps sounded occasionally on the landing. Joan listened to Ruth's regular, reassuring breaths. Ruth was here. She was alive. Joan almost didn't dare believe it.

"Can't sleep?" Ruth whispered.

Joan shook her head and then remembered that Ruth wouldn't be able to see her in the dark. "I thought you were asleep," she whispered back.

"I couldn't sleep after," Ruth said, soft. "For a long, long time. You keep seeing them, don't you?"

Joan rolled to face her. "I keep walking into that room," she whispered. "Where I found you . . . All that blood leading to the sofa. You pressing down on Gran's wound." She hadn't seen the others, but her mind kept conjuring horrors. Bertie with his throat slit, all alone. Uncle Gus and Aunt Ada bleeding out.

Ruth pushed Joan's hair from her face. "It's not as fresh for me," she whispered, "but I remember how I felt."

"You don't feel it now?"

"I do. It's just . . . different. Like a scar compared with a fresh wound."

Joan didn't know what to say. She felt hollowed out and so terribly lonely suddenly. For her, it had been last night. For Ruth, it had been years ago.

"I miss them," Ruth whispered. "God. *So* much. I missed you."

Joan had assumed that Ruth had found Gran, at least, in this time. Apparently not. She shifted closer so that she could hug Ruth, a little clumsily. Joan had barely even begun to miss them yet, she realized. It had only been one night for her. But there'd been so much pain in Ruth's voice. This was the same loss, two years apart.

"We'll undo it," she whispered into Ruth's shoulder. "We'll get them back."

"Did that Oliver boy promise you that?" Ruth whispered. "Because if he did—"

"No. He said it couldn't be done. Is that true?"

Ruth was silent. "Try to rest even if you can't sleep," she said finally. "Close your eyes, at least."

The evasion made Joan's stomach twist. "*Is* it possible to save them?" she said. "Is it?"

Ruth's arms squeezed tighter for a moment and then she pushed Joan away gently. "Close your eyes," she said. "You don't have to sleep. Just close your eyes and breathe."

Outside, the rain had finally stopped. Joan breathed in and out. She lay awake, listening to raindrops fall from the roof in long, slow strikes.

ELEVEN

Joan jerked awake, half caught inside her childhood nightmare—the old, old one, of the prison with the cold stone floor and the guard outside with heavy shoulders like a mastiff. She lay awake, shivering with it. She could still feel the scratch of straw under her shoulders. The smell of sickness and filth seemed to linger in the air.

It was just a dream, she reminded herself. Just the one she'd always had. It wasn't real. She was okay. She was here in bed. . . .

She opened her eyes and the memory of what *was* real hit her like a shock wave.

Aaron's voice cut through it, snide and posh. "Could I trouble you to pass me a pen?" His voice was weirdly grounding.

Through the bookshelf partition, Joan glimpsed the surreal image of Ruth and Aaron at the breakfast table, eating toast and drinking tea. There was a frosty tension between them, but evidently they'd formed enough of a truce to eat breakfast together.

"Identification," Aaron said, writing. Someone—probably Ruth—had stolen stationery from the post office. Joan recognized the logo: a tree, half in bare winter branches, half in summer leaves. "Money, clothes . . ." Aaron made an irritated noise and scribbled his pen onto the corner of the paper. "I can't work like this. I need a spreadsheet."

"You've only said three things," Ruth said. "Surely you can hold three things in your head."

"I cannot *believe* I'm here with you," Aaron told her. "I wish I were anywhere but here. I wish I were at home with a good book."

Joan dragged herself out of bed. She rubbed her eyes and stumbled around the bookshelf. "Hey," she mumbled.

They both looked up at her. "You look like death," Aaron said.

"Yeah, well, you look . . ." Joan waved her hand sleepily. "You haven't combed your hair."

Aaron pressed his hand to his chest, feigning a wound, and then went back to writing his list.

In the bathroom mirror, Joan *did* look like death—gray-skinned and glassy-eyed. She splashed cold water on her face and came up looking like death with a wet face.

The nightmare was still half there. As always, it felt more physical than a normal dream. Joan's stomach ached with remembered hunger. Her skin crawled with the desperate urge to escape. She squeezed the edges of the sink and took a deep breath. She wasn't there; she was here. Ruth was here. Aaron. They *had* escaped. They'd all survived. And as long as they'd survived, they could do more.

Back in the main room, there was a third cup of tea on the table and a slice of buttered toast.

"Thanks," Joan said gratefully. She slid into the spare chair. "So I've been thinking," she said. "About changing what happened."

"We talked about this," Aaron said. He wrote down *Travelcards*. He had old-fashioned, looping handwriting, like someone's great-grandmother.

"No, we didn't," Joan said. "You said it couldn't be done. But I don't believe that."

"Oh, you don't *believe* it," Aaron said. "Wonderful. We're all saved."

"I've been thinking about it all night," Joan said. "Monsters must change things all the time—just by traveling."

"Do you really not have a computer?" Aaron asked Ruth.

"Yesterday, we walked around in this time," Joan said, undeterred. "We talked to people. We affected traffic. For all we know, we accidentally prevented someone from meeting their one true love."

Aaron was disgusted enough to stop writing. "Their *one true love*?"

"Think about it," Joan said. "We walked around a lot yesterday. What if one of the times we crossed the road, we held up a car? What if some guy in that car was supposed to meet his future partner that day? Only we pressed the button at the lights. Now he arrives two minutes later than he would have. He never crosses paths with the partner. They never meet."

"You're talking about the small fluxes of the timeline,"

Ruth said. "Those changes are meaningless—the timeline smooths them over. It's like . . . It's like . . ." She leaned over and blew across her mug. The tea in it shivered and then stilled. "It's just like that. We change things, and the timeline restores itself. Whatever monsters do, the timeline keeps its basic shape. Important events stay the same."

"In your *true love* scenario," Aaron said, "the timeline would make sure that the partner was delayed too. They'd still meet. Nothing important would change."

Joan couldn't deny that there was a resistance about the world. She remembered those two envelopes falling to the ground yesterday; she remembered the feeling of the timeline stirring in response to her attempts to change it. But if the timeline had to resist, then surely there were times when it failed. "Are you telling me you've never heard the smallest rumor?" she persisted. "You've never heard any stories about events being changed? Not ever?"

"Never," Aaron said.

"I don't believe you," Joan said.

"Do you know what infants do?" Aaron said. "They drop things over and over and over because they have to test the physical properties of the world to understand it."

"You think I'm an infant?"

"No," Aaron said. "I think you're in denial about your family's deaths. You don't want to believe they're dead. You're desperate for any possible way to bring them back."

Joan couldn't understand him at all. "They're not even dead

yet!" she said. "They're not going to die for years and years! And I'm going to stop it."

"No, you won't."

"How do you know? You haven't even tried. What does it hurt to try?"

"*You!* When you realize that you can't, it's going to hurt *you!*" Aaron said. The words came out in a rush. Then he scowled as if he hadn't meant to say them out loud. He shoved his chair back. "Oh, do whatever you want. I'm going to get myself some proper nineties clothes."

"He's hot." Ruth leaned over and took the leftover slice of toast from Aaron's plate.

"Who, Aaron?" Joan said, startled. Ruth hated the Olivers. And Aaron wasn't Ruth's type at all.

"Is that why you're still with him?" Ruth said. "Do you like him?"

"*What?*" Joan felt herself starting to flush.

"Do you?" Ruth wasn't saying it in her usual teasing way. "Because I think he likes you."

"*Likes* me?" Joan said. Why was Ruth talking about Joan liking anyone? The last time Joan had kissed a boy, he'd killed their family. "He despises me. He—" She brutally cut off the train of thought. "It doesn't matter what he thinks of me."

Ruth's sharp expression reminded Joan of Gran's. "He's here. Olivers and Hunts can't stand each other. But he's still here, two days after you escaped."

"I saved his life," Joan said. "He thinks he owes me."

"He owes you?" Ruth said thoughtfully. "Huh. Okay." She bit into her toast and leaned back in her chair, chewing. "Okay."

"Okay?" Joan echoed. "Now you're fine with it?"

Ruth shrugged. "You saved his life. He owes you."

"Right," Joan said. And when he didn't owe her anymore, he'd be gone. And that would be that. They'd be out of each other's lives for good.

Someone had opened the windows, and from the light outside she guessed it to be midmorning. There was a muggy heaviness to the air. The room smelled of burnt toast and the wet-stone aftermath of the storm.

Aaron had left his handwritten list on the table: *identification, money, clothes, Travelcards, housing, school.* That last one gave Joan pause. *School.* She couldn't imagine going to school in this time. She couldn't imagine actually living here.

"He wasn't quite telling you the truth, you know," Ruth said into the silence.

"What do you mean?"

"There *are* rumors of events being changed. I'm sure he's heard them."

Joan's breath caught. "You didn't tell me that last night."

"They're only rumors. I've never heard of anyone doing it for real."

"What rumors?"

Ruth hesitated. Long enough that Joan prompted her. "What rumors?"

"Nothing specific," Ruth said. "But . . . people say things about the Liu family power."

Joan thought of something Gran had always said. "The Lius remember."

"Yes," Ruth said, "but some people say that it goes beyond perfect memory. They say that some of the Lius remember things that never happened."

The way she said it made Joan shiver. "So maybe . . . they're remembering changes in the timeline?"

"I don't know," Ruth said. "It's possible."

"We have to talk to them."

"They might not be willing," Ruth said. "Families don't like to talk about their powers with outsiders."

"I want to talk to them."

"All right, but . . ." Ruth looked Joan up and down. "If you're leaving this way station, you'll need a proper makeover."

"What's wrong with this?" Joan said. She was wearing a black T-shirt and jeans. Plenty of people on the street had been wearing T-shirts and jeans.

"Everything," Ruth said.

Downstairs, at the market, Ruth pushed clothes along a rack: *flick, flick, flick*. Two aisles away, Aaron was doing the same thing with a small frown.

Ruth pulled out a tartan miniskirt. "This," she said. She draped the skirt over Joan's arm. *Flick, flick*. "And this." A baby-blue sweater that looked like it had been shrunk in the wash.

"Really?" Joan said.

"And these." A pair of heavy black combat boots. Ruth added a new pair of black stockings to the pile.

The changing booth didn't have a mirror. Joan buttoned the skirt. It was high-waisted enough to hide her bandage. But the sweater floated above her navel, leaving a long stretch of bare skin. "I think this is a dog vest," she said to Ruth through the curtain.

"It's supposed to look like that." Ruth ducked in and pulled Joan out of the booth.

Joan stared at herself in the mirror. It was like she was wearing the sexy Halloween version of her normal clothes. Ruth uncapped an eyeliner pencil and defined Joan's eyes, heavy at the corners. When she was done, Joan hardly recognized herself.

"What was wrong with the T-shirt?" Joan asked.

"The cut was wrong." The voice was Aaron's. He came out of his own booth, and his eyes widened as he took in Joan's outfit. "That's . . ." He seemed uncharacteristically lost for words. "Good."

He himself had transformed into a member of a nineties boy band: ripped jeans, a bomber jacket, and a little gold earring. He should have looked ridiculous. He *did* look ridiculous, Joan told herself. Except . . . Aaron made the whole outfit look thought-out and expensive. For the first time in Joan's life, she kind of understood the appeal of a nineties boy band.

Aaron stepped closer to her—close enough that Joan could

feel the warmth of his body as he lowered himself to his knees in front of her. For a moment, she was weirdly tongue-tied. "What are you doing?" she managed. Aaron reached up and plucked a pair of scissors from a nearby table. Before Joan could protest, he sliced into her stockings. And then she wasn't tongue-tied anymore. "What the hell are you doing?" she said, outraged.

Aaron dropped the scissors and used his fingers to tear the slashes into bigger holes.

"That's not bad," Ruth said grudgingly.

"What—what if you'd cut me?" Joan said.

Aaron had finished tearing the holes, but he was still kneeling, looking up at her with his cool gray eyes. "I wouldn't have cut you," he said.

Joan wanted to accuse him of deliberately making her look as stupid as he did. But the Joan in the mirror looked unexpectedly good—almost as good as Aaron—like they could be in the same band.

It struck Joan suddenly that Aaron had saved her life too. He'd said that he owed her. That he couldn't leave her until he'd repaid her. But he'd saved her life at the Pit and again at St. James's Park. Surely, he'd paid her back twice over.

It took Joan a moment to remember what she'd wanted to say to him. "Do you know anything about the Liu family power?"

"Perfect memory," Aaron said. "Everyone knows that."

"Yes, but Ruth says that there are rumors of more. Rumors that some of them remember events that never happened."

Aaron got to his feet slowly, and then Joan was looking up at him. "I've heard the rumors," he said evenly.

"Maybe they're remembering events that have changed."

"I understand the implication."

"If events have been changed before, maybe they can be changed again."

Aaron sighed. "I understand the implication."

"Ruth and I are going to see them," Joan said.

Ruth shifted beside her, clearing her throat. Joan looked at her questioningly.

"I'm, uh, not exactly welcome in the Liu houses," Ruth said. "I've . . . Well, I've kind of stolen a few things here and there, and I guess I have a bit of a reputation. They wouldn't let me through the front door." At Joan's look, she said defensively, "They have some nice stuff."

"Justification enough," Aaron said, dry.

Ruth gave him the finger, but it was halfhearted.

"Well, just tell me where they are," Joan said.

"No," Aaron said heavily. "I'll take you."

Joan looked at him, surprised. He'd been so scathing about the idea. And he didn't look any happier about it now. He was scowling down at his new blue sneakers.

"Be careful," Ruth said. She sounded as though she didn't like the idea of being separated from Joan so soon after they'd found each other. Joan didn't like it either.

"You too," Joan said. "Be *really* careful, okay?"

Ruth nodded slightly. "Just keep in mind that the Lius don't involve themselves in petty power plays like *some* families." This must have been directed at Aaron, because he rolled his eyes. "But every family has their own agenda."

The Ravencroft Market had arcades running through it. Joan hadn't realized how big it was. Aaron led her down one arcade and then another. Each seemed themed. One whole arcade sold weapons of various eras: knives and swords and bows. Another sold spices that Joan had never heard of.

"This way," Aaron said.

The next arcade had a door at one end. It opened onto another nondescript human laneway. When Joan shut it behind her, the market sounds of people talking and selling cut off like someone had flicked a switch. No human wandering past would have suspected that a different world lay beyond that black door.

Joan touched the brass plaque on the wall beside it—a sea serpent coiled around a sailing ship. The same symbol she'd seen by the door to the inn.

"Are all monster places marked like this?" she asked.

"That symbol means that monsters from any family may enter," Aaron said. "This whole complex—the inn, the market, the post office—is a way station. Monsters from all families are welcome to come and go."

A way station. Joan remembered the monsters who'd arrived in the rain yesterday, wearing clothes from different times. She pictured places like this dotted around the city—safe places where monsters could travel in and out, unobserved by humans. Places to exchange currency and buy clothes, to meet people and relay messages. To eat and sleep.

Aaron had already started walking toward the mouth of the laneway. Joan followed him. She felt as though she'd just glimpsed a whole bigger world.

Outside, the remnants of the storm were all over the streets—puddled water and stray sticks and leaves. Joan's self-consciousness about her clothes started to fade as she realized that no one was particularly looking at them—or, at least, no more than people usually looked at Aaron. These clothes really did make them blend in more.

"Thank you for taking me," she said to Aaron a little awkwardly. "I know you don't believe we can change anything."

"I know you have to do this," Aaron said. Joan was reminded of his weary expression from last night. "Every monster goes up against the timeline."

"What do you mean?"

"Everyone goes up against the timeline," Aaron said. "Everyone tries to change something at some point."

What had Aaron tried to change? When had he gone up against the timeline? What had happened that had made him so weary now? Joan wanted to ask him, but something in his expression silenced her.

Just like yesterday, the nineties were everywhere. As they walked past newsstands, Joan glimpsed headlines: "New Disaster for John Major." "Steffi Poised to Win Wimbledon." On the cover of *Vogue*, the model had heavy mascara and thin eyebrows.

Aaron took the same kind of twisting route he'd taken to get to the monster inn: through parks and shops and church-yards.

"This isn't a shortcut," Joan said slowly, when Aaron doubled back.

"I'm avoiding security cameras," Aaron said. "Monsters don't like being captured on camera. There aren't as many in this time as in yours, but there are enough."

Joan took that in. The Hunts didn't like being photographed either. Joan had always thought that was one of their eccentricities. But it seemed this was another thing that was cultural.

Not long after that, Aaron turned into a narrow commercial street, full of jewelers and bespoke shoemakers. If Joan were to guess, they were somewhere north of Covent Garden. He stopped halfway up the street. "The Lius," he said.

The shop—if that's what it was—had no signage, not even a street number. The front was just a cool wall of frosted glass bricks. Patches of violet and green shimmered beyond the glass like the dart of exotic fish. In the summer sunshine, the effect was almost tropical.

As they stood there, a beautiful woman pushed past them, briefly enveloping them both in a scent that made Joan think of summer gardens. She pushed at the wall, and a piece of the glass moved inward—a door, its edges cunningly blended into the glass bricks. Joan caught a glimpse of vibrant color. Then the door swung shut, and there was only the wall.

"We need to be very careful," Aaron said. He had a relaxed hand in his pocket, but Joan was beginning to recognize his mannerisms now, and she could see the tense line of his back. "Nothing's free between families. If you want information from the Lius, you'll have to trade for it."

"I have money," Joan said. She'd sold the phone yesterday.

But Aaron was already shaking his head. "Something like this is considered a favor. It'll be a favor for a favor. And monsters take debts seriously. You'll have to pay what you owe."

"And after all this, what will I owe you?" Joan said.

Aaron's cheeks turned pink. "I told you. I'm the one who's in your—oh, will you stop asking questions so we can do this?" he said with an exasperated tone that was becoming a familiar part of their conversations.

Joan shrugged. She turned and pushed the wall where the woman had touched it. To her surprise, the door crashed open. She'd measured her effort for a heavy glass door, but in some genius of craftsmanship, it had been weighted to open to the lightest of touches. Joan's push had made it fly. She flushed, the violent entrance making her feel ridiculous. Distantly, she heard Aaron make a disapproving sound at her clumsiness, but she barely registered it as she stared around her.

The space inside was huge—far larger than it had seemed from the street. Light streamed from skylights. More light shone through the glass-brick wall, scattering into rainbows on the pale wooden floor.

The layout was a crisscross of white walls. It took Joan a second to realize that they were strategically angled away from direct sunlight. The slashes of tropical color that she'd seen from the outside were paintings, the streaky abstract kind that she'd always thought looked like children's finger paintings.

But these weren't painted by children. Perhaps aided by the layout of the room, perhaps by careful placement and progression, these paintings were intensely compelling—raw and mysterious. Joan found herself walking closer.

Just a few steps revealed a man, hidden by the angle of a wall. He was in profile, repositioning a painting, and he had Chinese features, handsome and grave. He looked up at Joan's approach.

"Ying?" It was the woman who'd entered ahead of them. She was even more beautiful now that Joan could see her properly. She was perhaps thirty, with flawless golden-brown skin. Her face was as delicate as a doll's. She gave Joan a casual up-and-down look that dismissed her, and then reconsidered the dismissal. She tilted her head. "Daughter?" she asked the man—Ying. "Niece?"

Ying's pause was long. "She is not a Liu."

Now that he was looking at Joan directly, she could see that his face was cut with deep, sad lines. His dark hair was parted perfectly and pulled back into a short ponytail. His clothing was both impeccable and slightly incongruous: shirt collar as white and rigid as porcelain, trousers a blue-gray linen that made Joan think of stormy seas.

Joan felt Aaron appear beside her. "Excuse me," Aaron said. "I want to trade."

Joan had thought Aaron would fit in perfectly here. He

didn't. Beside Ying, Aaron looked uptight and overthought. In here, he was as out of place as Joan.

"My apologies, but you'll have to wait," Ying said. His accent was Oxford. "There are people ahead of you in the queue."

Aaron's cheeks reddened. He opened his mouth, and then clearly couldn't bring himself say it.

Joan restrained herself from rolling her eyes. "He and I are here together," she said.

Ying had the face of a man who'd seen everything, but Joan saw a glimmer of curiosity in his eyes. "A Hunt and an Oliver together? How very Romeo and Juliet."

A flush crawled down Aaron's neck like an ugly rash. "Not that kind of together." He looked as though he'd eaten something he was allergic to.

Joan felt her irritation flicker like a fanned flame. Aaron had a knack for making her feel that way, it seemed. She bunched her hair into her fist to cool her own neck.

As she did, the woman made a small, surprised cry. "You've been cut!" she said to Joan. "My goodness. What happened to you?" She touched her own slim side.

Joan dropped her hand. The skirt had slipped and the bandage with it, revealing the edge of the sword wound. Joan wrenched her skirt up, wishing she were wearing more than the dog vest.

"What happened?" the woman asked. "It looks as though you were in a *duel*."

Joan caught Aaron's alarmed look. Apparently, questions

about sword wounds were dangerous territory. "It's nothing," Joan said. "It's just . . . paint."

"Paint?" The woman sounded skeptical.

Ying's smooth voice interjected. "My apologies. There *was* a wet painting by the wall."

"Oh," the woman said, uncertain now.

"Shall I have your piece delivered to the Ritz?"

"That would be convenient," the woman said. She inclined her head graciously.

Joan could feel her curious eyes on them as Ying gestured for them to follow him.

Ying led them on a winding path through the gallery. The angled walls reminded Joan uncomfortably of the maze at Holland House. Her heart stuttered each time they turned a corner; she half expected to find Nick's people waiting with weapons. But at the end of their walk, there was just a small staff kitchen.

It was incongruously cozy compared with the soaring gallery. Everything was covered in mismatched striped wool—the teapot, the legs of the chairs, knife handles, cushions. "My niece likes to knit," Ying said when he saw Joan looking. He went to a cabinet and took out a first-aid kit. He cut off a piece of clear tape.

"You lied for me," Joan said, accepting the tape.

"I didn't lie," Ying said. "There *is* a wet painting by the wall." His eyes crinkled slightly, although the rest of his face remained solemn.

Joan did smile, tentatively. She fixed her bandage, hiding it again under the edge of the skirt.

As she did, Ying put together bowls of love-letter wafers and fresh strawberries and shelled peanuts. With some careful jigsaw-puzzling, he squeezed all the food onto a tray. The impulse to feed guests reminded Joan acutely of Dad.

"Please." Ying gestured for Joan and Aaron to follow.

He led them through the back door to a beautiful, if overgrown, courtyard garden. It seemed to be the center of the Lius' residence: a square surrounded on all sides by buildings. A covered walkway ran between the courtyard and the buildings.

One covered section had been set up for a painter, with a table and an easel. Ying placed the tray on the table. His niece had been here too. The table legs wore striped tights in mismatched colors—blue and red, and green and pink. Joan caught Aaron glancing at them with mild horror.

The courtyard had a pleasantly casual feeling. Fern fronds encroached on the table. The air smelled of paint and jasmine. The sun had come out, turning the air thick and summery. There was no sign of yesterday's storm.

In the covered walkway, most of the doors had sneakers and flip-flops outside them. There were half-painted landscapes and portraits propped against the walls.

"One of my son's works," Ying said, and Joan realized that she'd been looking at the nearest painting. It was of a man standing outside the door of a little town house, his back to the viewer. "Jamie loves the hero myths," Ying said.

"The hero myths?" Joan said.

"The hero knocks," Aaron murmured, as if it were a familiar subject of art.

Joan was more shaken than she'd have expected. *Nick*. The painting showed the hero standing outside a monster's door. Even from behind, he didn't look much like Nick. He had light brown hair to Nick's dark, and an immense muscularity to Nick's human frame.

Joan had thought she'd understood that the boy she'd kissed at Holland House was a figure from legend. But seeing him like this—mythologized in a time before his own birth—made the hairs rise on the back of her neck.

"Joan," Aaron said.

Joan blinked at him. "Yeah." She pulled herself away from the painting with some effort.

"Please," Ying said. "Sit."

There were no proper chairs in the courtyard. Joan sat on the raised brick edge of a bed of violets. The brick was warm and dry. Ying sat on a low stool by the painter's easel. Aaron remained standing, leaning against one of the thick white pillars that separated the courtyard from its corridor.

Ying poured hot water into the teapot. The scent of green leaves made Joan feel acutely homesick, as did the little teacups he unstacked. The cups were decorated with multicolored birds. They had sweeping tail feathers and outstretched wings. Phoenixes.

"I've been wondering," Aaron said to Ying from his place

at the pillar. "You identified our families just by looking at us." It was a detail that Joan hadn't noticed. "A Hunt and an Oliver. How did you know that?"

"Most monsters are recorded in the Liu family records," Ying said matter-of-factly. "The two of you are Joan Chang-Hunt and Aaron Oliver. Joan is the daughter of Pei-Wen Chang—a human. And Maureen Hunt—the estranged daughter of Dorothy Hunt."

Estranged? That wasn't right. Everything else was, though. Joan folded her arms, feeling exposed and in awe at the demonstration of the Liu family power. Perfect memory.

"And you," Ying said to Aaron, "are the youngest son of Edmund Oliver."

It wasn't a question, and Aaron didn't answer.

"By Edmund's second wife," Ying said. "Marguerite Nightingale. The wife they executed."

"That's enough," Aaron said tightly. His back was very stiff. His mother had been executed? Joan forced her eyes from his face—she felt as though she were intruding on something horribly private.

"As I said, the Liu records are very comprehensive," Ying said. "But you didn't come here for me to tell you things you already know. You came here to bargain. So, let's bargain. What is it that you want?"

"Information," Joan said.

Ying inclined his head in acknowledgment. "Rules first, then. My family likes to keep things simple. We will have a conversation, and at the end of it, my family will be owed one favor."

"What favor?" Joan said.

"You'll know when we call it in," Ying said.

By the pillar, Aaron shrugged slightly at Joan. He'd apparently been expecting these sorts of terms. Joan didn't like them at all. Buying something unknown for an unknown price was a stupid thing to do. But there'd been no other leads. And if she could get *any* information to save her family . . . She nodded at Ying.

"Very well, then." Ying leaned over to the table and poured tea into the little cups. He passed one to Aaron and one to Joan. "What do you want to know?"

Joan sipped her tea, giving herself a moment to collect her thoughts. The tea was good—grassy and fresh and green. The kind of tea Dad kept in the freezer. "We've heard rumors," she said. "About your family's power."

"Perfect memory," Ying said. "That's common knowledge."

"There are rumors about hidden aspects of the power."

"I've heard rumors," Ying said thoughtfully, "about hidden aspects of the Oliver power." To Aaron, he said: "They say that the heads of your family can see more than other Olivers see."

For some reason, Aaron's gaze flicked to Joan, his expression unreadable. "We're not talking about my family," he said.

"No?" Ying said musingly. "Olivers see. Hunts hide. Nowaks live. Patels bind. Portellis open. Hathaways leash. Nightingales take. Mtawalis keep. Argents sway. Alis seal. Griffiths reveal. But only the Lius remember." The words were slightly chanted—the recital of a nursery rhyme. "The twelve great families of London," he said.

"I hope you're not expecting us to pay for that," Aaron said dryly. "Every monster child in London knows that rhyme."

Ying's face did that thing again, where he seemed amused without actually smiling. "The family powers are common knowledge," he said. "But you're asking about family secrets. If I were you, I'd be concerned that a Liu family secret might cost more than you're willing to pay."

"*I'm* the one making the bargain," Joan said. She was the one who'd wanted to come here. "Not Aaron. And I'm willing to pay."

Ying gave her a long look, as if assessing whether she really wanted to make the trade. "Have you ever heard of the *zhēnshí de lìshǐ*?" he said finally.

"The true history?" Aaron said.

Ying's eyebrows went up. "You know Mandarin?"

"No," Aaron said. "I know of the belief." He sounded disapproving.

Ying turned back to Joan. "Some people believe that there was once another timeline," he explained. "One that existed before our own. Some families call it the *vera historia*. Or the true timeline." There was a sad reverence in his voice. "We believe that the true timeline was erased, and that *this* timeline was created in its place."

"A fringe belief," Aaron said. "Everyone knows that the

timeline corrects itself. It's impossible for there to have ever been another timeline."

"Some of my family believe they remember fragments of it," Ying said.

Joan's breath caught. It was true, then. The Lius did remember changed events. "Do you?" she asked. "Do you remember it?"

Ying took a long moment to answer. "The Liu power is perfect memory," he said. "For some of us, our power goes beyond that. We remember small changes—the ordinary fluxes of the timeline. But only those of great power have glimpsed the *zhēnshí de lìshǐ*."

Joan leaned forward, eager. "If there were another timeline, then something changed it. Or someone."

"I'm sorry," Ying said, not unkindly. "But that completes our conversation. I've given you information about the Liu power. Now you owe a favor."

"No," Joan said. The conversation was just starting. She needed to know so much more. "How was the timeline changed? Please. I'll owe another favor."

"I'm sorry," Ying said. He refilled Joan's tea. "As I told you, my family likes to keep things simple. One debt is simple. Multiple debts are complicated. But please. Finish your tea and feel free to peruse the gallery afterward."

Aaron shifted from the white pillar. He came over to sit beside Joan on the edge of the garden bed. "Joan," he said softly. "He's met the terms of the bargain."

"We can't leave," Joan said. She was sure that Ying knew

more. "Aaron, I can't leave until I know."

Aaron bowed his head. When he raised it again, it was to look up at Ying. "I'll take on a debt," he said.

"No," Joan said. That wouldn't be fair. He hadn't even wanted to come here.

Maybe Ying would take something other than a favor. But what did Joan have to trade? She hadn't brought anything with her into this time except for a phone and her clothes—and she'd sold the phone yesterday.

The only thing she still had . . . She put her hand to her chest, feeling the lines of the necklace under the soft fuzz of her sweater. The man at the market had offered to buy it yesterday and Joan had refused.

Her hands shook as she unclasped it. It was the last thing she had left of Gran. She tried not to think about that as she offered it to Ying. "Will you take this instead of a favor?"

"I'm sorry," Ying said.

"*Please*," Joan said. "Please. I need to know."

"Need to know what?" Ying said.

"How to undo deaths."

The sad lines in Ying's face were like carvings in wood. "You've lost someone."

"Yes," Joan whispered.

"I can't help you with what you want to know," Ying said gently. "You don't owe me for telling you that you can't bring them back."

Joan couldn't accept that. "Something or someone changed

the timeline before," she said. "You have perfect memory, and you said that the Liu records are comprehensive. You must have heard something—some rumor, some whisper—about how it was done." She held out the necklace again. "Please."

Ying started to shake his head as if to refuse one final time. And then he frowned, leaning closer to get a better look at the necklace. Joan heard his breath catch. "Where did you get that?" he said softly.

Joan remembered the way Gran's hand had slipped from her wrist, leaving the chain behind. She'd barely been able to see it through her tears that night. "My grandmother gave it to me."

"May I?" Ying said. But instead of reaching for the necklace, he cleared the table, moving bowls and plates to the ground so that there was only the black tray left.

Joan draped the necklace across it. The gold pendant was very bright against the black.

There'd been blood on the chain after Gran had died. Joan had washed it that night in the shower. But she hadn't really looked at it—she hadn't been able to bear it.

Now she examined the pendant: it wasn't the silver-tongued fox of the Hunts, but something else. At first, Joan couldn't make out the intention of it. It was a creature with a lion's head and the talons of a bird. It wasn't much bigger than her thumbnail, but it was exquisitely detailed: three-dimensional and lifelike. It stood on a flat gold disc, ears up, head tilted in curious interest. The whole thing seemed to be solid gold.

"I never noticed you wearing that," Aaron said to Joan.

"It has a long chain," Ying said absently. The chain was gold too, and very fine. There were dark marks along it, as if the gold had been burned. Ying spread his fingers, touching four fingertips to the patches, and Joan had a sudden clear memory of touching the chain in those same places. The chain had been unblemished, and after she'd touched it, these dark patches had appeared. She'd thought at the time that the blemishes had been blood. But looking at the chain now, it seemed almost as if the gold itself had been transformed into something else. But *how*?

Ying looked at Joan again. There was something searching in his gaze, as if she hadn't really had his attention before this. And now she had it completely. Joan was unexpectedly reminded of the way Edmund Oliver had looked at her in the Gilt Room. His indifference had changed to interest, as if he'd seen something inside her. *The Hunts have been keeping secrets,* he'd said.

"What do you want to know?" Ying said.

Joan swallowed. Her heart was beating faster, and she wasn't sure why. "How was the timeline changed?" she asked.

"There are stories about the creation of our timeline," Ying said. "But they're myths."

"Myths?" Joan said. *The human hero is a mythical figure,* Ruth had said last night. "What myths?"

"They say that the King created our timeline," Ying said. "Using an object. A device. He destroyed the *zhēnshí de lìshǐ* with it and created this timeline in its place. Now this timeline is his timeline. Everything in it is just as he wishes it to be."

"What device?" Joan said. They were so close to learning what she needed to know. If there was a way to get her family back, she had to have it.

"All I can tell you is that it's held at a place called the Monster Court." Ying was still looking at her with that new attention. "The seat of the King's power. And you don't need to ask me how to get to it." He picked up the necklace, and, to Joan's surprise, placed it back into her hand, coiling it slowly before letting the end drop. "You have a key."

Joan stared at him.

Ying stood up. "We'll call on you when we need a favor," he said.

TWELVE

꘎

Joan and Aaron walked away from the Liu family gallery. Joan couldn't stop touching the necklace Gran had given her. Could it actually be a key to the Monster Court? The seat of the King's power?

"You talked about the King when we first arrived," Joan said to Aaron as they walked.

"Get that pendant out of sight," Aaron said, clipped. He was very tense. He'd insisted on walking back by a different route, and now he was checking over his shoulder.

"Why didn't Ying take it?" Joan wondered. She tucked it carefully under her sweater. "I offered it to him."

"He probably didn't want it anywhere near him," Aaron said. "And neither do I."

They reached an intersection. Joan pressed the button at the lights. Aaron's fingers twitched, as if standing still were intolerable.

"Why are you so scared?" Joan asked him.

"We need to get back to the market," Aaron said. His mouth was tight, and the pale press of his lips reminded Joan of how ill he'd looked when Ruth had spoken of seeing Court Guards at the hospital.

"Who is he king of?" Joan said. "All the monsters of England?"

Aaron didn't seem to want to answer. When he did, it was curt. "Our borders don't match what you'd think of as countries," he said shortly. "They were drawn in a different time."

What you'd think of as countries. Joan had that feeling again of seeing a crack through a curtain—a glimpse of another world. There was so much she didn't know—so much Gran had never told her.

A red Royal Mail van trundled past them. Aaron tracked it until it had turned the corner. He was watching every car that passed. The lights changed. "Come on," Aaron said. He'd already started walking.

"Aaron—" Joan said.

"Keep walking," Aaron said. He waited for Joan to catch up. "The King is never seen," he said, still curt. "He rules through the members of the Monster Court: the King's arms and executioners. We sometimes call them the *Curia Monstrorum.*"

Joan matched her pace to Aaron's. She tried to make sense of the pieces she had. The monster world had a hierarchy of authority. Ruth had talked about Court Guards; Joan guessed they were something like police officers. Above them were the members of the Monster Court. And above *them*, the King himself.

The King is never seen. Joan imagined an invisible presence that permeated the monster world. "Do you think it could be true?" she asked Aaron. "What Ying said? Do you think the King once changed the timeline? Do you think he erased the true timeline with a device?"

Aaron shot another reflexive look over his shoulder. "Don't *say* things like that," he hissed. He caught Joan's confused expression. "*True timeline*," he clarified. "Don't say those words in public."

They were walking alone beside the road. Hardly public. And Ying hadn't seemed afraid to say them. "No one can hear us," Joan said.

Aaron looked around before he spoke, and when he did, his voice was soft, as if he was afraid they might be overheard, even though there was clearly no one in earshot. "There is only one timeline. The King's timeline," he said. "Events are just as he wishes them to be. To speak of another timeline, to call it the *true* timeline . . . it's dangerous. It's—it's blasphemy."

"Blasphemy?" Joan repeated. It was an unexpected word for the context. She would have thought *treason* would be a better fit for a king. "But, Aaron, if—"

"*Please*," Aaron ground out. "*Please* can you wait until we're somewhere safe before you ask any more questions?" He ran a shaky hand through his hair. "What have we got ourselves into?" he asked, almost to himself.

The Ravencroft Market was busier than it had been when they'd left. As they wove through it, Joan finally saw how the main area was structured: divided into periods like the sections of a department store. Over there was the twentieth century; and over here the twenty-first, the clothes becoming less and less familiar in color and cut with each decade after Joan's own, until they were as strange as clothes from the distant past. It made Joan want to walk through to the far end of the market—to see the contraband technologies there.

"There are Court Guards patrolling the market," Aaron murmured. "Keep your head down." He ducked his own head, but Joan was curious enough to look around. *Monster police*, she thought. She remembered again Ruth's story of seeing Court Guards at the hospital.

She didn't spot any of them at first. And then she turned into an aisle where a man was saying mildly to a stall owner: "Give me all the cell phones."

The man wore a gold pin on his lapel: a winged lion, posed as if stalking the viewer, wings outstretched like a bird of prey. The stall owner was a middle-aged woman with purple lipstick and a matching purple jacket. The Court Guard's manner was easygoing, but the woman's hands shook as she put the phones into a box. She didn't look at him directly.

Aaron took Joan's elbow and moved her quickly past them. As they walked, Joan began to spot more and more guards with winged-lion pins. Stall owners looked on, white-lipped but not protesting, while phones and other devices were confiscated, as their tables were stripped bare.

"Technology out of its time," Aaron whispered to Joan as they reached the stairs. "Technically illegal, but Court Guards don't usually concern themselves with small markets like this."

Joan swallowed. "Ruth said she saw Court Guards after she spoke about the massacre," she whispered. "And I was overheard speaking of the massacre yesterday. Do you think they're looking for us?"

"If they were here for us, their attention would be on people, not technology," Aaron said. "It's just a coincidental raid. Come on."

To Joan's relief, Ruth opened the door to the flat on the first knock.

"There are Court Guards—" Aaron started to say.

"I know," Ruth said. "I've been watching them from upstairs."

She ushered them into the bedroom nook. There was a pull-down ladder in the ceiling.

Joan followed Ruth up the ladder and found herself in a rooftop garden. On one side, the market's glass dome rose like a sail. From up here, the leadwork ravens in the blue glass were the size of cats. Waist-high parapets enclosed the rest of the rooftop, reminding Joan of the Liu family's courtyard.

"You can see everything from here," Joan said wonderingly. Below, on the street, monsters were popping in and out of existence like soap bubbles. She didn't think she'd ever get used to that. Through the glass dome, the market was laid out in miniature. The guards looked the same as everyone else from this height—their pins too small to see. But Joan could tell where they were from the spaces other people left around them. And, even from up here, Joan could see how the guards had changed the atmosphere of the market. Customers were moving more slowly, heads turned to track them. Sellers were quieter.

"No one ever comes up onto the roof," Ruth said.

"Because it's ghastly," Aaron said. Someone had put potted plants up here, but they were long dead—withered to silver stems. The parapets were crumbling. He added, conceding, "Although, true—it's a comprehensive view."

Joan sat on a parapet, facing Ruth and Aaron. "We have some news," she told Ruth. "We spoke to Ying Liu. He confirmed the rumors. Some of the Lius remember another timeline."

Ruth's eyes widened. "He told you that?"

"That's the least of it," Aaron said. "Your cousin is in possession of contraband from the Monster Court itself. Did you know that?"

"*What?*" Ruth said. "No!"

Joan unclasped the gold necklace and leaned over to hand it to Ruth. "Gran gave it to me just before she died." She hoped Ruth wouldn't feel hurt that Gran had given her something.

Ruth didn't look hurt. She looked puzzled. She took the necklace and stretched it out against the bright white sky. She twisted it slightly, making the chain glint.

"Have you seen it before?" Joan said. "In Gran's house, maybe? Or did she ever wear it?"

Ruth shook her head. "Not that I know of. What are these dark patches on the chain? They almost look like stone."

"I don't know," Joan said. The question made her feel strangely uneasy. She remembered again how she'd touched the necklace after Gran had died: how, when she'd lifted her fingers, the gold underneath had been dull and dark. That couldn't be right, though, she thought again. She had to be remembering that wrong.

For some reason another memory came to her then: Ying Liu spreading his fingers to touch those dark patches. The way he'd looked at her searchingly afterward.

"According to Ying Liu, that's a key to the Monster Court," Aaron said.

Ruth jumped and almost fumbled it, as if he'd told her she was holding a snake.

"That's what he told us," Joan said.

Ruth's eyes were huge. "*This* is a key to the Court?" she said. "I don't understand. How is it even a key? It's a necklace."

"I don't know," Aaron said. "But look. The pendant is a sigil. It looks almost like a family chop."

Ruth held it up again, curiosity apparently overcoming fear. "I've never seen this sigil. . . ." She frowned, looking more closely. "What is it? A gargoyle? There are knots in its tail."

"A chimera of some kind," Aaron said. "But I've never seen it before either."

Ruth turned the pendant over. There was an indented, stamped image on the underside of the disk. The same creature, standing on a scroll. Joan squinted at the words. *Non sibi sed regi.* Latin?

"'Not for self, but for king,'" Aaron said.

"Those words don't belong to any of the twelve families," Ruth said.

"Maybe a lesser family's chop," Aaron said. "Or a French family's."

"But there's no name on it," Ruth said.

"What's a chop?" Joan asked.

Aaron reached into his pocket and took out a chain, unhooking it from a buttonhole. Joan had noticed the chain before, but she'd assumed it was for a fob watch. Now she saw that it had a little pendant figurine attached: a mermaid. But not a fairytale mermaid: there was something menacing about the tilt of her head, her clawing hands, the snakelike coil of her tail. It was the same mermaid that had been tattooed on Aaron's relative. The same outline Joan had seen through Aaron's wet shirt. The Oliver sigil.

Aaron mimed stamping it against the table and then handed it to Joan. "It's a seal."

There was a flat gold disk under the mermaid's tail. It had an etched image of the mermaid along with Aaron's name in mirrored letters. *Son of Edmund,* the chop said. Joan made out a Latin phrase: *Fidelis ad mortem.*

"Proof of identity," Aaron said. "Most monsters have one. In my family, we get them when our power stabilizes—when we're confirmed to be Olivers. We're buried with them when we die."

"Proof of identity?" Joan said. "Don't people forge them?"

"Not really," Ruth said. "They're handmade. The little scratches and imperfections are almost impossible to perfectly forge."

Joan took Gran's necklace back from Ruth. She examined

it. Ruth was right. It did kind of look like a chop. "Ying told us something else," she said to Ruth as she fastened it back on. "He said that the King erased the previous timeline and created this timeline in its place."

"Are you talking about the true timeline?" Ruth said. At Aaron's wince, Ruth said: "It's only blasphemy if you believe all that nonsense about the King being infallible."

"Some of us honor our oaths," Aaron said.

"Oh, give me a break from that fake Oliver piety," Ruth said. "Your family is a bunch of slithering schemers. You should just own it instead of pretending loyalty to the King."

"Fidelis ad mortem," Aaron said. "We live by it. You wouldn't understand."

"Yes, 'loyal unto death,'" Ruth said. "Clever that you don't say who you're loyal to. Everyone knows it's only to yourselves."

"Better than the Hunt motto. What is it again? 'Always running'?"

"Always *free*," Ruth said sharply.

"Can we go back to the important part of this conversation?" Joan said.

Aaron closed his mouth over whatever insult he'd been about to shoot at Ruth. He shrugged one shoulder, not quite sheepish.

"Ying Liu said that the King erased the previous timeline using a device," Joan told Ruth. "A device kept at the Monster Court." Joan tapped the pendant. "And now we have a way in."

She looked at the other two expectantly. Ruth was as silent as Aaron.

"Gran knew about the hero," Joan said. "That's why she gave me that necklace. So we could get into the Court. So we could find that device and stop the massacre."

"You want to break into the Monster Court?" Aaron said.

"Yes, of course," Joan said.

"You want to steal a device from the King?" Aaron said. "The mythical device that he used to create the kingdom he rules over? The device that—if it existed—he would protect more closely than any object in his possession?"

"I didn't say it would be easy."

Aaron laughed. "Joan. The Court isn't even *reachable*. It sits outside time. There's no way to get there without an invitation and an escort."

"Well, maybe that's what the necklace is for," Joan said. "Maybe it's not exactly a key. Maybe it's an invitation."

"I don't want to have this stupid conversation," Aaron said. "Getting in and out isn't even the issue. We'd be executed on the spot if we were even overheard speaking of this. What we need to do is to lie low. Find a safe place to stay and settle down in this time."

"Settle down in this time?" Joan said, incredulous. She thought about Aaron's list. *Housing. School.*

"Yes," Aaron said. And he was actually being serious about it—Joan couldn't believe it. "Our families were murdered," he said. "We were nearly killed too. We experienced something truly horrendous. We need to stop and take a breath."

"Gran gave me this necklace for a reason!" Joan said.

"You don't know that," Aaron said, sounding as frustrated

as Joan felt. "Dorothy Hunt is a renowned thief! She probably stole it without even knowing what it was."

"She told me we had to stop the hero!" Joan said. "She gave me that necklace to use it. She knew!"

"And was there a reason why she never told you anything else your whole life?" Aaron said. "Was there a reason she waited until she was dying to tell you anything at all?"

"We're not talking about that," Joan said. Couldn't he see that they might have found a way to save their families? "We need to make a plan to get into the Monster Court."

"We're not going to the Monster Court!" Aaron said, just as impatiently. "We're never going to the Court!"

"I'll go without you if I have to!"

"Oh, really? How are you going to do that? How are you even going to find it? *I* wouldn't know where to find it." Aaron turned to Ruth. "Maybe your family should have actually taught her something. Then she wouldn't have such stupid ideas about things."

"Will you shut up about that?" Joan snapped.

"No," Aaron said. "You almost fell out of this time twice yesterday!" To Ruth, he said: "That should never have happened! Your family never even taught her to be safe!"

"Gran wouldn't let us tell her what monsters were," Ruth blurted, as if surprised into honesty.

"What?" Joan felt as though she'd been punched.

Ruth saw her expression. "Oh, Joan. It's not like we—we just thought you *couldn't* travel. Most monsters can't if they have a human parent. Gran probably thought it would be kinder if you didn't know. I mean . . ." Her voice gentled. "I suppose she thought it would upset you too much to learn the truth of it."

"But . . ." Joan blinked, puzzlement overriding hurt for a moment. Gran *had* known that Joan could travel. Gran had known to wait up for Joan the night she'd first traveled. She'd *known*. "Don't the records say I can travel?"

"But that's what I mean," Ruth said. "The records said you can't."

"You thought she wasn't a monster," Aaron said.

"I didn't say that," Ruth said.

"A person who can't travel isn't a monster."

"Is that what you say about Olivers who can't?" Ruth sounded disgusted.

"An Oliver who can't travel is an oxymoron," Aaron said.

"Your family makes me sick," Ruth said.

Joan found herself standing. Her head was starting to hurt. She needed to think. "Where are you going?" Aaron said suddenly.

"For a walk."

"A walk where?" Ruth asked.

"I need to think." And she couldn't do that with all their bickering.

Joan left the monster street and walked until her head started to clear. She needed to figure out how the key worked and where the Court was. Maybe she should go back to the Lius.

The sun was out. She tipped her head up to feel it. She waited for some sniping comment from Aaron about the pause, but it didn't come. She'd forgotten for a second that she was alone. The silence gave her a strange feeling of relief and, unexpectedly, something closer to loneliness.

There were cafés all along the street. Joan picked an American-style diner with big windows and seats that got a bit of sun. Inside, tired tourists were eating hamburgers and hot dogs and all-day breakfast sausages and eggs.

Joan sorted through her money, carefully separating the monster notes from the human ones. When the waiter came, she ordered a pot of tea. Then she sat there, leaning her head back against the headrest and watching a couple argue over a map the size of a tablecloth. In thirty years, they'd have GPS and nothing to argue over.

The waiter returned with tea. "Thanks," Joan said as he set it down. Then, to her surprise, he slid into the seat opposite hers.

Her heart stopped. It was Nick.

THIRTEEN

Nick's hands shot out before Joan could react, clamping around both her wrists. Joan's heart pounded painfully. She heard the catch of her own breath. He looked just the same as he had two nights ago—the night she'd kissed him; the night her family had been murdered. His dark eyes were the same: serious and earnest. Just like when he'd asked her to stay with him.

"Do you remember what I told you the last time I saw you?" he said.

He'd told her he'd kill her if she ever stole time again. A shot of fear went through her. She tested the underside of the table with her knee. It didn't budge, even when she increased the pressure. She glanced at the neighboring table. It was bolted down. She couldn't kick the table over.

Nick looked casually out the window. People were walking past them, dressed for work, in the loose suits of this time. Joan followed his eyes from the window to the security camera above them, to another camera on the other side of the room. "Next time," he said, still soft, "I'll make sure we're alone."

"How can you be here?" Joan whispered. But there was

only one way. And like a storm hitting, her shock and fear at seeing him gave way to pure fury. "You're a monster too? After all you did, you're—"

"No!" Nick's jaw tightened. "I'm human."

"You liar!" Joan said. He was too good at lying. Everything he said was clear-eyed and true. "Only monsters can travel!"

"Only monsters and me. And I travel in a different way. *I* don't steal time."

"How, then?"

He didn't answer, and Joan shook her head in contempt. She thought about how she'd left Aaron and Ruth back at the market and couldn't believe how cavalier she'd been. If Nick's people found them, they'd be helpless.

Or maybe they were already dead. Maybe everyone at the inn and the market . . . Joan wrenched at her hands. Nick's grip tightened.

"Sorry," he said. He didn't sound sorry. "I can't let you touch me."

It was unbearable to be this close to him, to look at his familiar face, his serious eyes. Joan had looked at him so much at the house. She imagined what they must seem like to anyone glancing at them from the outside—a boy holding his girl-friend's hands at lunch. A few days ago, she'd have wanted that so much. Now they both knew that if he loosened his grip, she'd fly for his neck—cameras or not.

One question had been burning in her mind since that night. "Did you know they were my family before you had them killed?"

"No." Nick's eyes were still clear.

Joan made herself keep going. "Would you have killed them if you'd known?"

Nick didn't hesitate. "Yes."

It hurt like a physical wound. "We were friends. You and me. We were—" Her voice broke. He'd kissed her. She'd never kissed anyone before. "Why did you have to kill them? Why did you have to?" She could hardly recognize her own voice. The worst of it was that she felt it still—the pull toward him. "I *hate* you," she said.

This time Nick did hesitate, long enough for Joan to hear his hitched exhale. "I know."

Joan wanted to kick the table over. She wanted to hurt Nick like he'd hurt her. "You didn't have to kill them!" she said. "You didn't even know them! They were *people*! You're killing *people*!"

"They were stealing time from humans." His brown eyes were still earnest. "I couldn't allow them to harm anyone else."

Joan couldn't bear the earnestness. She couldn't bear being on the other side of it. "You killed all those people!" she said. "You didn't even give them a chance!"

And now those solemn eyes hardened. "You're wrong," he said. "Every monster who died that night had stolen time. Every member of your family. The Olivers. The other families." His voice went cold. "You know who didn't get a chance? The humans they stole from. All those people on the Tube. The tourists of London. People just walking down the street. Your people prey on them. But not anymore. I won't allow humans to be harmed. We won't be prey."

He'd never been prey. He'd seemed so vulnerable in the Gilt Room, a boy among monsters, and all that time, he'd been the deadliest thing there.

"Hello," a cheerful voice said.

Joan jumped, startled. It was a waitress. Joan had almost forgotten that they were in public.

"Ooh, didn't mean to scare you, love." The waitress had a Welsh accent and kind eyes. She pulled out a notepad and pen. Her name tag was cloud-shaped and said *Donna*. "What would you like?" she said. "We do breakfast all day. Bit of toast? Eggs? Everything on the menu is good except the porridge. Chef did something fancy with grapefruit peel and nutmeg today. I'd avoid it."

Nick shifted subtly, changing his grip on Joan, making it look more like they were holding hands. His posture changed too, loosening out of dangerous into something gentler. If it hadn't been for the tension in his jaw, the sharpness in his eyes, Joan might have thought he was the Nick she'd known. The volunteer she'd met in the Holland House library. She fought back a pang. That Nick had never existed. Joan was missing someone who'd never been real.

Donna looked at their clasped hands and smiled as if they looked sweet sitting there together. "What can I get you?" she said.

Joan made herself smile back. "Might need a bit longer." Donna's neck was bare. Joan found herself hunching, wanting to cover her own neck in sympathy. But Donna didn't know that monsters were real, that another London existed within her own. She didn't know that people could steal life from her just by touching her neck—and that this sweet-seeming boy was capable of a massacre.

"Sorry," Nick said to Donna apologetically. "I need a minute too." Sandwiched out of Donna's view, one of his hands had clamped down harder on Joan's wrists, grinding down, almost painful. He thought he was protecting Donna from her, Joan realized, and a wave of anger hit her again.

"All right, then," Donna said, still cheerful, "I'll be over there. Just give me a yell."

They watched her walk back to the counter.

"If you touch anyone in this room," Nick murmured, "I'll risk the cameras."

Joan dropped all pretense of smiling. "I'm not the one responsible for a massacre."

Now that Joan had seen a glimpse of the old Nick again, she could see something of him still in this new incarnation. The two Nicks shared a kind of serious quality, a calmness that Joan had found peaceful at the house.

She'd been on a school excursion once to a chapel built in the first century. They'd all been allowed to touch the rough stone wall of it—two thousand years old and still standing. Utterly solid, while everything around it had fallen. Joan had imagined its foundation stretching miles down into the earth. When she'd first met Nick, she'd been oddly reminded of that wall. This new Nick had that quality too, but in him it just felt like implacability. Now she knew why. He had a mission, and nothing would alter it. He wouldn't stop hunting monsters until every one was dead.

"If you're not here to kill me, then what do you want?" Joan gritted out.

Nick's eyes traveled down her neck. Joan flushed. "That's a nice necklace," he said.

Joan wrenched at her hands, but it was like tugging at a wall. Nick adjusted his grip so that he was holding her wrists with one hand and then slipped a finger under the chain. He tugged until the pendant slipped out from under Joan's shirt. He made a sound that wasn't quite amused, just a soft huff of air.

"I looked for this at the house," he said. And Joan remembered the audit he'd been doing—cataloging every object in every room. Joan thought about how Gran had given her the necklace with the last of her strength. She thought about Ying's widening eyes when he'd seen it. "You were looking for this all along," she said.

"And you had it all along," Nick said. "I'd never have guessed." He turned the pendant. His knuckles brushed against Joan's throat. She swallowed involuntarily, and knew he'd felt it when he lifted his eyes to hers. "I never guessed you were a monster," he said. "I watched over you at the house. I thought I was keeping you safe." He ran his thumb over the little pendant and his forehead creased. "I never thought you were one of them."

It hurt unexpectedly. She hadn't even known what monsters

were until that last day with him. "Was it hard killing all those people?" she asked. "Did you feel anything?"

"I did what had to be done," Nick said. And he was the new Nick completely when he said it, his gaze hard. Dangerous.

"Is that what you tell yourself to sleep at night?" Joan said.

Something flickered over Nick's face.

"Oh, you don't sleep?" she said. "I haven't much either since that night."

"Where did you find the necklace?" he said.

"What is it?" Joan countered.

He shrugged. "A gold necklace with a charming alphyn pendant. Made in the mid-nineteenth century, I'd guess."

"What's at the Monster Court?"

His posture stiffened. He pulled the chain gently until he found the clasp. His fingers worked, and then the chain and pendant were in his palm. They disappeared into his pocket. When he pulled his hand out again, he had a knife.

Joan's breath caught.

"I told you," Nick said. "I won't kill you here."

"You should," Joan whispered.

Nick tilted his head.

"I'm going to come after you," Joan promised. "I'm going to stop you from killing anyone else. I'm going to kill *you*." She'd never imagined she'd say those words to anyone—let alone Nick. She'd never imagined they could be true. She felt as though she were squeezing her own heart in her fist.

Nick's hand tightened for a moment over Joan's wrists. Then

he released her, slowly. He stood, knife ready if she attacked. When she didn't, he stepped back.

Joan gripped the edge of the table so that she wouldn't be tempted to try anything now.

"I mean it," she said. "You're dead."

He gave her his familiar solemn smile, the one that he'd given her all the time at the house. "Aren't we all," he said. "Somewhere on the timeline."

FOURTEEN

Joan ran back to the monster street. She wiped angrily at her face as she did. She hated that she was crying.

Being that close to Nick had brought it all back—all the feelings she'd had for him. Maybe still had for him. And in turn he'd told her the truth in that clear-eyed way he had. He'd have killed her family even if he'd known who they were to her. He'd have killed her if the cameras hadn't been there today. To him, she was a monster, and he'd been born to kill monsters.

And Joan was terrified too. Her mind kept throwing up images of Ruth and Aaron dead in the flat. Of everyone on that monster street lying dead—just like at Holland House.

She made herself take the long way, though, down side alleys and doubling back rather than running straight to the flat like she wanted to. She wasn't going to lead Nick to anyone.

For the first time, she looked for cameras, avoiding them like Aaron always did. Nick had pointed out the cameras in the café, and Joan was sure that was how he'd found her. She was beginning to understand why monsters hated cameras. If your enemies could travel in time, you never wanted to leave a record of where you'd been.

The market was bustling with people. Joan wanted to scream at them: *The hero is here in this time!* But she'd have sounded mad—like screaming that Superman was here.

She stumbled up the wrought-iron staircase to the landing. To her relief, she could hear Ruth and Aaron arguing through the door of the flat.

"—the only family without allies," Aaron was saying. "That's how much you're despised."

Joan pounded on the door and Ruth opened it mid-sentence. "I don't know what the Mtawalis see in your family," Ruth said. "They're too—"

"*Stop*," Joan said. She'd had it with their fighting. She slammed the door behind her and took a deep breath. "We have to stop this," she said. "Nick is here."

They stared at her—not frightened, but confused. "What do you mean?" Aaron said.

"Nick is here!" Joan said. "He's here in this time!"

There was a longer silence. "He can't be," Aaron said. "He's human. I saw him with my own power."

"Humans can't travel," Ruth said.

"I don't know how he got here!" Joan said impatiently. "But I'm telling you, he's here!"

"Are you sure?" Aaron said. "Are you sure it was him?"

"He took the necklace," Joan said.

Aaron looked at Joan's bare throat and went pale. "Why would he do that?"

Joan could guess why. Sometimes it felt as though she knew Nick as well as she knew herself. He was going to use the necklace to get to the Monster Court. To get to the same device that they were after. He was going to change the timeline.

Aaron had said it last night. *The human hero is the end of days for monsters.*

"You told us the myth," Joan said to Aaron. "You said that in the end of days, the hero kills the ancestor of monsters."

Nick's plan was as clear to Joan as if he'd told her himself. He was going to use that device to change the timeline. He was going to kill that ancestral monster. And when he did, no other monster would ever be born. Every monster would be erased from the timeline. Nick's purpose as the hero would be fulfilled.

Aaron didn't say anything, but Joan had seen that expression on his face before. He'd had it in the maze—when he'd looked down and seen the symbol of the hero on the back of a man's neck.

"No." Ruth shook her head.

She didn't want to believe it. Joan knew that feeling well.

"Gran told me about the hero that night," Joan said. "Ruth, she knew about him. She was expecting him, but . . ." She remembered what Gran had said. *I was supposed to have so much more time to prepare you. I thought I'd be fighting beside you.* "I think he came at the wrong time. She wasn't ready for him. She tried to tell me more, but she was too weak. She gave me the necklace. And now Nick has it. We have to stop him. We have to."

"What are we supposed to do?" Aaron said. "If he can travel, he's probably left this time already."

"We know where he's going," Joan said. "We know what he wants. We just have to get there first."

"The Monster Court." Aaron breathed it out like a fearful prayer. He looked toward the windows. The middle two were cracked open, allowing glimpses of white sky amid the rippling blue of the stained glass. "Listen . . . ," he said. "If you're right, then every monster is in danger. We need to trust the Court to stop him. I think it's time to seek an audience."

"Don't be a fool," Ruth spat. "I realize that you're an Oliver, so your instinct is to lick boots, but the Court can't be trusted. Court Guards have been hunting down survivors of the massacre. And you know as well as I do that only the Court can have altered the family records to conceal what the hero has done."

Aaron had glared at *lick boots*, but now he started to frown. "I can't make sense of it."

"Isn't it obvious?" Ruth said. "This is the King's timeline. Every event is how he wishes it to be. Or so the Court says. The King protects us from humans discovering us. Or so the Court says."

"You're perilously close to blasphemy," Aaron said.

"Then let me say it clearer," Ruth said. "The hero is proof of the limits of the King's power—a failure in the King's purported control of the timeline. If the King could have stopped the hero, he would have. Instead he can only conceal him from us. How's that for blasphemy?"

As Aaron's face lost all color, Joan had a strange feeling of almost knowing something. Like a word on the tip of her tongue, or like a dream that she couldn't quite remember.

"No," she said. "The King created this timeline. He used something to change the original timeline." That was true. She didn't understand why she was so sure, but she was.

And at the same time, she felt unsettled. Why *was* the Court concealing Nick's actions? And if the Court knew about Nick, why hadn't they already stopped him?

"We have to do something," she said. "I know there are things we don't understand about this, but if Nick gets to the Court before we do—if he changes the timeline—he's going to end us all."

"Joan . . ." Aaron looked helpless.

"No," Joan said. "No." She didn't want to talk about anything but a plan. Because, Nick aside, they had to get to the Monster Court. She *needed* that device. It was the only way to bring back Gran and Aunt Ada and Uncle Gus and Bertie. She needed it to undo what Nick had done.

"We can't get there before he does," Aaron said. "We can't get there at all. The Court sits outside time. It's inaccessible. Nick took the only way in. The necklace."

"There must be another way," Joan said.

"There isn't," Ruth said.

"There must be," Joan said. She needed to *think*. Instead she found herself helplessly remembering how Nick had slipped the necklace from under her shirt. How he'd looked at her. She tried to steady her breath—she didn't want to cry again. She remembered how his knuckles had brushed her throat as he'd worked the clasp from her neck.

The necklace . . . A vague memory came to her. Ying Liu hadn't been the first person interested in the necklace. Someone else had asked about it first. . . .

"When I first went to the market yesterday," she said slowly, "someone offered me money for Gran's necklace."

"So?" Aaron said. "Those stall owners buy and sell all kinds of junk."

"But it wasn't junk, was it?" Joan said. "It was a key to the Monster Court." Joan remembered the gleam of interest in the man's eyes. *Go on*, he'd said, *name a price.* "If he buys stuff like that," she said, "then maybe he sells stuff like that too."

"If he does, then he's mixed up in some dangerous things, and we should stay away from him," Aaron said.

"If there's even a chance . . . "

"Joan." Aaron sounded helpless and scared. "The King's power is absolute. We can't just . . ." He shook his head. He'd thought the term *true timeline* was blasphemous; Joan couldn't imagine how he must be feeling about going against the King more directly.

"You don't have to do this," she said to him. He didn't have to be part of this at all. "I'll go down there and find the stall."

But when she reached for the door, Aaron and Ruth followed her.

Joan pushed through the market. The Court Guards who'd raided earlier were gone, but they'd left behind an atmosphere of discontent and fear. One stall owner was crying as Joan passed her. The man who had stood at the stall with her earlier was nowhere to be seen.

"What do you remember of this guy?" Aaron asked Joan as they walked through what Joan now recognized as the twenty-first-century section of the market. There were clothes here that could have been from her own wardrobe at home.

"I think he was a Hathaway," Joan said. He'd had their muscular build. Aaron grimaced.

"You don't like that family?" Joan said. Aaron had been annoyed by the loud Hathaways at the inn.

"They're thugs," Aaron said.

The man wasn't at his stall; his card table was bare. Joan thought about the crying woman earlier. She turned to the seller at the next table—a woman with a bob of gray hair and a youthful face. "Excuse me," Joan said. "Yesterday, there was a man here selling phones." She hesitated, not sure how to ask if he'd been caught in the raid.

To her relief, the woman pointed to the far end of the market. "Down the back."

The back of the market was dingy and cold. There didn't seem to be a particular time associated with it. Some tables were selling fresh eels and fish on ice. Other tables had nothing on them at all.

Muscular men and women watched Joan as she passed. All Hathaways, she thought. There were animals with them. Dogs, mostly, but Joan glimpsed some cats and an animal that looked more fox than dog.

"I've never seen a dog like that," she whispered to Ruth.

Ruth glanced over. "It's not from this time."

"We can take animals with us when we travel?"

"We can take small objects," Aaron said. Which made sense—they'd arrived in this time with their clothes. "But only the Hathaway family can travel with animals," he went on. "Most of them travel with a familiar."

"A familiar." It was a word Joan associated with witches. "You mean a pet?"

"Yes, a pet. The most useless family power in London." Aaron's tone was contemptuous. He kept his voice very low, though, as if he didn't dare insult the Hathaways within their hearing.

The man who'd bought Joan's phone was at the very back of the market, where it ended in a smoke-blackened brick wall. From here, the rest of the market was just the curtained backs of stalls. Cardboard boxes lay about, discarded. There was a smell of old cabbage leaves and fish.

The man sat at an empty card table, asleep, his squashed face snoozing against the dirty brick wall. A tiny bulldog snored at his feet. The man was a little older than twenty, broad-shouldered and hulking. Sprawled out, he barely fit into the folding chair.

"*Him?*" Ruth said to Joan. She groaned. "Tell me *Tom Hathaway* isn't your guy."

The man's arms were crossed in sleep. There was a tattoo around one bulging bicep. Curled lines formed a two-headed dog, both heads meeting to growl at each other.

"You know him?" Joan asked.

Ruth grimaced. "Everyone at the Ravencroft Market knows Tom Hathaway. Used to be a Court Guard. Got sacked. Now he's a washed-up drunk who buys and sells phones."

"Fantastic," Aaron said.

Joan took a step closer. "Tom?" she called. The man and dog continued to sleep. "Tom Hathaway?" Joan said louder.

The man sniffed and twitched. "Mm?"

"Can we talk to you?"

"Mm." Tom smacked his lips, but he didn't open his eyes. "Get me a drink, love?"

Ruth looked at Joan and Joan mouthed back *From where?* Aaron rolled his eyes. He bent down and grabbed a half-drunk beer bottle from under Tom's own card table. He plonked it down.

Tom's eyes opened at the sound. He fumbled for the bottle and then swallowed down the remnants of the beer in one big gulp.

"Tom?" Joan said. "We want to buy something from you."

"Get me a drink, love."

"I think he's broken," Aaron said dryly. "When you pull the string, he only says one thing."

"I think he needs a coffee," Joan said. The bulldog was awake now, sniffing at Joan's shoe. She bent to stroke its soft head. It was very small for a bulldog, but clearly well cared for—sleek brown-and-white fur and a solid build. Better cared for than Tom himself, who had the crooked nose of a fighter and was barely conscious in the early afternoon.

"Tom, do you remember me?" Joan said. "You offered to buy my necklace."

Tom peered at her through cracked eyelids. He saw her bare neck. "You sold it to someone else?"

"Not exactly," Joan said. "Do you know where I can get another one?"

Aaron returned from somewhere with a paper cup of water. Tom took it eagerly and gulped. Then he wrinkled his nose. "Oh, what's this?" he complained. He offered his dog the rest of the water. It huffed, and then struggled to its feet. Tom tilted the cup so that it could lap inside.

"That necklace—" Joan started again.

"Look," Tom interrupted. "You want to buy a phone?"

Joan blinked. "No."

"You want to sell a phone?"

"No."

"Then fuck off."

"But the necklace—"

"I know what it was," Tom said. "Saw one once at the Court. But you're not going to find one in any bloody market."

Joan deflated. She'd hoped he'd recognized the necklace because he'd seen ones like it here. But it seemed he'd only recognized it from his past life at the Court itself.

Aaron realized it too. "He's just an opportunist," he said to

Joan. Tom's expression was blearily blank in response. Aaron clarified, sneering: "You took a chance when you saw it. You offered to buy it and hoped she didn't know what it was."

Tom shrugged. "Yeah."

"Let's go," Aaron said to Joan. He'd been surveying Tom and the dog, hand in his pocket like a landlord inspecting substandard property. Now he turned to leave.

Joan put a hand on Aaron's arm. "Wait," she said. "Wait." They couldn't just walk away. Their families' *lives* were at stake. Every monster's life was at stake, their own included. They *had* to get into the Court. "My cousin tells me that you were a Court Guard," she said to Tom.

"So?" Aaron said to Joan. "She also said he was fired." He looked disdainfully down at Tom, at the empty beer bottles clinking under his table. "Can't imagine why."

"We need to get in," Joan said to Tom.

From Ruth's gasp and Aaron's alarmed look, Joan realized she shouldn't have said it so bluntly. But she kept picturing Nick already at the Court. They couldn't let him get to that device.

Tom's face was still bleary. Ruth and Aaron's alarm hadn't touched him. "You want me to get you into the Monster Court?" he said.

"Can you do it?" Joan said. Her body felt tight with tension.

"Why do you want to get in?"

"None of your business," Aaron interjected.

Tom regarded Aaron. "You're an Oliver, aren't you?"

Aaron didn't reply.

Tom scratched at the crook of his jaw. "Could spot one of you anywhere. Nose in the air like you can't stand the smell of the rest of us."

"Can you get us in or not?" Joan said.

Tom closed his eyes deliberately. "No," he said, flat and final.

"Excellent find," Aaron said to Joan. He didn't bother to keep his voice down. "Really. Top-shelf."

But Joan wasn't ready to give up yet. She thought she was starting to get a read on Tom. "You haven't even heard what's in it for *you*," she said to him.

"Joan," Aaron said. "Let's just go."

Joan ignored him. She waited for Tom's eyes to crack open. "We're going to steal from the Court."

"*Joan,*" Ruth said, and Aaron swore.

"You are so fucking reckless," Aaron said.

But Tom's eyes were open properly now, a flicker of interest kindled. Joan was relieved. She'd read him right. And so had Aaron. Tom was an opportunist.

"You want in?" Joan said.

"Oh, for fuck's sake," Aaron said.

"*You're* not an Oliver," Tom said slowly to Joan.

"We're Hunts," Ruth said.

"Hunts." Tom rested his head against the wall, visibly relaxing. He looked intrigued. It was the opposite of how most people in the monster world had reacted to the name Hunt. Tom retrieved a half-eaten sandwich from under the table that the dog had somehow missed. To Aaron's obvious disgust, Tom took a big bite. "What're thieves doing with an Oliver?" he asked with his mouth full.

"He owes her," Ruth said. "She saved his life."

Tom took another bite. "And she's making him steal from the Court?" His bleary eyes brightened. "Making an Oliver break his vows to the King. . . . Guess it's true what they say, huh?" he said to Aaron, mouth still full. "Never get into debt to a Hunt. They'll screw you sore."

"What charming advice," Aaron said.

Tom leaned back against the wall, chewing. He seemed to be enjoying watching Aaron squirm. "I've heard that Hunts can steal anything from anyone."

Joan nodded. "Bet there were things at the Court that you wanted when you worked there." He was probably pretty annoyed that he'd been fired too.

Tom took his time finishing the sandwich. "I might be interested," he said finally.

"Really?" Joan said. She breathed out, relieved.

Tom seemed to come to a decision. He held out a big hand for Joan to shake. "Yeah."

"Okay." Joan took his hand. It was nearly double the size of her own. "Okay."

"Why are you shaking his hand as if you've made a bargain?" Aaron said to Joan incredulously. "You haven't made a bargain! You haven't even agreed on a price!"

"Oh, don't worry, sunshine," Tom said to him. "I'll open the big door. As long as your little thieves open the other doors, we'll be square."

"Ah, I see," Aaron said a little faintly. "The Hunts will steal what they want. You'll steal what you want. And I'll just continue to live my best life."

"Be ready in two nights' time," Tom added.

"Two nights?" Joan said. She'd been barreling through the conversation, her only concern to get into the Court before Nick. Now, though, she felt a wave of unease.

"That's when the gate opens," Tom said.

"The gate?" Joan said.

Tom nodded. "There's going to be a gala at the Court. Lucky you, huh? Last time the gate opened was centuries ago. And it won't open again for another century. It's like it's opening just for you."

"Lucky us," Joan heard herself say. But all she could think about was how she and Aaron weren't even supposed to be in this time—they'd overshot. *Lucky*. It didn't feel like luck.

With that new monster sense in the back of her head, Joan could feel the timeline stirring—as it had when she'd watched those envelopes fall.

And she couldn't have said why, but the unease bloomed into foreboding.

Back at the flat, Aaron was furious. "We're not doing this," he said. They'd left Tom at the market, already half-asleep again. "This is ridiculous. This is *not* a plan!"

"Well, not yet," Ruth said. "But I think he could get us in. He *was* a Court Guard. And if we have a way in, then we have the *start* of a plan."

"Were we looking at the same man? He could barely hold his head up!" Aaron's voice was shaking. "Do you have any idea what the Court will do to us if they catch us? And they *will* if we have to rely on that fool."

"We'll be careful," Joan said.

"Look," Ruth said to Aaron. "If we're wrong about Tom— if we're caught at the gate—then we'll get arrested. So what? We'll just make up some lie about gate-crashing the party."

"Arrested?" Aaron said. "Have you ever actually met a member of the Monster Court? Have you come face-to-face with one of the *Curia Monstrorum*?"

"No," Ruth admitted. "I've seen Court Guards."

Aaron looked at her with a bleak expression Joan had never seen on his face before. "One of them came for my cousin once," he said.

"You actually saw a member of the Monster Court?" Ruth sounded disbelieving. "One of the *Curia Monstrorum*? Which one?"

"Conrad," Aaron said. He answered the question in Joan's expression. "We call him the King's Reach. He's the King's authority in this time. He's responsible for enforcing the law two centuries into the future and three centuries behind."

"Kind of like a policeman?" Joan said.

Aaron's face went pinched. "Not really like that, no."

"Conrad came. In person?" Ruth asked. She still sounded disbelieving.

For a moment it seemed like Aaron was going to leave it at that, but then he set his jaw. "I was there. I was at school with my cousin Kit when Conrad came."

Joan glanced at Ruth. Her posture was still skeptical, but Joan could tell she wanted to know more.

"They say that Conrad was a Nightingale once," Aaron said. "When he ascended to the Court, he revoked all ties to his family. His loyalty is only to the King now. But he still has the Nightingale power. He can steal life from monsters." His tone was becoming more subdued. "And . . . they say he can do other things. They say he can force people to travel with him."

"He forced your cousin to travel with him?" Joan asked Aaron.

Aaron didn't seem to hear her. His attention was on something inside his own head. "Kit and I were walking back to our dorm room. When we turned the corner, Conrad was waiting for us."

Aaron swiped a hand over his mouth. "He told us to follow him outside. He took us to the pond down by the football field. Well, they called it a pond, but it's more like a lake. I didn't go down there much. People used to say it was haunted." Aaron's mouth twisted. "Conrad just stood there, looking at us. Then he said: 'Do you know why I'm here?' He was so casual. He said: 'Someone's been taking time at this school. Students who attend are eighteen percent more likely to die before the age of seventy-five than the general population.' He said that one day that anomaly would draw the attention of human authorities. He said that the King didn't tolerate mistakes like that."

"What did he do?" Joan asked, hushed.

"He just . . ." Aaron's hands curled into fists. "He told me to go to my room. I went. I stayed up all night, but Kit didn't come back. The police dredged the pond for him in the end. Because, see—" His voice cracked, finally. "See, back in the sixties, they'd found a boy's body in that pond. They thought maybe something like that had happened again."

"Oh," Ruth said, soft.

Aaron's hands uncurled and curled again. "We must have heard those stupid ghost stories a hundred times."

"You just walked back to your room?" Joan blurted. "You didn't try to help your cousin or anything?"

Anger flashed over Aaron's face. "What do *you* know about going up against the Court?" There was a horrible rawness in his voice. A tone that Joan didn't fully understand.

"Okay," Ruth said placatingly. "Okay."

"Shit." Aaron thumbed the corner of his eye. "We can't do this. We don't have a plan. We're not trained to fight. We have nothing."

"We're going to plan this," Joan said.

"We don't even know what we're looking for! We have no idea what this device looks like! We don't know where it will be! We wouldn't even know if we saw it!"

"You're right," Joan said. "Okay, you're right. You're right."

And he was right. They couldn't plan this knowing as little as they did. They needed more information.

Joan knew what she had to do.

The innkeeper was alone when Joan arrived at the inn. It was very late. Joan had left Aaron and Ruth asleep at the flat. Only the lights of the main dining room were still on. The wall of stained glass was dull without the backdrop of daylight. The cauldron of stew bubbled softly over the low-burning hearth.

"Was wondering when you'd come back," the innkeeper said. He was sitting by the hearth, reading a book. As Joan got closer, she saw that it was in a language with a non-Roman alphabet.

"Have you found her?" she said.

The innkeeper dug into his pocket and retrieved a folded piece of paper. But he didn't give it to her. "Dorothy Hunt is not a good person," he said. "I don't know what your business is with her, but you want my advice? Put this in the fire."

Joan held out her hand for it.

Without her phone, Joan had to ask for directions and then more directions just to get to Soho. By the time she got to the address, the night was cold and black.

She stood outside the door, feeling a wave of déjà vu. Aaron wasn't with her this time, but there was a plaque beside the black door: a sea serpent engulfing a sailing ship. This was a monster place.

The door opened onto a short dark corridor with soft lights along the floor; it reminded Joan of walking up the aisle of an airplane. At the end, there was a room just a little wider than the corridor, lit with golden chandeliers the color of candlelight. A gleaming wooden bar ran the length of the room.

Joan stood there, frozen. There she was. Gran. Sitting alone at the bar, drinking. She couldn't have been more than twenty-five years old, dressed for the nineties in black ankle boots and a black gauzy dress with a Peter Pan collar.

Joan had expected her to be young, but not quite this young. Joan was reminded again that monsters were time travelers. She imagined them, suddenly, living a few months in this year; a few months in that one. Skipping back and forth between decades at whim. She wondered if she'd ever get her head around all this.

Gran was beautiful young—a different beautiful from her older self. Her cheekbones were still sharp. She had Ruth's hair: lustrous, dark curls. Her eyes were the same luminous green as in Joan's time.

And she was alive. She was alive and she was here.

"I fucking hate this song," Gran said to the bartender conversationally. It was "Wind Beneath my Wings." Gran and Aunt Ada had argued about it once. They'd all been at a funeral for a distant cousin of Gran's. *You don't even know this song*, Aunt Ada had hissed to Gran. *I know bullshit when I hear it*, Gran had hissed back.

The bartender lifted his head and saw Joan. "Out," he said. "No kids in here."

"I just want to talk," Joan said. "To her. I just want to talk to Do—Dorothy." She stumbled over Gran's name, unused to saying it.

"I'm not selling you anything," the bartender said.

"I'm not buying," Joan said. "Five minutes. Please."

The bartender looked over at Gran, and Gran nodded slightly.

"Five minutes," the bartender said. "I'm setting a timer."

Joan took a deep breath and sat on the bar stool next to Gran's. She didn't know where to start. Gran lifted her glass, and Joan saw that her ring finger was bare. Joan had never seen her without her ruby wedding ring.

"I don't know you," Gran said, with her usual gruff impatience. "What do you want?"

"I'm your granddaughter," Joan blurted.

"Granddaughter?" Gran said. But her sharp gaze flicked over to Joan and then stayed.

"I look more like my dad."

"What's your name?"

"Joan. Joan Chang-Hunt."

"Chang. That's not a monster name." Gran gulped down her drink. "So Maureen's been messing around with humans. Christ."

Joan was shocked. Gran had never said anything like that to her before. Gran had always gotten along with Dad.

"You have something to tell me," Gran said. "That's why you're here. Just say it." And that was where Gran's harshness was coming from, Joan realized. Gran had known the moment that Joan had said "granddaughter" that something bad was coming.

The memory of Gran's agonized breaths returned to Joan in a rush. The slow, pained rise and fall of her chest under Joan's hands.

"Just say it," Gran said.

"You . . . Two days ago. Thirty years from now. You—you died. You were killed." Joan's voice shook. "The human hero isn't just a myth, Gran. He's real. He came and killed our family. He killed—God, he killed *so* many people."

Some of the harshness left Gran's face as Joan talked. Joan kept expecting the timeline to unravel as she told Gran the place and the time. But, just like with the post office, Joan could feel the timeline resisting. "Do you believe me?" she said to Gran. *Please believe me.*

"I believe you," Gran said, and Joan felt her chest loosen. She'd been tenser than she'd known. Gran called over the bartender to refill her glass.

Joan waited for him to leave again, and then lowered her voice. "Just before you died, you gave me a necklace," she said. "A key to the Monster Court. I think you wanted me to find a device that the King once used to change the timeline. To stop the massacre and save our family. But I don't know how to find it, Gran."

"The *transformatio*?" Gran said. "That's a myth."

"A lot of myths seem to be proving true lately," Joan said.

Gran's mouth turned downward. She always looked like that when she was thinking. When she was angry, she tended to look amused. When she was looking at a mark, her expression went blank.

"I always heard that the King keeps his treasures in the Royal Archive," Gran said. She tilted her head, and a trick of the light made her familiar green eyes seem cool—almost cold.

Joan hadn't expected Gran to be so forthcoming. The older version of her was much cagier. She'd have asked Joan a lot more questions before telling her anything at all. Perhaps that wariness had come to her in older age.

"Did I tell you anything else?" Gran said. "Joan, wasn't it?"

Joan started to shake her head and then realized there *was* something else. She hadn't been deliberately withholding it. She'd archived it, hardly let herself think about it.

Keeping an eye on the bartender, Joan whispered to Gran what Gran had whispered to her. "Just before you died, you told me that someday soon I'd come into a power. Not the Hunt power, but another. It was the last thing you said. You told me not to trust anyone with the knowledge of it. And I haven't, I swear. You're the only one I've told."

Gran's expression went blank. "A power?" She glanced up, and Joan realized, startled, that the bartender was standing a few paces away. He hadn't been there a second ago. He'd been drying glasses at the other end of the bar. "What kind of power?" Gran said.

"I—I don't know," Joan whispered. "I haven't seen any sign of it yet."

"Hmm," Gran said. Her expression was still blank. She made two scratching motions with her forefinger. It was one of their family signals—the signal to fetch someone. But fetch who? It was usually accompanied by a name signal. Three fingers up for Ruth. Thumb and forefinger crossed for Aunt Ada. Forefinger and thumb in a *J* for Joan.

Who did she want Joan to fetch?

Gran made the name signal with her left hand, but not one Joan had ever seen before. Her hand was curled, thumb at an angle. *C*? *G*?

It wasn't until the bartender put down his cloth and said "Excuse me" that Joan realized the signal hadn't been intended for her at all. Gran didn't realize Joan had understood it. She didn't seem to know that one day she'd teach it to Joan.

Gran's green eyes were narrow and speculative now. She was looking at Joan like she was valuable. But not like a person was valuable. Like something that could be sold for a very high price. *You can't trust anyone with the knowledge of it*, Gran had said. Joan's chest felt painfully tight.

"Is there a toilet down there?" Joan pointed in the wrong direction, deeper into the bar, hoping that would be less suspicious. She knew that the bathroom was near the front door. She'd passed it on the way in.

"Back the way you came," Gran said.

If you need to run, always imply that you'll return. Gran had taught Joan that. "You won't go, will you?" Joan said. "You'll be here when I get back?"

"Haven't finished my drink, have I?" Gran said.

Joan made herself linger, even though all she wanted to do was to get out of this room—get away from this version of Gran who wasn't her gran. Who'd looked at Joan like she didn't mean anything to her. Who'd told the bartender to fetch someone.

Joan turned slowly. Putting her back to this Gran made her skin crawl. She walked to the corridor and turned the corner. She walked past the toilets, and then pushed open the door out onto the street. And then she ran.

She looked back, once, at the end of the laneway. The bartender was standing in the doorway, staring after her. Joan ran harder. She didn't look back again.

Gran had warned Joan not to trust anyone. It just hadn't occurred to Joan that she'd been including herself.

As Joan ran, she started to sob as she hadn't since Gran had died. Some part of her had believed that everything would be okay when she found Gran again. She'd believed that Gran would take over and stop Nick herself.

But the woman back there hadn't been Gran.

Joan's gran was dead. She was really dead. She'd died two days ago, and Joan hadn't been able to stop it.

Aaron was awake when Joan got back. He was sitting outside the flat, looking out onto the empty market below. It was very late now. The tables were tarped, the food stalls shuttered.

"Where did you go?" he whispered to Joan.

"I found out what we needed to know," Joan said. "The King's treasures are kept in a place called the Royal Archive.

The device is called the *transformatio*. We need to include that in our research—find out if there are any physical descriptions in the myths."

Joan waited for Aaron to push back. *It's still too danger-ous. Even if we get into the Court, how are we going to get into the archive?*

But there was a different kind of frown on his face now. "Where did you go?" he said again, softer. "Joan, are you all right?"

"Course I'm all right." Joan was glad it was too dark for him to see her face. "Come on," she said. She held out her hand to help him up. "There's a lot to do."

And in two nights' time, they'd save their families. They'd save everyone.

FIFTEEN

Two nights later, Joan paced the market flat, waiting for Aaron and Ruth to finish getting ready. Aaron had styled them all. He'd found Ruth a sparkling platinum dress and Joan a forest-green gown with a plunging back. The heavy drape of it brushed Joan's legs as she paced.

Aaron emerged first from behind the bookshelf partition, hand in his pocket. A young James Bond. His suit was the same pale gray as his eyes. Joan tried not to stare. He always turned strangers' heads, but this sophisticated look had made him mesmerizing. It was hard to look away. *He doesn't fit here,* Joan thought, not for the first time. He belonged at a glamorous estate, not in this little studio flat above a market.

"Nervous?" he said, and Joan realized with a strange feeling that he'd been watching her too, that his gaze had sought her as he'd entered the living area.

She made an effort to stop pacing. The gold light of sunset had tinted the stained-glass windows, making the whole room glow: a low-burning hearth. She *was* nervous. "Yes," she admitted, and then wondered when she'd started to trust Aaron enough to be that open with him. "Feels so close," she explained. "Like maybe we'll have our families back tonight."

"Maybe." Aaron's gaze hadn't left hers. For a moment, Joan thought he was going to say something more, but he seemed to change his mind. He scooped up two shopping bags that had been resting by the bookshelf and brought them over to her.

"More clothes?" Joan said.

"Finishing touches," Aaron said. He took out a midnight-blue velvet box. Inside, there was a long string of pearls, knotted at the center with diamonds. Joan stared at him. "Verisimilitude," he said. "May I?"

Were the pearls real? Were the diamonds? Surely not. Verisimilitude.

Joan turned. She felt rather than heard him step closer—a change in temperature. She bunched her hair, tucked it over one shoulder, and ducked her head.

To her surprise, he draped the long heavy line of the necklace down her back rather than her front. She shivered as each pearl hit her skin, a splash of icy water. The pearls warmed quickly, though. She turned to find Aaron standing closer than she'd expected.

She thought he'd step back, but he stayed there in her space. His eyes seemed darker than they had a few moments ago. Joan's heart stuttered strangely.

"So what do you think?" she said. She tried to make it light, but they were so close that her voice came out unexpectedly intimate. "Will we pass for important people?"

When Aaron spoke, it was just as intimately, with no sign of his usual snide tone. "You're important," he said, his gray eyes very serious. "I know you want your family back, but your life matters too." Joan opened her mouth to protest, and he shook his head slightly. "Just . . . *Please* be careful tonight. The Court is a dangerous place."

Joan felt a stab of guilt then. She'd dragged Aaron to this point. From the beginning, all he'd wanted was to lie low, to be safe. "You don't have do this," she said, just as serious as he was. "You keep saying you owe me. But you don't. We both know that debt has been paid." Was there some special monster wording for this? "You're released," she tried. "I release you."

"Joan . . ." There was something complicated in his expression, something Joan couldn't decipher. He sighed and took a shoebox from another of the bags. He passed it to her. Inside, there was a pair of soft black flats. "In case we have to run," he said.

They got a cab to Victoria Embankment. Tom had told them that the gate would open at midnight, near Whitehall Palace.

Joan had been confused. Whitehall Palace had burned down three hundred years ago.

"It's just the physical location," Aaron had explained. "It's hard to keep track of what buildings are around when. If monsters say 'Newgate Prison,' we just mean where it once stood."

Now, as they walked up Horse Guards Avenue, Joan's chest felt tight. Even in daylight, there was something skeletal about

Whitehall's bleached buildings. Tonight, it felt like walking into the streets of the dead.

"I hate mires," Aaron said as they walked. "They give me the creeps."

"Mires are places where you can't travel," Ruth explained to Joan. "This one stretches from Westminster Abbey to Leicester Square. You can't travel anywhere, in or out, while you're here."

They'd scouted earlier to find a building recess with a view of the Banqueting House—the only part of Whitehall Palace still standing. The spot wasn't perfect—they were only shielded from the street by a railing. But as Joan settled into place beside Aaron, the darkness enveloped them. Down the road, clumps of tourists milled around the mounted sentries of the Horse Guards building, but the street was otherwise quiet.

Joan kept track of the time by counting Big Ben's strikes.

Ten o'clock went by. Then eleven o'clock. The temperature dropped.

Long after eleven, there was still no sign of a gate or of guests for the Court gala. The only warm part of Joan's body was her arm where it was pressed against Aaron's. She couldn't stop shivering. He must have been cold too. There was some room between him and the rail, but he hadn't moved from Joan's side.

"Maybe Tom got the time wrong," Joan whispered.

"Maybe he's a drunken fool who hasn't been a guard in years," Aaron whispered back.

Joan opened her mouth to answer, and then stopped.

Someone was emerging from the direction of Charing Cross. She nudged Aaron. Ruth was already looking.

The moon was gibbous, but offered little light. Only the person's silhouette was visible. Their gait as they passed was eerie—slow and gliding. Joan found herself holding her breath.

New footsteps made them all turn again, toward Parliament. Two more people were approaching. Men in Victorian top hats. And still more people from Horse Guards Avenue.

Big Ben began to sound. It was midnight.

The arrivals were all on foot. Some silhouettes were familiar, some alien—clothes from the distant past, or the future. Monsters.

Aaron's breath was coming shorter now. He sounded as nervous as Joan felt. She could just see his face, pale gray in the dark.

On Big Ben's last strike, the world seemed to still. The sounds of London ceased. No cars, no rush of water from the Thames. No insects in the air. Joan craned to look at the horse guards. They were sitting on their horses, still as ever. Terrified? Or had they been frozen in time?

"Look," Aaron breathed. He nodded at the junction between Horse Guards Avenue and Whitehall.

At first Joan wasn't sure if she was making patterns out of nothing, like seeing shapes in clouds. But something seemed to be changing in the junction. Shadows were shifting like smoke.

"What is it?" Ruth whispered.

Joan had seen it before—in paintings of old London. "It's

the gate," she said. "It's the Whitehall Palace gate."

The shadows solidified into a huge arch straddling Horse Guards Avenue. It was the arch alone, without the palace walls—the bare brick bones of it. Joan stared. Inside the arch, the stars were unaligned with the sky outside. Inside, the moon was full. And framed like a picture was Whitehall Palace, beautiful and whole, before the fire.

A lone figure came into view—on the wrong side of the gate. The figure stepped through, and a male voice rang out, theatrical and baritone. "Welcome to the Monster Court."

A murmur of excitement ran through the crowd. The road in front of the arch was full of people now, and more were arriving. The atmosphere was giddy in pockets, solemn in others. But above all, a strange tension hung over everything. Joan could feel why. Some sixth sense inside her—the monster sense—could feel the timeline straining fruitlessly against this unnatural beast. Whitehall Palace out of its time.

"I've never seen anything like this," Ruth whispered. "I always heard that the King had power, but seeing it . . ."

Joan scanned the crowd. Aaron seemed to know who she was looking for. "Those guards aren't moving," he whispered. "If the hero is here, he's frozen like the other humans. There's some kind of suspension over everything but monsters. I've never seen power like this either."

"This is the advantage that we need," Joan whispered back. "If Nick can't get in—even with that key—*we'll* get the device, not him. Then we'll just have to figure out how to use it."

"One thing at a time," Aaron said. "We're not in yet." He nodded at the gate, where guards were verifying people's identities before allowing them through.

Tom had explained how the gate identification would work.

"There'll be a guest list at the door," he'd said.

"And you can get us on the guest list?" Joan had asked.

"No," Tom had said, as if that were a ridiculous thought. "The guards have a book of personal marks. That's the guest list. Guests find their mark in the list and then stamp their chop next to it to prove their identity. But I know for a fact that the guard who checks the marks gets lazy late in the night. So just get into the line late, and then find a mark that's a near match to yours."

"And if we can't find a near match?" Aaron said.

"Then you'll get found out," Tom said. "He's lazy, not an idiot."

That had presented a problem. Joan didn't have a chop, and the other two couldn't leave a record of their real marks at the gate.

Tom had taken them down to a marina where narrowboats and barges with peeling paint bobbed up and down on brown water. His little bulldog, Frankie, had toddled behind him. When her stubby legs had struggled with the wharf steps, Tom had leaned down and bundled her under one arm.

"The Hathaways live on the canals and the river," Ruth had

whispered to Joan. "This is their territory."

Muscular men and women had eyed them from boat decks and from chairs set up along the wharf. There'd been a home-spun quality to the boats; most had obvious repairs. They'd all had the same symbol, painted on the cabin or as the weather vane: a two-headed hound, growling and black.

Real animals had been everywhere too—lounging on decks and running underfoot: dogs, birds, cats.

Tom had climbed down into a boat at the end of the wharf, Frankie still under his arm. He'd returned with a tray full of chops, the figurines dull and dirty.

"Tell me you're not a grave robber," Aaron had said.

"Don't be daft," Tom had said. "They came out of the river. Everything washes up on the foreshore. Even monster chops." He held out the tray. "Go on. Pick."

Aaron had gone first. He'd sorted through all the chops, dismissive until he'd finally found a bronze mermaid figurine.

"Not much of a disguise," Ruth had said.

"I'm clearly an Oliver," Aaron had said. "No one would believe anything less."

Ruth had gone next. She'd chosen a Patel family chop: a white horse, its chipped enamel showing glimpses of the bronze beneath.

Joan had picked out a figurine that reminded her of the sea serpent images beside monster doors. "A dragonara serpent," Ruth had said. Joan had turned it over. The underside had been etched with a name—*Lia Portelli.*

Joan gripped her figurine now as she waited in the queue. The gate arched behind the guards, creating a dark passage between this world and the next. Through the gap, Whitehall Palace gleamed, bone white as the Banqueting House.

Aaron stepped up to the guard. "Henry Oliver," he said.

The book of marks sat open on a pedestal like a guest book at a wedding.

The guard turned the pages with a white-gloved hand. Joan glimpsed caged-bird stamps for pages and pages, and then the Oliver mermaids.

Aaron ran a finger down the page, one hand in his pocket as if he were bored by the ritual. Then he reached for the golden ink pad and stamped his seal beside one of the marks.

The guard glanced down at the book. Joan held her breath. Now, at the crucial moment, the whole plan seemed stupid. It relied too much on one man's poor judgment, and on luck—the stamps would have to look reasonably similar.

"Pleasant evening," Aaron commented to the guard.

"The dates on both sides were chosen for the occasion," the guard said. He nodded at Aaron. "Welcome to the Monster Court." He waved Aaron through. Joan breathed out in relief.

Ruth was waved through next.

And then it was Joan's turn. She took her place in front of the guard. He was wearing a dark blue uniform with gold braid. This close, she could see that his gold buttons were etched with winged lions. She'd seen the same creature on monster currency. And again on the guards' pins at the market. The symbol of the Monster Court.

The guard himself was just as Tom had described him: curly blond hair under the braided guard's hat, and heavy-lidded eyes already dull with boredom.

The guard had barely glanced at Ruth's mark, but Joan's hands still shook as she reached for the book. She'd tried to memorize the features of Lia Portelli's chop: the sea serpent, the exact pattern of the rippling waves around it. The number of olive leaves in the border wreath.

The man held up a hand to stop her. "Please wait," he said. "We're changing guards."

"What?" Joan whispered. Her mouth was so dry, the sound hardly came out. *Do you have any idea what the Court will do to us if they catch us?* Aaron had said.

On the other side of the gate, Aaron and Ruth were waiting. They'd seen the guard speak, but apparently hadn't been able to hear any words. As the lazy guard stepped away, Aaron's eyes widened in alarm.

Joan's heart thudded as a new guard made her way through the gate. She had a neat blonde bun and hard eyes. She took her place by the book and then nodded at Joan. "Please find your mark," she said.

Go, Joan willed Aaron and Ruth. *Go*. But they just stood there, staring at her. Joan's heart sped up even more. If she was caught, they'd be caught too. They'd made it too obvious that the three of them were together.

The new guard looked Joan up and down. "Please find your mark," she said again, with more impatience.

"Portelli," Joan managed.

The guard turned the pages from the horses of the Patels until she reached pages with the Portellis' dragon-like sea serpent. Joan swallowed. She could see the differences at a glance, and she wasn't even an expert at looking for them.

She wet her dry lips and then pressed her stamp to the golden ink pad. "That other guard," she said. She looked over in the direction he'd gone, and held the line of sight. "He wasn't checking the marks very carefully."

"The one who was just here?" In Joan's peripheral vision, the new guard scowled and glanced over too.

The moment the guard looked away, Joan pretended to press her chop against the paper, hovering her stamp just above it. When the guard looked back again, Joan was lifting the chop up from an existing mark.

The guard bent and examined the two marks carefully— perhaps more carefully than she usually would have, after Joan's comment.

Joan wet her lips again. She could see Ruth's grim face over the guard's shoulder.

"'Marie Portelli,'" the guard read. "'Great-niece of Elizabetta.' I met your great-aunt in the 1700s."

"She's a force," Joan said, hoping that was true. Aaron had said that the other name on a chop was the closest head of family in your line. *An indicator of status*, he'd said. *The closer your relationship to a head of family, the higher your status.*

Maybe for Olivers, Ruth had said. *Hunts aren't like that.*

To Joan's relief, the guard seemed satisfied. She nodded and stepped aside. "Welcome to the Court," she said. She gestured for Joan to walk on.

The passage through the gate was about five paces long. Joan walked in, half expecting the guard to grab her by the collar—to say that someone had seen what she'd done.

One, two, three, four, five steps.

The change of temperature hit her at once—the air was humid and pleasantly warm. The smell of the Thames was stronger here: mud and brine.

Ruth took Joan's arm and pulled her away from the gate. "What happened?" she whispered.

"There was a change of guard," Joan said. "But it was okay. I just—"

"We saw what you did," Aaron said angrily. "Why didn't you just walk away?"

"I—I don't know," Joan said honestly. "I don't know." The truth was that it hadn't occurred to her. She'd just wanted to get in.

And she *was* in. She was here. She looked up wonderingly. The sky was full of stars. Aaron had said that the Monster Court sat outside time. What did that mean?

"I never thought I'd see this," Ruth said.

Joan looked over at the vast expanse of Whitehall Palace. She'd never imagined she'd see this either. Whitehall Palace had been London's Versailles—it was the city's great lost treasure. Beyond the main white building, there were glimpses of red-brick turrets and towers. The complex of buildings seemed to stretch for miles. This was where Henry VIII had married Anne Boleyn, and where he'd died. Where Charles I had been executed, and where his son Charles II had returned from exile to usher in the Restoration.

Joan stopped herself before that dangerous yearning feeling could start. She took a deep breath and released it.

"Look at that," Ruth whispered.

"I know," Joan said, and then realized that Ruth wasn't looking at the palace at all. She was looking back toward the archway: 1993 was still visible, the gibbous moon in the sky. The gate had been a bare ruin when they'd walked in. But in this time it was a gatehouse with three stories of windows and a pitched roof. It was too dark to see much of the skyline beyond the palace walls, but Joan imagined she could hear trees rustling in place of cars.

"It gives me the creeps," Aaron whispered.

"Really?" Joan wondered. It was so beautiful.

"We can't travel out of the mire," Ruth said. "We'll have to walk back through that gate."

It hadn't occurred to Joan that monsters might feel trapped if they couldn't travel. For her, it was something terrible that she'd done. Something she never wanted to do again.

"What would happen if we didn't use the gate?" she wondered. "If we walked out of the palace through another door. Would we end up in the 1600s?"

"I don't think we're in the 1600s now," Ruth said. She was still looking at the archway, her face pale. "This place feels as though someone took a piece of the world and suspended it in the middle of . . . of *nothing*. There's nothing around us. I think if we looked out one of those windows in the gatehouse, there'd be nothing." Joan must have looked confused, because Ruth added: "Can't you feel it? There's no time outside this place. It's like we're on a rowboat in the middle of the ocean."

Joan sought that internal monster sense. She could feel something, but not as viscerally as Ruth clearly did. To Joan, the palace just felt self-contained. She looped her arm through Ruth's, wanting to comfort her. "Good thing we're not likely to get invited back, huh?"

Ruth's mouth twisted up. "We weren't invited this time."

"Oh yeah," Joan said. "Oops."

The three of them followed the other guests toward the heavy black doors at the other end of the courtyard. The path was lit with floating globes the same color as the moon.

The guests' clothes were extravagant. What had been dark silhouettes from afar were revealed to be intricately embroidered silks and jewels. All around, people were speaking other languages: Joan caught snatches of Latin and something that wasn't quite French—some older version of it, maybe. Other people were speaking languages she couldn't even guess at.

Here and there, animals padded alongside guests—dogs and cats and stranger creatures. Joan glimpsed a leopard with a jeweled collar, and a snake wound around a woman's shoulders.

A bird strolled past with a strange bobbing motion. "Is that a dodo?" she whispered to Aaron.

"Don't stare," he whispered back. As they walked farther, he murmured: "Be careful. There are Olivers here."

"Anyone you recognize?" Joan asked.

Aaron shook his head. "Just stay away from them."

Joan remembered the last time she'd been among Olivers. "Because I'm half-human? You think they'd attack me on sight?" The Olivers could see the difference between monsters and humans if they were close enough. They'd know what she was just by looking at her.

"Attack you for being half-human?" Ruth whispered. "What has he been telling you? The Olivers are vile, but they wouldn't do that."

But they had, Joan thought. She remembered Edmund's cold, scouring gaze.

"Never mind that right now," Aaron said. "Just stay away from them. Don't let any Oliver close enough to see the color of your eyes." There was a strange intensity in the way he said it.

"It's not like they wear name tags," Joan said, puzzled.

"I'll point them out," he said.

They all fell silent as they reached the palace's huge arched doors, flung wide for the crowd to enter. The doors were black wood, Tudor roses carved into the top corners of the frame.

Joan crossed the threshold and then she was inside—in a great hall. She looked around in wonder. The room was lit with the soft light of floating chandeliers placed high up near the buttressed ceiling. At eye level, the walls were lined with rich tapestries depicting scenes of battle. Joan closed her eyes and smelled roses and violets—not artificial, but fresh, as if she were standing in a garden.

Ruth clutched Joan's arm. "Michelangelo's *Cupid*," she whispered. She pointed at a marble sculpture in a corner of the room: a sleeping child, raised on a plinth. "That sculpture launched Michelangelo's career. It was lost in the fire." Her eyes were wide. "Incredible."

It was all a wonder. Ruth pointed out more artwork, burned and lost: a Holbein, a Bernini.

But this wasn't Whitehall Palace—not really.

The chandelier above Joan broke apart suddenly, scattering through the air in individual glittering diamonds. As one flew close, Joan saw that it was a butterfly, but lit from within. Its wings sparkled.

Statues of dangerous creatures lined the hall: lions, leopards, dragons. Now, from under a window, a stone lion's tail twitched, making Joan jump. Then, in synchrony, all the statues stood up and roared, flames blasting from their upturned mouths. The flames made shapes as they crested, royal crowns. As sparks rained down, the creatures sat again like obedient dogs.

Servers wandered between guests, offering delicacies on silver plates. Joan took a couple of sweets from a passing tray. They turned out to be tiny marzipan lions, exquisitely detailed. They were too beautiful to eat. Joan pocketed them.

"Olivers," Aaron murmured. Joan blinked at him. He nodded

at a group of three men striding through the gauntlet of stone creatures. "Remember what I said?"

"Yes," Joan whispered. She'd stay away from them.

"Tom made it," Ruth said in a tone of relief.

Joan followed her gaze to a doorway. She saw then that this hall was the first in a series. Open doors offered glimpses of more wonders in the rooms beyond: glittering lights, people dancing. Where was Tom?

"Guards at each doorway," Ruth whispered.

Joan hadn't noticed that, but Ruth was right. It was hard to concentrate on security. Everywhere she looked, there were people in elaborate costumes from the Renaissance, from the Regency, perhaps from the future.

There he was, Joan saw in relief. Tom was in the next hall, standing by a silver fountain. It shone, lit from within, the water bright as moonlight. He looked unexpectedly good—he'd scrounged a dark gray suit from somewhere, and barely looked out of place in it. He'd even dressed Frankie up: she had a gray bow tie that matched Tom's own.

Aaron didn't seem as relieved. "He's got a glass in his hand," he said, disgusted. "Someone stop him before he's too drunk to work."

"Shit," Ruth breathed. She headed over.

That left Aaron and Joan alone. As they strolled up the hall, Joan found herself increasingly nervous. Everyone else at the party seemed to hold themselves with the same air of restrained power, as if they were used to wielding authority. It occurred to

Joan again that she was half-human. Could monsters take time from her—from the human half of her? She wished she had a scarf or a high collar to cover her neck.

She felt Aaron step closer. To her surprise, he offered his arm. She blinked at him. "We should try to look as if we're enjoying ourselves," he whispered. "Or we'll draw attention."

Joan was more grateful than she wanted to admit. She put her hand on his arm and let him draw her past the first set of guards. The hall beyond was vast—a ballroom. There were fountains bubbling with plum-colored wine. A harpist provided music. And Joan might not have fit in here, but Aaron did. In a room full of powerful, beautiful people, he still turned heads. It felt strange to be so obviously with him. His arm felt very solid under her hand.

"How will we sneak out of this party without anyone noticing?" she whispered. They needed to get farther into the palace.

Aaron smiled at her, small and real. "That part's easy," he said. "I've spent my whole life escaping events like this."

"You have?" Joan said.

Someone nearby spoke. "Truly a relief to be in a room without humans."

Joan froze. She knew that voice. The last time she'd heard it, there'd been a gun pointed at her head. She turned, catching a glimpse of Aaron's face as she did. He'd gone paper white.

Edmund Oliver stood a few paces away. Alive, and with the same powerful presence Joan remembered from the Gilt Room. He seemed barely younger than he'd been when he'd died.

As Joan stared, Edmund started to turn. She felt Aaron release her hand. *Don't let any Oliver close enough to see the color of your eyes*, Aaron had said.

Move, Joan told herself. *Move*. But she couldn't seem to. She remembered how Edmund had looked down at her with that cold gaze. His eyes had widened as if he'd seen something inside her, and then he'd ordered Lucien to kill her.

"Father," Aaron said.

To Joan's profound relief, Edmund turned away from her, searching for Aaron's voice. Aaron had walked away a few paces, closer to the harpist.

"Hello, Father." Aaron's posture was careless, one hand in his pocket. When Edmund's lip curled in distaste, Aaron smiled slightly. "Aren't you happy to see me?"

"How did you get through the gate?" Edmund said.

"How?" Aaron's posture still seemed careless, but Joan knew him well enough now to see the strain in his eyes. "I'm an Oliver. I'm your son. My chop bears your name. That's enough to get me on any guest list."

For a second, rage flickered in Edmund's cold eyes. "An Oliver?" he said. "You're not worthy of the name. I removed you from the line of succession. If I could have stripped you of your name too, I would have."

Aaron's casual posture didn't change. Joan could hear people starting to whisper. Heads were turning. Aaron must be hating this, Joan knew. He was always so careful about how he appeared.

Joan wanted to shove Edmund away—to stop him from speaking—but she knew that Aaron was doing this for her. He'd drawn Edmund's attention to keep him from looking too closely at her. She felt sick.

Aaron looked over Edmund's shoulder at a blond boy about his own age, standing at the edge of the dance floor, watching the scene in silence. "Our new heir?" Aaron's mouth lifted, but there was no amusement on his face. "I had no idea the pool was so shallow."

Edmund took a step toward Aaron. "Geoffrey knows where his loyalties lie." For a moment, Joan thought he was going to strike Aaron.

So did Aaron—he flinched. Edmund seemed to realize suddenly that he'd drawn a crowd. He grunted. And then he was striding away, the blond boy hurrying after him. Joan held her breath as Edmund swept past her, but he didn't so much as glance at her.

As soon as Edmund was out of sight, Joan closed the gap. "Aaron," she said, trying to offer thanks or sympathy—she wasn't even sure.

Aaron looked down at her for a long moment, and then his expression turned to the disdain Joan remembered from the Gilt Room. "I suppose you enjoyed the show?"

Joan was stung. "Of course not. Aaron, are you all—"

"Why are you still standing here?" Aaron interrupted.

"*Aaron,*" Joan said, but he was already pushing past her.

At the cascading fountain, Ruth looked impatient. Tom had shifted from drinking to eating, moving along a table laden with food. There were crispy pastries, folded origami-like into animal shapes: swans and deer. And food that Joan didn't recognize: papery wafers and little iced cakes that looked sweet, but smelled of savory herbs.

"Mm," Tom said in acknowledgment of their arrival.

Frankie sniffed at Joan and then Aaron inquisitively. Joan bent to touch Frankie's soft head. Her stomach was churning.

"Where the hell have you two been?" Ruth whispered.

"Nowhere," Aaron said.

Tom paused to scoop up a handful of the delicate pastries and shove them into his pockets. "All right," he said with his mouth full. "Let's go."

Tom led them back to the first hall, past the line of fire-breathing statues.

Edmund had gone the opposite way, but Joan was afraid of running into him—afraid of what might happen if he noticed her. Beside her, Aaron was silent. He didn't look at Joan when she tried to catch his eye.

They stopped in a room off the hall. It was small but ornate. The wallpaper was hand-painted with pink and gold flowers. One whole wall was a vast mirrored cabinet decorated in gleaming gold leaf. The other walls had display shelves.

Two other guests were already in the room, placing a vase and a small sculpture on an empty shelf. Joan saw then that the whole room was crammed with valuable objects, on shelves and laid on tables: necklaces, coronets, statues.

"Gifts for the King," Tom said.

"We didn't bring a gift," Joan whispered.

"I think that's the least of our indiscretions tonight," Aaron muttered.

As soon as the other guests left, Tom strode to the far end of the room. "Someone keep watch on the door," he said. He slid his hand along the back of the cabinet.

There was a click, and a section of the cabinet wall swung open, revealing a dark room behind it.

"Royal escape route." Aaron sounded grudgingly impressed. "Every palace has one."

"Quickly," Tom said. He bent to pick up Frankie. "Before someone else comes in."

One by one, they slipped into the room behind the cabinet. Joan was last to step into the dark space. She pulled the cabinet shut behind her with another click—and just in time. Muffled voices sounded through the wall a moment later.

The darkness was complete. Joan could hear her own breaths and the muffled voices from the party outside. She could hear Ruth fidgeting beside her, dress rustling.

Tom's voice sounded, barely audible. "Forgot to bring a torch."

More rustling, and then an illumination revealed Aaron holding his phone. "This won't last," he warned. "Battery's almost gone." He held it up.

Joan had thought that they'd entered a narrow space—had been hunched a little to accommodate it—but now she saw that they were in a vast room with red-draped balconies and wooden pews. High above, the ceiling seemed to be covered in gold leaf. *The palace chapel*, she thought wonderingly. King Henry had married Anne Boleyn here.

"Come on," Tom whispered. "We won't have long before the gate closes."

SIXTEEN

In spite of the danger, Joan couldn't help but feel a guilty wonder as Tom led them out of the chapel and into the palace proper. She'd always loved history. And, stripped of the showy costume of monsters, this real, lived-in part of Whitehall felt more of a marvel than the fire-breathing statues of the great hall.

These dark spaces were the suites of Charles II and his mistresses. The walls were draped with rich tapestries of men on horseback and women in long gowns. The beds were as ornate as cakes—all chocolate curls and flourishes. Some of the sheets were rumpled, as if their owners had just gotten out of bed.

There was a strange air of suspension about each room. Letters and ink lay carelessly on desks. Doors were ajar.

"How can the Monster Court be inside Whitehall Palace?" Joan whispered to Tom.

"It isn't always," Tom said. "Sometimes it manifests in other places. They say that the King steals these places for a frozen moment."

"How?" Joan said, but Tom only shook his head. "And where is everyone?" Joan asked. "Where are all the humans who live here? Shouldn't they all be here too?" Tom shook his head again, as if he didn't know.

They walked through curtained spaces, guided only by the light from Aaron's phone. They all fell silent as they entered a room with curtains flung wide. The view through the window was the Thames under a bright moon.

The river was closer than Joan would have expected. She remembered reading that the river had been higher in the past. Aaron made an unhappy sound. Joan felt it too. There was something disturbing about the scene—beyond the height of the river. It took her a second to understand what it was.

Nothing was moving outside. The river was frozen—every ripple still. Moonlight lay along it like spilled milk. Trees and low buildings were dim outlines on the other side of the bank.

"I hate this place," Ruth whispered.

"The timeline hates it too," Aaron said. "I can feel it."

"I always thought that the King was just a man," Ruth said. "But this kind of power is . . . I've never heard of anything like it." She gazed out at the frozen river. "What if everything they say about the King is true? What if he *can* see everything?"

"He can't," Joan whispered back, with more confidence than she felt. "Or we wouldn't be here. We wouldn't have got this far."

Ruth shook her head. She was still looking out at the view. The window's reflection made her face ghostly. "There's something wrong about this," she whispered.

"This place—" Joan started.

"Not just this place," Ruth said. "There's something wrong

about all of this. I feel as if we've got something wrong."

"What do you mean?" Joan said.

"I don't know," Ruth said. "I don't know. It's just a feeling."

Joan didn't know what she meant. To her, this seemed right. Gran had given her a key to the Monster Court. And now they were here. Now they were achingly close to bringing their family back to life. "We can't stop now," she said. "We're almost there." She looked at Tom for confirmation.

He nodded. "We're near to the lion's den now."

But Joan started to feel the wrongness too as Tom led them down a long stone gallery, half open to a formal garden. In the garden, there were statues of animals on pedestals—a chained leopard in carnival colors, a unicorn with a horn as sharp as a saber—dozens of them, garishly painted and gilded.

"Where is everybody?" Joan asked him again. "Where are the people who live here? Where's the King?"

"The King is never seen," Tom said. When Joan turned to him, he said: "When he wants something done, he sends a member of the Monster Court in his place."

Joan remembered the story Aaron told. "Like Conrad?" she said. The man who'd executed Aaron's cousin.

"Conrad," Tom agreed. "Or Eleanor. Or the one we call the Giant. Those are the three members of Court who come near the vicinity of our time."

"I overheard someone mention Conrad in the halls," Ruth said. "He's here tonight."

The others visibly shivered. Tom looked over his shoulder. "We need to be quiet now," he whispered. "Guards patrol much more regularly closer to the Royal Archive."

At the end of a stretch of smooth green lawn, they reached a staircase leading down. Joan stood there at the black mouth of it.

Tom left Frankie at the top of the stairs. He descended.

From below, there were startled sounds, then pained sounds, then no sounds. Tom reappeared and grabbed Frankie. "All clear," he said unnecessarily.

Tom led them down the flight of stairs. Joan's heavy dress swept against her legs as she descended. She felt as if she were walking down to a bunker. The air began to smell of mud and brine. Joan imagined the frozen mountain of the river just beyond the thick stone wall.

At the bottom of the staircase, four guards lay sprawled on a dark rug. Joan looked at Tom, impressed. He'd taken out four armed men by himself.

Tom bent and unbuckled a wristwatch from one of the guards. "Eleven thirty," he said. The new guards would arrive on the hour.

"Okay, let's go," Joan said.

Beyond here, Tom had no idea of the archive's security; he'd never been allowed to guard it. Ruth had hedged her bets by bringing a selection of tools. Joan was secretly hoping there wouldn't be *any* more security. How much security could an archive in the Monster Court even need? The gates only opened every century or so.

Aaron led the way out of the alcove at the bottom of the stairs and into the passage to the archive. At his low gasp, Joan looked up.

The passage was only about twenty feet long, and it ended in a wooden door with a winged-lion insignia carved into it. The door to the archive. But there was something between them and the door. . . .

At first, all Joan could see was a patch of bright white on the passage floor. As she walked closer, the brightness resolved into a snowy landscape. She stared. There was a slice of winter in the middle of the passage.

"What is that?" she whispered. Light shone on the snow. She looked up and saw a piece of daytime sky, dazzlingly blue. It didn't look like a London sky.

The stretch of snow was about ten feet across. Joan could almost imagine jumping over it. She put her hand out tentatively. The air pushed back. "There's a barrier." It felt like magnetic repulsion.

Ruth came closer. "Did you *see* that?"

"See what?" Joan said. But now she saw it too. Inside the wintry landscape, a shadow was moving on the snow.

An animal padded into view, tigerlike, with enormous arcing fangs. It was as big as a horse, and solidly built. The huge muscles of its legs shifted as it walked.

Joan gasped, and the animal turned as if it had heard. It looked right at Joan, seeming as shocked as she felt. Could it see her? She got her answer a second later. It snarled at her and leaped.

Joan heard herself shout. She twisted to run. But there were no claws or fangs. Instead, someone had caught her and steadied her. Aaron. "Careful," he said shakily. "Or you'll fall."

The creature circled back, snarling, tail lashing. Joan shuddered.

"That's a saber-toothed tiger," Aaron said disbelievingly.

"That's not just winter in there," Ruth said, sounding just as shaky. "That must be a hundred thousand years ago at least."

Tom reached into his pocket absently and took a gulp from a flask. "Shhh," he said as Frankie yapped frantically under his arm and squirmed, trying to get at the tiger. Frankie subsided to a low growl.

As the tiger padded out of sight, Joan put her hand out again. The barrier seemed slightly rounded, as if it was shaped like a sphere. She pictured this slice of winter as the thick wall of a bubble that surrounded the archive completely.

"It's like a moat," Ruth said. "A piece of another time standing between us and the archive."

"You really didn't know this was here?" Aaron said to Tom.

"I would have *told* you," Tom said, annoyed.

"What are we going to do?" Ruth said. "We can't travel through that. It would be a hundred thousand years just to walk into the Paleolithic period, and then another hundred thousand years to walk out."

"I think that's the point," Aaron said. "It can't be traversed."

Joan hoped no one had ever walked through it. Because a round trip—through the moat to the archive and back—would cost four hundred thousand years of human life. Had the King ever stolen that much? She felt ill at the thought.

"We need to go back," Aaron said.

"No," Joan said. "No. Wait." She needed to think.

"There's no way in. We need to cut our losses," Aaron said.

"The new guards will be here soon," Tom said.

Joan could *see* the archive's door across the strip of snow. It was so close. She could hardly bear it. Behind that door, there was a device that could bring her family back to life. The *transformatio*, Gran had called it. And Joan was standing a few feet away, unable to even touch the door. She couldn't leave.

"Joan," Aaron said.

Joan shook her head.

"Look," Aaron said. "Even if it were possible to steal that much human time, we still couldn't travel through that *thing*. We're on a mire."

A mire. Joan had forgotten about that. Monsters couldn't travel here—their powers didn't work in this place. Except . . . that clearly wasn't quite true.

The King's powers still worked: this bubble of another time was proof of that; the whole palace out of its time was proof. Maybe the family powers would still work here too. Maybe the Hunt power would work.

"Ruth," Joan said. There was a twig on the floor, tracked in from the garden. Joan bent to pick it up. The thought was still half-formed as she straightened. "Ruth, do you think you could put this in there?"

"What do you mean?" Ruth said, sounding confused.

Joan's own family power had diminished over the years. As a child, she'd been able to hide and retrieve things just like the rest of the Hunts. But as she'd gotten older, retrieval had become less and less reliable. She'd lost things that way. A jade bracelet that she'd been given as a baby. A cameo brooch that Mum had once owned. A few years ago, she'd stopped trying to hide things at all. Ruth's and Bertie's Hunt power had gotten stronger as they'd gotten older, but Joan's had faded away as if it had never really been hers.

"How does the Hunt power actually work?" Joan asked Ruth.

Tom interjected with a soft cough. He showed them the wristwatch he'd taken from the guard: 11:35. "Next change is twenty-five minutes away."

So they had twenty-five minutes. No . . . Joan calculated. *Fifteen* minutes, unless they wanted to run right into the new guards.

Joan tried again with Ruth. "How does the Hunt power work?" she asked. "I used to think that we put objects some-*where* else. But that isn't right, is it?"

"No," Ruth said slowly. "It's more like we place objects some*when* else."

"Do you think you could?" Joan nodded at the snowy land-scape.

"What, put something in there?" Ruth bit her lip. "I don't know, Joan. . . ."

Joan gave her the twig. "Can you try?"

Ruth's dubious expression didn't change as she turned to the snowy landscape. But she put one hand up to touch the barrier.

"I think . . ." Joan was still feeling out the idea. "I think it'll be just like all the other times you've hidden an object with your power. The only difference will be that you can see where you're putting it."

Ruth pressed the twig against the barrier in the familiar motion of the Hunt power. She shook her head doubtfully, and was still shaking it when the twig crossed through. Her eyes widened. Joan heard Tom gasp softly

Joan let out the breath she'd been holding. "Let it go," she whispered. Ruth did. For a moment the twig seemed to stand, suspended in the air, and then it vanished.

"Where did it go?" Aaron said.

"Well . . ." Joan tried not to feel too excited. Putting a twig in there was a long way from crossing the barrier. "I think the Hunts place objects into a moment in time. My aunt Ada puts mugs of hot tea into the air. When she takes them out again, they're always still steaming."

"I don't understand, though," Ruth said. "How does this help us? The Hunt power doesn't work on living creatures. I can't push you in there, if that's what you're thinking. I can't go in there myself."

"I know," Joan said. "I know. But . . . what if you could create a tunnel?"

Ruth looked at her questioningly.

"What if you had a . . . a tube of some kind?" Joan said. "Could you hold the inside of the tube in this time and the outside in *that* time?" She gestured at the snowy ground. "Do you think you could make a tunnel through to that door?"

"An object can't straddle two times," Aaron said. "It would be torn apart."

"I don't think it would be torn apart," Joan said. She'd seen her family's power her whole life. She'd seen the way objects disappeared piece by piece. "You just saw Ruth do it—that twig stayed intact as it crossed the barrier, half in here, half in there. Ruth held it together with the Hunt family power. The twig didn't disappear until she stopped touching it." She could hear her excitement making her voice shaky. She wanted this so much.

"We don't have time for this," Aaron said.

"*Aaron,*" Joan said. For the first time since the confrontation with Edmund, Aaron met her eyes properly. "We're so close," she said. "That door is right *there.* We could save them all. We could bring them back."

Aaron shook his head, clearly unconvinced. But he glanced at Tom's watch and sighed. "What can we use as the bridge?"

They ended up rolling up the rug from the entrance, keeping a center loop big enough for them all to crawl through.

Ruth's mouth was an unhappy twist as they lined it up with the door. "I really don't think the Hunt power can do this."

"I think it can," Joan said. *Please,* she thought. *Please work.* The archive felt so close.

"This is not even a proper tube," Ruth said. "We just rolled it up." But she was already facing the wintry moat. Frowning with concentration, she pushed the rolled rug against the barrier. Joan held her breath.

For a long moment, it looked like it wouldn't cross. "I don't think I can—" Ruth started, but as she said it, the rug abruptly breached the barrier, scooping into the thick snow. Falling snowflakes sprinkled the wool. Tom pushed out a sharp breath, as if he'd been holding his too.

It was clearly an effort for Ruth. Her jaw clenched tight as she fed the rolled rug over the snow.

"Hope that tiger wandered far away," Aaron murmured.

Joan hoped so too. She was pretty sure that cats were the same everywhere—even cats with giant saber teeth.

And then the rug hit the end of the snowy landscape and Ruth couldn't get it any farther.

"Keep going," Tom said.

"I can't." Ruth sounded strained. "I think it's stuck at the barrier on the other side."

"It's okay," Joan said. She tried not to make her voice sound as desperate as she felt. "Just try."

Ruth pushed harder—her arms shaking with the effort. She ducked her head and grunted.

"A little over ten minutes left," Tom said. "If we want enough buffer to get out of here."

"Ruth," Joan said. "You can do it. You can."

Ruth took a deep breath and squared her shoulders. She

pushed again, and this time they all gasped as the rug cleared the snow. Part of the tube was here in the corridor; part of it was inside the barrier. And when Joan knelt to look, she could see the door of the archive through the eye of it. She pulled a bobby pin from her hair and tossed it through the tunnel. It hit the door on the other side with a *plink*.

"Ruth," she said wonderingly. "You did it! It's a bridge!"

"Now, that's impressive," Aaron conceded to Ruth. "Didn't imagine that the Hunt power could do that." The considering way he said it made Joan look at him properly. Aaron had the kind of mind that was constantly sorting people, reorganizing them like a pack of cards—kings and queens and twos and threes. Joan suspected that all Hunts had been low-number cards to Aaron. Now they'd exposed a new aspect of the Hunt power to an Oliver. Joan felt wary. Gran would not have liked that.

"Olivers. Always underestimating us," Ruth said, but with a shadow of her usual bravado. "Hey, I don't know how long I can hold this, actually." Her hands were trembling.

"Go," Joan said to Tom. "Quick."

Tom nodded. He scooted through the makeshift tunnel fearlessly, Frankie following.

"Now you," Joan said to Aaron.

Aaron looked gray with terror, and Joan didn't blame him. If the bridge collapsed while they were in it, they might get stuck in the Paleolithic period.

"Joan." Ruth's hands were shaking hard enough to make ripples in the cloth.

"Go!" Joan said to Aaron.

"Joan, you too!" Ruth said. "Bloody well *go!*"

Aaron hurled himself in, and Joan dived after, close enough that he was nearly kicking her face. Cold hit her suddenly— such cold that her lungs stuck on the in breath. Wind howled. *I'm going to be stranded here,* she thought. *The tiger is going to attack. It's going to break the bridge!*

But then Aaron was dragging her out. Joan scrabbled with her heels to help him. She knelt at the edge of the snow, panting. She peered through the bridge to Ruth. "Are you all right?"

Ruth was breathing hard, and unevenly too. "Peachy," she managed. "Hurry?"

Joan scrambled to her feet. She could tell that Ruth wasn't going to be able to hold the bridge open long. Tom showed her the watch again. Ten minutes before the new guards arrived.

Before them, the door to the archive was surprisingly plain: thick polished wood with no apparent joinery—as if it had been cut from a single massive tree. But, plain as it was, there was a craftsmanship about it. The arch of the door fit perfectly into the stone wall. And the wood was so polished it seemed to glow. The only decoration was the winged-lion insignia on the middle of the door.

Joan reached for the heavy iron handle. She tried to turn it. It wouldn't budge. She tried the handle again. Then again. She felt a bubble of hysterical laughter leap into her throat. "The door's locked."

"Stop messing about," Aaron said. He snatched at the handle, bobbling it up and down. "It's bloody well *locked*."

"Who locks a door behind a Paleolithic barrier?" Joan said.

"Keeping *us* out, isn't it?" Tom said.

That was undeniable. Joan knelt again and called to Ruth. "You need to come through!"

"I can't." Ruth was still breathing unevenly. "And I really need you to hurry up."

Joan thought. "I need your picks, then. It's one of those big iron-key type locks."

Ruth's pause said a lot. "When did you last pick a lock?"

Joan swallowed. "A while ago." They both knew that Joan had never actually done it beyond the games Gran had had them play as kids. Padlocks at the dinner table.

Ruth's pick set hit Joan's knee. "You can't take long, Joan." There was careful effort in Ruth's voice. "I can't hold this open much longer."

"Okay," Joan said. "Okay." She got to her feet fast, sorting through the roll of picks. She squinted at the keyhole. "How are we for time?"

"Nine minutes away," Tom said.

"Okay," Joan said again. She took a pick from Ruth's kit and probed at the keyhole. To her surprise, the pick met something just inside. It felt like a metal plate. Joan's heart started to beat faster as she traced the shape of it. It seemed to cover the hole entirely. "Can I have some light?" she asked.

Light appeared from Aaron's dying phone. The battery icon was red.

Joan bent to examine the keyhole. It was big enough that she should have been able to glimpse the room beyond. But instead the phone's torch revealed a metal sheet just inside the keyhole.

"What's wrong?" Aaron said.

"I can't pick it," Joan said.

"I thought Hunts could pick any lock," Tom said. "That was the deal we made. I get you in the gate. You get me in there."

"You don't understand," Joan said. "It's not a lock. There's nothing to pick."

"What are you talking about?" Tom said.

"The keyhole is sealed up. There's no room to fit a key into it."

Tom peered at the keyhole and swore.

"We're out of time," Aaron said.

"No!" Joan heard herself. "No!" They'd come so far to get here, and the gate wouldn't open again for a hundred years. They were so close to saving their families. They were so close to where they needed to be. And someone had made this stupid, false, mocking lock. "No!"

"Joan—" Aaron said.

"*No!*" Joan slammed her hand against the door, frustrated and furious.

And something woke up inside her.

Not the Hunt power, but another. *Someday soon, you'll come into an ability*, Gran had said. *You can trust no one with the knowledge of it.*

Power poured out of Joan—invisible, but real and strong as electricity. She felt disoriented and unbalanced. She felt as if she were falling off a cliff.

There was a sound like ice cracking.

From far away, Aaron's voice said, "We need to go."

"Wait." That was Tom. "Look, she did it. The door's ajar."

The torrent of power ended abruptly, and Joan was left feeling shaken and drained.

Aaron and Tom were peering around the edge of the door, into the next room, but all Joan could see was the keyhole she'd touched.

The silver metal of the lock had become reddish and dull, as if the metal had been turned into stone. Cracks ran through it; the new material seemed too brittle for this form.

Joan had a sudden clear memory of the gold chain with those dark, stonelike patches. *I did that,* she thought. *And I did this.*

And then Tom flung the door open, and the lock disappeared from Joan's view.

"Good God." Aaron took a step back.

The smell hit Joan first. It was familiar and terrible: excrement and confinement. Joan knew it well. It was the smell from the nightmare she'd had since she was small.

The room was tiny, with stone walls and a vaulted wooden ceiling.

"What *is* this?" Aaron sounded bewildered.

There was a mattress on the floor with a thin blanket—too

thin for this cold stone room. A bucket had been pushed into one corner. A wooden desk was against a wall.

Joan made herself step inside. "It's a prison cell." Not the prison from her nightmares, but she knew one when she saw one.

"But where are all the King's treasures?" Aaron said.

Someone had been kept in here. There were brown bloodstains on the edge of the desk. Scuff marks on the stone floor. Someone had put up a fight.

Tom crouched to touch an indentation in the mattress. The mattress was so thin that his knee compressed it to the cold stone floor.

"Where is everything?" Aaron said. "Where are the books? Where are the records? Where's the *transformatio*? Isn't this supposed to be the Royal Archive?" He turned to Tom. "This is the wrong room."

"It's the right room," Tom said. "You saw the protections around it."

"But there's nothing *in* here."

"I can see that, can't I?" Tom growled. He'd been talking for days about what the room might hold. *They say that the King collects treasures from all of time.* Now, frustrated, he ripped into the mattress, as if something might be hidden there. When he found nothing, he hurled it against the wall. It hit the bucket, and something disgusting slopped all over the floor.

"Oh, for—" Aaron backed up from the spreading mess. "Oh, that's repugnant. Why did you do that? Frankie, *no.*" He called the dog back before she could bound over there.

And now Tom was pushing at the walls, apparently hoping to find a hidden door.

"Tom, stop," Joan said. "We can see what was in here."

A person had been here. A prisoner. Someone all alone, cut off from the world, behind a slice of winter from a hundred thousand years ago.

"For God's sake," Aaron said. He hoisted up Frankie with a grunt, staggering a bit, as if she was much heavier than he'd expected. "Come on. There's nothing here. We need to go."

But then Joan hesitated. The scuff marks and the blood said there'd been a struggle.

Blood on the corner of the desk and messy scuff marks on the floor beside it. Someone had struggled next to the desk. And, after that, there were long scraped lines all the way to the door, as if the person had stopped struggling. Had they been unconscious? Or had they stopped struggling for a reason? Had they accomplished something near the desk?

On a hunch, Joan bent to run her hand under the desk. An uneven notch had been carved into the wood to create a shallow ledge. There was something in it. Joan had a flash of hope that it might be the *transformatio*, but even before she'd slid out the object and pocketed it, she knew it wasn't. It was clear that this room had never held the King's treasures. And in their research, the *transformatio* had been described as an ornate golden frame—a doorway.

"Hey." Ruth's voice sounded from the other side of the moat.

The rolled rug connecting the archive to the rest of the palace seemed to shiver right out of existence for a second, leaving an empty expanse of white snow between them and Ruth. The rug reappeared again a moment later.

"Oh my God," Aaron said, voice shaking. He had both arms around Frankie, and he tucked her closer, seeming to need the comfort. "What if we get stuck in that time?"

"Go! While the bridge is still here!" Joan pushed at Aaron. He went without argument, diving through the tunnel, careful of Frankie. "*Go!*" Joan said to Tom. He jumped into the tunnel too, and Joan threw herself after him.

The second crossing was more terrifying than the first. One time when Joan blinked, she saw an endless field of snow in front of her instead of Tom's legs. In the distance, trees rose from the landscape—like great monoliths, stark and leafless against the blue sky. Joan hadn't known that trees could be so big. The cold hit her belatedly, like a physical blow.

Then the snow and trees were gone. Tom was in front of her again. Joan scrambled after him, and then strong hands were pulling her out—Aaron's and Tom's. And just in time. As Joan cleared the barrier, Ruth tottered backward and lost her grip on the rug.

Ruth's gasping breaths sounded loud in the quiet. "Did you find it?" she managed.

Aaron shook his head. "The room was a vacant prison cell. No archive. No treasures."

Ruth laughed, high, with a note of hysteria. "Oh, fuck."

"You were right," Joan said to her. Ruth had said that there was something wrong. Joan hadn't known what she'd meant at the time, but she understood it now. She felt it too. "There's something wrong about all of this. I got something wrong."

"No time for debriefing," Tom said. "We have *minutes* before the new guards arrive."

"And *look*." Aaron pointed.

Inside the slice of Paleolithic time, the rolled rug that they'd used as a bridge was lying on the snow. It hadn't vanished like the twig had. Would the Court guess that the Hunt power had done that?

"We have to get out of here," Joan said. "Right now."

SEVENTEEN

They clambered up the stone staircase and ran back the way they'd come.

Joan's mind was racing, and she could see that the others were trying to figure out what had happened too. They'd broken into the Monster Court. They'd thought they'd find the *transformatio*—the device that could change the timeline. Instead they'd found a recently vacated prison cell.

Who had been in that lonely cell? Joan wondered as she ran. *Why* had they been put in there?

She shook her head at herself. Whoever the prisoner had been, she couldn't help them. She hadn't even been able to help her own family.

She ran through suite after luxurious suite, until her breath was hot and painful in her throat. Was the *transformatio* somewhere else in the palace? *Was* there still a chance she could find it here and save her family?

No. She knew the truth. They'd had one shot at this. Any second now, the guards would be alerted. The only thing left to do was flee.

Joan ran hard, reaching the suite with the curtains flung wide and the view of the frozen Thames. Breath ragged and legs straining, she glanced over her shoulder to check on the others.

No one was behind her. She stumbled to a stop. Through the doorway, she could see that the previous room was empty.

Panic struck her like a blow. Where *were* they? She tried to remember when she'd last heard them running behind her. Not for a few minutes, she realized. But how had she lost them? Had they taken a different route?

She took a deep breath, trying to force the panic down. There was no time to look for them, or for them to look for her; the guards could arrive at any moment. Joan would have to find her own way back to the chapel and hope that everyone else would make it too.

A last look over her shoulder and Joan started running again. And almost collided with someone running the other way.

Nick.

For a split second, the shock of seeing him was overwhelming. Nick was here and solid and real. In the café, there'd been a table between them, but there was no barrier now.

Nick's face betrayed his surprise, but Joan reacted first. She used her momentum to drive her knee into his thigh. He hissed in pain, but he dodged her next kick and managed to hustle her backward. Joan threw her hand up to his neck, just as he pinned her against a wall. His thighs were pressed against hers, chest against her shoulders.

Joan's hand curled around Nick's neck, her thumb under his jaw. But he'd pulled a knife. It glinted in the moonlight, its tip pressed against her side. The sharp point of it hadn't quite penetrated the thick velvet of her dress, but she could feel the pressure of it threatening.

They both breathed in and out, staring at each other. He was dressed for the gala in a beautiful black tuxedo, his clothes tailored for once to his muscled frame. His crisp white shirt made his hair look darker. His silk pocket square was a perfect thin line. He looked *good*.

Joan could kill him right now, she realized with a shot of horror. At the Pit, Aaron had said that you could kill someone if you took more time from them than they had left. All Joan would have to do was concentrate on one big block of time, and Nick would drop at her feet, dead.

And Nick could kill her too. All he'd have to do was thrust that knife.

Nick's breaths sounded as loud and unsteady as Joan's. Over his shoulder, Joan could see that frozen tableau: the unrippling river, the unmoving trees. She felt just as frozen. She and Nick were standing at the edge of a cliff. One wrong move and they'd both fall.

Nick's knife arm felt very tense. "Did you get it?" he whispered.

Joan supposed she should lie, but she shook her head.

They were as close as they'd been when they'd kissed. But

where there'd been tenderness in Nick's face in the library, now Joan could only see pain. "You stole time," he whispered hoarsely. "You stole human life." In the Gilt Room, he'd told her: *I only kill monsters who steal human life.* His arm shifted, and Joan tightened her hand against his neck. *Do it*, she told herself fiercely. *Take time from him.* In turn, Nick's arm tensed even more.

As he shifted position, his arm ground into the wound in Joan's side. She flinched and gasped, and Nick's eyes widened. The pressure vanished. "You're still injured?" he breathed.

"What do you care?" Joan said.

There was a shadow of agony in his eyes. "Would you have stolen time again if I hadn't killed your family?" he whispered. He sounded raw.

Joan was surprised by the question. "No," she blurted. It had been an accident the first time. She'd never wanted to hurt Mr. Solt. She found herself suddenly and horribly close to tears. "How were you even in the nineties?" she said thickly. "How can you travel in time if you're not a monster?"

"I'm not going to tell you that," he said, in the flat way that he spoke about his mission.

It felt as though they were at an impasse. They were pressed tightly against each other, neither of them moving. There was a distant shout. Then another shout—more urgent.

"Someone's discovered your break-in," Nick said.

"I should kill you," Joan told him. For her family. She sounded as raw as Nick had. *Do it*, she told herself. *Kill him.*

Nick shifted again, this time careful not to jolt the sword wound. And Joan had the sudden absurd thought that if she just stood on tiptoes she could kiss him. "You won't," he whispered, that shadow of agony still in his eyes. "You don't want me dead yet. You want to kill me *before* I kill your family."

There were running footsteps now, getting closer and closer. Joan and Nick stood there in that lethal embrace, tucked tight against each other.

"Maybe I'll kill you twice," Joan whispered.

Nick's mouth lifted, wry. "Not even your King could manipulate the timeline as much as that."

The footsteps drew closer. Perhaps four rooms away. Three rooms away. Nick slowly lowered the knife. For a second, they were just standing there, Joan's hand still cupped around Nick's neck as though she were going to kiss him, Nick's hands loose by his sides.

Do it, Joan told herself. But she couldn't. She just couldn't. She heard herself make a helpless, pained sound.

"Joan," Nick said. And the guards were coming, but he was staring down at her, intense and desperate, as if they were the only two people in the world. "You know this is wrong," he whispered. "Look around you. They steal from humans. That's all they do."

Joan shook her head.

"Last time I saw you, you told me you'd come after me," he whispered. "That you'd try to stop me. Please, Joan. Don't. Just stay away from me."

Joan wanted to hold on to him. She released his neck, letting her hand drop to her side. "You're a hero and I'm a monster," she whispered. "There's only one way that story ever ends."

Nick took a deep breath. When he spoke, his voice shook. "I know."

And then he slipped through the door and was gone.

Joan stumbled through the palace, trying to stay out of the way of the guards. Her body felt too alive everywhere she'd been pressed against Nick.

Without the light from Aaron's phone, it took her ages to navigate through the chapel in the dark, and to find the hidden door behind the cabinet. She had to keep shaking off flashes of memory—how Nick had dropped his knife before she'd dropped her hand. How raw his voice had been. By the time she found the door catch, she was shaking.

Ruth was waiting for her. She grabbed Joan's hand and pulled her through. And just in time. Another guest entered just as Joan scooted inside.

"Hey ho!" the other guest said, cheerfully. She was a middle-aged woman dressed in robes and a gold headdress. "Dumping your host gift too?" The woman took a small vase from her robes and placed it onto a shelf. "I arrived a bit late."

Joan couldn't find an answer. She was relieved when Ruth spoke. "Uh. Yes," Ruth said a little artificially. She leaned against the cabinet, covering the click of its closure with a cough. "Yes, we arrived late too." She patted one of the vases on the shelf.

"Goodness," the woman said. "Where did you get that old thing?"

The vase next to Ruth was ancient: cracked and repaired. The woman's vase was in the same style, but glossy and new.

Joan looked around slowly. The room was full of artifacts—people's gifts for the King. Vases and necklaces. Bolts of cloth. Bracelets, urns, statues. Hundreds and hundreds of artifacts. Museum pieces from all of history.

You know this is wrong, Nick had said. *Look around you.*

"Where did you get that vase?" Joan heard herself ask the woman.

"What, this?" The woman shrugged. "A little market in Babylon."

"Babylon?" Joan said. The hairs rose at the back of her neck. Babylon had been at its height nearly four thousand years ago. A return trip to Babylon would cost nearly eight thousand years of human life. Joan stared at the woman. She looked so ordinary. Like someone's mum. Had she stolen that much human life to go to a party?

Joan thought about the stone statues breathing fire in the next room. The butterfly chandelier. All the marvels here. It occurred to her that they were probably future technology. Human technology, stolen by monsters. Was that what Nick had seen when he'd walked in? All these stolen things?

"Joan," Ruth said urgently. Joan blinked at her. The woman was on her way out the door, sparing a moment to give Joan a puzzled look over her shoulder.

For the first time, Joan wondered what would happen if she and Ruth were on the opposite sides of this. She quashed the thought as soon as it had risen, surprised at herself. She could trust Ruth with anything. And Ruth could trust her. Always.

"Joan, are you with me?" Ruth's dark hair was frizzing out of her fancy bun. Ruth's hair was always like that—it never wanted to stay in one place. "Are you with me right now?"

"Yeah?" Joan said. "Yes."

"Okay," Ruth said. "Because we can't get back through the gate. There are guards swarming all over it. Dozens of them. We're stuck here."

EIGHTEEN

Inside the halls, none of the guests seemed to know about the break-in. The music was still playing; people were still dancing and laughing. Ruth took Joan's arm, and together they strolled through the hall, past the guards at the doors.

The guards knew. They were alert and watchful, eyeing every person who walked past them.

Joan and Ruth stepped outside. The party had extended now to the courtyard. People stood talking softly by the light of the moon and the floating lamps. Servers moved between them with food and drinks on silver trays.

Ruth led Joan away from the crowd, into the shadows by the hall's stone wall. Her grip was tight on Joan's arm. On the other side of the courtyard, there were half a dozen guards by the gate. Not enough, apparently, to alarm the other guests, but enough to prevent escape.

Joan's attention was drawn to a man standing in their midst.

"Conrad," Ruth whispered. Joan hadn't heard that much fear in her voice since the night their family had died. "The King's Reach."

Conrad was too far away to see clearly, but Joan could see that he was blond, in his early twenties at most. There was an air of power surrounding him. And something about him made Joan think of the relentless cold of winter; of still, moonless nights.

"That gate is the only way out of here," Ruth whispered. "What are we going to do?"

Figures peeled away from the other guests: Aaron and Tom. Frankie trotted underfoot.

"Conrad is methodical," Aaron whispered. "He'll check everyone who passes through the gate. And when he finds us . . ." He swallowed. "He'll make a spectacle of us."

"There must be another way out," Joan said.

"There's no other way." Tom sounded bleak. "And there's no way to travel out—we're on the mire."

"There is a way," Joan murmured. "We just traveled to the paleolithic period and back." She looked at her cousin. "You need to create another bridge and get us out of here."

Ruth shook her head. Her fingers felt very cold on Joan's arm. "I can't feel the Hunt power right now. It's like I burned it out."

"You need to try," Joan whispered. "Please."

"If we try, we need to be very careful about where," Aaron whispered. "We're almost on top of Downing Street and the Ministry of Defence. Scotland Yard. If we come out in the wrong place . . ."

"I know where we can go," Tom said. "Follow me."

The guests in the courtyard began to murmur as more guards appeared from the halls. Joan could hear pieces of their conversations. *Something stolen*, she heard. *Guards found unconscious*.

Tom ushered Joan and the others along the edges of the buildings, keeping to the shadows. No one seemed to notice as they slipped out of sight.

"We won't have long," Tom whispered. "The guards will check everyone on the grounds. They'll realize fast that we don't belong here."

They walked quickly. The palace grounds seemed to be structured as a series of open yards, each surrounded by buildings. Soon they were in the working part of the palace. Joan peered through the windows of the heavy stone buildings as they passed. One was a kitchen with huge unlit hearths and benches where food could be laid out. Another had deep basins for washing.

It was all as eerily empty of people as the suites had been. And it was dark. The only light was from the moon overhead.

"There's a gate farther up," Tom whispered. "Not too far from where Trafalgar Square will be."

He took them through a courtyard full of chopped wood. Then past an elaborate brick building with open archways. "Stables," he said.

"Wait," Joan whispered. She ducked into one of the archways. There were dozens of stalls, pristinely clean. There were no horses in any of them. There'd been no animals on the grounds, Joan realized—except for those brought in by the Hathaways. The woodyard, at least, should have been full of rats and cats and foxes. Insects. But here, alone in the stables, she couldn't hear anything but her own footsteps, her own breaths.

At the back of the room, there were saddles and neatly folded blankets. Joan took a coiled rope. Then she rummaged through a box of tools until she found a hammer and a couple of nails.

When she reemerged, Aaron put a finger to his lips. And then Joan *could* hear something—footsteps in the far distance. Voices. "Guards," Aaron murmured into her ear.

After that, they walked in silence.

Tom took them to a wooden gate at the very edge of the palace, where two stone walls met. The gate was small and unadorned—more like a passage out of a back garden than a palace.

Tom drew the iron bolt quietly and pulled the gate inward. They all retreated instinctively from the gaping mouth. On the other side, there were silhouettes of buildings and a wide street. The moonlight seemed to barely touch any of it. Nothing was moving.

Joan felt a sick swoop in her stomach, as though she were standing on a high wall. There'd been something awful about the view of the frozen Thames, but now she realized that the horror of it had been mitigated by the window between.

Beside Joan, Aaron put his hand over his mouth as if he were going to be sick.

"There's nothing there," Ruth whispered. "It looks like there's something there, but there's nothing there. It's a void. All those silhouettes are just shadows."

"I know," Tom said. His gaze was averted; he couldn't even look at the view.

Joan could feel it too—the horror of it. Her stomach roiled. Her skin crawled. She had the feeling that if she stepped across the threshold, she'd fall and fall and fall forever.

She tried not to think about that as she passed Aaron the hammer and nails to free her hands. Then she started to work on the rope. She made a loop with it, the size of the gate. As she tied the ends together, Aaron seemed to understand what she was doing. He lined up one of the nails at the left top corner of the gate's wooden frame. At Joan's nod, he tapped it with the hammer.

They all stopped then, listening. Joan held her breath. There were no urgent voices. No running footsteps. No sounds at all. Joan counted to ten. Then she nodded at Aaron again. He moved over to the other corner and tapped in the other nail.

Then he helped Joan hang the rope around the gate. Earlier in the night, they'd needed a long rug to cross the stretch of snow between them and the archive. But Joan hoped that here a rope would be good enough. And she hoped it would be easier for Ruth to manage.

"I don't know about this," Ruth whispered. "I can't even feel the Hunt power. It's like—" She hesitated as if she wasn't sure how it felt. "It's like it's burned out of me. The Hunt power isn't supposed to open gates like this."

"Close your eyes," Joan whispered, "and try. Just try. One more time."

Ruth hesitated again. Her eyes were sunken with fatigue; her skin was almost gray. But she touched the rope with the flat of her hand and closed her eyes. Nothing happened for a long moment. "I can't—" she started to say, and then something flashed on the other side of the gate. Joan heard Aaron gasp.

For a second, the moon had been smaller, and in a different part of the sky.

Ruth must have felt it. She opened her eyes. Frowning with concentration, she pushed the rope against the wooden frame, straining. There was another flash, and this time it lasted long enough for Joan to see the buildings grow and shrink on the other side of the road. There was no way to know what year she'd seen.

Ruth was already exhausted. "I can't keep it open," she said.

"Okay," Joan said. "Okay. We'll have to jump across during the flash."

"You must be joking," Aaron whispered. "If the gate closes while we're crossing . . ."

"If Conrad finds us . . . ," Tom whispered back.

Aaron squeezed his eyes shut for a second. "All right," he said in acknowledgment. "All right. I'll go first." He stepped up to the threshold of the rope.

"Get ready." Ruth's face was strained with concentration. "*Now.*"

The gate flashed open and Aaron hurled himself through.

And then he was gone, and there was only the shadowy city on the other side.

"Did he make it?" Ruth whispered.

"Yes," Joan whispered back, even though she hadn't actually seen him get to the other side. The flash had been too brief. She needed to believe that he'd made it. She needed to believe that he hadn't disappeared into a void.

"I'll go next," Tom said. He stepped up to the threshold, Frankie in his arms.

Joan put her own hand up against the rope, willing her own Hunt power to activate. She couldn't feel anything of it. Her Hunt power had failed years ago. But she couldn't just stand here while Ruth burned herself out.

"Get ready," Ruth said to Tom. Then, almost as fast: "*Go.*"

The gate flashed again. And then Tom was gone.

"Two more times," Joan said. "Me and you."

Ruth took her time to answer. Her breath was coming in gasps. "You know I can't come with you," she managed.

"Yes, you can," Joan said firmly. "You didn't even try back there at the archive, but I bet you could have."

Ruth shook her head.

"I'm not leaving you here," Joan said.

"Don't be an idiot." The usual spark in Ruth's voice wasn't there. She sounded tired and flat. She started to push at the rope again.

"*Ruth—*" Joan said.

"Just fucking go when I say," Ruth said.

"I'm not leaving you here."

"Three," Ruth said. "Two. One."

The gate flashed into existence. Joan grabbed Ruth's free hand, dragging her through as she jumped.

There was a flash of horrifying nothingness, and then Joan was falling out onto a footpath. She hit someone's back. Aaron's. She steadied herself against him. For a long moment, she couldn't breathe. Whatever time they were in, she could hear cars.

And then she heard Ruth's voice. "You absolute *idiot*. You could have killed us both!"

Joan swallowed, almost in tears with relief. *"You're* the idiot."

"What if you'd fallen into that timeless abyss or whatever it was?" Ruth demanded. "What if you'd got yourself killed!"

Joan looked around. Whatever had frozen Whitehall at the stroke of midnight had lost its grip. Tourists and cars were moving again, wandering toward Big Ben and back the other way to Trafalgar Square.

Otherwise, everything looked just as it had when they'd left. The cars were still low and boxy; people's clothes were still loose.

"I think we're back in the nineties," Ruth said. "I was aiming for the night we just left."

"You did *great*," Joan said.

"Quiet," Aaron said sharply. "We're not safe yet."

They were drawing some attention from tourists walking past. Had they been seen jumping out of thin air? No. People didn't look shocked enough for that. Then she saw someone give her an up-and-down look.

"These clothes are really memorable," she murmured. Aaron and Tom could have passed without comment, but Joan and Ruth were obviously dressed for a gala.

Aaron swore. He stripped off his gray jacket, leaving him in a shirt and waistcoat. He passed the jacket to Joan. Tom passed his to Ruth.

Joan slid into it, remembering the other time she'd worn Aaron's jacket—terrified and cold, and covered in Gran's blood. Just like last time, she felt instantly better. The gray length covered almost three-quarters of her dress. Tom's covered even more of Ruth's. Joan caught Aaron looking at her as she straightened the hem. Maybe he was remembering that night too.

"Okay?" she whispered to him.

He nodded. His expression was difficult to make out. "Let's get out of here," he whispered back.

Joan craned to look farther up the road. The great gate into Whitehall Palace had vanished. In its place, there were dozens of people in dark suits.

"Guards," Aaron whispered.

Conrad was standing among them, illuminated by a street-light. His blond hair shone, reminding Joan of Aaron. Conrad bent to say something to a man with black hair and a very thin build.

"That man he's talking to," Tom whispered. "*That's* not a guard. I think that's one of the Patel family."

"We should get out of here," Aaron said. To Joan, he said: "The Patels can mire monsters in time—they can prevent us from traveling."

"Don't they have to touch you?" Ruth said.

"Not if they're strong," Tom said. "If they're strong then they can—" The man raised a hand and Tom broke off. "This guy's strong! Run!" he said.

But it was too late. The man made a sweeping gesture, encompassing the breadth of the street—from the Westminster end to Trafalgar. The world seemed to ripple around him, as if he were a dropped stone in a pond.

The ripple emanated out, too fast to avoid. Joan stumbled with the power of it. Beside her, Ruth and Aaron staggered. Tom flung a hand out for balance, but managed to keep hold of Frankie.

As if with some sixth sense, Conrad turned his head to them, unerring in the dark. He issued an instruction. Guards began to rush toward them.

"Run!" Tom said. He pointed to Trafalgar Square—crowded with tourists even this late at night. "Split up and *run!*"

Joan sprinted toward Trafalgar Square. At first she could hear the others' running footsteps, but soon she found herself alone.

In their planning, Tom had suggested a rendezvous in case they got separated: an ancient stone staircase in Wapping, once used by watermen to access the Thames.

It took Joan nearly two hours to get there. She jumped onto a bus at Trafalgar and stayed on it until she was sure that she hadn't been followed. After that, she made her way to Wapping on foot.

On the main street, she took a dark passage past the Town of Ramsgate pub to the foreshore of the Thames. She picked her way down the slippery stone stairs, trying not to fall in the dark. There wasn't much to the beach at the bottom of the stairs. It was tiny and sharp-rocked and stank of sea rot. Joan's feet crunched over sticks and pebbles and shells.

There was enough moonlight to see that the tide was out. No one else was on the beach yet. Joan squeezed her hands into fists, trying not to imagine that the others had been caught.

At the water's edge, Tower Bridge was unexpectedly close, still in its night lights. Nearby, on the water, Joan could just make out a bobbing rowboat, moored to something that looked homemade. Transport out of here, care of the Hathaways.

They'd all get on that rowboat, and Tom would take them to a Hathaway mooring for the night. They'd decide what to do after that.

Joan backed away from the shore and sat heavily on the old stone staircase.

There's something wrong about all of this, Ruth had said at the Court. *I feel as if we've got something wrong.*

Joan dropped her head into her hands. She could hear the river lapping against the bank. In. Out. In. Like breathing. *We've got something wrong,* Ruth had said. But the truth was, it was *Joan* who'd gotten something wrong. *She'd* made the others go to the Monster Court.

She'd been so sure that she was right. She'd been so sure that the *transformatio* would be in the Royal Archive that she'd risked everyone's life. But she'd gotten it wrong. Instead of a device that would save her family, they'd found an empty prison cell. Gran had given Joan a key to the Monster Court, and Joan had wasted it.

As always, the thought of Gran brought back that terrible night. Sometimes, it felt like all Joan's memories of her family had been overridden that night. When she thought of Gran, it was always of Gran in that room, dying.

Think of something else, she told herself. But the memory kept going. Gran's last words. *You're in very grave danger. Someday soon you'll come into an ability. A power.*

Joan remembered how she'd stood outside that wooden door. She'd slammed her hand against the lock and power had poured out of her. And after she'd touched it, the metal had been as dull as stone—as if she'd somehow returned it to ore. She thought about the dark marks on the necklace. What had she done to that lock? To that chain? Had she transmuted the metal? Was that her power—to change metal into stone?

Joan clenched and unclenched her hand, trying to feel for that strange power again. But whatever she'd done at White-hall, she couldn't feel a spark of it now.

She wasn't sure how long she sat there before a low whistle made her jump. She turned. Tom's bulky silhouette was at the top of the stairs. "Don't get up. I'll come to you," he called down softly.

He jogged down the slippery stairs with the sure foot of a boatman. Frankie trotted behind him with cheerful huffs.

Tom got person-size and then Tom-size, stumbling up to Joan, all muscles and dopey good humor. "All right?" he said. "Took me a while to get here."

"I'm fine. The others haven't arrived yet," Joan said. "What if they've been caught?"

"I saw Aaron around Temple. Ruth too. Don't worry. They're not far behind." Tom's battered face cut into a smile. "Here." He unhooked a woman's handbag from his shoulder and opened it to show Joan that it was bulging with pork pies. "Stole us some breakfast."

Joan pictured him taking time out from dodging the palace guards to snatch a purse. Then she pictured him emptying out the keys and cash to make room for something he really valued. In spite of her worry about Aaron and Ruth, she found herself wanting to laugh. Apparently, you could rely on Tom to keep things simple.

She felt in her pocket. The marzipan lions she'd taken from the palace hadn't fared well. One was missing its tail; the other was missing its head. Oh well. She offered them to him anyway. "If Ruth or Aaron brings some drinks, we'll have a proper picnic." She patted the step and shuffled over to make room for him.

Tom grinned, but he didn't sit down as Joan had expected.

"And the other thing?" he said. "You have that too, right?"

Joan looked up at him. "I—" She hesitated. "What?" The sky was a predawn gray now. A trick of the light had put Tom's mouth in shadow, removing some of the usual slackness from his expression.

"I thought it would be in his bedding," Tom said. "Did you find it under the desk?"

Joan stared at Tom's silly face. Except that right now, his eyes were strangely sharp. The scar across his eyebrow was a pale slash in the morning light. He looked more like a thug than ever.

She *had* found something at the Court. Something wedged into the notch under the desk. She'd forgotten about it in the rush to escape.

"I don't know what you mean," she whispered.

"Let's not insult each other," Tom said, almost gently. "Neither of us was going to leave that room empty-handed. And you made the first move to leave."

Joan got to her feet slowly, careful to telegraph her movements in case he took it as an attack. Tom had seemed a gentle giant—not stupid, but slow and a little clumsy at times. Right now, though, he didn't seem so slow. And if he wasn't slow, maybe he wasn't clumsy at all.

Joan put her hand against her pocket. She could feel the thing she'd found—a square of lightweight plastic. She'd barely glanced at it before she'd pocketed it; it had been white, with no markings. She'd dismissed it as unimportant when she'd retrieved it, but now she wondered . . .

"Whatever you think I have," she said, "I don't."

Tom's expression seemed so sharp now that he could have been a different person.

Joan remembered suddenly how she'd met him. *He'd* approached her. He'd called out to her at the market when he'd seen her necklace—he'd known it was a key to the Monster Court. Later, Ruth had said that he was a former Court Guard. Everyone at the market knew, she'd said. Had Tom deliberately spread information that he'd been a guard? Had he known Joan would turn to him, needing a guide inside the Court?

Tom gave her a crooked smile. "You know they used to hang pirates here?" His tone was casual, but something about the way he said it made Joan's heart thump. "They hanged Captain Kidd right there." He nodded at the stone wall at the back of the stairs. Green algae covered two-thirds of the stone, an ominous sign of how high the Thames could climb. "This place isn't much in this time," he said. "But it used to be like Victoria Station here. Kids running around the docks. Whelk sellers calling out their wares. 'Whelks, whelks, penny a lot!' And the river so full of boats that we'd all be bumping up against each other."

Tom took the last steps in a casual stride. Joan stumbled back. Water splashed. She looked down to see that the river was pooling around her feet. The tide was coming in.

"They had to hang Captain Kidd twice," Tom said. "First time, the rope snapped and he thumped down into the mud.

The whole crowd thought he'd get a reprieve. That since the rope had snapped, he'd be spared. But he wasn't. He was hanged again, and the second time it took." His eyes had glazed, as if in memory, but when Joan shifted her weight, they sharpened again. "And afterward, they put him on a pole and let the Thames take him three times. Three tides."

"What do you want?" Joan said.

"What did any of us want?" he said. "To get to the Royal *Archive*." He almost spat the word. "But he wasn't there."

"He?" Joan felt like a complete idiot then. She'd assumed that the archive had been a room somewhere else in the palace. It hadn't occurred to her that the archive and the prisoner had been one and the same. Did that mean . . . Joan blurted: "*He's* the *transformatio*? He's the device? He's the one who can change the timeline?*"

Tom made an impatient sound. "There's no device. The *transformatio* really is just a myth. There's no way to change the timeline." He held out his hand. "But I know he left something in that room. Give it to me."

Joan wanted to take another step back, but she couldn't. The staircase was blocked by Tom's big frame. Behind Joan, the river was rising. The water swirled around her feet, lapping at the bottom of her dress. She put her hand in her pocket and closed her finger and thumb over the plastic square. "I'm a Hunt," she warned him. Had they ever mentioned her lack of the Hunt power in front of Tom? "If I hide it, you'll never find it."

"You won't do that," Tom said.

"Step back or I will."

A male voice in the distance made them both tense. "Maybe if we'd gone through Cheapside, as I'd said, we'd have been here ages ago."

Aaron. Joan breathed out, relieved. She'd never been so glad to hear his tetchy tone.

Then, less distantly: "Guards were all over the square mile, you idiot." Ruth.

"It's three against one now," Joan said to Tom. But it wasn't. Not quite yet.

"Do you even know what you found?" Tom said, low and intense. "It's a message. But you won't be able to decode it."

"Oh, but you could, I suppose?"

"Yes," Tom said. "The message was meant for me."

Joan hesitated then. "For you?"

Ruth and Aaron's bickering was getting closer. In a second, they'd be upon them. Tom would glance up, and Joan would have a moment to shove him off the stairs.

Still she hesitated. What was she missing? "Why would the prisoner have left you a message? Who was he?" And why had Nick been looking for him? There was too much that Joan didn't understand.

Tom shifted on his feet, as if weighing his options.

"Don't come any closer," Joan warned him. "I'll use the Hunt power to hide it."

"You won't use the Hunt power," Tom said.

"Why do you keep *saying* that?"

Aaron appeared at the top of the stairs. "Oh good, you're both here," he called down. He started to descend.

"Because you don't have the Hunt power," Tom said. He bent close and put his mouth to Joan's ear. "I saw what you did to that lock," he whispered.

A chill rippled through Joan's body. *Someday soon you'll come into an ability*, Gran had said. *A power. You can trust no one with the knowledge of it.*

Tom straightened just as Ruth came into view too. Then, as though Joan weren't any kind of threat at all, he turned his back on her, deliberately. "You took your time," he called up to the others.

Joan stared at his broad back. Aaron had already begun descending the slippery stairs. ". . . guards are everywhere," he was saying.

"Hey, just stay up there," Joan called up to Aaron. She felt cold all over. Aaron would have more leverage if he stayed above them. *Tom's not who we thought*, she wanted to say. *Ruth was right—I got something wrong about this.*

But something about the way Tom had said *the message was meant for me* gave her pause. "Just stay there," she called up again, because Aaron was still walking down. She kicked up water to show him that the river had reached the bottom step. "Tide's coming in."

"No, we have to go right now," Ruth said, and now she was picking her way down too. "While there's still some darkness to hide us."

"Guards are *everywhere*," Aaron said.

"We can't go to the Hathaways," Joan said. No way were they getting into a boat with Tom. No way were they going to the Hathaways, where they'd be entirely in Tom's power. But neither did Joan want to escalate this—not until she knew what was going on.

And now, finally, Aaron slowed his descent. "Your family didn't come through?" he said to Tom.

Tom shrugged. He turned back to Joan, looking at her as intently as she was watching him. Maybe wondering why she hadn't ratted him out yet. Joan was kind of wondering that too. *The message was meant for me.*

"Our shoes are getting wet," she said to Tom quietly. That wasn't quite true. The tide had only risen to Joan's step. Tom's feet were still dry.

Tom shifted his weight. He was a big man, but looming above her, he looked like a giant. If there was a scuffle, Joan knew who'd come out best. The stairs were lethally slippery with lichen. And Hathaway territory was the Thames and canals. Tom had grown up on the water.

Joan raised her voice to address Aaron. "Where can we go?"

"If not the Hathaways?" Aaron said. It was more than one question.

Tom didn't take his eyes off Joan. But to her surprise and relief, he backed up a step. "Not the Hathaways," he agreed, answering one of them.

Joan didn't dare blink as she climbed above the tide. She half thought Tom would try something while she was off-balance, but he didn't move. He hadn't touched her when they'd been alone together either, she realized slowly. He'd threatened her, but he hadn't hurt her. He could have easily taken what she'd found by force, but he hadn't. She couldn't understand it.

"We need to go somewhere *now*," Ruth said.

"Not an inn or a human hotel," Tom said. "The Court will have guards all over them."

"We can't go to my family. They'd turn us all in," Aaron said.

Ruth usually took any opportunity to bait Aaron about the Olivers, but she only said tensely: "Then where?"

"There's nowhere else to go," Aaron said. "Nowhere off the Court's radar. They have access to every human record. They have spies everywhere. They know every—" His mouth snapped shut suddenly. From his expression, he'd realized something.

"Aaron?" Joan said.

Aaron's gaze lifted to her face. There was an intensity in his expression that wasn't usually there. Without knowing why, Joan found it hard to breathe under the weight of his attention.

The river washed in and out. A bird chirped and was answered by another. Morning was coming upon them fast. And still Aaron just looked at Joan. "Aaron?" she said uncertainly.

His gaze left her finally, turning to the water. "There's a

safe house in Southwark," he said. "The Court doesn't know about it."

"How do you know?" Ruth said.

"My mother told me," Aaron said. His tone was final. It was clear that no more questions were allowed. He turned and walked up the stairs.

NINETEEN

———◦———

The sky was still mostly gray as they walked from Wapping, being even more careful than usual not to get caught by security cameras.

Beside Joan, Ruth was quiet. Joan was worried about her. Ruth had already been exhausted back at the palace, and now she was out of breath just from walking.

Joan put an arm around her, trying to take some of her weight. But she knew that if anything happened, Ruth wouldn't be able to run.

"How far is the safe house?" she asked Aaron.

"Not far." Aaron glanced at Ruth. If Joan didn't know better, she'd have said he was worried too. "But we'll have to cross the river." To Tom, he said: "Are you sure your family can't spare a boat?"

"They can't," Joan said flatly.

Aaron blinked, but to Joan's surprise, Tom backed her up. "We'd be seen crossing the river by boat."

Joan could feel the wary tension between them. She hadn't told the others what had happened at the watermen's stairs. She didn't even know why. The sensible thing would be to get herself and the others away from Tom.

The message was meant for me, Tom had said. Joan had been turning those words over and over in her mind. It hadn't even been the words; it had been the way he'd said them.

She couldn't make sense of it all. Gran's key to the Monster Court. The cover-up of Nick's killings. Rumors of a device that could change the timeline. An empty prison cell where the device should have been. *The message was meant for me.*

Joan felt as though she'd found pieces of a puzzle but didn't understand the picture they'd make when fit together. There was still something missing. Something she didn't understand. But what?

"It's almost dawn," Aaron said. "We need to get to the other bank before daybreak." He chewed his lip. "We're close to Tower Bridge."

"The bridges will be watched," Ruth said.

"We might be lucky," Aaron said.

As they approached Tower Bridge, Aaron swore under his breath. Blue lights flashed from parked police cars. There was a police checkpoint at the bridge. Cars and pedestrians were being questioned and searched. "Those police are monsters," Aaron whispered. "Most of them, anyway."

"How is that possible?" Joan said.

"The Court places monsters high up in human circles."

"Won't all these Londoners find this strange?" Joan said.

"They're used to it," Tom said. "In this time, there are IRA bombings for years on either side of us." He ran a hand over his face. "If there's a checkpoint here, there'll be a ring of security around London. Court Guards will be all over the Tube."

It was true that the motorists weren't asking questions as the supposed police peered through their windows. As Joan watched, a car was allowed to roll through. A police officer beckoned the next car with a gloved hand. "They're letting people through," Joan said. "What if we just walked down the footpath? How would they know we were the ones?"

"We can't be seen," Aaron said tightly. "There are Olivers and Griffiths among the guards."

Ruth breathed a curse. "The Griffith family can induce truth," she whispered to Joan tiredly. "Any monster who passes through will be stopped and questioned."

"We're losing night," Tom said.

"We could try the tunnel to Rotherhithe," Ruth said. "It isn't far."

"That tunnel was closed to foot traffic more than a century ago," Aaron said. "Only trains use it now."

"There are still ways through it," Ruth said. "If we're quick, we'll make it before the first train."

Joan exchanged a glance with Aaron. The last thing Ruth looked right now was quick.

Ruth guided them away from Tower Bridge to a round brick structure, filthy with caked dirt. Tufts of grass sprouted from cracked concrete around the brick.

"Lavatory?" Aaron said dubiously.

"Ventilation shaft," Ruth said. With two fingers, she mimed walking up onto the roof of the shaft, and then climbing down and down and down.

Joan could feel Ruth shaking with exhaustion as she and Tom boosted her up. Tom hoisted himself up next, one-handed, his muscles shifting with the effort. He'd tucked Frankie under one arm, and she craned inquisitively over his shoulder.

"I'm fine," Ruth mumbled. "I'm fine." But she seemed to be saying it to herself, hoping to make it true.

They climbed down—three levels at least. Ruth's gasping breaths got louder and louder. By the time they got to the bottom, her arms were shaking so much that Tom had to help her down the last rungs of the ladder.

"Are you all right?" Joan whispered.

Ruth nodded. "Listen for trains," she managed.

They were in an underground tunnel with a high, curving ceiling. Strips of metal arched overhead at regular intervals. Down the tunnel, the effect was of concentric arches. The wall was lit with old-fashioned swan-necked lamps. Train tracks ran along the ground.

"Don't touch the tracks," Ruth warned. "They're electrified."

"What happens if a train comes?" Joan asked.

Ruth gestured ahead. Between each pair of lamps, there was a recessed archway. There wasn't one tunnel, but two, Joan realized, with the archways connecting them.

There was a glint of something bright near Joan's foot. She

wiped at the ground with her shoe. Under the dirt, between the tracks, there were tiles: white and blue, with a winding floral pattern.

"There used to be a market down here in the 1800s," Aaron said. "People sold souvenirs in these archways. There were fortune-tellers. Monkeys."

"Don't tell me you came slumming down here," Ruth said.

"Tourists and slum dwellers are the best people to steal time from," Aaron said. When Joan looked over at him, he shrugged. "What?"

You know this is wrong, Nick had said. Joan thought about standing among all those gifts to the King. Those marvels, those horrors. She was struck with a sudden and intense yearning—so strong that, for a moment, she was afraid she was trying to travel. But it wasn't a yearning for a different time. It was for Nick—for the Nick she'd known before all this.

She remembered again the time he'd rescued the wasp. It had been stuck in the Gilt Room, rattling behind a curtain. *Kill it*, one of the tourists had said, but Nick had captured it in a cup and released it outside. *It's just in the wrong place*, he'd said.

Joan had trusted Nick's judgment: his moral compass. Just being near him had made her feel like the person she'd wanted to be. And now . . . She folded her arms around herself.

She was so morally compromised now. It had been at the back of her mind all the time since the Pit. She remembered telling Gran all those years ago that she wanted to be Superman. *You're a monster*, Gran had said.

As they walked down the tunnel, Joan became aware of a humming sound getting louder and louder. "What's that noise?" It didn't sound like a train.

"The pumps," Ruth said.

"We must be under the river," Aaron said.

Joan looked up at the ceiling. The air smelled of damp concrete. It was scary to think that the Thames was roaring over them. It reminded Joan of the wave of power that had engulfed them as they'd fled Whitehall.

"What exactly happened to us outside Whitehall?" she said. "What did that man do?"

"He hit us with the Patel family power," Aaron said. "He mired us in time. We won't be able to travel again until the strike wears off."

"It wears off?" Joan said.

The was a pause before Aaron answered, as if he'd heard something strange in her voice. "Eventually," he said.

"Difficult to say how long we'll be stuck in this time," Tom said. "Could be a day. Could be months."

"One of the Victorian-era Hunts stole a Patel chop once," Ruth said to Joan. "The Patels mired her for years. Forced her to live in a time she'd been in before."

"What happened?" Joan asked. Aaron had told her the rules—you couldn't be in the same time twice. The timeline didn't allow it.

"What happens if you're in a tunnel and can't get out of

the way of a train?" Aaron said, dry.

"We don't know what happened to her," Ruth said. "People who meet themselves in time vanish. Some people think that the timeline flings you away into its outer reaches. Or that you vanish into nothingness."

"It's rare," Aaron said. "The timeline doesn't allow you to jump into a time you already occupy. And if you get too close just by living, you start to feel an intense urge to leave. But you *can* live your way into it—whether by being mired or stubborn. The Olivers say that if that happens, you get pushed outside time itself."

Outside time itself. Joan shivered, thinking of that shadowy abyss of nothingness outside the walls of the Monster Court.

"What's the point of speculating?" Tom growled. "Either way, you're gone."

That seemed to silence them all. They walked through the tunnel, listening for trains. Joan imagined what this place must have looked like in the 1800s—lit up with gas lamps and crowded with market stalls and tourists in suits and long dresses.

"Are we going to talk about what else happened at the Monster Court?" Ruth said finally. She was flagging. Her voice was getting more and more hoarse and tired.

"What's there to talk about?" Aaron said.

"We didn't find the device," Ruth said. "We can't change the timeline."

Joan glanced at Tom and found him looking back at her. *There's no device,* he'd said at the watermen's stairs. No device meant no way to save their families. Joan couldn't bear to think about that yet.

"What's there to talk about?" Aaron said again. "We failed. We came out empty-handed. We barely escaped with our lives. And now Conrad is after us. We'll live out the rest of our lives running from godforsaken time to godforsaken time. And one day we'll turn a corner, and Conrad will be standing there."

Ruth said: "Listen, if you're going to—"

Joan held up her hand to quiet them. There was a glint of light ahead. A train?

"We're almost through," Tom said, and Joan realized that she was seeing daylight. From bank to bank, it didn't take long to walk under the river. And outside, dawn had finally broken.

The tunnel emerged where a train would have—right into Rotherhithe Station, platforms on either side. There was a security guard on one of the platforms. He paced away from them. From his posture, he seemed both cold and bored. He was clearly waiting for trains, and not expecting anyone to walk out of the tunnel.

Monster? Joan mouthed to Aaron.

Can't see, Aaron mouthed back. He needed to see the man's eyes, Joan remembered.

Silently, Ruth pointed out one camera and then another one.

Tom boosted each of them up onto the opposite platform. Before the guard could turn, they tiptoed up the stairs, and then they were out of the station, on the south side of the river.

The south bank was more industrial than in Joan's time. The breeze across the river smelled like tar. As they made their way west, Joan felt those jolts of alienation and familiarity that she was beginning to associate with this time. London Bridge and Tower Bridge looked just the same, but the Shard was missing. The Millennium Bridge was missing.

Ahead of her, Aaron held Ruth's elbow to keep her steady, solicitous and gentlemanly. Joan wondered—not for the first time—which period Aaron had actually grown up in. He sometimes seemed to slip into manners from another age.

Or maybe he wasn't from anywhere. Maybe monsters just traveled and traveled through the past and the future, never stopping for long.

"You haven't told them," Tom said softly to Joan. Joan wasn't sure if it was a question or an observation. Even more softly, he said: "They don't know about that power of yours either, do they?"

Joan shivered, remembering again how she'd slammed her hand against the lock. Power had poured out of her. And when she'd lifted her hand, the metal had turned into ore.

They'd fallen a little behind the other two, and now Tom slowed even more. Joan was suddenly very aware of his muscled bulk. "Walk faster," she said.

Tom smiled crookedly, but he lengthened his steps again just enough to keep pace with the others. His gaze turned to the river. "You can almost imagine that you can see the territories of the great families from here," he mused. "Olivers and Alis in the west. Nowaks and Argents north. Griffiths and Mtawalis south. Patels and Portellis, east. Lius, the center. Hathaways, the river. And the Nightingales . . ." He paused slightly. "Anywhere they please."

He'd missed a family. "And the Hunts," Joan said.

"And the Hunts," Tom acknowledged. "Always moving around the edges of other monsters' territories. As a child I used to think they were running from something."

Ahead of them, Aaron and Ruth turned into a narrow alley. "Stay in front of me," Joan warned Tom. The buildings here were built close and sunless. Warehouses and converted factories.

"You need to give me what you found," Tom said softly.

"What it is?"

"I told you. It's a message."

Joan shook her head. "I'm going to need to know more than that."

A muscle jumped in Tom's jaw. That was the only warning Joan had before the sudden burst of violence. In one fast movement, Tom had closed the gap between himself and the others. He threw Ruth and Aaron into a wall with easy strength.

Before Joan could react, Tom was shoving her too. Joan's shoulders hit the wall. After a stunned moment, she dove at him. He pushed her back again, almost casually, with one big hand. Joan was furious with herself. Tom had shown her exactly what he was at the rendezvous, and she'd just—

A car door slammed nearby. Joan froze.

Tom stared at Joan meaningfully, one finger at his lips. *Shhh.* He released his grip on her. She realized then that Tom had pushed her—and himself—into a doorway recess. Aaron and Ruth were in an identical recess opposite. Anyone looking from the street would see an empty alleyway.

Two more car doors slammed. Then footsteps sounded.

Joan risked peering around the recess. About twenty paces away, a woman and two men were walking into the alley from the street. Joan pulled back again, heart thumping. They were all wearing pins with the winged-lion insignia. All three were easily Tom's height, although not quite as muscular in build.

"How much longer?" one of the men said. "We've been patrolling all night."

"There was a sighting near here," the woman said.

"There've been sightings all over. You ask me, they've already escaped this time."

"They were hit by Sai Patel himself. They're still here," the woman said. "Conrad pulled guards in from all over. Took me out of the Victorian era. If he did that, he needs them found."

The footsteps got closer. Joan could hardly breathe. In the doorway opposite, Ruth and Aaron looked terrified. The doorways were too shallow to hide any of them completely. If the guards just looked—properly *looked* down the alleyway—they'd see all of them standing there.

"Do you believe the rumors?" the woman said. "Of strange powers used in the archive? Something forbidden." She lowered her voice. "Something *wrong.*"

"Above my pay grade," the man said.

"What about that other tip-off, though?" the woman said. "About a half-human girl with a strange power? That can't be a coincidence."

Joan couldn't breathe at all now. They were talking about *her*.

In the opposite doorway, Ruth's face creased with confusion. She had no idea what the guards were talking about—not about the power and not about the tip-off.

Joan had a suspicion of where the tip-off had come from. *Dorothy Hunt is not a good person,* the innkeeper had said. Joan's gran would never have hurt her. But the woman in the bar . . . Joan remembered how that young version of Gran had looked at her: as if Joan were nothing to her. Horribly and annoyingly, Joan felt tears prickling. She clenched her teeth, forcing them back.

"Wouldn't mind that reward, though," the man said.

"A favor from Conrad himself," the woman said. "Imagine that."

The tips of their long shadows reached Joan's feet. Tom touched Joan's hand to get her attention. *Ready?* he mouthed to her. Joan was almost too tense to nod. Tom gave her a slight smile, trying to be reassuring. *Me first,* he mouthed.

The shadows stayed motionless. The moment seemed to stretch and stretch. If not for Tom's chest rising and falling beside her, Joan would have thought that time itself had frozen again. She began to shake from unused adrenaline. Beside her, Tom's muscles were smooth and ready as though he could have waited all day in that tensed posture.

A sudden loud noise made Joan jump. It sounded like the

squeaky music from an old-fashioned video game.

The woman groaned. "Just because we're in the nineties doesn't mean you need a stupid ringtone," she complained.

"There was a sighting near Rotherhithe Station." It was the second man—the one who hadn't spoken yet.

And now, finally, sounds of movement. The shadows began to retreat.

"Were they caught on camera?" the first man said.

"If they'd been caught on any camera, we'd have them already," the woman said. She sounded impatient.

"Get in," the taciturn man said. "Conrad wants—" Then the car door slammed shut, and his voice cut off.

Joan waited while the car drove away, the rumbling of it quieting until the alley was silent. Beside her, Tom relaxed, slowly, his body loosening. He'd saved them, Joan thought. He'd protected them from the guards.

Joan couldn't make sense of it. He'd pretended to help them to get into the archive. Then he'd seemed about to betray them. And now he'd saved them instead. He could have turned Joan in—there was even a reward—but he hadn't. Why?

As she turned, she found herself caught in Aaron's direct line of sight. He was still in the doorway, and he was looking at her in the same intense way he had at the watermen's stairs.

Before Joan could say anything to him, Aaron abruptly pushed away from the door. "Come on," he said. "The safe house is this way."

TWENTY

The safe house was unexpectedly homey. There were family photos on the hallway walls, the kind only interesting to someone's mum: a little girl dressed as a pirate, her dad kneeling to tie the eye patch; the same girl older and asleep next to a napping cat. A whole-family shot: Mum, Dad, girl, and a new baby.

Joan stopped abruptly in the hallway. Had they broken into someone's actual home? Aaron hadn't had a key. Ruth had had to pick the lock.

Aaron stumbled into her back, and Joan turned just enough to put a finger in front of his lips, not quite touching him. He gave her an incredulous look. Behind him, Tom lifted his head—alert.

They listened. Nothing. No creaking floorboards, no whispered phone conversations with the police. No water running, no fridge buzzing.

A minute passed. Two minutes. Aaron's expression shifted from incredulous to irritated.

"Oh, for heaven's sake," he said finally, in his normal, superior voice. "There's no one here. It's as I told you. A safe house."

"Sorry if I didn't want to just blunder in," Joan said, but her heart wasn't in it. No one was home. The house was too cold, the air too stale. If the family in the photographs had ever lived in this house, they weren't here now.

"How *did* you know about this place exactly?" Ruth asked Aaron.

"It doesn't matter," Aaron said. That was even less information than he'd given at the watermen's stairs. Again there was a flatness in his tone that brooked no questions.

They trooped in, shoes loud against the floorboards. The hallway opened into a cozy sitting room. Aaron collapsed onto a fat little sofa piled with cushions. Frankie huffed and flopped onto the floor next to him. She seemed as tired as the rest of them. Ruth stopped at a bedroom door, looking longingly at the bed.

"Lie down," Joan told her. "I'll check the place out."

The house was simple enough: sitting room, one bedroom, kitchen, bathroom, separate toilet. Joan opened every cupboard big enough to hold a person—flinging them open at first, SWAT-style, and then opening them with more and more sheepishness. So, no one was hiding in the airing cupboard, then.

In the kitchen, animal magnets and postcards covered the fridge—Spain, Cornwall, Wales. Joan plucked off a postcard from Dover. *Wish you were here* floated above the cliffs. She flipped it over. The writing side was blank, the fifty-pence price tag still stuck to the corner. She opened the fridge. Empty and dark.

A little wooden table was nestled into the corner of the room. At first glance, it had seemed battered—as all kitchen tables were. But Joan could see now that the top was unmarked and dusty. Had anyone ever eaten at it? She replaced the postcard and folded her arms around herself. The whole house seemed creepy suddenly. An empty movie set. A furniture display room.

"Hey," someone said behind her.

Joan jumped and spun around. Tom gave her an apologetic look from the open pantry. "Tea?" He held up a packet of Tetley's, the box almost comically small in his huge hand. He was the picture of harmlessness.

Joan stared at him warily. She still wasn't even sure why she'd let him in here—after what had happened at the watermen's stairs. He'd shown that he was dangerous, and yet . . . She remembered again his intensity of feeling when he'd asked her for the message. But he hadn't hurt her when he could have taken it by force. And then he'd saved them from the guards. And, more than any of that, she kept thinking about the way he'd said those words. *The message was meant for me. . . .*

"Why didn't you turn me over to the guards?" she asked him. "It sounds like there's a reward."

Tom put the tea on the table. "I would die before I'd help the Court," he said flatly.

Joan searched his face. He'd proved himself an outstanding liar, but she didn't think he was lying now. His mouth had twisted slightly as he'd said *Court*. As if he hated the word.

Joan ran her hand over her face. She had to think, but she

was so tired. She was so bloody tired. She wanted to lie down right here in the kitchen and sleep for days.

"I'll make tea," Tom said. "And we should eat as well."

They really needed to talk. But Joan nodded. "All right."

"How do pork pies and marzipan sound?" Tom said.

"Like heaven," Joan said seriously, and he nodded, seeming too tired or too tense to smile.

Tom took the pies from his stolen purse. He opened and closed cupboards and drawers, pulling out plates. His bulky body seemed to fill the kitchen, but he moved with surprising nimbleness as he rinsed and filled the kettle.

Joan put the marzipan lions onto a plate. They were just smashed paste now. She found some mugs for the tea. It didn't take long, and when she was finished, she leaned against the fridge door.

She found herself unwilling to shift the mood back into something more dangerous again. But she knew that she had to.

"Who was he?" she asked. Tom stilled, his broad back to her. Without the clattering of plates and cups, the room was suddenly very quiet. "Who was the prisoner in that cell?"

"I told you," Tom said. "The archive."

"Who was he to *you*?"

Tom turned finally, but he didn't answer. He had a boxer's body, with big arms and broad shoulders; he was intimidating, even when he was relaxed.

"If he'd been at the palace, would you have brought him back to the rendezvous?" Joan asked.

"No," Tom said. That should have ended the conversation,

but Joan was pretty sure she understood now.

"That room he was in," she said. "The bucket. The mattress."

A muscle jumped in Tom's jaw. "I saw the room."

"He was a prisoner," Joan said. "But he left you a message. He knew you were coming."

She was watching closely enough to see agony cross Tom's face, and then she knew for sure. She'd felt it herself every moment since the massacre. The inability to save someone you loved. "You went there for him, didn't you?" she said. "You went there to rescue him."

"Yes." Tom's shoulders rose unsteadily. He was trying to keep his composure. Joan knew that feeling too. She'd barely been keeping it together since her family had died.

She took a deep breath. She felt in her pocket for the plastic square she'd found. She held it out to him. "You were right," she said. "It was under the desk."

Tom grasped it at once, closing his fist over it, as though afraid she might take it back.

"What do you think the message will be?" she asked him. "Do you think there'll be something about the *transformatio*?"

"No," Tom said, almost gently. "The *transformatio* is a myth." It was what he'd said at the rendezvous, but Joan was sure now he was telling the truth. She felt her stomach drop. "Let's go into the sitting room," he said.

"The sitting room?"

"We'll need some space to watch."

Aaron was asleep on the sofa. He looked deceptively angelic like this. His lashes were as long as a girl's. "Aaron," Joan said softly. She felt bad about waking him. None of them had slept much over the last few days. She touched his shoulder.

He opened his eyes. He blinked and then gave her a heart-meltingly sweet smile. "Hi," he said. Then he seemed to realize where he was. He grimaced. "Oh." He sat up, running a hand through his hair. "What time is it?"

"Still morning," Joan said. "We need to talk. Tom . . ." She looked over at him. Tom was watching her, warily. "Tom's been keeping some things from us."

"What things?" Ruth said. She was standing in the bedroom doorway. She looked exhausted. Her face was still gray.

Tom hesitated and then uncurled his fingers to reveal the little square of plastic.

"What's that?" Aaron said groggily. He started to frown. "Where did you get that?" He seemed to recognize it. "That's— that's *illegal*. That's incredibly far from its time."

"I found it in the prison cell," Joan said. "Tom thinks it's a message. . . from the prisoner."

Aaron's eyes were narrowing. Joan could see him making connections. The change of plans at the rendezvous. The way Tom had been standing over Joan on the steps.

"His name is Jamie Liu," Tom said. "He's been a prisoner of the Monster Court for . . . well, I don't know how long, from his perspective. From mine, three years."

"What exactly is going on?" Ruth said, and she might have

been tired, but her voice was sharp and suspicious. "What do you know?" she said to Tom.

"I think you should play the message," Joan said to Tom.

Tom pushed the coffee table to one side and rolled up the rug. Joan could feel the tension in the room. Tom's size alone was part of it. His muscled bulk seemed to fill the whole space.

He looked at the corners of the room, the placement of the sofa, as if assessing angles. "Stand back," he said. He waited for them all to shuffle away. Then he put the plastic square at his feet. The square seemed to shimmer.

A small chessboard appeared, floating in midair. It was the strange type of chess Joan had noticed in the Serpentine Inn: the kind with elephant and sailing-ship pieces instead of bishops and rooks. For some reason, seeing the board made Tom's expression soften. "Just because you beat me that first time," he murmured.

"It's a game?" Ruth asked.

"It's a password," Tom said. "One that only two people know." He placed a white pawn, and then a black one, and then kept going, alternating between white and black, his fingers moving with unhesitating confidence. The pieces clacked against the board just as though they were real. But Tom wasn't quite touching them, Joan saw. And when he tossed aside the first pawn, it vanished like a popped bubble.

He was replaying a game, Joan thought. Recalling every move without effort. Whoever had set this password had known he would. Joan thought about the drunk idiot he'd seemed to be just a few days ago. The real Tom Hathaway was turning out to be an entirely different person.

Finally, the white king stood alone, surrounded by black. Tom moved a knight into checkmate.

And then the board was gone. For a moment, a number floated in midair: 10.

And when that was gone, Nick was in the room.

"Run!" Joan shouted.

Tom's arm shot out, catching Joan as she tried to flee. "It's okay, it's okay." He steadied her.

"It's *him*!" Joan screamed at him. "It's the hero!"

"He's not really here," Tom said. "It's just a recording."

Nick didn't look like a recording. He looked as real as anything in the room. Joan's heart was pounding. Aaron had tried to run too. His back was pressed against the wall. Ruth was behind the pushed-back sofa. Her eyes were huge, breath coming fast.

Nick looked deceptively unthreatening. He was sitting in a wooden chair. And now that Joan wasn't freaking out, she could see what Tom meant. Nick was young—fourteen, maybe. And he wasn't here in this house. He was in the kitchen of a different house. There was a microwave, a fridge.

Movement in the kitchen became a man, walking toward Nick. He was clearly a monster. Nick was wearing a T-shirt and black jeans. But the monster was dressed for a different century. He wore a suit and a top hat. He removed the hat now, revealing sleek black hair.

He placed the hat carefully on the kitchen counter and stood in front of Nick's chair.

Joan swallowed. *"Run,"* she whispered to the man, even though it was pointless if this was only a recording.

Without warning, the man slapped Nick hard across the face.

Joan gasped. Nick lifted his head slowly. The slap had bloodied his mouth. Joan closed her eyes, not wanting to see what happened next. In a way, having her eyes closed was worse. She remembered how Nick had shoved the sword into Lucien—in and then out. She remembered how he'd hurled the blade into Edmund's chest. She remembered Lucien's blank face.

She remembered Gran, lying dead on the sofa.

There was another sharp crack. Joan's eyes flew open again. She'd expected to see the man dead, but he was still standing over Nick, and now there was more blood—all over Nick's nose and mouth.

"What is this?" Joan could hear the horror in her voice. It didn't make sense. It had taken Nick just seconds to kill Lucien.

Expression cold, the man drove his fist into Nick's jaw. Nick rocked back, just taking it. His arms were bound to the armrests of the chair, Joan realized.

The man struck him again. And now, finally, Nick reacted. "Please," he whispered. Blood was running down his chin, down his neck. His nose looked broken. "Please, no more. Please—"

"Stop," a woman's voice said.

The scene froze. Or at least Nick froze, mouth half-open, pleading. The man wasn't frozen. He looked over his shoulder at someone out of frame. "I can get him there," he said.

"No," the woman's voice said. "Start again."

The scene vanished, leaving the sitting room empty. Joan stared at the space where Nick had been, sickened. After the massacre, she'd imagined hurting him for what he'd done to her family. But actually *seeing* him get hurt in front of her . . . hearing the crack of breaking bone . . . She wanted to throw up.

A number floated in the air: 15.

Nick was in the chair again, face uninjured. The monster stood over him. Joan could hardly breathe.

"Who shall I kill first?" the monster said to him. "You have so many siblings. Should I go youngest to oldest, and kill your parents last? Or the other way around?"

"Leave them alone!" Nick said. "They're—"

The monster struck Nick's face, breaking his nose again. Joan flinched hard. A terrible dread began to fill her chest.

"Stop," the woman's voice said. "Start again."

The number 93 floated in the air.

"What *is* this?" Aaron said. "He's the hero. Why isn't he fighting back?"

Joan was beginning to understand, and it was more horrifying than she wanted to believe. When Nick appeared again, she crawled closer to him.

This time, he was on his knees, shaking. The chair was on its side, rope still tied to its arms. Nick seemed to have escaped it, but he hadn't gone far—he was kneeling by a dark-haired woman and man on the floor. His parents, Joan guessed. They were dead. They had the same stillness that Lucien had had, that Gran had had.

Where before Joan had tried to run, now she couldn't get close enough. Nick's expression was a mix of disbelief and devastation. Joan knew exactly how terrible that moment felt.

At the sound of footsteps, Nick scrabbled up, grabbing for a knife on the kitchen counter.

"Now that's what I like to see," the monster said. "Some initiative."

Nick backed up, the knife shaking in his hand. *Throw the knife*, Joan willed him, and then wondered at herself. Whose side was she on?

"Look at you," the man said, sounding amused. "Armed with a knife. And here I am with only my bare hands." He held them up in mockery, as though Nick were arresting him. He was still advancing. "But then, I killed them with my bare hands, didn't I?"

"You—you just touched them," Nick said uncertainly. "You touched their necks. And they fell."

"That's right," the man said. "Because I'm a monster."

"A monster?" Nick still sounded confused.

"I stole your parents' time from them," the man said. "All that they had left in them. Just like I've stolen from hundreds of people before them. Just like I'm going to steal your life from you."

"You're not well," Nick said. The man was within arm's reach of Nick now, close enough for Nick to stab him. "You're not a monster," Nick said in that serious way Joan was so familiar with. "You're a human, and you're sick. You need help."

"Stop," the woman's voice said.

Once again, Nick froze. And then Joan was sure. She breathed out slowly.

The monster turned again to the woman out of frame. "With respect, must we use this boy? How many times have we killed his parents? He's always so *virtuous* afterward." He spat the word *virtuous* as though it were a curse. "Perhaps a different human . . ."

"This is the boy," the woman said. "Not in spite of his virtuousness, but because of it. When we break him, that quality will turn into righteous fury." The glee in her voice made Joan want to scream. "Now do it again."

210

Nick was in the chair, voice hoarse. "You don't have to do this. You—"

"Stop. Again."

1100

There were more bodies on the kitchen floor. Joan couldn't bear to look at them this time. *You have so many siblings,* the man had said to Nick.

Nick had talked about his family; he'd said that they'd all

lived crowded together in a tiny flat. He'd never liked talking about himself, but he'd talked to Joan.

And now Nick had his knife to the man's throat. *"Why?"* His voice sounded raw. He was sobbing.

"Because I'm a monster," the man said. "They weren't the first and they won't be the last."

To Joan's shock, Nick shoved the knife into the monster's neck. As he fell, Nick's knees seemed to give way too. He made an agonized sound in the back of his throat that Joan would never forget as long as she lived.

"No," the woman's voice said. "Again."

1922

The kitchen was gone. Nick was standing on a street corner. He was far younger than he'd been in the other scenes. It was dusk, and the road was shiny with new rain. Cars flashed by, their lights briefly blinding.

When the monster walked past, Joan almost didn't recognize him. He was in modern clothes this time: an ugly Christmas sweater and a blue anorak.

Nick was fast: a striking snake. One moment the monster was walking by, the next he was kneeling, arms twisted up behind his back.

"Do you remember me?" Nick said. This time, his voice didn't shake. He was so young. Joan's heart wrenched for him.

The man's laugh was brief. Nick snapped his neck. When Nick turned, his eyes were bright with triumph.

A woman stepped into the frame. She was blonde and swan-necked, with the kind of face Joan had only ever seen on marble statues. Her imperious posture seemed out of place on that dreary London street. She belonged, Joan thought, on a throne.

The woman spoke. The approval in her voice was at odds with her cruel, cold face. "You're ready," she said to Nick. "You're perfect."

Joan's palms hurt. She was digging her nails into them. She'd drawn blood, she saw distantly. All the hero stories started the same way: *Once upon a time, there was a boy who was born to kill monsters.* But it hadn't been Nick's destiny at all. He hadn't been born to it. Someone had done this to him. Someone had *made him* into the hero.

"She was the woman you saw in the hospital, wasn't she?" she said to Ruth.

"Yes," Ruth whispered.

"Who *is* she?" Joan said.

"I don't know," Ruth said. Joan looked at Tom and Aaron. Tom shook his head slightly. Aaron seemed dazed.

"What we just saw . . . ," Aaron said. "That shouldn't have been possible. You can't be in the same time twice. It's a fundamental law of time travel. You shouldn't be able to change the timeline like that. But they killed his family over and over—"

"And over and over and over," Ruth murmured.

"It isn't possible," Aaron said. "How could it have been recorded? What family power can do that?"

Nick had been tortured and then rebooted so they could do it all to him again, over and over and over. . . . He'd been remade. How many times had they killed his family? How many times before they'd broken him? That last number had been 1922. Joan couldn't stop shaking. She rounded on Tom. "Did you know about this?" she demanded furiously. Because if he *had* . . .

"No!" Tom said. "I had no idea that the hero was—was *constructed*."

"You said this message was left for you! Left for you by—" Something that had been nagging at Joan surfaced. "Jamie Liu . . ." She paused.

Aaron appeared beside her, footsteps silent on the carpet. Joan could see the wheels turning in his head just like they were turning in hers.

"Ying Liu has a son named Jamie," Joan said slowly. "We saw his paintings in the Liu gallery. They were all of the hero."

Tom's jaw worked. He couldn't seem to stand still. He shifted his weight, fists clenching and unclenching. "Jamie always loved the stories of the hero," he said. "He was the foremost scholar of the myths."

"Was?"

"He found out something he shouldn't have," Tom said. "Something about the hero. Something he wasn't supposed to know. And the Court just . . ." Tom swallowed. "Took him. They just *took* him. It was a long time before we were even able to discover that he was still alive—that he was being kept by the

Court. That they were using him to keep their stupid records."

The Lius had perfect memory, Joan remembered. She should have realized that the archive was a Liu.

"We always knew that he was going to disappear," Tom said. "It was in the Liu records. But I *promised* him I'd protect him. I told him I'd keep him safe. I told him I'd change the timeline somehow."

"You've tried to rescue him before," Joan realized. "You became a guard to get into the Court."

"I never saw him in the Court," Tom said. "I tried, but I never got as close as I did tonight."

Joan remembered what Aaron had told her once. *Everyone goes up against the timeline. Everyone tries.*

"Jamie knows me," Tom said. "He knows I won't stop until I get him back." His voice cracked. "That fucking mattress was still warm."

As he spoke, the air in the sitting room seemed to shudder again suddenly.

Joan shuddered with it. "Tom," she said. She couldn't stand to see any more from the device. *Please*, she thought. But when the image resolved, it wasn't Nick.

Tom stumbled closer. A man in his twenties was standing in the middle of the room. He had Chinese features and a gentle quality. The kind of person who'd help an old lady cross the street, Joan thought. Her next thought was that he looked ill. His face was gaunt; the skin under his eyes looked bruised.

"Jamie," Tom whispered. He lifted a hand to touch the man's

face. But there was nothing to touch. His fingers went right through.

"Hello, Tom," Jamie said. He was in the prison cell. Joan could see the thin blanket. The cold stone floor. The sight of them gave her the swooping, sick feeling that she'd had when she'd been in there. The feeling from her old nightmares. She imagined she could smell the room again. Fear and sickness and death.

"The guards told me that no one would ever get into this room," Jamie said. "But I knew you would." His eyes crinkled, fond. "I love you."

I love you, Tom mouthed back, even though Jamie couldn't see it. Tom's expression was raw: an open wound. Joan felt like an intruder watching him.

"Who'd have thought researching fairy tales would be so hazardous?" Jamie's chuckle turned into a pained hitch. He rubbed his chest absently, as though his ribs hurt. The angle of his fingers looked wrong. They'd been broken and hadn't been set properly, Joan thought. Tom's own hands clenched into fists.

"Tom," Jamie said seriously. "I found something I shouldn't have. The hero is real. And he's going to kill more people than you can imagine. He'll commit dozens and dozens of massacres by the time he's done. But what he doesn't know is what you just saw. That he was *made* into the hero. He was made into this."

There were echoing footsteps suddenly, real enough that Joan and Ruth both turned to the kitchen. But the sound was coming from inside the recording. From the muffled quality, someone was approaching Jamie's room.

"The woman who made him—who brought me here. She believes no one can stop her," Jamie said quickly. "But she's wrong. She thinks she made the hero perfectly. She didn't. She made a mistake with him. He can be stopped."

"On your feet," a voice called through the door. "She wants you in the chair again."

Fear passed over Jamie's face. He forced a smile over it when he looked back at the camera. "Tom, you need to stop looking for me," he said. "You need to turn your eyes to what's really important. The hero *must* be stopped."

Tom shook his head. "No," he whispered.

"Yes," Jamie said, just as if he'd heard Tom's voice. "You can . . . for me." His smile gentled into something real and soft. "You hate goodbyes, so I won't give you one," he said. Tom was still shaking his head. Jamie kept speaking. "As for me . . . a Liu doesn't need goodbyes. I can see you perfectly even now. I remember every moment that we were together. Every touch. Every conversation we ever had. For me, you're always here."

The recording ended.

They sat there for a long while in silence: Aaron and Tom on the sofa, Ruth slumped in a chair.

"What are we going to do?" Joan said finally.

"What can we do?" Aaron said. His voice sounded flat. "We should wait out the Patel hit and then just . . . disappear. Live quiet, unrecorded lives. Pretend we never saw what we just saw."

"You mean give up?" Ruth said.

"What choice do we have?" Aaron said.

But it wasn't just their own families. It was all those other people who were going to be killed—dozens and dozens of massacres, Jamie had said. It was the human time that Aaron and Joan had stolen to get here. It was Jamie Liu, being kept in that cell.

And it was Nick and his family.

"In that message," Joan said, "Jamie said that Nick had been made wrong. That they'd made a mistake."

"If it was something that could have helped us, he should have just told us what it was," Aaron said.

"He's a Liu," Joan said. "He's the Royal Archive. He could have told us lots of things."

"And?" Aaron said.

"And the most important thing—the thing he chose to tell us—was that a mistake was made."

"Well, he didn't tell us enough," Aaron said. "And we can't exactly go and ask him for more information, can we?"

Joan looked at Tom. He'd realized it at the same moment she had. She could see it in the shadow of resignation that crossed his face.

"Yes, we can," she said.

TWENTY-ONE

Joan wanted to go immediately, but Tom refused. "We're not waking him up at the crack of dawn," he said.

That gave them a chance to get cleaned up, at least. Joan had a shower. There were clothes in the bedroom wardrobe in various sizes—some new with tags, some pre-worn and laundered. Who had this safe house been prepared for? Aaron had said that he'd learned of this place from his mother. How had *she* known about it?

More questions. Joan sighed. She found a pair of jeans that fit, and a T-shirt that said *Crystal Palace FC*.

Aaron looked pained when she reemerged. "A football T-shirt?" he said.

Joan was surprised to find herself smiling in response. Only a few days ago, she'd found his grumbling annoying. "It fits," she said.

"Is it indicative of your own taste or the selection in there?" Aaron said. "No, don't tell me. I'm afraid to know." He headed to the bedroom with a mild air of doom.

Ruth joined Joan. "What's the bet he'll come back out in

those same clothes?" she said. She looked better, Joan thought. She'd had a nap and woken with more color in her face.

"How are you feeling?" Joan asked her.

Ruth sighed. Her hair was flat where she'd been lying on it. "The Hunt power still feels burned out of me," she said. She added, very soft, "Do you think it'll come back?"

Joan reached up to fix Ruth's curls. She didn't know. But Ruth had burned herself out to save the rest of them. Ruth would have stayed there at the Court, as long as Joan had gotten out. Joan's throat felt tight at the thought. "You should stay here and rest."

"I'd rather be busy." Ruth poked Joan's foot with hers, and grinned when Joan protested. "Anyway, I think we should keep an eye on him." She looked over to the kitchen. Through the open doorway, Joan could see Tom sitting at the table with Frankie in his lap. Frankie looked sleepy—she'd eaten two of the pork pies. Tom stroked her head absently; he was staring at nothing much.

"You don't trust him?" Joan said. "I do. We saw him laid bare today."

"No, I mean we should keep an eye on him for *him*," Ruth said. "When you speak to someone you love before they know you . . . Well, it isn't easy."

Joan looked at her. Did Ruth know that Joan had gone to see Gran? But Ruth's expression had turned inward. *Everyone tries to change something*, Aaron had said once. Did everyone try this too?

They headed out soon after that. Conrad had apparently assumed they'd gone to ground. The police blockades on the bridges were gone, and there were fewer guards around.

Joan found herself walking with Tom. He'd scooped up Frankie and tucked her into his zipped jacket. She snored, squashed-faced, against his shirt.

"I think you'll have to vouch for my cousin," Joan whispered to Tom. "Apparently she's banned from the Liu houses."

Tom's eyebrows went up. "For what? Theft?" When Joan nodded, he seemed more amused than concerned. "I was banned from their houses for a while," he said. There was a nostalgic smile in his voice; it seemed to be a good memory. "Don't worry about it," he said. "You're all with me."

With all their precautions, it took a couple of hours to get to the Liu property.

Tom guided them to a back entrance—a narrow alley between high brick walls. Joan was beginning to associate such places with monsters. There was a black lacquered door in one wall. A Chinese phoenix had been carved into the wood, its long tail sweeping almost to the ground.

Tom's lighter mood from earlier had vanished. His huge frame was tight with tension. Still tucked in Tom's jacket, Frankie wriggled until Tom lifted her out. Once on the ground, she pawed eagerly at the door. When Tom didn't open it, she barked at him, sharp and impatient. Tom bent to stroke her brown-and-white back. "I know," he murmured to her. He straightened slowly. "You know," he said, not looking at anyone, "Jamie might not be able to help us. He's younger here in 1993. He's barely even started this journey."

"He's already painting the hero," Joan said. "He's already interested in him. He might know *something.* Give us some clue."

Tom's jaw worked. For a moment, Joan thought he was going to refuse to open the door. Frankie seemed to sense his reluctance. She jumped up, her paws against the door, and barked again, even more urgency in her squashed face.

Tom sighed. He fished a key from his pocket with the air of someone who had permission to come and go as he pleased. But his hand shook as he slotted the key into the lock and turned it. Joan wondered when he'd last used it. He pushed open the door.

"Oh," Joan breathed. She'd seen the front of the Liu property—the gallery and courtyard—but she'd underestimated the size of the estate.

Before them was a garden, artless and overgrown. The house had to be close, but by a trick of perspective, the greenery seemed endless. They could have been in the countryside. Wild crocuses and honeysuckle poked through the long grass. Joan closed her eyes and took a deep breath. Bees hummed. Somewhere, water was trickling. The air smelled of honey and sunshine.

Tom was a contrast to the serene garden. He shifted back and forth with the contained energy of a boxer. "Remember," he said, "in this time, he hasn't been taken yet—he hasn't been forced to become the *archive.*" He almost spat the word. "He won't know that the hero was created by monsters. He won't even know that the hero is real yet. It will all just be stories to him. Fairy tales."

"You don't have to do this," Aaron said.

Tom's jaw tightened. "No shit." He nodded toward the garden. "He'll be down by the water. He loves the water."

Tom led them all along an overgrown path and down rocky steps to a burbling stream. It would have been the perfect place for a picnic, sunny with dappled shade from the oak trees above.

By the stream, a boy of about fifteen was sitting on a rock, his jeans rolled up, bare feet in the running water. He was painting fish in bold orange strokes that seemed to magically turn into living carp as his brush moved. Like his paintings in the gallery, this one seemed more alive than the world around him.

Tom held up his hand before anyone could speak. He stared at Jamie's back and swallowed. Frankie didn't wait. She bounded down the hill into Jamie's lap, knocking the paintbrush from his hand.

"Hey!" Jamie laughed as Frankie barked, delighted, licked his face, bounced away, and barked again. Joan had never heard Frankie so vocal. On the last bounce, Jamie caught her before she could tumble into the water. "Who are you?" he said as Frankie wriggled in his grip, trying to lick his face again. "Hello. Who are you?"

Tom stood there, staring at them both. Joan couldn't imagine how he felt. If she hadn't known that this boy was the man from the message, she'd never have guessed. The man had been gaunt, every movement slow and pained. This boy was vibrant and full of vitality.

"You okay?" she asked Tom.

"No," Tom said. But he made his way down the hill. Frankie barked at his approach. The boy turned. In his shoes, Joan would have jumped half a mile, but the boy's expression just turned polite. "Oh, hello." He turned and saw the four of them. "Oh wow." He pulled his headphones off. "Sorry, I had that blasting." The headphones were attached to what looked like a slim silver purse. There were little boxes scattered around, all with colorful album covers. Music cassettes, Joan realized. The silver purse was a cassette player.

"Are you Jamie?" Tom said. His face was all cheerfulness as he introduced himself and the others. Joan remembered how it had felt when Gran had looked at her like a stranger. Tom showed no sign of what he must have been feeling. "Your dad said you might be down here."

"Does he need help in the gallery?" Jamie went to stand, but Tom shook his head.

"No, actually. We need your help. We heard you'd done some research on the hero stories."

"Uh . . ." Jamie seemed puzzled. Frankie was finally settling down. Jamie stroked her head. "You've come way too early. I've only just started researching them. So . . . Maybe go forward five years or so," he suggested. "I'll know everything by then."

Tom's throat worked. "Sure," he said. "But we'd love to chat now too. Because, see. We, uh . . . We're . . ." His amazing composure seemed to fail him. "Uh, well . . ."

Joan slid in before Tom's hesitation could get too weird. "We're collectors. We want to buy a painting," she said. "From the hero series. Your dad said you could tell us about it. Right, Tom?"

Tom shot her a look of mixed thanks and disapproval. "Right." So Tom lied to everyone except Jamie. Noted.

"Really? I've never sold anything before." Jamie looked so happy that Joan felt bad about the lie. Well, she would have felt bad. From the expression on Tom's face, they were going to have to buy every Jamie Liu painting in the gallery. "I really like your ring," Jamie added to Tom.

Joan saw it then. Tom turned his head from Jamie's view, just long enough for the mask to drop. He recovered quickly, turning back with a smile. "Thanks. My husband designed it."

Tom kicked off his shoes and sat, mirroring Jamie's posture. Tom's body was usually intimidating, muscles bulging from his shirt. But with Jamie Liu, he looked utterly unthreatening. He'd put himself down on an incline. It made him and Jamie almost the same height.

Joan followed suit, peering at Tom's ring as she sat. She'd never really noticed it before. It was dark metal with a scoured finish. Now she saw what had caught Jamie's eye. Etched lines ran over and under the band—images of hounds and phoenixes. They had the same quality of vitality, of life, that Jamie's paintings did. The same quality as the tattoo on Tom's arm.

Joan flattened her hands on the ground. The grass felt cool and dry. "We're really interested in the stories behind the paintings," she said to Jamie. "We were all saying that we didn't remember the hero stories very well."

"Oh, there are loads of them," Jamie said, face brightening with enthusiasm for the topic.

"Can you tell us about them?" Ruth said.

"Oh." Jamie didn't seem to know where to start. "Well . . . Different families tell different stories. The Patel and Hunt stories are mostly adventures. The hero fights mythical beasts like krakens and giant serpents. That sort of thing. In their stories, he only starts fighting monsters like us later in life."

"Huh," Joan said. Those were the stories that Gran had told her.

Aren't these just the Hercules stories? she'd said to Gran once when she was about seven. She'd been snotty-nosed and precocious as a kid. Gran had just waved her hand. *Oh, those ancients,* she'd said. *Always stealing our myths.* Now Joan felt her eyes well up unexpectedly. She'd hardly been able to think of Gran since the massacre without remembering her terrible last moments. This was one of the first times she'd remembered Gran just being Gran.

"The Mtawali stories tend to be fables. You know, with lessons attached," Jamie continued. "And the Oliver stories are mostly horror. I guess they enjoy terrifying their children before they fall asleep."

Aaron usually hated people talking about his family. But there was mild approval on his face at this. *God, the Olivers are weird,* Joan thought.

"We were trying to remember a particular one," she said.

"Where the hero has a flaw."

"A flaw?" Jamie said.

"A weakness."

"You mean like an Achilles' heel?" Jamie said. "Sorry. He doesn't die in any story I've read."

Waste of time, Aaron mouthed to Joan.

"Although . . ." Jamie hesitated. "There is one thing. It's not exactly a weakness. But it is a vulnerability, perhaps."

Aaron lifted his head. "What is it?" Joan asked.

"The Liu stories are romances," Jamie said. "In our stories, the hero was once in love with a girl."

Aaron grimaced and dropped his head again. But Joan's stomach twisted. "A romance?" she said. "The hero stories aren't romances."

"The Liu stories are," Jamie said. "We love a tragic romance." At the word *tragic*, the sick twist in Joan's stomach worsened. "Have you ever heard of the *zhēnshí de lìshǐ*?" he said.

"The true timeline," Joan said.

"Some families call it that," Jamie agreed. "The Liu stories say that in the *zhēnshí de lìshǐ*, the hero was an ordinary boy in love with a monster girl."

"A monster girl?" Joan echoed. The sick feeling was getting stronger.

"You know the theory of the timeline?" Jamie said. "That when we make changes, the timeline repairs itself? It returns to its natural shape."

"Yes," Joan whispered. She had a feeling that she didn't want to hear what was about to come next.

"The Lius believe that our timeline still tries to return to its true shape—still yearns for the shape of the true timeline. We believe that if people belonged together in the true timeline, then our timeline tries to repair itself by bringing them together. Over and over and over. Until the rift is healed."

"Like soul mates?" Tom said.

Jamie smiled at Tom. "Yes. If you believe in fairy tales."

On the way back to the safe house, Tom was very quiet. Frankie hadn't wanted to leave the garden. She'd lingered by Jamie's side, and had whined miserably when she'd realized they were leaving him behind.

Joan was quiet too. The first time she'd gone to Holland House, it had felt like a compulsion. She'd seen the name on a signpost and she'd *had* to go there. She hadn't been able to think about anything else. And then she'd met Nick, and it had been like she'd already known him. Like she knew him better than she knew herself.

"This doesn't help us kill him," Ruth said as they walked. "It doesn't help us stop him."

"I told you this would be a waste of time," Aaron said.

Our timeline tries to repair itself by bringing them together, Jamie had said. *Over and over and over. Until the rift is healed.* Joan had been drawn to Holland House while Nick had been there. Nick had found her in 1993. They'd collided with each other at the Monster Court.

She remembered how he'd touched her cheek. How he'd looked at her. What it had felt like when he'd kissed her.

But if the timeline was trying to repair itself, it was doomed to failure. This was a rift that couldn't be healed. Nick had killed Joan's family. Nick had been conditioned to loathe monsters.

"So, what now, then?" Ruth said.

"Now nothing," Aaron said. "Now we wait for the Patel power to wear off, and then we get out of this time and live our lives in hiding."

Joan pressed her fingernails into her palms—over the cuts already there. She let herself feel the bite of it. Gran had told her the truth that night. *Only you can stop the hero,* she'd said.

In a way, Joan had always known what she'd have to do.

Back at the safe house, Tom went straight to the bedroom. He left the door open at Ruth's insistence. "I'm fine," he said tiredly. "Well, no, I'm not. But I'm just going to sleep. That's all."

It didn't take long for the others to fall asleep too, Ruth on the sofa, Aaron on the living room rug. They were all so tired.

Joan was tired too, but she found herself staring at the photos on the living room wall: the mother, the father, the little girl, and the baby.

Joan had loved her family so much. She hadn't understood how much until they'd died.

She closed her eyes. Bertie had been the same age as her, and the gentlest of all the family. He'd hated arguments. When they'd been little, he'd always wanted to play games that they could all play—he'd never liked people to feel left out.

Uncle Gus had been the family fusspot. *Be careful out there, my love,* he'd say every time any of them left the house. He'd put vegetables in everything—even desserts. *You have to look after your health.*

Aunt Ada had been the smartest of them, except for maybe Gran. She'd never made anyone feel stupid, though. She'd been kind. She'd been a good teacher.

And Gran . . .

Joan squeezed her eyes shut tighter, remembering again how Gran had struggled for breath that night.

You want to kill me before *I kill your family,* Nick had said to Joan.

Joan didn't want to kill him at all. She couldn't lie to herself anymore. She'd been in love with him from the moment she first saw him. She'd been in love with him before that—in a whole other timeline.

He's going to kill more people than you can imagine, Jamie had said.

Joan stood a moment longer in the living room, looking at Ruth and Aaron. She could see Tom through the open bedroom door. Lying there like this, they all seemed as vulnerable as children.

Joan slipped into the hallway. As she reached the front door, a sound behind her made her turn. It was Aaron. He closed the door to the living room softly. Even without sleep, he was angelically beautiful. Almost too good-looking to be real.

"Let me come with you," he whispered.

"How did you know I was leaving?" Joan said.

"I just knew."

For a weak moment, Joan imagined saying *yes, please, come with me.* He'd been with her all this time. But this was going to be dangerous, and she'd risked the others enough. He'd helped her so much already.

"I have to go alone," she whispered.

Aaron dipped his head slightly. "You know where to find him?"

Joan nodded. "Where and when."

Outside, the sun was setting. Low-angled light filtered in through the wavy glass by the front door. It made Aaron's hair gleam gold. "Joan," he said, "you need to know that if you undo the massacre—"

"He has to be stopped," Joan said. "Whether our families can be saved or not. He can't be allowed to slaughter people."

"I know." Aaron took a step closer. And then he was right there in her space, filling her view completely. "I know."

"Aaron—"

"Listen to me, *please*. If you actually manage to do this, if you stop him before he starts—"

"No, I—"

"*Listen* to me," Aaron said. "If you change the timeline, I won't know you anymore. It'll be like we never met."

"We'd meet," Joan promised. "I'd make sure we did."

"*No.*" His tone was serious and urgent, with none of his usual undercurrent of irony. "Joan, if you somehow remember this, remember what I'm saying now. You have to stay far away from me. From me and from my family. Never let me close enough to see the color of your eyes."

"What are you talking about?"

"My family can see the difference between monsters and humans," Aaron said. "But our power runs deeper than anyone knows. Some of us can tell family from family."

He'd just told her an Oliver secret, Joan realized. Aaron, who protected and defended his family, always. He'd told her something no one outside his family was supposed to know.

"Because you'll know I'm a Hunt?" Joan whispered. "You'll hate me for it?"

Aaron didn't answer, but Joan knew the truth. For monsters, blood didn't come into it. Family was power and power was family. And she didn't have the Hunt power.

"In a human sense, they're your family," Aaron said. "You love them and they love you."

"I'm not a Hunt, am I?" Joan said.

"As children, monsters can have more than one family power," Aaron said. "We can have powers from both sides of the family, powers that jump a generation. But as we get older, the only power that remains is the power of our true family. When our true power stabilizes, we undertake a trial to affirm which family we belong to."

"I never did that," Joan said.

"You're supposed to undertake the trial around the time you turn twelve," Aaron said. "I was nine."

"Nine?" That seemed horrible to Joan. To have someone say that you didn't belong to half your family anymore. What if you had brothers and sisters who manifested a different power? Did you all get separated?

"I was so proud of myself." Aaron sounded contemptuous of his younger self. "I'd manifested what we call the true Oliver power—the ability to differentiate family from family. It's rare among us. But after I did . . ." Shadows flickered over Aaron's face as a car passed, its lights shining through the wavy glass. "After I did, they took me into a room. There was a man in there with his hands bound, in a cage with thick iron bars." His breath shuddered in his throat. "They . . . they shocked him with a cattle prod until he looked into my eyes. They told me that if I saw anyone like him again, I was to kill them. Or inform the Court if I couldn't do it myself."

Joan flashed back to Edmund staring into her eyes before telling Lucien to kill her. Then she remembered how Aaron had stood between her and Edmund at Whitehall Palace, shielding her from Edmund's view. How Aaron had taken Edmund's abuse to keep Joan safe.

"I never saw anyone like him again," Aaron said. "Until I saw you in the maze. Until I was close enough to see your eyes."

"What am I?" Joan whispered.

"I don't know," Aaron said. "All I know is that if you undo the massacre, you can't ever meet me. You can't ever trust me. I won't know. I won't remember what—" He cut himself off. Then he ground out, "I won't remember what you mean to me."

Joan felt horribly close to tears suddenly. His gaze was slanted away from her. "Aaron . . ."

"No, don't," he said. "Please."

"*Aaron*," she said. She touched his hand. He was always so warm.

Then he did meet her eyes. There was such intensity in his face that for a long moment, Joan thought he was about to kiss her.

He took something from his pocket. Joan's eyes were blurring. It took her a few blinks to make out a small object: a brooch in the shape of a birdcage. The base of the cage was richly decorated with flowers. Inside, a brown bird sat on the perch, head raised as if in song.

Aaron ran a finger down the edge of the brooch—gentle, almost reverent—and then gave it to Joan. "I found it in the bedroom wardrobe," he said. "It was my mother's."

"Your mother was here?" Joan whispered.

Aaron shook his head, but not in denial—as if he couldn't bear to talk about it. "Can you turn it over?"

Joan did. The brooch had a brass back with a simple pin clasp. Two numbers had been hand-engraved. The first was crossed out: ~~100~~. The second was in a different hand: 50.

"The Mtawali family has the power to transfer time into objects," Aaron said. "Travel tokens, we call them. You can use this one to travel up to fifty years without taking time from anyone. I know," he said before Joan could protest. "I know. Morally, it's the same as taking the life yourself, but it will feel different to travel this way. I promise."

Joan didn't believe that. Stealing life was stealing life. But all she could think about was that this might be the last time she saw Aaron—whether she failed or succeeded.

"When you're ready," Aaron said, "just think about the time you want to go to. Do you remember how it felt to jump?"

Joan closed her eyes, trying to remember that feeling of yearning from the Pit. She hadn't let herself feel it since that day.

"I've figured out where you're going, you know," Aaron whispered. There was a shift in the air. Joan felt his hand brush against her cheek gently, just for a moment. "You're going home," he said.

Home. It had been a long time since Joan had believed she could go home. But at the word from Aaron, she wanted it desperately. And *this* was the feeling of the jump, she remembered. This yearning feeling.

Nothing happened, of course. The Patel power hadn't worn off yet. "I wish I didn't have to go," she said.

Aaron didn't reply.

Joan opened her eyes. She was still in the house. But it was subtly different. The pictures on the wall had changed. The wavy glass of the window was clear and flat.

And Aaron was gone.

TWENTY-TWO

On the surface Holland House seemed just the same. Tourists wandered the grounds eating ice creams and sausage baps. Costumed guides chatted to tour groups about the gardens and the house.

Except that Joan didn't recognize any of the staff. And they all had a watchfulness about them—everyone from the ice-cream seller to the guides. A watchfulness and a military bearing.

Joan had guessed right. She knew Nick as well as she knew herself. According to Aaron, tourist sites were often traps for humans. After the massacre at Holland House, Nick had turned this tourist site into a trap for monsters. Anyone who came here with the intention of stealing time would be caught.

In the front garden, Thomas the peacock pecked furiously at Joan's shoes. "At least you haven't been replaced," Joan said to him. He cawed back at her in his harsh dinosaur way. He was well fed and in an unusually good mood, tail feathers relaxed. Nick was looking after the house, it seemed.

A woman's voice sounded from the terrace, unexpectedly cheerful. "Joan!"

Joan looked up. "Astrid?" she said, surprised and relieved to see a familiar face. Astrid had been one of the other volunteers at the house. She was half-Chinese like Joan, and half-Kenyan—tall and Black, with the straight-backed posture of a ballet dancer.

Astrid ran up to her. "What are you doing here? I thought you were only here for the school holidays." She threw her arms around Joan.

How long did Astrid think she'd been gone, Joan wondered. When was this? She hugged Astrid back. "I'm just visiting," she said. "What about you? I thought you—" She stopped as she felt Astrid's grip shift. She glimpsed a syringe.

Joan tried to struggle free, but it was too late. A needle jabbed into her side like a bee sting. And then everything went black.

Joan woke to pain. Her head ached. She blinked her eyes open.

She was lying on her side on a stone floor. Her heart started to pound. The far wall was iron bars. She was in a prison cell, just like the one in her nightmares.

No, not quite. That cell smelled of sickness and death. This one didn't smell of anything but clean stone.

Joan shook her head, trying to clear the bleariness. She tried to orient herself. Beyond the iron bars, the corridor archi-traves had a familiar pattern: fleurs-de-lis.

This was the basement of Holland House. When Joan had volunteered at the house, there'd been staff rooms and kitchens down here. Now, someone had kitted out one of the staff rooms into a prison cell.

Joan tried to reach up to touch her aching head, and realized for the first time that her hands were cuffed together in front of her. Her heart stuttered with panic. She tried to wrench her hands apart.

"Hello, Joan."

Joan turned fast. It was Nick. Of course it was. He was standing in a corner of the cell, in a slouch that looked very close to relaxed. Only a slight tension in his shoulders betrayed that he was feeling anything more.

"How's your head?" Nick asked.

Joan didn't want to admit to any physical weaknesses. "Bit over-the-top, isn't it?" she said. "The whole dungeon thing?" To her relief, her voice came out dry and calm. She surreptitiously felt her pocket, but the Mtawali travel token was gone; there wouldn't be any easy way out of here. She glanced around the room. There were no windows, no obvious ducts. It would take her a few seconds to get up. Another few seconds to rush him. And she'd seen how fast he was when he attacked.

She tried to push herself up to stand. Something tugged at her leg. She tugged back and realized that her left ankle was locked into some contraption jutting out of the wall. "Oh, *what?*" It looked like a chain from a medieval torture chamber. And then a wave of panic hit, claustrophobia combining with the setting. Her hands were trapped, and now she was locked to the wall as well. For a second she felt as though she really were in the prison from her nightmare. She fought the chain wildly. "Get it *off*!" The chain jerked her back again and again like the jaws of a live animal. Under it all, the fog of the drug lingered like sleep.

"Sorry, Joan. I can't let you hurt anyone." Nick hadn't moved. But there was a shadow of something in his eyes now. Concern? Confusion? He hadn't expected her to react quite like that to the chain. "I can't unlock that. I can't allow you to touch anyone. So you'll need to calm down."

Calm down? She'd love to see him if he were trapped somewhere like this. Inadvertently, she remembered him in that chair, mouth bloody, begging for mercy for his family. She squeezed her eyes shut, trying to breathe.

She thought about how Astrid had run right up to her, as if the staff had had an alert out on her. "You knew I was coming?" she said.

"You told me you would," Nick said. "I believed you." He shifted his weight. "So what's your plan? I assume you came to kill me."

"No," Joan said. "*No*. Nick, I came here to talk."

"To talk," he said flatly. He didn't believe her. "What about?"

"You."

His lips compressed. He'd never liked talking about himself. Joan hadn't known why until she'd seen those terrible recordings. "My people are prepared for any attack," he warned her.

Joan felt a wave of hurt. Did he really think she'd launch

some attack on him in a house full of tourists? There were ordinary people outside. Did he really think she'd do something like that?

Another voice sounded from outside the cell. "We won't get the truth out of her without artificial help." It was Astrid, straight-backed and grim. When they'd volunteered together, Astrid had run activities for the kids. She'd been a competitive fencer, and she'd shown the kids how to fight with foam swords. She must have been there on the night of the massacre, Joan realized. Had any of the other staff been with Nick too? Allies of the hero? Joan swallowed. Apart from Nick, Astrid had been her closest friend in the house.

"I don't want to drug her again," Nick said to Astrid.

"We need to know what she's planning," Astrid said. "You said it yourself. She's dangerous. She wants you dead. And there are tourists here. We're responsible for more lives than our own."

They left Joan alone for a little while. She examined the handcuffs. With some effort, she took a bobby pin from her hair and had a go at the lock, concealing her movements behind her crooked knees. She hadn't gotten very far before Nick and Astrid returned.

Nick tossed Joan a bottle of water.

"What's this?" Joan asked.

"Water," Astrid said. "With something in it. Almost as good as the Griffiths' power."

The Griffiths could induce truth, Joan remembered.

"There's no such thing as a truth serum," she said.

"Not in this time," Astrid agreed. "Drink. At least a quarter of the bottle."

Joan unscrewed the cap and drank half the water under Astrid's narrow gaze. She was thirsty, and she wanted them to know that she wasn't hiding anything. "How long will it take to work?" she asked. But, to her surprise, she could already feel it.

Warmth and relaxation spread through her, from her chest to her fingertips. Rather than truly relaxing her, though, she felt the same muffled panic as when she'd inadvertently tried to travel.

"Don't fight it," Astrid said.

But Joan couldn't help herself. She fought the blurry feeling as she'd fought the chain. She'd never liked feeling out of control.

"What's your name?" Astrid said.

"Joan Chang-Hunt." It came out in a weird forced burst. The drug really could compel her, she thought with a shot of fright. She hadn't expected it to work like this. Her mouth felt separate from her brain.

"Is your father human?" Astrid said.

Joan was shocked by the question. She shook her head, trying to clear it. The movement felt wobbly. "I—" She clenched her teeth together. The desire to answer truthfully was as intense as the need to breathe.

"Stop fighting it," Astrid said. "Where's your father?"

"I don't know!" Joan blurted. That was the truth, she

realized, relieved. She had no idea where he was right now.

"Is he human?"

Joan struggled not to answer. It was even harder this time. "*Yes*. Stop asking me about him!"

"All right," Astrid said to Nick. "You can talk to her now."

After Astrid left the cell, Nick sat down with Joan, just out of reach, his back against the iron bars.

They watched each other for a while. The strange thing, Joan thought, was how familiar Nick's presence felt. Something about him made her think of safety, of home. That wasn't real, though. Maybe it had been real in some other timeline, but not in this one.

"What was your plan in coming here?" he said.

"To talk," Joan said. "To talk to you."

His mouth turned down. "To distract me while someone attacks us?"

"No."

"Is someone here with you? Is someone else coming? Are there weapons involved? Explosives?"

"No," Joan said. *Explosives?* "No. *No*." Did he really think so little of her? But he'd already made it clear that taking any time at all was the same as murder in his eyes. It was why he killed monsters.

Joan remembered the look on his face when he'd found his family dead in his childhood house. She thought of Gran lying dead. Between them, there'd been so much blood. "Nick," she said. She let the compulsion speak the truth for her. "I came here to talk to you. That's the truth. You know I can't lie right now."

His eyes were as cold as when he'd addressed Edmund Oliver. "Talk, then. What do you want?"

What did she want? There were too many answers to that question. She wanted her family back. She wanted none of this to have happened. She wanted to be with Nick. She couldn't lie to herself. Not with the drug in her body. Not with him right here. She wanted him, even after everything that had happened between them. Even after what he'd done, she still only ever wanted to be in a room with him. She hated it, but she couldn't deny it.

To her relief, the drug didn't know which answer to force from her. She could pick one true thing. "Peace," she said. "Between monsters and humans."

"Peace?" Nick was still leaning back as though relaxed. But his mouth tightened. "I killed your family, Joan. Are you saying you could ever forgive me for it?"

"No," Joan blurted, forced to answer.

Nick seemed to stop breathing for a second. "No," he said softly.

"Just like you could never get over the fact that I'm a monster," Joan said.

Nick's answer took longer to come this time. "No," he said. Something about the pause made Joan wish he'd been compelled to speak the truth too.

But he didn't need to take a truth drug. He never lied—not directly. Joan's breath hitched. So there it was, the harsh truth of it.

If Jamie's story was true, then Joan and Nick had been together in another timeline. If the story was true, then the new timeline was still trying to repair itself by bringing them back together, over and over. But it was doomed to fail. What was broken between them couldn't be fixed.

"I'm not talking about peace between you and me," she said. It hurt to say it.

"There'll never be peace between monsters and humans," he said. "Not as long as monsters steal time. And you can't help yourselves. You all crave it."

Joan shook her head. She didn't.

"You crave time travel."

The compulsion answered for her. "Yes," she blurted. She pressed her lips together. She'd barely admitted that even to herself. The method of travel was a kind of focused yearning, and the yearning was always there in the background. It had been there as long as she could remember, in her love of history. "I can control it." She was relieved to hear herself say it. If the compulsion allowed it, then surely it must be true.

"Can you?"

"*Yes.*" Joan sat up and tried to inch closer to him. Her heart thudded when he pulled back his feet fast. "Stop. Stop asking me questions," she said. "I can't stop myself from answering. And I have to tell you . . ." She took a deep breath. "You told me about your family. The man who killed them—"

"Is dead."

"I know. You killed him."

"Every monster knows that," he said. "It's in all your child-hood stories."

Joan had never thought about how Nick might see those stories: his own suffering as a fairy tale.

"You broke his neck."

Nick stilled. That wasn't in the stories.

"You were tied to a chair before they died," Joan said. "You were tortured."

Nick sat up slowly from his slouch. The pretense of relaxation had ended. "You shouldn't know that," he said, soft and dangerous.

"It . . . it was recorded," Joan said.

Nick clearly hadn't expected her to say that. "*What?*"

"I'm so sorry, but I saw what he did," Joan said. "Your whole family was killed. I saw them. Nick, I'm so sorry he—"

"Stop," Nick ground out. "*Stop.*"

But Joan couldn't. "You have to know what they were actually recording." She wet her dry lips. "They were recording the process of making you into the hero."

Nick's eyes hardened. The only sound in the room was their breathing. Joan was very aware that the walls of the basement were five feet thick. The basement had once been a wine cellar. You could scream and scream down here, and no one would ever hear you.

She had to wet her lips again before she could speak. "The . . . the stories say that you were orphaned by monsters and destined to kill them. But you weren't destined. You were *crafted*. You were made into this."

"*Stop*," Nick said, and Joan felt a surge of real fear at the look on his face. She was suddenly very aware that she was trapped in a room with the slayer from her childhood stories.

But the drug was still working. It forced her to keep speaking. "They didn't just do it once," she said. "They killed your family over and over. They reset the timeline so they could torture you over and over."

"Stop," Nick said again. "Stop *lying*."

"I'm not lying. You know I can't."

"Drink the rest of that bottle."

Joan's stomach was churning. There was a good chance that she'd throw up if she drank. But she unscrewed the lid and took a deep breath, then forced the rest down. It sloshed unpleasantly in her gut.

The drug took effect even faster than the first dose. And this time, the out-of-control feeling was worse. Joan had the urge to babble anything to Nick. To say truths that he hadn't even asked for.

"You—you were made by monsters." She was stumbling over the words now; they came out faster than she could speak them. "They killed your family as . . . as a kind of origin story. To motivate you to hate us. Then . . ." She made a guess. "Then you were trained in how to identify us, how to kill us." She could see in his face that she was right. "Nick, you resisted them. You didn't want to become this. They had to do it over and over until you broke."

"You can't change the timeline over and over. It isn't possible."

"I can't lie," Joan said desperately. "You know I can't!" He *had* to believe her.

Nick shifted out of his relaxed posture to his feet, fast and smooth and lethal. Joan found herself scrambling back.

"Nick," she said. *"Please.* You have to believe me."

"Please?" he said, looking down at her. "Is that what your victims said at the Changing of the Guard?"

Joan shook her head.

"No, they didn't beg, did they?" he said. "They didn't even know what you'd stolen from them."

Joan's next breath stuck in her chest. He really was going to kill her.

But instead of moving closer, he took a step back and then another. He opened the cell door without a word and locked it behind him. Key first, then a heavy bolt. Panic ran through Joan at the sheer claustrophobia of it. "Nick!" she shouted. But he was already out of sight. Could he still hear her?

Whether he could or not, the drug was still hammering at her to speak. Joan screwed her eyes shut, trying to *think* around the desire to say truths. Nick hadn't believed her. She couldn't blame him. Who'd want to hear what she'd told him? That everything he knew about himself was a kind of lie?

The truth was, she'd never thought he'd believe her. But

she'd had to try. She'd had to know if there could be any chance of a better ending.

Now she felt around on the floor until she found the bobby pin. As she did, the drug worked at her harder. It was going to make her narrate her escape, she realized, a hysterical laugh bubbling up. She struggled against it, but, just like before, the desire to speak was overwhelming.

She needed to placate it with a different truth.

"The first time I met you . . ." She could hear the raw emotion in her own voice. She closed her eyes. The drug wasn't just forcing her to speak; it was forcing her to feel it. "The first time I met you, it was like I already knew you," she said. "Like I'd known you my whole life."

There was no response from Nick. She hoped he wasn't there.

"Wherever you were," she said, "I wanted to be there too. You were like the sun. I was always turning toward you."

There was a slight click as the spring gave on the lock. She blinked out of her reverie. *Focus*, she told herself.

"You kissed me that night," she said. "I'd never wanted anything so much. Later, I thought maybe you'd been playing me the whole time. But then, at that nineties café, I started to wonder. . . . Because you didn't kill me, even though you knew I'd stolen time."

She heard footsteps and then Nick was looking at her through the bars. Joan's heart skipped a beat at the sight of him. He hadn't left.

"The Liu family has a story," she said. "They say that there was once another timeline. One that existed before our own."

"I know what you're doing," Nick said. "You're working on those handcuffs. It's pointless. You're not leaving this cell."

"Don't you feel it?" she said. "Don't you feel that this time-line is wrong?"

If he did, he wasn't showing it. But the drug didn't care. It forced more words out. "The Liu story says that in the original timeline, the hero was just an ordinary boy in love with a monster girl," she said.

"Stop," Nick said.

"They say that if people belonged together in that first timeline, then *our* timeline will always try to bring them back together. They say that—"

"Joan, *stop.*"

Joan wanted to laugh. "I can't. Your stupid truth serum is making me talk and talk and talk. I think you'd have to kill me to make me stop."

His hands came up to grip the cell bars then, knuckles whitening.

"Oh, you don't like that idea?" she said. "Why not? You killed everyone else."

"You've taken time." He sounded formal. He'd said those words to other monsters just before he'd killed them. "You can't be allowed to harm another human."

Joan twisted the pin just like Gran had taught her. She almost had it.

"So you're going to kill me, then?" she said to him. "Or will you ask someone else to do it?"

Something dark and dangerous crossed his face. No, he wouldn't let anyone else touch her.

"What's the alternative?" she asked. "Keeping me prisoner here? Turning me in to the police? What are you going to say to them? 'She touched their necks'?"

"I'm sorry, Joan," Nick said. "I don't believe that we're— whatever it is you think we are. The fact is, I should have done my duty a long time ago. The fact is that you're a monster, and as long as you're alive, you'll hurt people."

There was a click as the left cuff finally released. Joan shook it off. With another *click-click*, she had the right cuff off too. She showed Nick her free hands.

"It doesn't matter if you're cuffed or not," he said. "You don't have any time to travel with. And if you travel without time, you'll die."

"You can't keep killing us," Joan said. Her throat felt so tight. "I can't let you."

"You're locked in that cell," Nick said. "You need human time to travel. And I won't let any human in there with you."

Joan braced herself. She wasn't sure what she more afraid of—this next bit working or it not working.

"You're right," she said. "I do need human time to travel. But I've had a hunch about something since I woke up in here." She could hear the fear in her voice now. "I'm not just half-monster. I'm half-human too."

Nick's eyes widened in realization.

Joan reached up to touch her own neck.

"Joan, don't!" The words sounded torn from his throat. Joan wondered if he even knew he'd said them.

Joan wrenched time from herself. Distantly, she could hear Nick fumbling with the key. But the loudest sound was her own screaming. When she'd taken time from people, they hadn't seemed to feel it, but this was like tearing into her own flesh. She fell to her knees in agony. How much time had she taken from herself? She had no idea.

The door burst open. Joan let herself look at Nick for a fraction of a second longer than she should have. She'd always yearn for him, she knew. Just like the need to travel was always in the background, so was her need for him.

She gave in to the other yearning.

TWENTY-THREE

The cell was dark and very cold. Joan crouched where she'd fallen, grief overwhelming the relief of escape. It wasn't that she'd lost Nick, she told herself. She'd never had him, not in this timeline, not after what had been done to him. Not after what he'd done to her.

She felt around in the dark. There was no resistance from the shackle. Joan was relieved. She'd been afraid it would come with her.

She took a tentative crawling step, and her shoulder hit the wall, making her grunt. She felt bruised all over.

She had a flash then of Nick shouting to her: *Don't*. What had he meant? Don't what? *Don't take time from yourself*? More likely *Don't escape*. She remembered what else he'd said. *I should have done my duty a long time ago.*

Joan swallowed back tears. Her eyes were adjusting to the darkness now. The far wall was still iron bars and a door. Joan touched her hair. No more bobby pins. The one she'd been using was in another time. She was going to have to pull the wire from her bra.

But when she went over to look at the lock, the door swung open at her touch. It wasn't locked. Wasn't even properly shut.

Somewhere, at the back of her mind, a warning bell sounded. This wasn't right. Nick would have posted a guard here.

When had she landed?

She half expected alarms to go off as she stepped out of the cell. But there was no sound. She walked down the corridor, through the old staff room, up the short flight of stairs.

As she surfaced into the house, a dry dust smell hit her, along with the more usual notes of wood and wool. The silence was eerie.

Joan's apprehension grew as she walked. The first room she came to was completely unfamiliar.

It took her a while to understand that it was the Breakfast Room. There should have been a roped-off dining table, with a replica Georgian breakfast: plum cakes and buttered toast and jam. But all the furniture was gone. The great tapestries of Bacchus and Venus had been stripped from the walls.

The house was still grand, of course, even naked: the walls were flocked velvet; the ceiling was a geometric marvel of gold and white. But with no one here, the grandeur had a feeling of impending dereliction. A house like this needed a staff to maintain it. Without them, the house would fall apart.

Through the bay windows, the sun was setting. Joan had a shuddering feeling of déjà vu, remembering the last time she'd stood at bay windows here, looking out onto the falling night.

How far had she traveled? If she walked out of the grounds, what would she see? Had she traveled a year? Five years? Ten? For all she knew, she'd stolen all the life she had left from herself. She could drop dead before her next breath.

She really, *really* couldn't think about that.

The house seemed empty, but that didn't mean that the grounds were unpatrolled. The library had a decent view of the surroundings, and from the color of the sky, there were about twenty minutes of light left.

Joan made her way through the China Room. That had been stripped too. The curator, Murray, had been so proud of the Holland House china collection—all those paper-thin cups with matching rose patterns.

Gran had died two rooms away.

Joan's breath hitched. She forced herself up the stairs. On the next floor, the door to the Yellow Drawing Room was open. The Gilt Room was visible just beyond. No Olivers this time. No Nick. Just two empty rooms.

Joan opened the library door. For a split second, she expected it to look just as it had when she'd left it: shelves of leather-bound books. Reading chairs.

But, of course, whoever had stripped the house had been here too. Only the bones were left: a long corridor of empty shelves. The ceiling was still a deep evening blue, speckled with gold stars. Joan had always loved it.

Through the window, the Dutch Garden was weedy and overgrown. The only movement was the wind in the leaves.

The house seemed abandoned. Joan drew a finger through the dust on the windowsill.

The last time she'd been in this room, Nick had been here too. They'd sat together in this same dusk light. Then he'd touched her cheek, and they'd kissed.

And then . . . Her breath shuddered out. Then they'd heard the sounds of monsters arriving.

Maybe in the true timeline she and Nick had kissed that night too. Maybe they'd both pulled away and laughed a bit, and then maybe they'd kissed again. Maybe afterward, they'd walked through the gardens, and on to Kensington. Gotten a kebab and an ice cream. Maybe they'd promised to see each other the next day, and the day after that.

The sound behind her was soft, a footstep against the wooden floor.

And then Joan really did understand why she'd come up here to the library, why she hadn't already left the house. She was always drawn to him. She supposed he was drawn to her too. The timeline would never stop trying to repair itself, as long as they were both alive.

She turned from the window. Her stupid heart leaped at the sight of him.

Nick was in shadow as he approached, but Joan could see that his hair was longer. He still looked the same, though— film-star handsome, dark-haired and square-jawed. And he still radiated that same otherworldly goodness. The hero to her monster.

It wasn't fair, she thought. They'd never had a chance in this timeline. They should have had their whole lives together, but now there was only this.

"Stop," she blurted. As though she could stop what was about to happen.

To her surprise, he did stop, just a few paces from her.

He'd set it up like this, Joan realized. The empty house. Just her and him here alone. No one watching, no potential collateral. No more excuses for what had to be done.

"You were standing by that window the first time I saw you," he said. His voice was the same as ever. Steady and deep as calm water.

"I remember," Joan said. She couldn't bear this. She couldn't fight him yet. She wasn't ready. There had to be enough time left in her for another jump. Maybe a bigger one this time.

Nick stumbled closer, as though he couldn't help himself. "Please," he said. "Please don't take any more time from yourself." Of course he knew what she was thinking. They'd always been in accord.

The step had brought him into the last of the light. Joan saw then what the shadows had hidden. He was only a little older. But his expression was different. Where last time, he'd been resolved, now he looked raw and unsure. Like the night they'd kissed.

"I had a long time to think," he said. "To wonder how much time you took from yourself."

Joan braced herself. She'd expected a terrifyingly fast attack—something like what he'd done to Edmund Oliver. But he was just standing there, hands open and unthreatening by his sides. *Now,* she thought. He was going to do it now. But still he stood there. The tension was unbearable.

He took a shuddering breath. "Joan," he said. "The first time I saw you, I knew what your voice would sound like before you said a word."

Joan stared at him. The memory came back to her in sharp clarity. Nick had walked into the library, head bent over an open book. Joan had been charmed by the careful way he'd cradled the book, protective of its fragile corners. She remembered how he'd looked up and seen her; how his eyes had widened just before she'd spoken.

"I knew what your laugh would sound like," he said. "I knew you were a restless sleeper, that you kicked off the sheets, even in winter. I knew you put fresh ginger in your tea. I knew that if you were faced with two choices, you'd always choose the right one over the easy one."

"Nick . . ."

"This timeline is wrong, isn't it?" he said.

"I . . ." For a long moment, Joan couldn't speak, even with the remnants of the truth drug demanding it. She'd been braced for anything but hope. "I . . . When I first saw you, I felt like I'd known you my whole life." Her own voice came out sounding horribly vulnerable. She quashed the hope ruthlessly. *If you were faced with two choices, you'd always choose the right one.* But she hadn't, had she? She'd done terrible things.

Nick took another step closer, and Joan backed up

unthinkingly. Something like agony crossed his face. He lifted his empty hands, showing her that he wasn't armed. But he'd never needed to be armed. He'd started out in the Gilt Room unarmed. "The last time I saw you," he said, "you told me that we were together once."

Joan couldn't take her eyes off him.

"I said that I didn't believe you," Nick said. "And then you took time from yourself. You screamed. I—I thought you were dying. I still hear it in my dreams." He wanted to come closer, Joan could see, but he stood there, rooted to the floor, hands still half-raised.

Joan quashed the hope again. There wasn't going to be a happy ending, she reminded herself. She was a monster and he was a hero. Everyone knew how that story ended.

Her next breath felt too heavy. Nick saw that too. He always saw everything. He wanted to reach for her, she knew. She could read him as well as he could read her.

But it wasn't *her* he wanted to reach for. Not really. He wanted the other Joan. The Joan who made the right choices. *That* Joan had died in the massacre, along with her family.

The Joan who'd lived was a monster now—in every sense of the word. She'd stolen time. Even now, some terrible part of her wanted to travel and travel, crossing decades like pirates crossed seas.

"What are you doing, Nick?" she said. Didn't he know that drawing this out was torment?

Nick lowered his hands slowly. "I don't know." He sounded

as raw and lost as Joan felt. "I've always put the mission first. I never allowed myself anything more."

It sounded like a lonely life. Joan remembered the kitchen where Nick had found his family dead. The fridge behind him had been covered with photos—Nick and his brothers and sisters blowing out birthday candles, laughing at the camera.

She remembered his spartan locker in the Holland House staff room.

Now, in the silence of the library, his breaths sounded unsteady. "I never allowed myself to feel anything," he said. "But then I walked into the library that day. And I saw you."

Joan remembered how he'd walked through the door that day. And when he'd looked up, she'd *known* him.

"Someone changed the timeline," he said. "But they couldn't make me forget you. Not completely." His dark eyes were intent on her, as familiar as her own heartbeat. "I love you, Joan."

Joan heard herself make a soft choked sound. How could something she'd wanted to hear so much hurt so much? No matter how much she wanted to travel in time, it was nothing to how she felt about Nick. From the moment they'd met, she'd only ever wanted to be near him.

"Don't," she whispered. It was too much to bear.

"I know," he said. There was so much pain in his voice. "I know how much you hate me."

Joan shook her head, even though it was true. She hated him. She loved him. There was a rift inside her, and she was being torn apart by it. She took a breath and barely controlled it. "It isn't me you remember," she managed. "I'm not her—I'm not that other Joan." The Joan from the true timeline, who'd made the right choices, who'd probably never stolen time in her whole life.

"I know who you are," he said.

"You *don't*." She suddenly couldn't bear the way he was looking at her. "I've stolen so much time," she said hoarsely. She didn't even know how many people she'd stolen from. Had to be hundreds. Maybe even a thousand. She and Aaron had been in the Pit for ages. And she'd used at least thirty years from the travel token to come here. For a second, her revulsion at herself choked her breath.

And then Nick did step closer, as though he couldn't stop himself. Joan could almost feel the warmth of him in the cool air of the abandoned library. If she reached out, she'd be able to touch him.

She clenched her fists instead. "Whoever we used to be, we're not those people anymore," she said. "If you feel anything for me . . . If—if I feel anything for you . . ." She watched his eyes darken as he realized what she was saying. "It's just a remnant of another timeline. We're different people now."

"What they made me into?" he said.

"*Yes.*"

"And what I made you into?"

Joan's breath stopped in her throat. She couldn't take her eyes off him.

"I'm sorry," he whispered. "I'm so sorry, Joan."

"I did those things," Joan whispered back. He'd killed her family, but it had been her hand on the back of innocent people's necks. It had been her choice.

"I don't even know how many people I've killed," Nick said, soft. A confession. She could hear it in his voice then too. He was as sick at himself as she was at herself.

"I wish . . ." Joan swallowed. "I wish we could be different."

"What if we were?" Nick said.

"What do you mean?"

"We can't change what we've done," Nick said, "but . . . we don't have to be the people we were made into." He sounded shaky. "You told me once that you wanted peace between monsters and humans."

Joan stared at him. The woman in the recording had said that she'd chosen Nick because his virtuousness could be twisted into righteous fury. The woman had thought she'd made Nick perfectly. But she'd been wrong. Joan understood that now. There was something incorruptible at the core of him. Something good that not even two thousand attempts at torturing and breaking him could erase.

"Do you really think it's possible?" Joan said. She wanted peace more than anything. She was half-human, half-monster. She didn't just want peace. She felt broken without it.

"I can't bring your family back," he said. "But if we can make this timeline better, I want to try."

Joan knew then. She wasn't in love with that other Nick— the Nick who'd never been the hero. She wasn't that other

Joan. She was in love with *this* Nick—the Nick who'd suffered unimaginably, and turned that suffering into wanting to protect people. And who still, even now, could imagine a future that was different.

She took the last step and reached up to touch his face. He let her, unflinchingly. "Can I kiss you?" she whispered.

He made a soft sound and reached for her with a kind of desperate relief that made Joan's heart jump. He was bare-necked, she realized as he pulled her into his arms. All she'd have to do to was slide her hand to his neck, and he'd be dead. His trust almost undid her.

"I've loved you since the moment I saw you," she said. Since then and before that. Now and forever.

"I love you," he whispered back. "I always have."

Joan closed her eyes. She could feel tears starting as his mouth touched hers. And the timeline responded. The monster part of her sensed it as her mouth opened under his: a shift in the world, as though vast jagged pieces were knitting together. The timeline was repairing itself.

Just for a second, she let herself *feel* it. She imagined that she and Nick could really have this. That they could be happy.

And then she opened her eyes and unleashed her strange power on him.

He huffed a shocked breath into her mouth. "Joan?" He tried to pull back, but Joan tightened her arms around him. She knew what she had to do.

Joan drew power from the depths of herself, and her power

responded as if it had been waiting for her call. *Something for-bidden,* one of the guards had called it.

In a way, Joan had always known what her power could do. She hadn't transmuted the metal into stone; she'd turned it *back* to ore. She'd unmade it.

And now she unmade Nick.

There was nothing gentle about it. Power poured out of her. His body jerked and shook with it. His face became a mask of pain. *Joan,* he mouthed. *Joan, please.* Joan forced herself to keep going, even as he started to scream.

She was properly crying now. Around them, the house started to shake.

Joan unmade him. The force of it shook the walls. Plaster cracked and dust rained down around them. She unmade everything Nick had done, and everything that had been done to him.

She unmade the lives Nick had taken. She brought her family back.

She unmade Nick until he wasn't the hero anymore. Until the Nick she loved was gone.

And, at the end of it, everything had changed.

EPILOGUE

The last weeks of summer were long and warm, even as the leaves started to turn. Everyone agreed that it had been the loveliest London summer in years.

In the city's parks, wildflowers bloomed later and longer than anyone could remember: sweet peas, daisies, violets, and honeysuckle.

Joan missed the end of it. She'd come down with what Gran worried was the flu and Uncle Gus thought might be heatstroke.

But Joan knew it wasn't a human illness. Unmaking Nick had pushed her power beyond its limit. She'd burned through every last spark of it to change the timeline. Now, whatever ability she'd had to unmake things was gone. She could feel the absence inside herself even after her body started to heal.

And her power wasn't the only absence inside her.

She dreamed of him. Sometimes he was in the Holland House library, sometimes tied to a chair in his childhood home. Always, he was screaming, begging her to stop. Joan woke shaking and reaching for him, words still thick in her mouth.

I'm sorry. I'm sorry. I'm so sorry. I love you.

If the dreams were bad, though, being awake was worse. The last moments at the house came back to her over and over. She remembered how Nick's eyes had widened. How his chest had shuddered as he'd started to scream. She remembered the look on his face as he'd realized that *she* was doing this to him. That she wasn't going to stop. She'd told him she loved him. She'd kissed him. And then she'd torn him apart.

Too weak to get out of bed, all Joan could do was lie there and remember and remember and remember.

No one else did.

"Holland House?" Gran felt Joan's forehead with the back of her hand. "You mean the old ruins in Holland Park? Why would you want to go down there?"

"I mean Holland House! The house in the park!" Joan tried to sit up, but Gran coaxed her back down.

"There's nothing there, love." Gran sounded worried. "You still have a fever. I'm going to call Dr. de Witt again."

Joan had never been a good patient. As soon as she was strong enough to stand, she pronounced herself well and headed straight for Kensington High Street.

She made it halfway up the street before she stumbled back to Gran's, half-dead on her feet.

"Serves you right," Gran said, but her voice was gentle. She guided Joan back to bed.

But maybe willing it to be true made it true, because Joan

got stronger and stronger every day after that. As soon as her legs would hold her, she headed to Holland Park. She went back the next day, and the next.

The morning that Dad was due home, she felt almost her normal self again.

When she came into the kitchen that morning, she found most of the family already up.

Joan paused in the doorway, feeling the same shock of relief and disbelief that she felt every time she saw them now.

Uncle Gus was at the stove, stewing pears. As she watched, he plucked fresh pears from an empty fruit basket and tossed the peelings over his shoulder, where they vanished into thin air.

He spiced the pears with a heavy hand—Gran's side of the family liked strong flavors. No matter where Gran was living, her house always smelled the same: of cinnamon and saffron and cardamom and cloves.

"I bet I could steal the *Mona Lisa*," Ruth was saying to the others. She was using Gran's broken radiator as a window seat. Her curls were a stiff black cloud around her face. "You're not seriously going to eat that," she added as Gran took a bite of toast. She groaned. "Oh, that is *wrong*."

"Dorothy, throw it out," Aunt Ada said. "Please."

"I like it like this," Gran said.

"It's burnt!" Bertie said.

"I like it burnt."

When they'd been dead, Joan had dreamed about them. She'd never been able to conjure all the little details, though. Gran's hair was a gray cloud, frizzier at the ends. Her dressing gown was frayed at the hem. And she may or may not have liked burnt toast, but there was a sly, amused quirk at her mouth as she ate it. She always enjoyed horrifying people.

Beside her, Aunt Ada was spreading Marmite onto a slice of pale toast. She was in a white suit, and there wasn't a spot of Marmite on the suit or her plate. Joan had asked Ada once how she always stayed so immaculate. Ada had grinned and kissed the top of Joan's head. *It's just confidence, love.*

"Anyone could steal the *Mona Lisa*," Gus said to Ruth now.

"I'm not talking about snatching it from the old man's hand," Ruth said.

"I wouldn't do that," Gus said. "What do you take me for? I'd properly steal it too."

"It's only a copy, anyway," Bertie said.

This drew everyone's attention.

"One of the Venetian families bought the original," Bertie said, as though he was surprised that they didn't know. "Paint was still wet."

"You sure?" Ada said. "I heard the Nightingales bought it—same deal. Paint wet."

"How many of them did Leo sell?" Bertie said.

"Yes, but the point," Ruth said, "is that I could steal a painting from the Louvre." She saw Joan in the doorway then. "But I would never do that," she added, singsong, "because theft is wrong."

Teacher's here, Ruth would sometimes say when Joan came into a room. She'd always said it fondly, almost with pride, as if she were saying *Joan's an astronaut, actually.*

She jumped off the radiator and slung an arm around Joan's shoulder. "Right," she said. "Last day in London. What do you want to do?"

Joan felt a familiar flash of fondness, along with a pang of something sharper. How many times had she come into a room and felt the conversation halt and change like this? *Joan doesn't like shop talk. Not in front of Joan.*

"I—" she started.

"I know, I know. You have to go somewhere first, and you'll meet me after." Ruth bumped Joan's shoulder gently. "Where do you keep going?"

"Nowhere fun," Joan promised. She took a piece of toast from Ruth's plate. "You finished with this?"

"No," Ruth grumbled, but she didn't really sound grumpy. She'd been more worried than she'd let on by Joan's illness.

"Take some fruit if you're planning to walk," Uncle Gus said. He plucked a blood orange from Gran's fruit basket and gave it to Joan. "You need to keep up your vitamin C."

Joan had forgotten that detail too. Uncle Gus thought that vitamin C could heal everything from the common cold to a broken leg. Her smile wobbled, and she swallowed hard. She'd missed them all so much.

The blood orange was sweet-scented and heavy, red as a sunrise. Perfectly ripe. And out of season, she realized slowly. Oranges were winter fruit. Maybe it was imported. Or maybe someone had traveled to winter. She looked back up at Gus.

"I'm fusspotting, aren't I?" he said.

Joan shook her head. "Nah." She managed a proper smile. But she put the orange back in the bowl. "I'd better get dressed."

Gran was sitting on the front doorstep when Joan left the house. She shuffled over to let Joan pass her.

"Geraldine from two doors down just walked past with a cat on a leash," Gran said. "Big ginger tom with white paws. Woman must be having a midlife crisis." She drank her tea. "Will you be home for dinner? I'm making treacle pudding."

On impulse, Joan bent to give her a hug. They weren't really a hugging family, but after a surprised second Gran put her mug down and hugged Joan back. *The formidable Dorothy Hunt*, Aaron had called her once, but in Joan's arms she felt fine-boned and fragile.

"Wouldn't miss it for the world," Joan said.

Joan remembered when she'd first returned to Holland House—a week ago now, still so ill that her legs would barely hold her. Her first glimpse of the house had been as much of a shock as seeing her family alive again. *The old ruins in Holland Park*, Gran had called it. But nothing could have prepared Joan for the reality.

The west wing was gone. The library where Joan had met Nick. Sabine's Room, where Gran had died. The east wing was still there, but gutted. All that was left was the facade, now wrapped around a hostel. Joan had wandered inside in a daze and found a modern building, unrecognizable in layout. Where the Gilt Room had been, now there was a dormitory in cheerful kindergarten colors.

A pamphlet in the information office had said that the house had been bombed in the war—twenty-two times in one night. Joan took the pamphlet to Roger's Seat, the hidden alcove overlooking the Dahlia Garden. The house might have changed, but she still knew some of its secret places.

There, curled up and half hidden by a curtain of leaves, she read about the new history of the house. In her own timeline, a private company had bought Holland House in the 1950s and turned it into a museum. In this timeline, the house had been destroyed before that could happen. The burned husk had been sold to the Royal Borough. It was all there on the page, in black and white with citations.

Joan had sat there for a long time. Whatever the pamphlet said, she knew that she'd done this. When she'd altered Nick's history, she must have altered the history of the house too. It had just had the bad luck to be in the proximity of her power.

And she couldn't help but ask the question: If she'd done this to Holland House, what other changes had she inadvertently made to the timeline?

Now, on her last morning in London, she walked the familiar path from Kensington High Street to what was left of the house.

Where do you keep going? Ruth had asked.

Joan didn't know why she kept going back. Penance, maybe. The heaviness in her chest made more sense when she could see what she'd done to this place she'd loved. But it wasn't just that. There were memories here that were nowhere else. She could walk through the gardens and imagine that he was here with her.

As Joan walked, she was joined by joggers and people pushing prams and walking dogs. There was a football field where the maze had once stood, and she could hear the distant smack of the ball, people shouting, the ref's whistle.

After the long summer, the weather had finally turned. It was cool and drizzly as she walked past the house's facade, past the little café, past the old icehouse. In the other timeline, food historians had churned ice cream within its thick walls, using fresh fruit from the kitchen gardens. In this timeline, it was a gallery space.

Joan lingered in the covered walkway between the icehouse and the old orangery. This bit was new—built after the rest of the house had been bombed. There were murals all the way down the wall, depicting a garden party in the Victorian era.

Joan's favorite was the one where the partygoers were in an elaborate formal garden—ankle-high hedges creating intricate green loops. Women in voluminous skirts lounged against a central fountain. Whoever had painted this couldn't have known the house, but they'd captured the mysterious atmosphere of the old gardens.

Joan stepped closer. She could almost have kept walking

into the painting, she thought dreamily.

She caught herself with a sharp breath before the tug of yearning came.

Almost automatically, she grounded herself in the details of the moment—as Aaron had taught her. The smell of wet stone. The patter of rain outside the colonnade.

Footsteps.

Déjà vu washed over her. She turned toward the sound, knowing already that it wasn't Nick. She'd have recognized the rhythm of his step. Still, her heart skipped in disappointment at the confirmation.

The newcomer was a soberly dressed man, perhaps twenty years old. He shook his umbrella carefully into the garden and then made his way down the walkway, stopping at the mural beside Joan.

His face was pale and Chinese—familiar, Joan thought. But recognition didn't come until he stepped closer to the painting with an air of intent interest. He'd been an artist, she remembered.

Jamie Liu had been gaunt as a prisoner, but in this new timeline he was solidly built and healthy. He had an expensive haircut, and he was dressed for colder weather than it was—gloves and a dark blue trench coat.

I've met you, Joan wanted to blurt out. Except that she hadn't met him. Just like she hadn't met Nick, hadn't met Aaron. Sometimes, the weight of remembering, when no one else did, made her feel like she was going mad. She'd seen people lying dead in these gardens—except that she hadn't. Her family had died here—except that they hadn't.

"I love these paintings," she said a little awkwardly. She needed to hear him say something. She knew what his voice should sound like, and she needed the proof that her memories were real. "You almost feel as though you could step into the party."

"That would be nice." To her relief, his voice was the pleasant treble she'd expected. He turned to her, seeming curious but not uncomfortable. "It certainly looks like they were enjoying better weather."

She smiled tentatively. "I'm Joan."

"I remember," he said.

The Lius remember. Joan shouldn't have felt as shaken as she did. She stared at him.

Jamie gestured toward the garden beyond the walkway. "Shall we go for a walk?" He offered his umbrella to her.

Joan found her voice. "It's not that bad out."

"I know, but . . ." Jamie looked up at the gloomy sky. "I don't much like the wet."

Joan remembered him as a boy, bare feet splashing in the lake. *He loves the water,* Tom had said. What had happened to him as a captive? Whatever it was, he seemed changed in this timeline. The clear-eyed boy who'd painted fish by the lake had been replaced by a man with a wary but polite demeanor.

He held the umbrella solicitously over Joan as well as himself as they walked, even when she protested that she didn't mind the rain.

They took the path around the old orangery. Through its arched windows, Joan could see people preparing for an event, setting tables with shining silverware and flower arrangements. In Joan's memories, there'd been potted orange trees in this part of the garden—outside in summer, to be put back inside the orangery in winter.

"I don't remember much," Jamie said. "The Liu power only gives me fragments of the other timeline."

Looking at his gloved hands, his coat, Joan wondered. "What *do* you remember?" she asked.

"I remember that the hero was real."

Joan heard her breath shudder out, half relief and half pain. Just hearing someone else speak of him felt like a broken taboo.

"I'm sorry," Jamie said. "I know what he was to you."

"I had to do it," Joan whispered. "My family . . ." She swallowed. "I had to."

They passed the summer ballroom. Joan kept her eyes on the path, afraid to see sympathy in Jamie's face. There were rosebushes here, a little overgrown.

"I know," Jamie said gently. Joan heard him breathe in and out. "I remember my captivity," he said, and Joan's heart twisted, remembering the boy he'd been. She turned back to him.

"Does Tom know?"

Jamie shook his head. "When I left home today, he was painting the boat. Green paint all over him." For just a moment, as he spoke of Tom, there were no shadows in his eyes. He looked almost like his younger self. "Tom's happy in this timeline," he said. "I have you to thank for that."

How do you Lius stand it? Joan wanted to ask him. *How do you stand remembering when no one else does?* But she could see how Jamie stood it. The same way she was going to have to. He just bore it.

"Thanks to you too," she reminded him. "You got that message to us. You told us the hero was made."

"Did I?" Jamie sounded uncertain.

He didn't remember, Joan realized. A strange loneliness washed over her. She thought about the day they'd all gone to see him. Her, Aaron, Ruth, and Tom, sitting by the pond. She remembered how warm the sun had been. How glad she'd been that they were all there with her. Whatever differences they'd started out with, they'd been a kind of team in the end.

But Aaron would never remember that day, and neither would Ruth or Tom. Not even Jamie remembered it all.

"I don't remember leaving a message, but . . ." Jamie hesitated. His gloved hand was tight on the stem of the umbrella. "I know she's still out there. The woman who took me captive."

The woman who'd made the hero. Did she remember what she'd done, Joan wondered. Did she know what Joan had done?

Whether she did or not, *Joan* knew.

"It's different this time," she promised Jamie. "If she comes back, we'll be waiting."

Jamie didn't exactly look reassured, but he met Joan's eyes and nodded. He tested the air with one gloved hand and pulled the umbrella down. The rain had stopped.

They stood there together, watching the sky clear. There

were ruins here by the path, crumbling brick arches covered in ivy. These ruins had been in the previous timeline too, the remains of some long-forgotten structure.

Joan looked beyond them to the house. From this angle, she could see scars on the brick walls where the west wing had been. From this angle, she could see how much of the house had survived: twenty-two bombs in one night, and these walls were still standing.

There was a little blue appearing now between the clouds. The sun was coming out. Joan lifted her head to feel it.

ACKNOWLEDGMENTS

So much heart and work went into this book, and I'm so grateful to everyone who helped to bring it into the world.

Thank you so much to my family for your endless encouragement, love, and support: Dad and Jun, thank you for your help with translations and names; Ben, thank you for brainstorming with me and coming up with ideas for the powers; Lee Chin, Moses, Wennie, and Nina, thank you for all your encouragement over the years.

Thank you too to the friends who were there from the beginning. This book started at a dinner where we all discovered that we'd been thinking about writing a book. It's been amazing to see so many wonderful books written since that night—and I'm sure there'll be many more to come. Thank you to Bea Thyer for being the best host that night as always; to C. S. Pacat for all the years and years of amazing brainstorming sessions, problem-solving, and manuscript swaps (this book couldn't have been written without you!); and to Shelley Parker-Chan, I'm so happy that we're on this journey together—who would have thought we really could make our dreams come true! Thank you too to Anna Cowan for the many great writing sessions and chats, and for your insightful feedback over the years.

To my lovely and brilliant Clarion class of 2015, I couldn't have written the first draft without the kick-start of our 300-words-a-day pact. You all inspire me—Jess Barber, adrienne maree brown, Zack Brown, Pip Coen, Bernie Cox, Rose Hartley (thank you for hosting lovely writing retreats and for your great feedback on the draft!), Nathan Hillstrom, Becca Jordan, Travis Lyons, Evan Mallon, Eugene Ramos, Mike Reid, Lilliam Rivera, Sara Saab, Dayna Smith, Melanie West, and Tiffany Wilson. I miss you all, and I wish I were reading your stories right now.

Thank you so, so much to my wonderful agent, Tracey Adams, and the whole team at Adams Literary—Josh Adams and Anna Munger. Tracey, you changed my life with one phone call, and you've done more for this book than I could have imagined in my wildest dreams.

Christabel McKinley, thank you so much for sharing the book in the UK and Australia—I appreciate all your hard work and enthusiastic support so much. Thank you also to Stephen Moore and all the other associates.

At HarperCollins in the US, huge, huge thanks to my fantastic editor Kristen Pettit, and to Clare Vaughn and the whole brilliant team. I so appreciate your insightful edits, your vision, and all your support. Special thanks to the production editors, Caitlin Lonning and Alexandra Rakaczki; the designers, Jessie Gang and Alison Klapthor; the cover artist, Eevien Tan; the production managers, Meghan Pettit and Allison Brown; the marketing director, Sabrina Abballe; and the publicist, Lauren Levite. I'm so proud of the book we all created together. You've made it so much more than I had imagined it could be.

At Hodder & Stoughton in the UK, thank you so much to my wonderful editor Molly Powell, and to Callie Robertson, Kate Keehan, Lydia Blagden, the cover artist Kelly Chong, and to the whole amazing team for all your great work and your vision for the book. Heartfelt thanks, as well, to the wonderful Anissa and everyone at FairyLoot. Working with you—and Hodder & Stoughton—to create the gorgeous FairyLoot special edition has been a dream come true.

At Allen & Unwin in Australia, thank you to the whole amazing team—Kate Whitfield, Jodie Webster, Eva Mills, Sandra Nobes, Liz Kemp—and everyone else who has worked on the book. I'm so grateful for all you've done. It's wonderful to have such a fantastic local publisher and local support.

Huge thanks also to the teams at Eksmo in Russia, Penguin Random House in Spain, Piper in Germany, and Vulkan in Serbia.

I'm also immensely grateful to all my friends at Education Services Australia—I couldn't have written this book without your support and encouragement. Thank you especially to my podmates, Alison Laming, Susan Trompenaars, and Jessica Boland, who were there every day, for every step of my writing journey—from the boring stuff to the stressful stuff to the fun and exciting stuff. I appreciate your support so much. Thank you as well to Kelly Nissen and Noni Morrissey (thank you for believing that this was going to happen long before I believed it!). To Emma Durbridge, Madeleine Daniel, Stacey Hattensen, and Tilka Brown, thank you for all the writing chats. To Jill Taylor, thank you for teaching me so much. To Libby Tuckerman, thank you for giving me such flexible work hours—I wouldn't have been able to finish this book without your support.

Thank you to Naomi Novik for showing me that publishing a book was possible and that maybe I could do it one day too. Naomi, I'll never forget seeing Temeraire in a bookshop for the first time and thinking, *I know the author of that! I know someone who wrote a book!* Thank you for all your help and enthusiasm over the years. Thank you too to Francesca Coppa and Gina Paterson for teaching me so much about writing. I still use those lessons in everything I write. Thank you to Zen Cho for being a sounding board for last-minute peace-of-mind checks. And thank you to Diana Fox for fixing the beginning of the book. You were 100 percent right about the solution.

To Warren Leonard, thank you for understanding the book so completely and for getting to know it inside out—as well as I do. All your fantastic questions pinpointed plot holes and helped me to resolve and strengthen the worldbuilding and the backstory.

To Liana Skrzypczak and Bec Miller, thank you for our many wonderful writing sessions and chats on all those weekends.

To the lovely and talented Pandas writing group—Elaine

Cuyegkeng, Kat Clay, Aidan Doyle, Likhain, Emma Osborne, Sophie Yorkston, and Suzanne Willis—thank you for the dinners and crits.

To Alex Hong (I miss your writing!) and Melissa Siah, thank you for keeping me company in my research by going on the Lost Palace tour with me on a drizzly London evening.

To the Friends of Holland Park, thank you for taking the time to give me a wonderful tour of Holland House and Holland Park.

To Sarah Rees Brennan, thank you so much for all your encouragement. Eliza Tiernan, thank you for the support when I was on submission (and the genius donut strategy). Amie Kaufman, Jay Kristoff, and Astrid Scholte, thank you for generously sharing your knowledge and experience with a debut. I appreciate it so much. Tashie Bhuiyan, thank you for being an encouraging and welcoming face after my book deal was announced.

To the Clarion 2015 instructors and administrators: Chris Barzak, Saladin Ahmed, Jim Kelly, Karen Joy Fowler, Margo Lanagan, Maureen McHugh, and Shelley Streeby. I learned so much from you in those amazing six weeks. I wish I could do it all over again.

To the Life at Springfield writing workshop (Kinchem Hegedus, instructors Karen Joy Fowler and Nike Sulway, and all the participants): thank you for reading an early version of the prologue and chapter one and providing great feedback.

Finally, I would like to acknowledge the Traditional

Custodians of the lands on which I wrote much of this book, and to pay my respect to their Elders, past, present, and emerging: the Bunurong and Wurundjeri Woi Wurrung peoples of the Kulin Nation.